Taken by the Pikosa
WARLORD

Xiveri Mates Book 7

Elizabeth Stephens

Contents

Guide to the Tribes of Sucere Earth

— Sucere Earth —
Sucere *(soo-jer-ray)*
The term used to describe the Earth of the future following the total decimation of the planet due to climate related catastrophes that first depleted the global potable water supply and led the Water Wars. The surface of Sucere Earth is unlivable, except to a few surviving species that managed to evolve to adapt to harsh desert climates, scorching heat, and virtually no rainfall.

— Warlord Tribes —
Pikosa *(pick-oh-sah)*
The Pikosa tribe occupies the cave systems of Sucere Earth and survive by enslaving weaker tribes, mining minerals from the rocks deep underground, hunting 'crocodiles', and using the subterranean pools for water supply and to grow a meager selection of plants. Tribe members are characterized by medium brown/bronze skin, black hair, and dark eyes.

Wickar *(wick-are)*
The Wickar tribe is a fully nomadic tribe whose hordes ride atop Sucere 'elephants' and 'horses' and whose primary means of survival is through raiding and pillaging other tribes, including other warlord tribes, as well as hunting the surface animals. Tribe members are characterized by tanned white skin, golden blonde and brown hair, and colored eyes.

Kawashari *(kah-wah-shar-ee)*
The Kawashari tribe inhabits the mountains of Sucere Earth whose highest peaks still have fertile ground. Tribe

members are characterized by tan white and brown skin and red hair. Red hair is a coveted feature among the Kawashari but, because of this, many of their tribespeople are inbred.

— Captive Tribes —
Tanishi *(tahn-ee-shee)*
The Pikosa word for "little ones," this term describes the humans of the past who are now thrust into this new Sucere Earth. Tanishi come from all countries of Earth as we know it and though most speak another language as their mother tongue, they all also speak English. They are the only diverse tribe.

Omoro *(oh-mohr-oh)*
The Omoro tribespeople are characterized by dark grey skin and grey and silver hair. They are roughly the same size as the average Tanishi and occupy tribes in rocky and mountainous regions on the surface of Sucere Earth.

Danien *(dan-ee-ann)*
The Danien inhabit cave systems only and, as a result, have extremely pale complexions and white hair and are extremely susceptible to sun sickness.

إلى حبي الأول. لغة.

Ila hubbi el'awal. Lugat.
To my first love. Language.

إليزابيث ستيفنس

Elizabeth Stephens

/

Halima

A ripping sound. No. It isn't a sound, it's just *ripping*. Ripping the world. Ripping me. Crrrrrack. Right down the middle.

The pain of it shocks my whole body, like I've been punched in the chest and that fist tastes like metal and blood and is screaming my name. It must be my name because even through the warped pronunciation that my ears reject, I recognize that name. I know it on a deep, fundamental level. Just like I know that I have a soul and that soul is pulled together by skin and this combination of soul-wrapped skin is what makes me human.

I'm human and my name is Halima.

"Halima!"

Her pronunciation is all wrong. It's a deep haa — not a short ha — followed by a laam, yaa, meem and rounded off with a ta'marbouta. But the woman screaming can't help her pronunciation because she's speaking English and my name is Arabic.

English. Arabic. Huh. Strange that, so instinctively, I know the differences between them.

"Halima, can you hear me?"

Yes, I can hear you, but my name is not ha — *with a flat a* — limb-uh, *my name is* hhhaah-leem-a, *as my mother once spoke it.*

Mother.

I can place the word's meaning, but can't seem to conjure the memory of the mother who first told me my own name. The mother who was once mine. When I reach for her, all I see is a hand drawing a *ha* so elegantly — that flattened roof over the generous curve below — but it's only drawn in this way when the letter exists in isolation...

ح

The hand rustles the paper beneath it as it draws the *ha* again, but this time with a pointed roof that slopes down before reaching back up to form the *laam* that is the second letter of my name. *Yaa, meem,* and *ta'marbouta* follow. It's light brown, this hand. The same light brown as mine. Halima, she writes for me.

حليمة

I reach again through the fog of my memory, past the chasm of so many vocabularies competing for voice — Cantonese, English, Wolof, Farsi, Turkish, Hindi, Korean, French, Spanish, and my mother tongue, Egyptian Arabic — but when I reach, reach, reach to grab it, that hand changes, becoming larger and callused and menacing and a darker brown than it was.

It stretches towards me from up above, grabs onto the front of my shirt, heaves me upright and then pulls harder. I fly. I lurch. I gag. I choke. I can't breathe. My eyes roll back and my stomach pitches as I'm dragged out of some kind of bed or maybe a bath — a glass case full of liquid that's an unnatural, neon blue.

"Halima, can you hear me?" The voice screeches over the sound of screeching.

I clear my throat, draw on my knowledge of English, and answer. No, I don't. I choke.

My lungs sear and my torso revolts. I feel like I was reborn in a blue goo that sticks like sap instead of in the womb of a mother that I no longer know.

I squeeze my eyes shut again and reach, reach, reach for the image of that hand drawing an elegant *ha* and I know that if I can just get there, everything will be alright, but...

"Haddock!" The woman roars and her dark hand is met with a second one, this one lighter and larger and rougher.

"Will she survive if you remove the breathing tube?"

The woman's face comes into view on my next blink. Dark brown skin, head just as bald as the man standing beside her. Her eyes are bright white and so are her teeth, but when she looks at me, I can see a pupil that's fully blown, subsuming the brown iris that guards it.

The man beside her has white skin and is equally, terrifyingly hairless. It makes me wonder what I look like. Am I just as bare and exposed as all the others? Do I, too, lack the visual markings needed to identify me?

His green eyes roam over my face. His mouth is pursed into a murderous line, lips thin in contrast to the woman's at his side. An alarm sounds somewhere behind him — *another* alarm. Something crashes, metal tears, voices scream in so many clashing intonations.

My gaze swivels listlessly to the corner of the room, following the man called Haddock's stare to a cluster of bald people standing in the corner. *Where are we?*

The room around us is big and full of shattered tanks that are either empty or full of blue goo swirled with a darker, more terrifying color. *Blood. It's blood.*

I cough, though there's something in my mouth choking me that I can't speak around, and the sound brings Haddock's attention back to me. He blinks several times and shakes his head quickly.

"We don't have a choice, Kenya," he says to the woman.

I'm on my side, on some kind of table. It's hard and I can hear it bending beneath me. Behind me, hands work at something in my butt and then free it. My butt cheeks clench together. My pants are drawn back up over my hips.

"She matters," Kenya says sternly, tone one of reprimand.

Haddock bites his front teeth together and spits, "We all matter. That's why we were chosen. But right now, we need to get the fuck out of here before they breach."

"I have orders from the general, doctor. Just do it!"

"They've breached!" Comes a new voice, another woman this time.

She has no hair and skin that seems unnaturally pale. Based on her accent alone, I'd have guessed she was Korean. Without hair or even eyelashes, it's hard to discern anything about any of these beings. We're all the same bald, wet things, covered in sticky blue on top of grey uniforms that have words stitched into the lapel.

Kenya Pettis. And then beneath that. *First Lieutenant.*

I glance at Haddock's shirt. *Haddock Schwarzmann. Doctor. Surgeon.*

And then I glance down at my own shirt. Upside down, it takes me a few seconds to put the letters together. They're written in the Roman alphabet, having been transliterated from Arabic.

Halima Magdy. That's my name. But perhaps, more important, is what's written below it. *Etymologist. Interpreter.*

I am Halima Magdy.

I am the interpreter.

And I can't breathe.

I start to shake as I become aware of the reason for my restricted breathing. *There's something in my mouth.* The man curses, but his hands are strong and sure as he maneuvers my head and then... *Pain.* That ripping returns. *Ahlan wa sahlan,* I think, welcoming it back.

Haddock pulls and the object comes out from between my teeth, feeling very much like it excoriates my insides as he rips it free.

My back and chest heave when the tip of the thing finally clunks off of my bottom lip. I writhe and buck on the table, trying to grab ahold of that elusive next breath.

My eyes roll back. There are hands on my chest, pressing. I black out. And then I'm awake and there's a man's mouth on my mouth. He's breathing and I'm gasping and he wrenches back at the same time that the woman grabs my hands and pulls me off of the table. I land on my knees.

"Halima, listen to me." My head spins. I fight the urge to vomit. "You are one of three hundred and forty-four people selected to survive the climate apocalypse and subsequent water wars that destroyed the earth.

"We've been asleep for the past four thousand years. It should have been eleven, but we were woken up by a species of humans who survived the wars and what came after." She shakes her head. Her upper lip is sweating. Her entire face is sweating. I'm sweating. "They've evolved."

Fear. Her tone is pure fear. I can feel it screech in the breath that scrapes its bloody nails down my nostrils and throat before settling in my lungs and squeezing.

"They shouldn't be here. They weren't supposed to survive. No one was. But they have and now they're going to take us. They've killed most of our soldiers and, from what I've seen, every male commander that we had. Leanna was the colonel, but she's the highest ranking officer left. She's our general now. She sent me to get you."

She glances over her shoulder, shaking mine as she moves. "Your orders are important. The most important I'll deliver today, so listen to me, Halima. I know that you don't know who you are.

"Memories were wiped when you went into the Sucere Chamber — that's where we are now. The only selective memories left behind for any unranked Sucere member are those pertaining to your skill. Do you know what you are?"

I nod, mute, and glance down at my shirt. With a shaking finger, I point to my left breast.

"Yes. Good. You're the interpreter."

The interpreter because on the Sucere Chamber, there is only one.

Not mutarjima but *al*-mutarjima. *Meem-taa-raa-jeem-meem-ta'marbouta. Jeem* has always been my favorite letter. Just like a *haa*, but with the dot up above it. *A sacred letter.* Someone said that to me once, but I don't know who. My memories no longer carry the sound of their voices.

"Your orders are to stay silent. Do *not* attempt to communicate with them. Just listen. Learn. We need to know their weaknesses so we can exploit them when the time is right. It's our only chance to kill them and escape and we need you for that. Halima, when you..."

"Kenya," the male barks, tapping one foot on the ground again and again. He's barefoot. We all are. "We're running out of time."

"They're here!" The woman in the corner's barely finished speaking before the doors explode open and *they* come in.

Bronze skin. Inky black hair. Thick belts dripping with weapons lace around their waists. Shoes lace up their ankles.

They come like a storm, holding swords and spears and whips. The whips, they sing. People — *my* species of people — scream as the frayed leather ends of *their* whips find our sensitive flesh. Kenya forces me down, throwing her body over mine. I'm in shock for a fountain of reasons, this only one among them.

Then, less than a heartbeat later, she's ripped away from me and I'm dragged up onto my feet.

Pain shoots through my shoulder and continues to tear apart my lungs as I'm dragged by a man — by a *male* creature I can't see — down tunnel after tunnel.

There are bodies everywhere, pressed against me on all sides. Most are the bald humans in the grey uniforms. The rest are the monsters hurting us.

I try to catch the different names, different professions, different trades, trying to build a tower of reason in my mind, but the tower is made of splinters. Reason is too hard to find.

There's an architect and an urban planner, a biologist and a geologist, a paleontologist and an anthropologist, an electrical engineer and an aerospace engineer. There's even a woman with enormous blue eyes whose shirt says *artist*. I wonder distractedly what kind.

The rocks under the sensitive soles of my feet are cold and craggy. I stub my big toe while shoved from behind. Eventually, the lights around us change. The air changes. The heat that was so oppressive dissipates, comes back with a vengeance and then dissipates again. *We aren't in the Sucere Chamber anymore.* Maybe we haven't been for a while. Somewhere along the way, we *descended*.

We're in caves. The tunnels are narrow and frightening. Some of the violent warriors carry live flames — torches — but they aren't needed by the time the hallways widen since the walls here are recessed with fire pits high above my head, but not so high above theirs. Them. They're tall.

The woman I recognize from the previous room stands beside me and rattles like stone in a cage. I glance at her shirt.

Jia Kim. Botanist.

She's crying without making any sound and when I reach down and clutch her hand, she holds me back firmly, desperately, without question. She doesn't know me and I don't know her, but we're together now. Each one a little less alone.

As we descend further into the ground, I'm forced to think of Hell.

In ancient Mesopotamia, the Sumerians believed all souls went to Kur, a large hole in the ground just like this. Maybe this is Kur, I start to think, but when we're finally forced through an opening into an enormous cavern, I'm no longer certain. Kur is described as a dark, miserable place. But here? This cave? It's simply beautiful. *Zay al foll.* As beautiful as jasmine.

Light punches into the cave through a single opening in the ceiling in strokes of pure gold. I can see sand and dust particles dancing through the light that illuminates the full expanse of the cave in brilliant shades of brown and blue topaz.

A river splits the center of the space and on its other side, flat, smooth stone leads up to a single massive rock and the towering throne mounted on top of it — and the creature occupying it.

But even Hades was beautiful in some depictions... Maybe, it's even the beauty of this place that makes it that much more horrible.

I'm not sure where I am — I'm barely certain of *who* I am — but I'm afraid. Perhaps fear is my only truth.

I'm shoved further into the cave, as big as any cathedral, and as I sweep my gaze around, I can see that the space is full.

People — creatures — are everywhere. *Everywhere.* Men and women with bronze skin, black hair and whips in their hands stand around the perimeter of the massive chamber. They watch us as we enter and I think fleetingly of Kur and Hell and Dante's nine circles.

Hell is heat and fire and Kur is dreary and miserable, filled with demons and dust. Hearts are weighed on Anubis's scales in Ancient Egypt and in Tibet, one must serve in Narakas deep in the earth until one's Karma has achieved its full result.

How heavy are our hearts?

How much karma did we waste?

What did we do in our last lives that was so *wrong*?

Jostling bodies part in front of me and through their curtain I finally get a clearer picture of the man on the throne, and any lingering uncertainty I had about whether or not this was the final Judgement, is erased.

Here we are. This is it. Purgatory has reached its conclusion. Because even though I can't remember the face of Allah, I know the word and its definition. And I know it's counter in the underworld. Hades. The Devil. Baal the Prince. Azazel.

He sits in the center of this new world on top of his throne watching us as we're brought in to face him, waiting impassively to deliver his verdict. Anubis, the devourer.

I catch a second glimpse of the creature when I'm shoved forward, closer to the river's edge. It's the jangling sound that pulls my attention up. He's holding a chain in his right hand and when he jerks it, the woman caught on its other end flies off of the rock beneath his throne and lands hard on the smooth landing below it.

Cupping her cheek, she rears up with fire in her gaze that makes me think that, in one past life, she might have been a Valkyrie even though in this one she's wearing the same grey uniform as the rest of us.

Her pale head is bald, but her cheeks are flushed bright pink. It stands out against the grey and drags my attention down...down...to the red that covers the rest of her.

"Is that blood?" Jia, at my side, whispers. "Oh god, what did he do to her?" She's shaking as we reach the river's edge — or I am, but I don't let go of Jia's palm.

I don't know her, but I don't let go.

"Gedabegulibetihi pondari tenirodiki!" Comes the shout from behind me. I can't interpret it, at least not fast enough to avoid the surge of pain that slashes across my back.

I'm too shocked to scream. Too shocked to do anything but absorb the pain of what feels like a thousand knives slicing me from my right shoulder blade to my left hip. I nearly fall off of the stone bridge that crosses the river — would have, had Jia not caught me and pulled me to the safety of the stone on the other side.

I black out, but when I come to a moment later, I'm wavering on my feet, grey-uniformed people spread out to my left and right. As we're forced into a shaky line, Jia crushes my fingers in her grip. She's sobbing forcefully now, enough for the emotion to shake her chest. She tries to clap a hand over her mouth to stop the sound and stop drawing attention to us, but it doesn't help.

She screams when the flash of the whip comes for her and drops onto her knees. I fall beside her, refusing to let go of her hand as her grip goes slack in mine.

"It's alright, Jia," I whisper hoarsely, but it's a lie. It's not alright. Anubis devours the souls of those who aren't worthy to pass on into their next life.

The sound of laughter and rattling chains echoes across the cavern. The chain in Baal's hand isn't the only one present. There are other beings in here besides us grey-uniformed victims and the whip-wielding demons intent on torturing us.

As my gaze flits around, I notice that there are other species present — at least two, from the looks of it.

Slighter beings with charcoal-colored skin almost blend into the walls and stand in complete contrast to the creatures with blue-hued skin and white hair that falls in ratty knots to their waists.

They aren't like us — the fact that they aren't bald or wearing uniforms all but confirms it. And they definitely aren't like the demons. They look so different from us, from *them*, from each other, I wonder...I'm lost in wonder...I don't know what to think.

I close my eyes and think of those hands, tracing that letter called *jeem*. Tracing my name. Spelling it for me for what might have been the very first time. How many times have I drawn it for myself since? And in how many languages?

I am Egyptian, but I am the interpreter. It's my job to find the weaknesses of the monsters containing us and liberate the captives. *All* the captives, I decide then, regardless of their species, creed or color. They won't die here because I am Halima the interpreter and I will not die here and I will bring them with me.

I will not die here. This is not Hell. Anubis can be defeated.

The thoughts settle the pain in my back, reducing it to a dull throb. Opening my eyes, I inhale in two jerks that rip at my lungs, that tear up my heart.

But Jia's hand is still in mine and I focus on it with everything I have as Baal finally descends from his throne. He makes his way down the line of people and, at every person, he nods to one of the four opposite corners of the chamber.

On his command, that person is taken away and locked into chains that attach them to the other people crowded there.

There are a few exceptions.

Four women are pulled from the crowd and taken somewhere else. The first has a full, round figure and a rich brown skin tone. The second is very tall and thin. The third has my skin tone, but doesn't look Egyptian or Middle Eastern — she could be South American, but I'm not sure.

The fourth is petite, but I don't see her face or her name tag until she's dragged too far enough away for me to identify anything about her. All I know is that all four women didn't look bad, even bald and dripping wet and all I can hope is that they were not taken by the Devil for their beauty.

Even though I don't know how beauty is defined in this new world, I have other words in my vocabulary that are far more frightening. Words like power. Words like rape.

Jia gasps and, when I follow her gaze, I lock up, too. Baal has reached Kenya in the line and regards her now with greater consideration than even the four women he removed. Too much consideration.

Kenya meets his gaze with a ferocity that terrifies me because it's threatening and she's our captain. She gave me my orders. Haddock had been prepared to leave me. For as long or short as it lasts, I owe her my life.

And then the Devil does something truly horrible. He smiles. He smiles and his teeth flash white against his face. His smile is beautiful and I'm sucked beyond the River Styx straight into Hades by the man who holds the moniker himself.

"Memo lithan togo na. Memak haren higo no." His voice is a rich rumble that makes my abdomen squeeze.

Jia says something next to me, but I can't hear her. I'm concentrating, gears in my mind slowly coming to life as I recognize some of the words. Not all of them — not even half — but just two.

Lithan. Haren.

Lithan...

Lithan lithan lithan. It sounds like the old English word for *travel*. That word later evolved to *laedan* in the fourteenth century, which meant *to guide* and later found its heart in the English word *leader*. Leader. Is that what he's calling Kenya now?

How he knows she's a leader is beyond my comprehension as is the fact that, even though most of these words are *not* anything I've heard before, some of these words are most definitely rooted in English and Spanish and others, Arabic. Fascinating. Meanwhile, much of the grammar seems to be Amharic. Incredible.

"Ero, ellama merimerikeganma," another of the giants shouts. I don't understand any of the words, but my focus attaches itself to the first. *Ero.*

Ero. Ero Ero Ero.

He has a name and it's not Baal, not Azazel, not Hades. And if he has a name, that means he's just a creature, just an animal like the rest of us. He can bleed. He can be gutted.

Ero, the animal, looks back at the woman tied to his throne. He gives an order that prompts another barbarian to release her. Grabbing Kenya violently by the back of the neck, he throws her towards the throne and snaps his fingers.

A single spear is tossed onto the ground and lands directly between Kenya and the other woman. Instincts I know not to ignore tell me that this is Leanna, our general, and that Ero has identified the two highest ranking officers left among our people. But how? And what is his plan? Why did he release Leanna and why is he giving these fighters a weapon?

"Fugcha," he orders and I gasp.

"What is it?" Jia says. "Halima, what is it?"

"He wants them to fight," I whisper back.

Kenya is first to move. She lunges for the spear, but she doesn't attack Leanna. She throws herself at Ero.

Leanna moves a split second later and gathers the loose end of her chain. She spins it around her head like a propellor and wields it like a flail at the same time that Kenya feints and thrusts up at Ero's stomach.

He doesn't move until the last second. Until just an inkling of hope trickles in that these two warriors might be able to beat him.

But even though he's weaponless, he *is* the weapon. He stands two heads taller than Kenya and one of his hands could easily wrap all the way around her throat. He catches the chain when it comes at him and even though the tail end smashes into his shoulder and a red welt appears beneath it, he doesn't flinch.

At the same time, his other hand catches the spear just beneath its pointy metal tip. He stops its path inches from his ribbed abdomen. His limbs move in perfect sync, his gaze half distracted.

The Devil-worshipping demons around the cave laugh, though it takes me a moment to identify it as such. Laughter. Typically a term used to describe joyous sounds, sounds of mirth. But this sound could not be farther from it. This is a terrible sound, one that reaches into chests and snuffs out all tendrils of hope and happiness like plucking dandelions.

He grins and when he starts to laugh too, I feel my soul whither a little, retreating deeper into my body where it will be safe.

While he laughs, Kenya and Leanna try to retract their weapons, try to attack, try to free themselves in any way, but they're stuck and he's laughing and they're all laughing and Jia's shaking so badly at my side that our sweaty, sticky palms remain locked together through adrenaline alone.

Ero rips back his left arm and Leanna, unwilling to relinquish her weapon, goes flying. She hits the stone ground just twenty feet in front of me and, when she rolls onto her side, I see that her back is covered in brutal welts and slashes. Her grey shirt is shredded. *How many times did he whip her?*

Tears well in my eyes as I look towards the monster, rage making me sweat even more. My heart kicks like a boot to the chest. I wish I could kill him. *I will. But I'm not ready yet.*

He drags Kenya in towards him by the spear and catches her by the throat when she falls. Lifting her by the neck, he tosses the spear over his shoulder absently where it's caught by a younger male warrior before Ero tosses her just as easily onto the ground next to Leanna.

"Tekaroella haremu."

Haremu? Like Harem? The thought jolts and I feel shouts of protest surge up into my mouth as two female demons lead Leanna and Kenya away, but then I remember... *Don't give yourself away. They cannot know what languages you speak...* So I cage angry, violent words behind my teeth.

La'a. No. Nein. Ayi. Bu. Non. Net. I close my eyes, reach for a language that feels distant to me, settling on Turkish, then begin counting to a hundred. Bir, iki, üç, dört, beş, altı...

Very quietly, I hear a soft, shaky voice whisper, "Hana, du, se, ne, daseos..." I'm counting out loud and now Jia's counting with me in Korean. I quickly make the switch. "Yug, ilgob, yeodeolb..."

She laughs lightly and frantically under her breath and squeezes my hand so hard I think she might break my soft bones. Then I'm sure of it when I feel a shadow — a hot, enormous shadow — fall over us. I open my eyes and look up.

A wall of bronze is the first thing I see. It's covered in reflective brown and pink scars. They cover every inch of him. Some thin and fresh. Some old and thick and badly healed.

The thickest one starts at his lowest rib and travels down, disappearing into his dark brown pants. They're woven fibers, but I can't tell beyond that what material they are, just that they're stained. *Is that Leanna's blood? Kenya's?*

He's twice my height. That's all I can think when I first look up at him. I'm wrong — at least, I hope I am — but it's still what hits me first. And even though I hate him, his size alone gives me pause, makes me shiver, makes me want to lay all my secrets bare so that I don't have to be punished by him when he figures out that I'm here for a rebellion.

And for revenge.

I pull my lips into my mouth and bite down on them. As I do, I notice a downward flicker of his. His mouth is large, almost comically so, and a dark, delirious pink. The wells of his eyes cast dark shadows across his cheeks, which are high and cut like shards from the black and green stones glimmering in the cave walls around us.

Like his heavy eyelashes, his hair is inky black and falls down to his swollen shoulders. Tangled and raging, his curls rush like the River Styx. *You are not Charon. You are Ero. You can be defeated.*

Jia was shaking before, but now my own tremors are all I can feel as I finally force myself to meet his gaze, only to find that he's not looking at me. He's not looking at Jia either, but at our locked hands.

I shake so badly that it pulls Jia further towards me. Without warning, the disturbed look Ero wore fades and he drops onto his haunches.

His massive body is an occultation of the light trickling down from above. The scent of blood and sweat and salt perfume his skin. He smells like War itself. I want to close my eyes, but I'm riveted to the motion of his bloody knuckles as he produces a dagger from the belt at his waist. Short, it has a leather handle and a blackened blade.

He shouts an order that I can't interpret and a demon approaches with a torch in her hands. Sweat pours from my armpits down my sides, down the back of my neck, and from the curve below my breasts as Ero takes his dagger to the open flame, movements deliberate and slow as he waits for the pointy end to glow bright red.

"Oreyo yasibalu yaruella?" He chuckles and I hate the sound. It's lovely and all I can think of is Lucifer. *Lucifer was an angel once.*

He holds his blade up before his eyes and, seemingly satisfied, brings it closer and closer to Jia and me. We both cringe away from the heat radiating out of the glowing steel, but in order to escape it we'd have to release each other's hands and we don't. It isn't one of us, or the other, but both.

We don't know each other, but we don't let go.

Ero's mouth twitches, but this isn't a male to make false promises. He brings the blade in closer and closer until it touches the insides of both of our wrists at the same time.

The sight of it burning my flesh comes before the sensation of pain and my fingers lock when I should have spent those precious seconds trying to pry them open and get away.

My brain lurches, but is slow to fire or maybe it's just that the pain in my back makes this fresh agony hard to feel. Jia screams and collapses forward, but she doesn't let go of me. She still doesn't.

And I still don't let go, not even as the smell of burning flesh wafts up to greet me. It clashes with the scent of the blue goop still clinging to my uniform, which reeks of antiseptic, but also with the stranger scents lingering beneath the blood and sweat and salt on his skin.

Woozy, I waver and strangely, I think that he smells like war, yes, but he also smells like Anubis. Just like Hades would in my dreams. He smells like minerals and grass and metal, like salt and like sea. He reeks of survival, of regret, of a paradise lost. He smells like an angel that fell. He smells like ruin.

Where there is ruin, there is hope for treasure.

The thought collides with the pain and pushes it back. Reduces it to rubble. A voice — an actual voice — whispers those words in my head and I *know* that voice. I know it.

Ebi. *Father.* Father said that. He was repeating the words of a poet he loved and that poet was called…was called…I stretch further into the memory, but come up short.

"Where there is ruin, there is hope for treasure." I hear the words out loud, but this time in my own voice.

"Woga eh?" He rumbles, but I don't answer or let myself be shocked by the nearness of his voice and his overwhelming presence. So sad. So ruined.

Instead, I close my eyes and let tears leak down my cheeks and I cry for him, for this Anubis, Charon lost at sea.

I cry for this place with its ruined soul and I repeat words that come to me, "My soul is from elsewhere, I'm sure of that, and I intend to end up there." It's the same poet…something…something Jalal…el…something. He was my father's favorite.

"Woga eh?" I open my eyes to see his chiseled face, his brow furrowed.

He must not like what he sees in mine because he bares his teeth at me like an animal, lips peeling back in rage. He yanks the brand away from my skin and Jia's and a surge of breath rushes into my lungs along with the rich, overlapping tastes of pain.

"Kedejiniliste?" His intonation tilts up in a question. I don't understand the word, but I know he wants me to repeat what I've said.

I open my mouth, but as I look up at him and meet his bitter gaze, the words catch in my throat. I shake my head.

Khara. Khara khara khara. I know immediately that I made the wrong choice. It's in his eyes. They're storm cloud grey, reflective of the color of the dark blade he returns to my arm, but my arm alone.

"Just let go," Jia whimpers, pained, but still trying for me.

But I don't let go. I don't speak or answer her or him, but I refuse to let go, just like I refuse to look down and see my skin burning. I just focus on the feeling of Jia's soft hand in mine.

The mistake of my open defiance gets more grim the longer I stare into his eyes. A vein pulses across his forehead. The muscles twitch in his steely neck. His jaw sets and he presses his brand more fully below the wound he already made just below my elbow crease. Harder and harder and harder...

My eyelids flutter. He repeats his question, but I don't repeat myself. And it no longer has anything to do with the fact that the pain has blotted out the memory of the poem, making it impossible for me to recite, and everything to do with the fact that another word creeps front and center, past thoughts of mother and father, past thoughts of ha and jeem, past thoughts of language and who I am or what, and settles calmly in the center of my being.

Together. A reminder that Jia's hand is in mine and even though memories have forsaken me for all the value that they had, there are new memories to be made, new foundations to fight from. I am not here alone.

We're here together.

And if I'm wrong and he *is* Anubis of this new world, it will be *together* that our hearts are weighed.

We'll find a way.

"Together," I whisper. "Hamkke," I repeat in Korean.

Jia's hand squeezes mine harder and through the scent of burning flesh and the pain that threatens to eclipse all else, I hear her whisper, *Hamkke* back.

"Kedejiniliste," he snarls between his teeth.

But my head is foggy. Reality beats a lazy retreat and I rock onto my heels and let my head fall back as I continue to endure.

I endure until the pain gets so overwhelming, I don't feel it anymore. Dizzy, I open my eyes and in Amharic, I whisper, "Anidi laye."

Together.

His nostrils flare and his storm cloud eyes glaze over with fear disguised as violence and they are the last things I see before the dam breaks and the pain trickles in and drowns me.

2
Ero

Finding the Tanishi over thirty days ago has put my warriors in a good mood. The energy of our cave system has changed. There's more laughter. More chaos. More bloodsport. It's beautiful.

Tanishi means *small one* and I watch one of the Tanishi men fight one of my warriors now. This Tanishi tried to hoard rations and this is his punishment.

If he survives.

And if not, then he'll make excellent feed for the crocs that live deep in this cave system and who need to be appeased from time to time.

The warrior in the ring connects her heel with the Tanishi's stomach. When he howls in pain, she laughs. We all do.

Croc feed it is...

These Tanishi are so weak and small — even smaller than the Danien and the Omoro — but, like the other small captive races, they're good laborers, and their small statures make it possible for them to mine the cracks and crevices in the cave system.

They've even wiggled in to find new routes through to farther reaching water sources. It's good work, even if some of it has been unsanctioned — though I would never admit to it. Most unsanctioned searchers end up as croc feed, anyway.

One of the two Tanishi at my feet shifts, her chains clanking. She is the Tanishi leader, though the other female leads them, too. I could tell by the way the pale-skinned one looked at me. So much to see in those eyes, especially considering that, at first, the Tanishi were all the same disgusting soft, wet, hairless masses that we found crawling out of those tanks.

There were so many of them, it was lucky that some were dead in their tanks and others were impossible to revive and that, for the rest, they are easy to kill when we need to.

Had all survived, their numbers would have easily overwhelmed us and that's not a risk I can take. If any of the captives ever realize that they outnumber us six to one, then we could have trouble.

And I do not believe in trouble.

Only rules.

Only obeying.

Only submission.

The leader with the pale skin shakes her chains again. I glance down at her absently. I thought about stripping her naked to humiliate her — and all of them — but in the remarkable time we've held her and the other Tanishi captive, their skin has toughened up and their hair has grown all the way down to their shoulders. So have their nails. I frown in disgust down at her hands where her cracked fingernails look like claws.

Despite that, her hair is red — a coveted color among the Kawashari. We could use her as bait and slaughter part of their horde, steal their resources. They grow foods high in their mountain dwellings that we haven't seen in years. Raiding one of their nagamas would be an ultimate prize.

So until then, I don't need one of my warriors going after her in the meantime. Even my most insatiable warriors know not to rape any stolen women. They know how I feel about using sex as a weapon of war. It only leads to disease, which spreads and kills even faster than Wickar and Kawashari tribes, snakes and desert crocs.

After our last losses, finding so many easily subjugated people to replenish our dying numbers feels good. Once we weed out the weak, we will use the strongest among them to breed.

The two Tanishi at my feet will become breeders, but only if I'm able to break them. The Tanishi with the red hair surges against her chains. *Perhaps, not this one. Croc feed, then…*

I release her chain, nodding and giving her permission to step into the ring and take the place of her fellow Tanishi. She obeys and fights and even though she doesn't win, her skill is improving. *Would be a shame to feed her to the crocs.*

I order Lopina to carry her back to the protected females and treat her wounds. Already, this is a step forward, closer to having her underneath me or one of the other males. She doesn't fight me, but fights on my command.

Good girl.

The fighting ring clears as the other chained Tanishi leader shouts curses up at me. She seethes against her chains and I could punish her for it, but I don't want her to get used to punishment exclusively.

Punishment should remain erratic, spliced in with the occasional reward. Create unease. Create a complete lack of stability. Make them shake just to be near me. Make them afraid. Yes, so afraid. It's a game. My favorite one.

For now, I withdraw my whip and hold it towards her in a threatening grip. She flinches, holding up one arm, and my warriors laugh when I stand and slide my whip back into its sheathe.

"Imitina togari," I tell her. *Not today.* I toss her a wink.

She shrieks at me and her teeth glow white against her skin, which is a particularly alluring shade that reminds me of the large trees we were once able to grow. They haven't grown in years, since the Nigusi fell when I was a child, the Nigusi I once served... I try not to read into it as a bad omen.

I snarl back at the female whose skin is colored in reminders of loss. Even if I don't plan to physically torture her today, I can't allow her outward defiance or what she triggers in my memory. *Failure.*

No. Nigusi don't fail. Not unless they intend to swim with the other worthless prisoners among the crocs.

I snarl and bite the air in front of her face, moving at a speed these little Tanishi don't ever seem prepared for. She falls back, grip slipping on the stones below her so that she tumbles down to the flat arena landing.

My warriors laugh and the fighting ring breaks, warriors returning to their stations. I stand as they disperse and take a tour of my mines, ordering Wyden to remain where he is so he can watch the leader. I do not trust her. Then again, I don't trust him.

I trust nothing but my own intuition.

I follow it now.

My feet pull me through the largest mines towards the sound of shouting coming from one of the smaller ones. Fires built into the walls reveal an unusual sight.

Three of the Tanishi are standing up against one of my warriors. He holds a whip and brings it down on the thigh of the Tanishi on the left. The man falls, but is quickly replaced by another.

The Tanishi female has both hands outstretched. She is speaking to her fellow Tanishi in whatever language it is that they share and as she speaks, more of them step from their posts and crowd beside her.

I frown.

She is not a leader and she is smaller than the rest and even her shaky voice carries little authority, but whatever she is saying is enough to rally them.

I approach and several of the Tanishi lose their confidence. They fall to the ground. A female begins to cry. A male begins to shake. The whipped male eyes me with threats in his pitiful gaze and I prepare to kill him, but am distracted by what's *behind* him.

The Tanishi were defending an *Omoro* against one of my warriors.

They were not defending their own.

My frown becomes more severe and I kick the whipped Tanishi in the ribs. He buckles and I push him aside with the toe of my shoe.

I shove two more Tanishi away from the Omoro, noting their miserable stench, so that I can reach out and grab him. The Omoro male cowers away, a miserable old man, and his thin legs collapse like twigs.

I grab his shoulder and yank him forward. He's thin, nearly frail. Sick. I can see it in the yellow of his eyes and the boil that's formed on the side of his neck and I hiss.

Cave sickness spreads. He could kill every creature here.

"He has cave sickness, Nigusi," my warrior, Warren, says at my back. "The Tanishi here were trying to help hide him."

I nod once and pull my sword out of my belt. It's clear my warrior was doing what he was trained to do by eliminating him. The end a lone slave would meet on the surface would be brutal. The end he would meet with the crocs would be better, perhaps, but not by much. And I cannot allow the disease to spread. Because once caught, there's no curing it.

I meet the old Omoro man's gaze and he nods once. "Giwehela," I whisper between us. *Discarded.*

He tips his head forward so slightly I almost miss it on a blink. Then he closes his eyes, exhales, surrenders. I plunge my sword through his breast bone in a hard, rapid motion. He's dead instantly. The caves are protected.

"Giwehela unjay," I repeat. *Discarded successfully.*

"Giwehela unjay," comes the reply from the warrior behind me.

"Take him to the crocs," I order.

Warren steps past me and scoops up the corpse, flinging the body over his shoulder. I turn and prepare to follow him out of the cavern, but see movement out of the corner of my eye that stops me.

The Tanishi who had been speaking before places her hand on the shoulder of an Omoro female. She leans in close to her, wrapping the female up in an embrace I've never seen before. I study it in profile.

The Omoro seems somehow less confused than I feel and holds the Tanishi back, even going so far as to drop her forehead onto the Tanishi's shoulder.

She is crying, the Omoro, and the Tanishi has her mouth pressed to the long, dark strands of the Omoro's hair. Her lips are moving and it looks *dangerously* like the Tanishi is speaking to her.

That isn't possible. Tribes do not share tongues. I shake it off, but I cannot allow this strange display to continue. There is no unity. No solidarity. There is only living and dying alone.

Moving rapidly, I separate the pair and lift my hand, prepared to strike the Tanishi, prepared to kill her if she does not survive the blow. She lifts her hand like she'll try to defend herself against me and my gaze snags on her forearm where she bears a series of marks. Burns.

I made those.

A fleeting memory touches my conscious. Torturing the newcomers. Instilling fear. Yes. Yes... I remember now. This female had her hand locked in that of another Tanishi's and she refused to release her.

The solidarity I hoped to burn out of her, burns within her still.

I tortured her, waiting for her to release the other woman. She did eventually, but only after she passed out. Before that though, I could have sworn she said a word that she has no way of knowing. A word that, if spoken, could turn to action and could bring everything I've worked for down.

An ancient word that strikes like a viper, venom implanting a memory I thought I'd excoriated directly into my skin, my mind, my soul. *Anidi laye.*

That's what the Nigusi I served once said right before he was gutted. He told us that we would die if we didn't learn to work together.

Together.

Anidi laye.

He was wrong.

It's about separation, keeping the tribes apart, never assimilating and never letting them unite. Their numbers, together, would overwhelm my warriors. And language is the key to that.

My hand twitches as I reach for the Tanishi. I grab the Omoro female instead. I grab all the Omoro and push them from the chamber without looking back at the strange female with the frail form, the mocking scars and the ghosts of ancient Pikosa warlords trapped in her eyes. She will die soon and by my hand. But not now.

I need to consider her strange marks that look dangerously like signs…signs spelling a word she had no way of knowing but that she said, that I heard.

Anidi laye.

No, the mark is just a mark. It spells nothing.

These are not signs. If they were signs, then that would mean she is something of importance and she's a captive — unimportant by her very nature.

That's not what signs mean. If she bears a sign that I see, then that means that sign is for me.

I growl audibly as I look back at the female, examining her face as she slowly lowers her raised hand. Her skin is lighter brown than mine and darker brown than the pale Tanishi beside her. Her hair is dark, though not so dark as mine, and falls to her shoulders in curled tangles.

Nothing special. Nothing at all. Too small to be a breeder and if she is touching tribe members that do not belong to her, too stupid and too dangerous to be anything besides feed for crocs in the future. So yes, I will kill her.

My gaze flashes to her arm and the mark that stands out there like a beacon, like a reprimand directed at *me*. *For* me. I frown.

Anidi laye. But what does it mean?

Yes, she will die.

Soon.

Soon, but not today.

I hasten from the cave quickly.

3

Halima

"Do you see this? This is lodestone. Are you looking, Halima? Halima," Chayana squeals. She knows I'm not.

She huffs, "You don't even understand how stupid this is. We're pulling magnetite and hematite out of the caves with our bare hands. If they knew that there was a banded formation of lodestone here — *magnetized* lodestone — they'd have been using it by now. Or maybe they haven't seen it. Or do you think they're too stupid to realize what it is?"

She releases a loud squawk — a sound I know is as close as she gets to rage — before changing topics faster than a mosquito swept up in a strong wind.

"I mean do you know how rare that is? Magnetized lodestone? I mean look! *Look!* Halima, Haddock. Are you looking?"

I glance at Haddock and see him watching me with his lips curved up in a smile. Giving me a quick wink, he sidles up to my right. His shoulder presses against mine, a pleasant sensation, even if he stinks. We both stink. So far, the warriors in charge haven't given us enough water to thoroughly wash ourselves in and we've been here over thirty — maybe even forty days by now.

It's...unfortunate.

Especially considering that one of the stranger side effects of coming out of stasis after roughly four thousand years is rapid hair and nail growth, including hair...everywhere. My armpits look like shrubbery and don't even get me started on the small forest between my legs.

Haddock's reddish-brown hair falls to his shoulder blades and his reddish-brown beard has a whole host of things stuck in it that I'd rather not think about. Still, he's not a bad looking man with his muscular arms and thick black eyelashes and green-brown eyes.

I don't know who I was before I went into that sleep cell, but whoever I am now is a sexual creature. Captivity hasn't stopped my libido any and even though I'm not particularly attracted to Haddock, I find myself staring at him more and more often and getting increasingly...restless. Maybe it's just the contact I'm missing. The human connection. The intimacy. Who knows. Either way, I bite my bottom lip and wink back up at him.

He inhales deeply and gives me a warm smile.

"Are you guys listening!" Chayana practically shrieks. "Look!"

She uses a lump of the black rock in her hand to beat at the wall until a lump of darker black rock breaks off. Then she shuffles over to where I'm standing.

"Give me your hand. You've got some magnetite there, right?"

"Um. I don't know. I'm not the geologist. I'm the interpreter."

She isn't listening to me. It's not her strong suit. "Wait, what?"

Her face scrunches up, her enormous eyes crinkling at the corners. They're light brown and completely stunning, made more so by the new, wild growth of her curly eyelashes. Her dark hair falls to her mid-back, slightly less curled than mine, but just as dark. She was Hindi by birth, but now she's what the warriors call *Tanishi*, just like the rest of us.

And she's the geologist.

And the Pikosa are the warriors who've enslaved us.

She laughs as she plucks the stone in my hand and tosses it over her shoulder. "You're hopeless at this. That's granite. Even though it's a useful resource, these Pikosa guys only want us mining for iron ores. You see the difference? Haddock. You've got some hematite there, don't you?"

"Uhhm..."

She rolls her big eyes and grabs his wrist, yanking him towards her. "Yes. See the difference? This has a greyish hue. Your granite was yellowish."

It was? "Oh yeah. I see." I don't see.

"You don't see," she deadpans.

"Oh no. I see." I don't and I don't want her to launch into an explanation of the difference between the different grey rocks like she's done a thousand times before.

"Clearly you don't. The difference is..."

"I know a poem about granite."

"What?" I know she's asking for clarification, but I take it to mean she wants to know what the poem is.

I speak up loudly before she can tell me about the properties of magnetized heratite or megnalite or blablaite. "You are a ruby encased in granite," I start.

Chayana makes a face and shakes her head. "That's nice, but this mine has no rubies. *This mine has magnetized lodestone!*"

"Chayana," Haddock says. He reaches across my body and lays a hand on her shoulder, shushing her in a calming way I haven't mastered yet. "Just tell us about the lode...loud...whatever you're holding."

Haddock is also not the geologist. Haddock is the doctor.

Chayana hesitates, like she wants to defy him and launch into her tirade about the different rocks she finds all so fascinating, but fortunately for us, she decides against it.

She makes her squawk sound again, only a little softer this time, and unfurls Haddock's fingers from around the rock — the hermit rock? is that it? — in his palm.

It's a big palm. Rough and broad. Paler than mine is, but not by much. My mind wanders out of boredom and I try to picture what it would be like to act on my fantasies. To swap caves with Michel, Haddock's current cavemate, and...and what?

I don't have any memories of what it's like to be with a man, but I know that sex is defined as the coupling of two adults and that it *can* involve a penis entering a vagina.

I have a vagina, defined as the elastic, muscular part of the female genital tract and, given that he would appear male, I assume that Haddock has a penis, or the organ of copulation in higher vertebrates. Maybe, I should just ask him if he would like to…to copulate? Is that what women in this new world do?

"Halima, are you paying attention?"

I jerk, realizing that I've been staring at Haddock's hand and not the small pebbles in it. They're…levitating. *Levit* from the Latin meaning *light*, yet this is stone. "How…"

"Lodestone is a naturally magnetized chunk of magnetite. Oh and hey, get this. You'll enjoy this, Halima." She nudges me with her elbow. "The first magnetic compass was actually made out of lodestone. And did you know that the word lodestone actually means course? Or like…course stone? Heh? Hehhh?" She elbows me again twice more and I blink at her, shocked.

"You're right. In Middle English, lode means *journey*."

"Ha! Isn't that great? Who says a geologist can't be the linguist, too?"

"Not really a question of linguistics, but etymology."

She makes that squawk again and before she thinks to rebut, I quickly amend, "But yes, your point holds."

"Seeeeee?"

I nod, smiling along with her, more interested now. "Could you break up more of that lodestone so we can share it with the other prisoners?"

"We should be using it to separate the iron ore from the other minerals in the sediment. If we just took it out and then pulverized it immediately, we could use these natural magnets to pull out the iron ore without having to go through this shit."

She holds up her hands and I cringe, curling my equally broken nails into the heels of my hands. Her fingertips are bloody and torn, scratches covering her palms. Her feet are worse, but I don't look at them because it makes me think about the pain in mine.

A loud clack of laughter behind us makes us all jerk. Haddock turns, jaw setting. Chayana's light seems to dim. It's depressing. For as annoying as I find her most of the time, I need her enthusiasm. I need it like the little bit of light that filters in through some of the cracks in some of the larger caves. Pressing my face up to that light, I find myself remembering that there was once something called happiness. It's a memory — a hope, a *yearning* — strong enough to buoy me.

I slide my messed up fingers over her wrist, hoping to divert her fear back into excitement. It's all she has. It's all *we* have on these endless days and bitter nights. Kur is truly a dreary place. The longer we're kept in the dark, the more I believe that the Mesopotamians had it right.

"Can we use the small pieces for idiots like me who can't tell the difference between a hermit rock and a journey stone?" I offer.

She blinks, uncomprehending, then her lips jerk up to the left. "That's a great idea. I didn't think about that. Here, take this one for now."

The laughter gets louder behind us and Haddock turns and limps to the opposite cave wall quickly. One of the warriors whipped him in the leg a few days ago when we were trying to stop the Pikosa from killing an old man of the Omoro tribe, not that it helped. Ero stabbed him anyway and had one of his warriors throw him into the river. *Hades. Azazel. Monster.*

Panicked about meeting that same fate, I stumble to the bucket in the center of the room and make a great show of dumping the few rocks into it that aren't the journey stone just as a Pikosa warrior appears in the entry. He's still talking over his shoulder with a second Pikosa warrior when he shoves Jia, by the scruff of her collar, into our room.

He turns without ever even looking at us and makes his way back down the tunnel. I exhale. Chayana exhales.

Haddock says, "Jia." He goes to her and skims his hand down the back of her arm in an affectionate gesture.

Jia smiles around at all of us but her gaze quickly flits to me. "Hamkke," she whispers. *Together*, in Korean. The word in any language has become a sort of talisman for us Tanishi to carry.

"Together," I whisper back in English so the other two can understand.

"Together," Haddock says, before quickly turning his attention back to Jia. "Are you alright?"

"I'm fine." She nods, tucking her hair behind her ear. Unlike my hair and Chayana's, hers holds no curl. Just tangles. "I was in the separating room. I don't know why they brought me here, but I come bearing gifts."

"The separating room. Gah!" Chayana makes her squawk and goes to the wall where I watch her fingers trace a rift in the stone, slightly blacker than the surrounding grey rock. "If we could just use this, we wouldn't have to separate at all. We could use the lodestone as magnets to pull the iron ore directly out of the…"

"Okay, okay Chayana." Jia shakes her head and futzes with her bangs. She's the only Tanishi I've met so far that's actually bothered to try to style themselves. Her attempts were…sort of successful. "But wait just a second. I have toothbrushes and they're poking me."

Lifting up her shirt, she unfolds the elastic band at the top of her pants. Half a dozen sticks fall out, clattering onto the rocky floor. She bends to collect them and holds a stick out to me. My eyes light.

"Is it really time for a new toothbrush?"

"It is indeed. Marlene and I managed to steal some more stems. It's crazy. They have an entire sassafras field and it's clear that they use the leaves and the roots, but not the stems. We were able to collect almost eighty stems. We should be well stocked for the next few months, if we can keep them hidden."

The thought that we could be here doing this for many more months makes me immediately depressed. Just as quickly, I shrug that thought off.

The biologist and the botanist found us some twigs.

The geologist found us some new rocks.

It's toothbrush day. And here under the Devil's reign, it's important to celebrate the little things.

"And don't forget your toothpaste." She unfolds a small leather square and sprinkles some calcium powder onto the end of my root.

"I could kiss you on the mouth, Jia," I tell her.

"Only after you brush your teeth," she quips.

Haddock laughs lightly and as Jia opens her mouth to say more, a loud crack fires into the space, making my already sweaty chest melt.

I turn to see a Pikosa guard — one that I don't recognize — standing in the open entry of this small cavern. *This is it. Heaven help us. We're about to be slaughtered over a sack of toothbrushes!* But he just scans the four of us until his gaze settles on me.

"Nia." He speaks in Pikosa, but even if the word didn't closely resemble the ancient Amharic word for *come*, the directive would have been obvious.

I don't hesitate. I don't dare. I'm not that brave. Others are, but I'm not one of them. I'm just the interpreter and I'm still terrified that the Pikosa might realize that I know what they're saying. What will they do to me then? Skin me alive? Eat me? Twice now we've been fed meat and both times, I've been terrified to know it's origins. *But that hadn't stopped me from eating it…*

I look back over my shoulder just as the tunnel curves. Chayana's light is dead. Haddock is staring after me murderously. Jia offers me a small, depressing wave.

"Together," I mouth, hoping they hear me.

"Hamkke," Jia mouths back before the cave swallows her up.

The Pikosa warrior leads me through a maze of tunnels. They overlap and branch off in dizzying arrays but I know where all of them lead. We're in the Northwest cave system, one I know like the back of my hand because this is where they shoved all of us Tanishi.

This particular tunnel leads to the central cave — the one where I was branded, the one that has a river running straight through it. My heart starts to patter with both excitement and fear.

Fear, because the burn mark on my right forearm is gruesome. A series of jagged lines all wrapped up and twisted together.

Excitement, because as the rich scent of minerals reaches my nose, the air around me thickens with a refreshing mist. It's cool here.

As I pass through the narrow opening and step into the vast cavern, the scalding temperature of Hell retreats and is replaced by something almost bearable while sunlight punches down through the cave's main overhead opening in strokes that look like pure gold. I fixate on it until I see *him*.

He's back again today. He isn't here every day, but when he is here, the soldiers are more aggressive and restless, like they've got something to prove and whatever that thing is, is terrible, is rage, is violence.

They fight each other. They fight prisoners. They fight prisoners against each other. They bet. They laugh. Ero doesn't. He glares around at everything, paces and gives orders. Occasionally, he sits on his throne. I don't… I don't look at him when he does that.

Whenever he's here, Leanna and Kenya are, too. I don't know what he does to them when they're gone and the selfish part of me hopes never to know. But from what I can see of their rapidly diminishing forms is that every day, they look a little more haggard, a little less fierce, a little more broken.

I have to get them out.

Haddock says Ero's trying to use them to break all of us. He says we can't give in. I don't know what he means by that, but the others do, so I don't ask. I'm supposed to understand *everything*.

I feel pressure. We're plotting. Of course, we're plotting. But we aren't closer to actual plans. Somehow, that feels like my fault, like I've failed them.

With the crowd gathered around Ero's throne, I can't see much of Leanna or Kenya in their chains. I'm one part guilty, two parts grateful for that. I don't want them to look at me and make me feel like I've failed over and over and over again.

"Nia!" The guard shouts and, before I can react, he returns to where I'm standing stuck staring at Ero and grabs my arm.

He drags me to the edge of the river, near to where it feeds out of the cave system through a pitch black tunnel and continues its journey. Sometimes, I imagine what it would be like to follow it and let my body go wherever it's taken some of the other discarded captives before. And then other times, I imagine drowning.

Here, a group of prisoners with skin so pale it's near translucent wash Pikosa clothing. The Pikosa call these captives, *Danien*. The Danien and the Omoro are the only two other tribes represented here.

While Danien have long white hair and pale white skin, the Omoro are their opposite. They have dark brown-grey skin and charcoal-colored hair. It's fascinating how each tribe, aside from us Tanishi, manages to look so homogenous.

Omar thinks that somewhere in the last four thousand years, tribes formed and those tribes completely sequestered themselves from other tribes in order to survive. They inbred. Bad traits were passed down to some tribes while other tribes kept up a certain level of genetic diversity by harvesting only the strong and weeding out the weak.

Omar is our geneticist.

Ryden is our anthropologist and he agrees.

Given the lack of overlap between the tribes' spoken languages *and* the fact that these languages share roots with our ancient tongues but still manage to remain entirely distinct, I'd say they're probably right.

"Nia!" The guard shoves me down to the river's rocky edge where I take the empty space between two Danien women and ignore the blood on the rocks beneath my folded knees. *What happened to the Danien who was here before me?*

The Danien next to me hands me a pair of trousers well-lathered in soap. The woman working across the river from me rinses out the garment handed to her before passing it to the next Danien kneeling in line beside her. That Danien wrings it out.

Simple enough.

I submerge my hands in the cool water and have no luck containing my sigh of pure pleasure. The female across from me trills quietly — almost sounding like a laugh — but when I look up and meet her gaze, she looks away.

I smile at her anyway and we continue working in *near* silence. No one seems to be paying attention to us, though — no Pikosa anyway. They're all gathered in front of the throne watching the fighters battle, which is a good thing, because the clamor disguises the sounds of the Danien whispering quietly to one another. No one can hear them. No one but me.

And they're plotting. No, they're *beyond* plotting. They're already in the *planning* stages.

I listen with my ears cocked as the female beside me says to the other Danien females in the group, "If we want to escape, we need…tomorrow…tools…" I don't understand every word, but I understand enough to know that this is an escape plan and I want in on it.

My entire being is riveted to their conversation as they debate which tunnels to take out of here, how to distract the guards and where they'll go when they reach the surface. Surface. *Sur face.* Origin French. From the sixteenth century word directly translating to *on face.* I wonder what it's like...

I think of the gold light and imagine paradise.

"We could cave the Northwest tunnel," the female across from me says, "...distraction..."

I tense.

And then she whispers, "I think this Tanishi can understand us."

The woman next to me recoils from me like I'm going to punch her. I hold up both hands and open my mouth but evidently the wiring that connects languages together in my brain is not also attached to my ability to reason.

I should have denied the accusation, or even confirmed it and immediately told her that I mean no harm...but instead, I open my stupid mouth and stutter in my crude imitation of the Danien tongue, "Speak Danien...bad?"

I should have expected what she'd do next, but I didn't. And when I mean to run, I don't, leaving me open to attack. The Danien kneeling on the river's edge leans forward and pushes me hard.

I release a loud squawk, reminding myself of Chayana for one gleeful second before my hands flail out, I lose my balance, the fabric in my fingers disappears down the tunnel and I go tumbling after it.

I hit the water with a slap, a sharp rock hitting my left arm hard and spinning me around. I flail and kick and sputter, mouth breaking through the surface of the water as I stretch for the rocks on the other side of the river. I go under again and inhale a deep lungful of wonderfully refreshing water as a new, fresh memory comes catapulting from the dark.

Sand beneath my toes. Laughter. Voices saying my name in the pronunciation that belongs to me. Water rushing over my head, my mouth opening as if to scream and more water rushing in. It burns. But before panic can set in, strong hands lift me up and shake me.

"You don't know how to swim, Halima! Don't go near the water, habibty…"

There are no hands now though. There's only hard, slippery rock and my flailing fingers reaching, stretching, praying to catch one. I do and manage to haul myself up.

"Father?" I gasp, coughing to clear water from my lungs, but when I manage to blink my eyes open enough to see, the Devil's cold grey eyes are watching me.

4
Ero

A Tanishi's just been pushed into the river. I roll my eyes and laugh loudly, even though my stomach muscles tense. I'm up on my feet as two warriors rush forward ahead of me, but I wave them back when I see that the Tanishi in question has managed to grab hold of a large rock anchoring her to the river bank.

My stomach muscles release and then clench all over again when her face appears above the frothy water and she says a word. I don't know the word or understand her tongue, but it's her dazed look of hope that drags me through thorns. *She's looking at me like she knows me, like I'm someone she trusts.*

Meanwhile, I haven't been able to stop thinking about her. Her strange behavior with the Omoro, the word she shouldn't have known — all of them — the defiance in her strange, frightened stare and her strength despite the fact that her body looks to have been built from sand more than bone.

The sign carved in her arm — a sign of my own making.

I frown down at her, fingers twitching as I debate casting her down the dark tunnel. Dark hair. Dark eyes.

She must register that I am not the savior she's hoping for, because she releases the boulder she's clinging to and slips under the rapids again. The river's pull is strong, so I have to be quick to catch her before she's lost forever. *Why not just let her fall?*

Balancing carefully on the smooth, slippery rocks beneath me, I thrust my hand into the cold water and grab for skin. Finding some, I pull her out.

I have a hold of her wrist and her body dangles uselessly on the end of her arm. I draw her in, like a fish on a line, but my gaze catches on the brutal scar covering her forearm from her elbow halfway to her wrist.

I did that.

And the mark is getting darker. It spells a word that does not exist. *But it's a word that once did.*

Anidi laye.

I frown. "Impossible," I sneer under my breath.

My gaze flashes to her, as if expecting an answer, but she just chokes and sputters up water. My desire to kill her doubles and my grip on her wrist twitches. I should let go. I should just let go. Ignore the mark. It's just a mark. Not a sign. It's just a wound. Not a message from the scarred earth written in scars.

She coughs and droplets of water hit my cheek. "The current is surprisingly strong, isn't it, Tanishi?"

The water's spray on my bare knees is cool. My kilt is short and breathable against the mine's heat. In the village, I'd wear linens or training leathers, but in these mines, the kilt is the most I can bear. Why these new prisoners don't work naked and choose to keep their filthy rags is one of many things I'll never understand about them.

She kicks her legs in a useless motion underneath the water's surface. It's clear that, without my hold, she'd drown immediately. I glance towards the darkness of the mountain, thinking about what would happen to her if she fell and actually made it to the tunnel's end. Thinking again that I should drop her.

This time, my hand doesn't twitch at all.

She will die, but…not today. Not yet. Not now.

"Following the river will not lead you to the village, Tanishi. It would take you straight to the crocodile den. You could only hope that you'd drowned by the time you reached it."

I shake my head, gaze straying to the mark, trying to remember the last time I wrote anything down. Trying to remember why the Nigusi of my youth said what he did. Annoyed that I'm even considering his words here in this world in which he died a coward, so weak he barely even existed.

I am Nigusi. There is no *anidi laye*. There is only my rule or the crocodiles.

I clench my hand even harder around her wrist and her head falls back. She swats at me with her free hand, clearly in pain as she tries to relieve the pain likely tearing through her shoulder. She's lucky it's even still in the socket.

"Even an adolescent crocodile would be able to eat you in two bites. You'd have more luck with an adult. Maybe you'd live a few more days in its stomach."

The Danien on my left flinches and I look up and meet her gaze. I read panic, terror and stronger than both, guilt. I laugh and stand, pulling the Tanishi up with me. As I walk toward the throne, I grab the Danien by the dirty white hair on her head and drag her along.

Ellar steps up beside me. "What is it, Nigusi?"

"The Danien threw the Tanishi into the river."

"How do you know?"

"I can read it in her eyes."

Ellar laughs, slapping her hand to her thick, muscular thigh. "Want me to throw the other Danien in as a warning? A little meat for the crocs?"

"Too skinny to bother the crocs with." I throw the Danien down onto the stone landing in front of my throne and shove the Tanishi down beside her.

The Tanishi leaders chained to my thrown become immediately agitated in a way that I don't like. It suggests, once again, that this minuscule Tanishi female with the easily broken skin is of some importance and I don't read *leader* in her gaze. If it were there, I would be able to see it.

The Tanishi leader with dark brown skin tries to lunge off of the rock, but the chain binding her to my throne has almost no slack and yanks her back. She says words in Tanishi to the female on the ground and I can't have that.

I pull the whip from my belt and allow the leather tip to unfurl. It makes a swatting sound as the six loose ends hit the stones below. My wrist twitches towards the small, scarred Tanishi's back while I glare up at her dark-skinned leader, in challenge.

This will be a turn. To know if I can break her using her people. It would never work for me. I'd sacrifice any of them. But she retreats in a way that fills me with elation. How much more easily her subjugation will come when I wound and maim those under her control. *Good girl.*

"Where do you want the Danien?" Wyden says, approaching with the other warriors to form a loose arc around us as they wait for the bloodsport to continue.

Kneeling on the stones, the wet, scarred Tanishi is shaking like a loose sheet in a sand storm. So weak. Pathetic. I feel at ease, seeing her like this and I smile. It's insane that I imagined for even a second that she could be an omen. She is nothing. Worthless. The scars on her arms are just that. Scars. And they are only the first to come by my hand.

The scarred Tanishi turns her face to the side and she watches the Danien on hands and knees beside her with enormous, round eyes. She licks her lips. Her face, light brown when I pulled her from the river, is now ashen, the hollows beneath her eyes as dark as bruises.

And then she speaks.

She *says* something to the Danien. I glance at the Danien's face to see a similar surprise. Similar, but less. As if the Danien knew this already and isn't surprised to hear the Tanishi speak, but is surprised by *what* the Tanishi says. I flinch back.

I. flinch. back.

I have never flinched before except in the bloodiest of battles to avoid the cut of a sword. I glance around. None of my other warriors saw what I just saw. This act of pure chaos. *She spoke. No… She spoke* again.

Two different tongues that do not belong to her came out of her mouth, I'm sure of it. My gaze flies to the mark on her arm and I feel suddenly sick. Scar or sign? Sign or scar? My previous certainty is shaken just as quickly as it arrived.

Destroy the Tanishi. *Destroy her!* I know that I should. I know it with every fiber of my being. But that knowledge does not translate to the movement of my arm. Instead of slashing towards her, I twitch to whip the Danien instead.

If I'd had just an extra second to pull back, shake off my doubt and strike for the Tanishi, I could have killed her — wounded her badly, at least — and spared myself everything that came after.

Everything...

Instead, the moment hangs like a noose, time looping back on itself like waves on the rocks. My arm moves in a practiced motion, muscles slick from the heat in the mines more than from the exertion of the movement.

I've done this many thousands of times before. I've whipped prisoners since I was a boy. I know the weight of the leather in my palm, the worn, warm material of the grip, the sound of the leather slicing through the air, the slight *hiss* as it passes by my ear, the wet tear of broken flesh.

It's what I hear now, much louder than I remember ever hearing it, but it isn't the Danien's skin that's being flayed, as intended. It's the Tanishi's. *What has she done?* Just as I bring the whip down, she throws her tiny frame across the Danien's body.

She throws herself to cover the Danien and her skin tears open in a bloody mess and I blink, remembering that this was the same female who clutched the terrified Tanishi's hand in her own, the same female who tried to rally her own kind to stand up for the diseased Omoro, the same sick creature who offered a disgusting display of comfort to a female outside of her own tribe.

And now, she's done it again.

"Nawh!" The dark-skinned Tanishi shouts while the pale-skinned leader says, "Haylemah!"

My warriors laugh somewhere in the peripheries, but this isn't fucking funny. The tribes do *not* speak to each other. The tribes do not protect each other. The tribes only protect themselves and the individual within the tribe only protects itself. To give away one's strength, in this world, means death.

And she sacrificed herself willingly.

And she speaks their language.

And she speaks mine.

Mine.

The word lingers in the droplets of blood leaking down her back. So many of them. Skin as thin as this should have been eradicated civilizations ago. Even the Danien would not bleed so quickly.

The wild and rapid movements she took, coupled with the jerk of my own hand, made the gash in her skin appear unevenly beneath the bite of my leather. Her tunic is shredded around the right shoulder, but my whip didn't make it all the way across her back. From here, it looks...it looks...

No. No no.

I lunge for the female and grab a torn corner of her shirt. I rip it down, tearing away the fabric so I can see the full expanse of her narrow back.

The wound is a garbled mess on her shoulder, tags of flesh overlapping one another but, when I squint and tilt my head, I see that the wound spells a word in the ancient Pikosa text, one we no longer use but that is of the same bloody script scarring on her arm...and it looks...it looks like...

El-li.

I hiss, recoiling so quickly that I send stones scattering beneath my steps. They trickle and dance, sounding like bells before they stop chiming. I drop my whip and the leather thunks down dully on the stone battleground beneath my feet. My gaze roams over her back again and again, the inflamed skin appearing bright red and much clearer than it was the first time.

Two vertical slashes followed by a jagged loop spell the word *el-li.*

Mine.

I frown harder, the urge to kill her strong, but not strong enough. No longer can I risk avoiding the signs.

I *cannot* avoid the signs.

Not when they've appeared more than once. The first one was a warning, but this one feels very much like a threat and I'd be a fool to turn my back on it.

I grab her by the hair and wrench her off of the Danien, onto her feet. I lift her against me, so that her back is shielded by my front. I cannot allow the other Pikosa to see this. No one can see this. *No one.* I don't know what it will mean if they do. I know only that it will bring madness down on us and I cannot allow one captive to be the reason for my undoing. *Never.* I am Nigusi of this tribe.

I will kill her. But only once I decipher the signs or dismiss them and ensure she can bring no ruin onto me, even in death.

"Where are you taking the captive, Nigusi?" Wyden says as I stomp past him, keeping the Tanishi captive clutched tightly against my chest.

With one hand wrapped around her throat, the other around her bony hip, I lift her up against me so that her filthy feet barely graze the floor as we move.

I can feel her thin throat working beneath my palm. Her skin is too soft for this place. Weak. Disgusting. *El-li.*

Mine.

My chest heaves, breaths coming harder and hotter, scorching my lungs. I must be wrong. I must be mistaken. The signs that brought the Pikosa tribe to my feet would not lead me to this frail creature.

These cannot be the same signs that caused my hand to choose an axe over a sword when I fought a dozen warriors to claim the empty Nigusi seat. Nor can they be the signs that told me to follow the river past the crocodile pit and revealed the village cave system to me. The signs that led me to intercept the Omoro convoy, where we brought in the largest group of prisoners the Pikosa tribe has ever seen until the Tanishi…

All of these signs were clear.

Just as this one is.

And just like those, this sign speaks to me on a cellular level, deep beneath scar-riddled flesh where small uncertainties linger and fester in caves too narrow for my meaty hands to reach.

Wyden runs his hands over his hair, which is braided down the middle of his head and shaved on both sides. He watches me curiously and watches the Tanishi in my grip even more curiously. *Wyden cannot be suspicious already. He will need to be watched.*

"Get the prisoners back to work," I hiss, taking the East tunnel where prisoners do not go. Those that try, never come back.

The captive starts to writhe as I approach its entrance — fear of the Eastern tunnel, well hammered into her. *Good girl.*

I shake my head and sneeze. Her ragged black hair falls to her shoulders in tangles and tickles my nose and right cheek.

I hold her slightly away from me and turn left, off of the path that leads to the village and to the private quarters I keep on this side of the river, in the mines. The light slap of running feet greets me as I reach my grey doorway, fit my fingers to the enormous round stone blocking it, and pull the heavy weight aside.

That slapping sound reminds of a time when I was a young warrior in training, and the ill-fated Nigusi warlord I'd served. He'd been a fair master, I'd thought, but he'd been slaughtered by the challenger who took his place, so in this sense, he deserved to die.

He'd been the one to speak of foreign things, like anidi laye.

"Brin, bring me fresh linens for the Tanishi. The captive stinks."

The young Pikosa warrior-in-training glares harshly at the female in my grip. Hatred of the captive races is instilled in all warriors at a young age. He starts away from me just as quickly, giving me a deep nod that suggests he's unhappy with my command, but he'll do it anyway. He has no other choice. Not if he wants to survive.

I hesitate as his back retreats from me down the long tunnel leading to the village, but like the same tickling of her hair against my cheek, there's a tickling in my throat that makes me issue one more order.

"Bring me a healing kit and more salve." I can smell the blood on her torn flesh and I...it bothers me.

"Healing salve, Nigusi?"

I hiss, "Don't make me ask again." My chest heats. I don't like the sensation.

"Of course, Nigusi." I hear him, but I've already turned away, shoved the captive into my quarters and rolled the stone doorway back into place, sealing us within.

My quarters here in the mines are small. Three simple rooms with natural archways connecting them. I release the captive and step past her into the first room, equipped with just a series of metal hooks where I hang my kilt and armor, plus a series of drawers that house my whips and daggers. Conspicuous, I'll have to move them if I expect to keep the captive here. *Wait...what? Keep her here?*

The captive makes a small sound, like she's in pain. I glance at her over my shoulder and sneer, "You're dripping on my rug."

She keeps her eyes on the ground and her hands clasped around opposite elbows. She's shaking. *Weak.* Her grey clothing — the same grey rags all the Tanishis wear — is soaked through with river water. The water is rich in minerals and I can scent them on her skin and hair now, but the cloth wrapped around her is itself, disgusting.

"Undress," I tell her. When she winces, I grow cold and sneer, "I know you can understand me. Don't try to pretend you can't."

She still doesn't react except to press her lips more firmly together. It's very red, that mouth, tinted with a purple hue. It draws my attention. *Draws and captures.* I jerk my gaze up from her mouth — a mistake — and meet her gaze — a trap.

I narrow my eyes and inhale deeply. My shoulders roll back and my stomach muscles clench all on their own. Attempting to disguise the strange tremor that flutters up my left hand, I unbuckle the strap at my shoulder and let the supple leather fall away from my skin. I hang the pauldron on one of the hooks behind me without breaking her gaze. Without it, all that's left is my kilt and when I touch the heavy belt buckle securing it in place, she tenses.

I didn't whip her on the flagellation stone when I should have and now her distress stays my hand again. My fingers drop to my sides. I cross my arms over my chest and lean against the rocky entrance to my bathing chamber. I watch her. *Her eyes are black as pitch.* I watch her even after she drops her gaze and the tremors in her shoulders and back become more pronounced.

She wipes her palm off on her pant leg nervously as she glances continuously to her right. She's looking into the other room — at the bed, maybe? I follow her gaze to the large sand-stuffed mattress on a heavy metal frame. A linen sheet is balled up at the foot of the bed. I don't use it. There's no need, even though the air in here is fresh and cool.

Light trickles in through the shafts that lead all the way up to the surface and dust particles twist through it so slowly. I find myself often entranced by the way that dust and sand moves through the light before I remember that I am a warlord and warlords have no such concerns.

Despite the surface conditions, the air from above smells clean by the time it filters through so much mineral-rich stone. Despite the surface conditions, the air that reaches us is also cooler than it is in the mines where we keep prisoners.

Here, I can breathe. Even more than in the village, I find it more possible here than anywhere to…just…take a breath…and release.

And I brought a captive into this domain. Into *my* domain.

El-li. Mine.

Mine though she shouldn't be.

My fingers curl into my bicep. I'm uncomfortable. I don't like this. I don't like any of it. I don't like *her* and I like her silence the least.

"Speak," I shout.

She jumps and looks at me and, for a single, suspended moment, I imagine that I see something else — someone else — beneath this frightened and fragile exterior and that someone is a warrior, just not the one who will ever wield a sword. And then the moment passes and she is this shell of a creature once more.

She points into the bedroom, but not at the bed or at the light leaking in through the ceiling in three dozen different places. She's pointing at the metal cart against the wall. On top is a pitcher and a platter.

I laugh darkly and nod once. "Go. Take what you please."

Her lack of hesitation surprises me. Not to say that she doesn't hesitate — she does — but not for as long as I had hoped she would.

She goes directly to the water, bypassing the platter entirely, even though it's been recently restocked. Brin and my other fledging warrior, Tenor, are the only two allowed inside this space. My space. *El-li.* Mine. The word haunts my thoughts.

When she turns, clumsily fumbling for the cup, she knocks it to the ground. She bends to retrieve it with her right hand and pulls the flayed skin on her shoulder. She stops halfway to a crouch and hisses, then straightens and takes the pitcher from the table just like it is. She gulps water down like she hasn't had a drink in days.

I watch her throat work. Watch water leak from the corners of her mouth and drip off her chin, down her neck, down past the torn collar of her shirt where I can see her prominent clavicle. Prisoners aren't fed well, but she still looks thinner than she should.

I glance at the platter and there's a strange prickling in my fingertips, like I want to reach for that food for her. Like I want her to reach for it.

She sets the pitcher down quickly and wavers wildly on her feet. Her hands fumble for the metal table and, catching it, hold on tight. I close the distance between us, taking slow steps until I feel her heat. It's suffocating and takes effort for me to push through it. It feels like I'm wading through a sandstorm. But I've done that before, too, and she's no sandstorm. She's just a little, shattered thing.

I catch the outsides of her upper arms between my hands and I squeeze *gently*. Maneuvering her while she's dizzy like this is easy. She goes where I push and I push her back through the entry chamber and across it, into the next.

In this final chamber is a void hole built into a small nook and hidden behind a stone curtain and, before that, is a pool filled with fresh clean water carried in from the river just beyond the wall. It eddies directly into this room, creating a pool of fresh water for me and me alone. Mine. I frown. And now I'm giving it to her.

My fingers curl and flex as I release her and step back. "Clean yourself. Soap is in the metal case. Put your clothes in the chute."

I point at the small hole in the stone wall to my left. It leads down to lower chambers of this cave system where we compost everything from inedible parts of the plant to animal feces. Given the state of her clothing, I suspect they'll make a good addition.

"I don't want to see them again. Fresh linens will be brought for you. Use this to dry yourself and to staunch your wound."

Metal drawers fill a metal frame on the wall to my right. I go to it and pull a linen towel large enough for me from the top drawer. It will fit her like a blanket.

I turn from her and cross the entry again, moving to the bed. Lying on top of it, I can see the full lay of my chambers. I drink from the plastic wine skin, reclined and relaxed as I watch the captive dip her toes into the cool water.

She makes a small sound, something like a whimper, even more like a sigh. My lips quirk and I exhale through my mouth, savoring the rich and velvety texture of the wine.

She glances at me and then glances around the room. Looking for a way to shield herself from me, perhaps? She won't find anything and seems to realize that. Her shoulders slump forward as she brings her hands underneath her tunic to the waistband of her pants. She pulls them down in a rush and I'm shocked by how well formed her legs are. Unlike her torso, they have supple muscle definition and make her look more robust than her thin torso and chest give her credit for.

She carefully works out of her tunic next and my gaze slides down her side, noting that her legs are long compared to the rest of her. And even though she has little in the way of breasts, she has hips and a small, taut rear. *The kind I could explore, my cock teasing that tight entrance. She'd be so tight, given how small she is.* I shift on the bed and rearrange my swelling cock beneath my kilt. I dismiss the thought.

I don't find her attractive and I don't molest prisoners.

That is how disease spreads. That is how tribes fall.

Only the strong will join and she might be the weakest captive I've ever seen. I'm just…out of practice. How long has it been since I've been alone with a woman? The thought troubles me. I dismiss it.

I don't look away though.

I drink and I watch and I drink some more. She lowers herself into the water and uses the soap from the drawers I directed her to. *She speaks our tongue. Understands it, at least.* My suspicion is all but confirmed.

She detangles her hair with her fingers. I'm finished with my wine skin by the time she moves to her back. She attempts to massage soap gingerly into her wound. It clearly pains her. Her face is riddled in lines that don't belong on her skin which, free of filth, shines smooth.

Her face is…thoughtful. Expressive, in a way Pikosa faces are not. I can read her even more effortlessly than most. Every twitch, every nuance.

I smirk at that.

Funny, that I can read her while she can understand me. We are, in this sense, a perfect counter to one another. *Mine.*

I wrench my gaze away and look somewhere else, but there isn't anywhere else to look, so I look back but she isn't there.

I jerk up and stalk into the bathing room. She's against the wall, examining the entrance in the cave wall where the river flows in. It's a narrow entrance covered by a grate, but I worry for a moment that she might just be small enough to slip through.

It would be dumb of her to try even if she could. But then again, the sight of her back makes me frown. If I were in her position, how would I react? My back has just been flayed and she knows, just like I know, that I will have to kill her some day. Right after I'm done deciphering the signs and putting them behind me. What incentive does she have *not* to try to escape?

I glance up at the ceiling. The skylights filter in the sun that torches and scorches the surface. Too narrow for any approaching warriors or surface beasts to slip through. But what of her small, agile form?

No. That thought is even dumber.

These skylights are so narrow, not even the smallest Tanishi could find her way all the way to the surface. It's meters and meters away, besides, and no Tanishi is stupid enough to try to escape top-side. *But what if she doesn't know what awaits her…*

I frown harder, thinking back to the discovery of these Tanishi. There was a strangeness surrounding it. Everything from the blue gel cases we found them in to the larger cave surrounding them. It was a cave system unlike anything we'd ever seen before. Unnaturally smooth, with built in doorways that sometimes, but not always, moved. Huge stone slabs propelled by magic.

There had been that terrible screeching sound we thought at first could have been some new undiscovered terror, but then it stopped and the little bald creatures survived their tubes and we retreated from the unsettling cave as quickly as we could, never looking back.

But then later, after their hair and nails grew disgustingly long, their leaders proved harder to break than any other we'd encountered before.

It's as if they don't know the natural order of things. Pikosa, Wickar and Kawashari at the top. Captive tribes at the bottom. It's as if they think they're *equal* to us and that they might break free and start a tribe of their own. That they might avoid becoming croc fodder.

No. These Tanishi could not be so stupid. They're half our size and weak, besides. But they do *know* things. They've been remarkably resourceful at creating more comfortable caves for themselves. They haven't died of disease. They've even kept their teeth cleaned through methods unknown. We use the bristles from the bay plants, but they don't have access to the green rooms. What do they use?

She reaches her arm through the grate and I stiffen, thoughts pulled away from danger as she approaches it. "They can taste your blood on the river water," I grunt. "The crocs. Get away from there unless you plan to be eaten."

She releases the grate, but not with any urgency. She turns to me and I have the odd urge to draw a reaction out of her. Only one thing has so far. I take my hand to my belt and release it. She looks away as my kilt falls to the stone below.

I unlace my shoes, the leather falling away from the thick, rubbery soles and wade into the water. It rises quickly up to my chest. I slide onto the bench seat ringing the pool and watch as she tentatively perches on the edge of the bench across from me. Smooth stone, it's chilling under my bare ass and thighs.

"You try to leave through the river, you'll get swallowed whole," I say. She doesn't answer, just gives me an avoidant glance and returns her attention to her soap.

"Or you could try to shimmy up one of the holes in the cave and try your luck on the surface." I have to laugh at that.

The holes are too narrow, but even if she *could* somehow find a way up through the jagged, narrow cracks, she'd never make it to a village where she might consider herself safe — an Omoro or Danien tribe might take her in, if she reached one, but I have my doubts. Besides, between the sandstorms, sand snakes, and the nomadic Kawashari hordes that roam near our lands, she wouldn't make it far.

"So what is your plan? I won't let you leave through the door."

She gives me a look, one that riles me and makes my cock think twice about the fact that she's a worthless captive and continues trying to work her soapy fingers through her hair.

I notice, as her hands flit around her face, that her fingernails are jagged and cracked. I wade to her and reach past her to one of the bottom drawers. It opens noisily, contents rattling around. I push aside tubs of soap and a few small daggers before finding a file. I grab her left wrist.

She balls the fingers of her free hand into a fist and tries to hit me with it. Surprised, I don't notice the gesture for what it is at first. Not until I recognize the expression on her face.

I laugh, "You can't possibly think to fight your way out of here." The thought is, frankly, hilarious. I laugh hard, trying to picture her with her little fists going up against my youngest warriors. "Your fist has no effect."

Meanwhile, if I hit her with intent, her death would be instantaneous.

For whatever reason, that thought makes me feel strange. Almost proud? Not at the thought that I could kill her, if I wanted, but the thought that, against so many obstacles, I could keep this slight creature *alive*.

I shake my head and return my stare to her hands, her light-colored palms and their dark-colored lifelines.

Forcibly unfurling her fingers, I take the file to her fingernails and remove the excess, one at a time. Grabbing her feet below the water, I push her back onto the bench and do the same to her toes. It feels strange, caring for her.

"There, better." I shove her back and watch her expression scrunch as she tries to make sense of what I've just done, maybe trying to figure out why I haven't hurt her.

It's a question I haven't answered yet myself and I don't plan to now.

I shake my head and lean back, letting the wine run through me and stretching both arms across the warmer rock above the water's edge.

"You will have to speak to me eventually."

She reaches behind her, fingers fumbling over the stone ledge. She doesn't break my gaze but rather lifts a single eyebrow again as she takes back her bar of black soap and works it into her skin.

The black suds glisten against her shoulders and, even though she doesn't say anything at all, I can still hear her. Because she looks at me as if to say, *I don't think so.*

I answer her out loud. "We'll see about that, Tanishi."

And with that slight challenge, I realize just what she's done. She's given herself a few more moments to live because how can I kill her without knowing what her voice sounds like in the Pikosa tongue?

5

Halima

This is bad. Real bad. Khara as I'd say in Egyptian Arabic. Complete and total shit. And I mean that literally.

My first escape attempt is through the poop hole. Not the chute built into the wall that leads down into a real scary kind of blackness, but through the hole built directly into the ground that Ero, and now I, shit into.

Granted, I've only taken one poop into the poop hole since he trapped me in his room last night, but it was enough for me to be able to notice a very small, soft glow coming from somewhere deep down, wherever the poop hole goes.

Which is where I'm headed to now.

Except the glow that looked faint and inviting from above looks real menacing from where I am now, with my arms and legs splayed, shimmying down the poop-lined stone.

I've reached the bottom of the thirty foot shaft and I can see that it empties out into a kind of poop and pee trough that slopes down. That's fine and all, and I might have made the short drop out of the shaft onto the trough if I hadn't also noticed the very distinct sounds of Pikosa people chattering in the background.

This is a work room. And, judging by the words I hear now, which sound an awful lot like *samad* and *k'oshasha* — the Arabic word for fertilizer and the Ahmaric word for dirt — I'm kind of thinking that these people are turning their king's shit, among others, into something useful.

And, if I keep going, maybe they'll just include *me* in whatever they're concocting. A shit pie to feed their people that I have no desire to be a part of.

My right shoulder burns from where Ero stitched my shoulder back together and my arms and legs are shaking from the effort it takes to cling to the inside of this rocky poop tunnel.

Alas, I have no other option but to climb back up the way I came, wash off in Ero's self-cleaning pool and hope he doesn't notice that I will have used all his soap to get this smell off of me. Because it stinks. I stink. I've never smelled anything worse in my entire life than the poop trough below me, separated from the soles of my feet by about a body's length. And I *refuse* to make that drop. Better take my chances with the crocodiles.

I glance up at the dark opening high above me. Up, I must climb.

I reach for the next hold above my head, my slick, sticky, stinky fingers slip and the plan I had to climb is flushed in an instant.

My hands and feet lose purchase all at once and I slide angrily down the shaft, bumping knees and scraping elbows, before eventually landing in the poop trough in a heap. Poop and other disgusting liquids splash around me and a surge of bile pushes into my mouth.

A Pikosa woman screams. And then several more Pikosa scream. Swallowing brutally, I glance around, the wet tips of my hair sticking to my neck and jaw. My instinct is to reach up and brush my hair away from my face, but my hands are even more disgusting than my hair is, covered in poop and droplets of my own blood. Instead, I ball my hands into fists and clench all my muscles together tight as I wait for someone to grab me and hurt me.

But no one does.

I blink around at the people in the room and yes, they're all Pikosa and yes, they're all staring, but no one dares approach. I hold my hands up, fingers splayed in a submissive gesture, but one of the males closest to me jumps back, bumping into the woman standing behind him and knocking the pitcher out of her hands and to the floor.

The ceramic pitcher shatters and clear liquid spills everywhere and the woman releases a loud string of words I don't know yet, but that I know are curses.

There's a small panic with Pikosa rushing around trying to contain the spill, giving me enough time to look around this chamber. It's larger than any of the other working mining caves up above with the exception of Ero's cathedral.

Four long tables stretch across the cavern, made out of the same metal material everything here seems to be made out of, and a dozen Pikosa work at each one, but these aren't the big, hulky Pikosa I'm used to seeing. They're bigger than us Tanishi, sure, but they aren't all muscles as the warrior males and females seem to be. *Maybe I can fight my way out of here.*

The thought is laughable. I actually start to laugh, but that causes me to inhale and taste some of the shit that's sprayed onto my mouth. My gag reflex kicks. I choke down my next breath, unfurl my legs and step down onto the floor with renewed determination.

I might not be able to fight, but I will not die here.

Alone and covered in poop.

So I run. I skirt the spilled liquid and run around the edge of the room to the cave's only entrance and, amazingly, the Pikosa near me all scramble madly to avoid me, rather than trying to contain or kill me. I make the most of it, lunging at Pikosa as I charge towards the open entrance that leads into yet another cave.

Even larger than the last, this cavern has high, vaulted ceilings. A fine mist hangs in the air and the only smell of shit in this room is the smell that I carry with me. I keep going.

Pikosa might not have been in that last cave, but there are plenty of them in the next one. This one fascinates me, and I quickly realize that we prisoners have been working only one small part of this cave system — the roughest part — but beneath the layers and layers of this cavernous universe, there's so much more and all of it, unexpected.

Because here, there are *plants*.

Vegetation grows here in abundance. Dirt and plants cover the floor and vines crawl up the walls and over the ceiling, gluttonous for the light that beams down bright and beautiful from huge openings in the ceilings.

One of the men harvesting berries from one of the lower vines looks up. He shouts, "A Tanishi's escaped!" That causes panic. Another man runs towards me and I scream in panic and throw up my hands when he reaches out to grab me.

He latches onto my shoulders but then he takes a breath. His brown eyes bug out of his head and I watch as his throat jerks, and then his whole body jerks, and then he turns from me and throws up on the thick, scratchy vine plants behind him.

The king's poop is a shield against his own people, I realize with glee, so I keep running.

I make it out of that cave and into one that's dark, illuminated only by light coming from each of the caves that branch off of it. Operating on a hunch, I head up, down the narrowest, darkest tunnel.

I don't cross any Pikosa — a good thing — but the cave gets darker and darker — a bad thing — until it gets so dark that I'm running almost blind and have to skim my hand along the craggy wall as a guide.

"Khara," I whisper at the sound of voices behind me. They're still faint, but the Pikosa know this cave system better than I do, so I don't doubt their ability to catch up with me quickly. I pick up my pace, immediately stubbing my big left toe on a rock.

"Khara!" I shout, bouncing up and down on my right foot. I lose my grip on the wall and yelp, "Khara! I'm going down!" And I do. I hit my shin on the rock that just numbed my toes of the same foot, so I don't feel the pain right away or all at once.

It comes in waves. Really horribly painful waves. The kind that make you hold your breath. It *hurts*.

My hands scramble over the floor, but there are more rocks here, all of them sharp. I roll onto my side and then onto my back and for a moment, I just lay there, in severe pain, hoping my foot isn't broken while the rest of me is covered in poop from the man who holds my life in his palm, like a little bird. *Where have all the birds gone?*

I start to laugh. I mean, there are tears coming out of the corners of my eyes — from the pain — but there's laughing tears mixed in there, too. This is so stupid.

What were they thinking, the people who put us here? That the water wars would wipe everyone out and there would be nothing left but a lush earth ready for repopulation and that we would be the ones to do it? Without challenge?

It's unnatural, trying to shoot us humans forward through time to a time when the water wars are a thing of ancient history.

The Water Wars, not the water wars...

The humans that I've met have heard stories from the generals, trickled down in whispers passed from one cave system to the next.

Haddock had a chance to meet a man called Tino in a cave he worked twelve days ago. Tino is the last surviving male leader left. He's a lieutenant — *was* a lieutenant — so he got to keep his memories of the world before. He told Haddock such fantastic stories. I wish I could have heard them for myself.

Tino told Haddock about wars that consumed the entire planet as countries fought over an ever diminishing water supply until eventually, bombs were dropped that couldn't be undropped, water sources were spoiled at the source, disease spread rampant and the deserts that once covered a third of the earth spread and spread and didn't stop spreading until they took everything.

I guess the world leaders who decided on Sucere didn't think the humans left would divide, separate, tunnel, fight. But now? These Pikosa? They've fought ruthlessly, over thousands of generations, for survival. They've earned their survival. And what have we earned? What have I earned? What horrible thing did I do to earn me this?

How much karma did I waste?

How heavy is my heart?

How many Narakas do I need to endure before the afterlife finally takes pity on me and swallows me up into the blissful dark?

A shuffling sound. Scattering rocks. I open my eyes and brace, ready and waiting to either get slashed, grabbed, beaten, or attacked — but when I open my eyes, there's no one. Just two specks of light that loom strangely low in the darkness surrounding me, almost the color of pitch.

And then those specks move, shutter, *blink*. Khara! That's a face!

"Khara!" I throw out both hands and the face looming so low flinches back. The body it belongs to scutters away and I exhale, relieved, until I remember that I'm here despite everything and I have every intention of doing exactly what the ancestors of the Pikosa did to get themselves here.

They fought.

So, I'll fight.

"Wait!" I lurch up, aware that I'm speaking in English again — the common language among us Tanishi.

I blink, focusing on the body shifting against the shadows. Dark grey skin, near black, whoever it is blends in with their surroundings, down to their dirty, stained teeth. Everything except for their eyes, which are enormous and white and, in the center, bright green. *Can they see in the dark?*

Omoro. I flit through the Omoro words I've heard in passing. I don't have much to work with. My focus has been almost entirely on the Pikosa.

As of now, I've heard Omoro spoken maybe twice — once when we were trying to keep Ero from killing the Omoro man with the swollen lymph gland. Haddock says that the man's infection might have been transmissible. I didn't care. I'd still been determined to save him.

And then I remember the girl I'd comforted after... she'd been Omoro. She'd been so sad. She'd let me touch her and gather her to my chest and for just a moment, we beings whose differences are so great as to nearly make us an entirely different species, had felt like one spirit.

From that briefest of interactions, I gleaned that their language has French roots — not French from France, but in the roots, I hear Acadian, almost as if these were Cajuns propelled forward in time with the rest of us Tanishi, then dusted in grey powder.

I can't think of any concrete words in Omoro, other than their word for *water* — sounds like the French *eau*, with a g. Geau. As if it were meshed with the Spanish *agua*. I shout it now because I can't think of anything else.

"Geau!"

A slight recognition in her gaze stalls her long enough for me to scramble for Cajun words and shout them all out quickly, "Wait! Please, wait!"

And the Omoro waits. Crouched against the cave wall opposite me, I see it — *her?* — blink. I hold out my hand and she shuffles back, then I remember I'm covered in shit and lower it to the ground. Non threatening. Appear non threatening.

I choke back another laugh. Me? Threatening? Ha.

"Can you show me how to get to the Tanishi?"

A shuffle back. I realize that the sentence I used is far too complicated considering that these are not Cajuns, nor are they French. They're Omoro. Boil it down. What am I attempting to communicate, in its essence?

"Tanishi go?"

Confusion. I can sense it more than I can see it. It's followed quickly by fear because there's echoing in the tunnel behind me. I start forward, towards the Omoro, glancing in the direction of the Pikosa and hoping that the Omoro in front of me understands my urgency.

I edge forward a little more and try offering her a smile in the hope that this sways her to overlook the poop I'm wearing as a cloak.

But instead, her gaze snags on my mouth and she says the last thing I'd have expected. "Dinte."

Dinte. Could be *dintel*, Spanish for *lintel*, or dinte, Spanish for ten. French for *dent*, teeth, or French for *dentelle*, lace...hmmm....

I shake my head, hesitant to make a stab with this. Instead, I wait, letting the pressure build, knowing that I'm already dead, no matter the outcome of whatever happens next. I just want *her* to feel that pressure and, hopefully, react to it.

She presses back and even more shadows fall over her form and I realize that there's an offshoot from the main cave system behind her that I didn't see.

She reaches up a hand. Her palm is a lighter color, just a shade darker than mine is. She brings one soot-colored fingernail up and then taps her teeth.

I grin. "Dinte," I repeat. Tooth or teeth. "Dinte netteyer? Dinte limpiar?" I say, trying to stab in the direction of both Spanish and Cajun words for *clean*.

She nods, evidently understanding one of them and in a voice soft as ash, repeats. "Dinte nettoyo. Comon nettoyo Tanishi dinte?"

I grin. "I can give you," I answer, miming the action for brushing ones teeth. "Take me to Tanishi and we give all Omoro teeth clean. All."

I don't know if any of these words translate to her tongue, so I try them first in Cajun, then in Spanish, then in French, for good measure. I speak them in long sentences, then in short ones that communicate only roots and meaning.

I keep speaking as my nerves rise and the sounds in the tunnel behind me get louder and louder and the Omoro watches me longer and longer without moving, without responding, without flinching.

For a moment, I entertain the idea that she's actually just trying to keep me here to *ensure* that I get caught and I tense, waiting for it to happen but stubborn, too, unwilling to move.

The shouting in Pikosa echoes down the tunnel. "This way! I can smell her!" Offff course they can.

I meet the Omoro woman's gaze, finding that recognition, sure that she's the one whose soul I connected with once when I tried to help her tribesman. *Words are a pretext. It is the inner bond that draws one person to another, not words.*

Father.

Was that male her father? The thought hits me in tandem with my father's voice and I'm filled with a deep, painful longing.

He's quoting his favorite poet again. Jalal...Jalal...I shake my head, struggling to remember and fighting against the attempt. It's distracting me and though I'd love nothing more than to sink into it and remember father and mother and beautiful things like beaches and calligraphy, I need to be here, fully covered in the Devil's shit, reaching for understanding in a language I was never taught to speak.

Words are a pretext. It is the inner bond that draws one person to another, not words.

I attempt to convey my spirit to hers while withholding everything else — my panic, the beating of my heart, the ache in my shattered shoulder, my left foot and shin.

"Anidi laye," I tell her, though I know she does not understand. And in a language even more distant to her, I say, "*Law semahti, alhaony.*" Please, help me.

"We're close!" Comes the Pikosa cry, so loud it sounds like they're already right on top of us. Seconds, that's what it will take before they are.

My eyes flutter. She flinches back and then all at once, she lunges towards me and grabs my arm, not giving a damn about the poop.

She pulls and I happily let her lead me into the blackness of the next tunnel. It gets darker and I stumble. I can't see anything, but she knows exactly where she's going.

Soon we're forced onto our knees and she releases my arm long enough for us to crawl through an opening so narrow it makes my soul catch in my mouth, and then fall down. *The Hmong word for epilepsy translates to, when the spirit catches you, you fall down.*

My mother had epilepsy.

The memory of this knowledge catches me, just like the expression. I remember that I learned about the Hmong in my medical anthropology class in university. I remember reading a book with that same title — *When the Spirit Catches You* — and though I cannot remember the contents of the book, I remember that I then found it absolutely mesmerizing, and even the pain of it beautiful.

"Ouch. Khara," I spit as I slide down a short tunnel, scraping the heck out of both of my forearms and my already tattered knees.

Water splashes beneath my palms and shins, frightening me because I don't know how deep the pool becomes or where it ends.

Luckily, the pool is shallow and short and before I have time to truly panic — or mount a resistance to wherever she's taking me — the Omoro is pulling me up and out of the water and out of the narrow tunnel we'd been crawling through into a cave I've never been in before.

It looks completely unlike all of the others and it takes my eyes a moment to adjust and my brain another moment to understand what I'm seeing and find the right words for it — in any tongue. Because, the light isn't coming from lanterns or fire pits or cracks in the cave walls that breathe in air from the surface.

The light comes from *candles*.

They decorate every inch of the cave, mounted high and low. Some are lit, though most are laying against the floor in stacks. The colors range from grey to purple, but most are a soft green, like moss. There must be hundreds of them. Thousands.

I haven't seen anything like this in the caves before and I want to stop and ask questions, but too quickly, the Omoro pulls me into another narrow tunnel.

We scramble up and scrabble down and do this a dozen more times until suddenly — WHAM! — we're in a mine system that I find familiar.

"Dinte," she repeats as we stand against one wall, both breathing hard.

She holds my wrist and stares into my eyes and I take a moment to admire the fact that, despite the strange — to me — color of her skin and the paler grey shade of her hair against it, she's actually quite...human looking. Quite pretty.

Huh.

I wonder...how does she see me?

I still don't know what I look like. The thought makes me grin because who cares? It doesn't matter and down here in the dark, it *definitely* doesn't matter.

"Dinte," I repeat.

I nod, and then I touch my chest. I'm still naked. Her gaze drops to my fingers and then my breasts and then my sex.

"Halima," I tell her. I point to her.

She doesn't speak, doing that waiting, waiting, waiting thing again. Again, she gives in. "Frey."

"Frey. Ana asad," I tell her, another Egyptian expression of greeting. I hear it momentarily in a man's voice before it recedes. I reach...but my memories, like those birds, have flitted away to live in some other time, some other universe where they have some other destiny.

My jaw works and I swallow a lump. My throat is dry. Everything tastes like piss and khara and a little like the bile that keeps crawling up and down the back of my throat. I mean to hold Frey's gaze, but I break it instead.

Her hand tightens around my wrist. She speaks in full sentences and I start to fill in the gaps that exist in my comprehension. With each word, I understand her a little better. By the end, I register her meaning.

She's thanking me for what I did before for her friend — not father — and she knows that I took a lash for a Danien. She knows I'm being kept by the warlord and wants to know why he hasn't killed me yet.

I shake my head and shrug my shoulders. "I don't know," I tell her in as many words as I can.

She nods and her eyes narrow, glowing reflective green again in the dark. Her head twitches and she cocks one ear up. "We go."

I nod, but before I move forward and lead her toward Jia's cave and the place I know she stashed some of the sassafras toothbrushes, I take Frey by the wrist.

"I can teach you Pikosa," I try to communicate to her. "We can learn together to escape them."

She blinks at me, tilts her head. "Escape," she answers.

I smile. I just can't help it. "Yes. We will escape *anidi laye.*"

Her face scrunches in confusion. I reach from her wrist to her fingers and lace my fingers through hers. "*Anidi laye.* Pikosa word. Together. Escape *anidi laye.*"

She swallows hard and offers me a small smile. Her grey tongue peeks out from between her fuzzy teeth. "Andinila," she answers.

I laugh as softly as I can, but the sound is still a little too loud, a little too hysterical. A little too hopeful, too. "Anidi laye."

"Omoro, Tanishi anidi laye." Her expression turns to flint and her eyes become distant. I wonder if she's thinking about Ero and the man that he killed in front of her eyes. It's clear she had affection for him.

"Together." I nod and I know that her words and this moment have changed everything. We'll escape together.

But I need to get her some toothbrushes, first.

6
Ero

"She did...she did *what*?" I'm one hundred percent certain I've misunderstood one hundred percent of what Lopina just said.

She's staring at me with every attempt at keeping her mouth from forming either a grimace or a grin. All of my other warriors are keeping their distance, careful to avert their gazes. Other than Lopina, only Ellar and Wyden have the courage to step forward. Ellar, because she is trusted. Wyden, because he is competition.

Wyden stands just behind Ellar with his arms crossed, a muscle in his jaw ticking. Ellar opens her mouth to speak, but Wyden cuts in, "This is why we need warriors stationed in the lower cave systems. Our people working the fields aren't warriors. They couldn't stop her."

When he stabs his finger towards me accusatorially, a flicker of rage ignites at the nape of my neck and works its way upwards rapidly into my thoughts before shooting back down my arms.

My right, dominant hand twitches. The motion does not go unnoticed by Wyden. His face flushes. He shuts up with a sneer.

My jaw clenches and I have an impossible time loosening the hinge. "*Our* people are not warriors? The Tanishi weighs less than a box of hair. A Pikosa child should have been able to stop her and you're saying we need *warriors* to stop her? *My warriors?*"

I rise from my throne and jump down onto the stone landing beneath my throne. "Perhaps, I should throw her into the pit against *you* and let her take your place."

I knock into his shoulder hard enough to throw him off balance as I move past him. He stumbles back a step — just the one — but I only mean it as an insult, not an attack, and an insult is how he takes it.

His arms tighten over his chest and his sheathe slaps the outside of his kilt when his left thigh spasms. It's his most obvious tell — one I exploited when I fought him for the throne a decade ago.

That was when we shared a tender, boyish trust between us. That was before I gave him that scar. A single downward stroke that cuts from his forehead to his chin. The scar is faded, but still visible when the light catches it. *Unlike the Tanishi's scars, this one doesn't spell anything. If it is an omen, it's not an omen that is mine.*

"Did you put her back in my chambers?" I ask Lopina as she hustles to catch up to me.

"No," she answers, causing me to stop dead in my tracks. I turn to face her from the opening to the Eastern tunnels.

"What the fuck do you mean, no?"

"I mean *no*. We haven't caught her yet."

We spend the next *four fucking hours* tracking down my Tanishi. *My* Tanishi? I shudder. *The* Tanishi. And in the end, we don't have to bend over backwards to find her. She just...appears.

I have half my fucking war party scouring the tunnels, trying to crawl through narrow crevices to foreign places our larger bodies cannot reach. When we fail again and again, I send in the Omoro and the Danien, but they all return empty-handed. It causes a strong rift of stress to tear through my thoughts that I'm not used to.

Stress when the filtration system breaks. Stress when Wickar scouts or caravans are spotted by our scouts. Stress when crocodiles try to breach the upper cave systems. Stress when I think Wyden or Gerarr will make a play for the throne while I'm still sitting on it.

Sure.

But this stress? This stress is all new and I'm not sure what to do with it. It's not stress that belongs to me, but that belongs to her. Did she fall into the river again? Did she try to wriggle her way through a narrow shaft? Was there a cave collapse? Is she buried under rubble? Did she try to escape to the surface? I'll have to punish her when I catch her, doesn't she know that?

My right hand flexes and curls, remembering the weight of the whip against my palm. But it also remembers another sensation.

We shared a bed last night, the Tanishi and I. I mean, she slept in my bed. We slept on opposite sides of my bed, but she was still in it. We did not touch, but I still felt...her.

I was aware of her in ways unfamiliar to me. She, on the other hand, seemed to sleep soundly, unconcerned by my presence. Undisturbed by it. Does she not know that I will, eventually, have to kill her?

Does she know that I did not sleep and it was because of her? I have not shared a bed before.

I watched her sleep. She looked so serene.

"Ero, we found her!" Ellar shouts.

I leave the team of Danien I'd been ordering behind and charge after Ellar through the caves. The long, lynch rope braid she wears slaps between her shoulder blades before whipping over her shoulder when she turns to look back at me.

"She made it back to the main cave. She does not seem to be hiding. Should I have her executed?"

"No."

She nods, happy to take orders from me in ways Wyden isn't. She makes space for me to advance and I see Lopina standing on the other side of the river on the rocky landing, holding Wyden back.

"Wyden!" I roar.

He turns to look at me — all the warriors in the room do — but I'm looking at her.

There, crouched on top of my throne, are three Tanishi. Two in chains and one in...one in — *What. the. fuck.*

My jaw works. I don't believe it. She not only escaped my chambers, but she did so *naked* and now she's here, out in the open, making no effort at all to hide herself. She's speaking to her Tanishi and, with her back to me, they see me before she does.

I charge over the river and the two Tanishi in chains shuffle back so that they're flanking my throne. The one with the red hair says something to my female and she nods, but with hesitancy. Then my Tanishi turns around with surety.

"Get down from there," I roar, knowing that she can understand me.

She doesn't hesitate as I thought she might, but ambles awkwardly down from the raised stone and drops onto the arena floor.

Interesting that as I approach, the stress that was so heavy in my chest begins to dissolve...

I close the distance between us and reach out to grab her arm. "What the fuck were you..." Fucking *sands* — the *smell*.

I lurch back, releasing her, while a sound of pure disgust — and a dose of bile — ripples up and down the back of my throat.

I look at my hand where brown smears decorate my palm. That same brown covers her from head to toe and fuck, the smell wafting from it...it almost smells like...

A crack of laughter breaks my concentration and I turn to see Warren standing there, a hand covering his mouth. He shrugs in response to my glare. "You asked us why we *couldn't* catch her, but that wasn't the right question. The right question was why we *didn't* catch her. No one wanted to get close enough to touch her.

"We thought about just killing her, but then we couldn't figure out how we'd get rid of the body. I guess we could've just dragged her with a whip into the gator pit, but imagine the stink she'd have carried through the tunnels. Not like she hasn't done enough of that.

"We don't know where she's been. The farmers found her in the filtration caves, but they lost her in the Northern tunnel system. She just..." He shrugs again, crosses his arms and stares past me at the Tanishi. "She just showed up here. We don't know what route she took."

This is troubling.

I glance at the Tanishi, intending to interrogate her but I can't do it here. The other Pikosa still don't know that she can speak our language and if they find out, it'll be my end as Nigusi and nothing is worth that.

Coming close enough to her to touch, I hold my breath, push aside thoughts of bedlam and doom and grab her shit-painted arm.

Ignoring the shocked and bewildered stares — and yes, some laughter, too — from my warriors, I drag her out of the main cave. The temperature increases as we wind through the Eastern tunnels, but her skin still pebbles under my touch.

"Why is she still alive?" Wyden's voice cracks through the silence. Is he following me? Here? Toward my private space?

"You dare," I hiss as I turn to face him, careful to keep my body between him and my Tanishi.

"You need to kill her, Ero," he says, refusing to call me by the title that I earned through bloodshed.

"You need to remember your place, Wyden. Get back before I gut you here and now."

"What is she to you?" His stare tilts down and I snarl, hating the way he watches her, "Get out!"

Behind me, she whimpers and staggers as she tries to escape my rage. I notice that her gait is uneven and when I look down, I see that she's in pain. Again. This creature has almost no defenses and an unnatural propensity to hurt herself. It makes me want to chain her to me all the time, just to keep her close. *Safe. To keep her safe.*

"She will be your reckoning, Nigusi," he says, backing slowly away.

He's right. Still, I say, "Look at her again, and she will be yours."

I shove the Tanishi down the tunnel, but her weight sags against me. She's stumbling, particularly on her left foot. *Fuck.* Her toes are badly swollen and the soles of her feet are tracking blood. My frown cuts even harder towards my jawline.

I sweep her legs, lifting her up into a cradle hold, filth and all and, before I know what I'm doing, I'm in my own chambers, rolling the stone door closed and finally alone, I head to the pool and lower myself into the water with her in my arms.

I wash her body and hair thoroughly, taking care with the stitching on her shoulder. I tried to stitch her carefully and in a way that would make the word I thought I saw seem less convincing — erase the sign — but in the daylight filtering in through the cracks up above us and echoed in the torches ringing my walls, I can see that my work was not met with success.

The scar from a previous whipping forms the complete letter, but it's the curve that I created that adds the second syllable. The one that brings the word together.

Together.

My frown has never been more cutting as I wrench her clean body from the water, take a towel to her skin and toss her onto my bed. She flops there like a damp rag, utterly boneless.

She does not try to fight and I find this momentarily disappointing until I remember that, despite not being a warrior, she is still lethal. The havoc she reigned in my mines is still ongoing.

I wonder if I should go back, but the moment I step towards the entrance, she sits up, looks at me and — *in my own fucking tongue* — shouts, "Antebelik!"

She reaches for me with her burned arm and I blink longer than I should, using the darkness to escape it.

"Wait!" She says, repeating the word again.

I storm to the foot of my bed, wishing I had the ability to crush her, but her burned arm is still raised, forming a barrier cast by spells of her own making.

"What did you say?"

She takes a breath and I hang like a victim from the edge of her lips. Especially now that she smells like minerals again — my minerals. How can I use the same minerals on my own skin and have it produce such a different scent? I'm so distracted, I see her lips moving before I register her answer.

"I'm graceless. I went down the stink pipe." And there it is. Perfect Pikosa pronunciation coming from a Tanishi's throat, but the words are all wrong. She speaks in Pikosa yes, but from a time that came before.

It takes me several moments to understand her meaning. And when it does, my mouth does something strange and unprecedented, twitching up when it should be forming a grimace or a frown.

"You went down the toilet shaft?"

She takes a moment, blinking at me with her enormous round eyes. Her eyelashes are so hypnotically dark, it makes the darkness of her gaze that much more stunning.

A moon wrapped inside of another moon.

Fuck. My blood heats as I look at her — *look at her* — for what might be the first time. She's a female and she's naked in my bed and she belongs to me.

I rip my gaze away from the distraction her fuckable body presents and focus on the tray of food and the wine skin beside it.

"Yes," she says quietly, "I did."

"That was very foolish."

I hear her shift on the bed and my treacherous gaze returns to her body. She makes no move to cover herself and seems half as afraid as she did before.

What game is she playing at? She should be terrified. I'm a male and have all the power over her. But she isn't acting like it.

She licks her lips again and I fight the invasive urge to bring her water from the tray on top of the drawers to my right. I fold my arms across my chest to prevent myself from acting on the impulse as I watch her carefully formulate her response. *Thinking of the words or trying to decide what will least likely get her sent to the surface?*

"Maybe," she says and I hate that answer. I hate it a lot.

"What did you do while you were gone? I hear you were gone for hours."

Another pause. She bites her lip. "I fell into a jungle room. Then I was lost. I escape...but into big cave..."

"You're lying." I can feel it singing through me. Some part of what she's said is a lie, but I'm not sure which part.

"No..."

"You are."

I rub my chin as I watch her, perturbed that she's watching me back. "How do you know our language?"

She licks her lips again and I can't stand it. I move to the tray of food and hand her both the tray and the wine flagon. Maybe some alcohol will loosen her tongue, I think, but really I just don't want her to look so hungry anymore. I grunt and pretend not to hear her as she thanks me.

I take the box of healing supplies in one hand and pull up a seat close to the edge of the bed. While she chokes on a swig of wine, I grab her legs at the knees and pull her feet over the edge of the mattress.

She has cuts all over her feet. Its *impressive* she was able to keep going with how deep some of the stones in her feet are embedded. And her swollen toe? It's clearly broken, yet it didn't seem to slow her down at all.

I want to ask her how she ran on injuries when even some novice warriors cannot. I want to ask her why she didn't stop, if she feels pain, if someone harmed her, if she intended to be found and why, *if she intended to come back to me.*

I bite my tongue and apply healing salve to her tired, broken feet, grateful for the distraction.

"How do you know our language?" I repeat before I can hear the incriminating words of gratitude fall from her dark red lips.

"I learned you," she answers in Pikosa. She has almost no accent. Almost.

She reaches for the meat on my tray and I watch her alternate between that and balls of fried rice. She doesn't touch the wine again and my mouth quirks.

"Drink," I tell her. I need her loose, relaxed, willing. *And then I could sink into her so easily* — No. I cut off that thought.

"It tastes transcendent. What is it?"

Transcendent? I give her a funny look. "You use ancient words."

"I do? Which ones?"

"Transcendent. This is not a word I've heard in years."

"Oh. What does it mean?"

"It means something has passed this mortal realm and is lost to the skies. Like magic."

"Ahh. I see. Why is this an ancient word? Why no more?"

"Because there is no magic. There are only signs."

"Signs?"

I wince. I hadn't meant to say that and grunt, frustrated with myself. "These signs are not meant for prisoners like you," I sneer, then change the subject. "How do you know these words when we no longer use them?"

She doesn't answer. She doesn't eat. She just watches my hands as I set the healing salve aside and begin wrapping soft cloth around her feet.

I create a splint for her largest toe from two stiff pieces of leather and bandage them into place. A solution, but it's not a long term one. She'll need more support than these little twigs if she's going to heal right. I'll have to make her some shoes…

Shoes. I cringe. *No captive has ever been given shoes before.*

I pause and repeat my question more gruffly, "How do you know the words?"

She lifts her gaze from my hands to meet the line of my eyes. It's unsettling, her ability to look at, into, and through me. Every time, it's as if she's searching for something and every time, I'm a little more intrigued by the various striations I see in the darkness of her stare. It's a stare that's far too enlightened. *Transcendent, perhaps.* Because the signs in her eyes spell my name clearly.

"Speak," I bark.

She nods, takes another swig of wine, then corks it while cringing from the taste. Then she looks at me with that irritating look and I fall still, and quiet. The only sound is the distant trickle of water through the rivers deep beneath us. I wonder if she can hear them.

"Do you have any idea where we Tanishi come from?"

I get chills. *Chills.* It's never happened to me before. Not that I can remember. I've got the bandage wrapped tight around her foot. Her toes twitch when my hands clench. I release her even though there's no reason for me to and I don't like it.

"You came from the tanks in that strange cave."

"Cave?" The Tanishi says. She shakes her head. "It was no cave, Ero."

I suck in a breath. Her words are frightening, but not so frightening as the sound of my name on her breath. Ero. She whispers it softly, like that softness is something I deserve from her. I shudder all over and shoot back on my stool, putting more distance between us.

"Yes, it was. A smooth cave, likely carved out by water," I insist, trying to mask my doubt with severity.

She just makes a face. "Truly? But what about the *seeran*?"

"*Seeran?* I don't know this Tanishi word."

She chews on her bottom lip, considering before she says, "The sound. There were sounds. Loud thunder."

I narrow my gaze, not liking the implication of her tone, like she knows something I don't.

"The horn," I offer, but it's a hollow offer.

An animal was ruled out. A horn, Ellar had offered, but I knew better. It would have taken fifty Pikosa blowing on a series of horns to produce a sound like that.

"No, Ero."

Ero. There it is again, my name spoken as a cruel incantation.

Her eyes are guileless and I hate that. I hate it almost as much as I hate the sight of blood seeping through the bottom of her bandages as she kicks her feet. So fragile. She will break apart in my caves just as so many captives have done before her.

But none of them have belonged to me.

Thrusting up suddenly, I go to the racks of my clothing hanging against the opposite wall and grab a pair of my sandals. That and a knife.

The Tanishi starts but I just glare at her and start hacking angrily away at the leather as I retake my seat. "What was it then, Tanishi?"

"Halima," she whispers.

I close my eyes, willing myself to unhear her. "Speak your truth, *Tanishi*."

She makes a small sound, but I don't read her face. I don't want to see that disappointment.

"Let me tell you a book."

"We don't have books. There is no writing." I purposefully don't look at her arm.

"Then I speak badly. I mean to tell you a history."

History. History is not something we dwell on. There is little to tell other than tales of violence. I grunt and she must take that for acquiescence because she bravely presses on.

"There were once *seetees*," she starts but I don't know this word.

We negotiate and she explains a concept I don't grasp. Surface dwellers who lived, not in stone structures or mountains that protected them from sand storms and ferocious predators, but in towering constructs made of wood and glass because in this land, sand storms were rare and the Tanishi were the greatest land predator.

I balk at that. "You lie. Tanishi are weak."

"Shh," she says, shocking me to the point that I'm not even given a chance to punish her for her insolence. "Just hear. In these *seetees*, all tribes lived together."

Anidi laye. There's that wretched word again.

I fight not to look at the mass of scarred skin ruining the perfection of her arm and I fight even harder against the sudden, shocking wave of guilt that accompanies it.

"They did not fight until the day the rivers dried. Water became less. Strong tribes came to take water. They stopped speaking. Tribes became smaller and smaller. But before this happened, right when there was the first fight, tribes were still together. Together, tribes picked a few from each tribe to go into special water…"

She struggles and I struggle to understand what she means, but we push on. Together.

"The people in the special water were put in a big…" I don't understand and again, have to debase myself and ask for clarity. Frustration mounts, and it only increases with her explanation.

When she finishes describing this thing she calls *Sucere*, I'm left to understand that she means the people in the special water pods were put into a large boat…but

I've never seen a boat like the cave we stole these Tanishi from, so I must be mistaken and I hate being mistaken. I hate being unsure. And right now, the ground beneath me is made entirely of small river stones. Every step forward I take, I slide down, down, further down into madness.

Meanwhile, Halima — no, the Tanishi — just nods and speaks animatedly, her hands playing an instrument composed of only air. "The special water was put onto the boat along with *tek-no-lo-gees* that will help the together tribe build back a *seetee* and to live good lives again."

"What are these things — teknologees?" I grunt and when she completes her explanation, I understand that she means instruments of magic. Things I have heard of, but that haven't existed in the Pikosa tribe for generations, if they ever even did.

She goes on, "The boat was built to live thousands of years. For four or five thousand years, the people in the tanks slept. They thought, when they experienced light again, the surface will be empty of tribes.

"They thought, in the light, they could build their *seetees* — that they could use their instruments of magic to rebuild what was lost to war. But they did not find light on their own. Their boat was raided by Pikosa tribe and the Pikosa tribe knows only war. They were taken and made Tanishi. Made slaves…"

"You make no sense!" I shout, rising up onto my feet.

Rage and frustration *and fear* make me reckless and bold. I reach forward and shove her chest, placing all five of my fingertips against her sternum and pushing. She flies back with so little effort on my part, her back hitting the sheets. I scan her body and want nothing more than to shut her up violently, but I don't fuck Tanishi.

I don't know what enrages me more — that I don't fuck her, or that I want to.

I spear my hair with my fingers, take the tray from her and in an act of pure petulance, fling it across the room. The stone shatters against the rock wall and falls to the ground in pieces. I kick them aside as I stalk across the carpet to the exit. I need to leave before I do something terrible —

Try to make sense of her words. Try to believe her.

"You will tell me the truth when I return," I threaten as I roll back the entrance to my chambers. "I don't want to hear any more of this *history* or your lies. I only want to know how you speak our language — the words that come from before."

"Because I come from history!" She shouts after me, sitting up on the bed. Her cheeks are flushed with color that makes her look striking. "The only untruth I told is that there were once Pikosa. The truth is that you Pikosa were once Tanishi."

I slam the door shut and in the hall, am left breathing hard. I'm panicked. I'm also worried. I don't fully understand this history she described, but I know that she was telling the truth. I know it just like I can read her soul. She is an honest soul. Painfully so. What pathetic creator made her this way? Where did she come from? Because her story seems too fantastical to bear.

"Nigusi?"

I jolt, jerking up and glancing to the right. Tenor is standing there, her hair falling in four long braids down to her hips. She watches me warily, Brin just behind her.

He has his hand on his sword hilt. Tenor is touching her whip. I sneer at both of them, though I mean it as a grin.

"You do not need to fear me, young warriors."

They ease as I speak, even though I speak with a forced calm I don't feel inside at all.

"You are Pikosa. You are like me..." My mind flashes with thoughts — images I can't quite conceptualize of these towering, megalithic *seetees*. Not villages. Seetees.

Pikosa history does not extend so far back for me to have ever heard of these fantastical creations. Pikosa history does not extend back much at all. Only a few generations. Only until the next Nigusi falls.

I shake my head, trying to clear it. *There were no Pikosa, because you were once Tanishi.* It can't be. Such small things. How could we have come from them? It's confusing. She must be lost in her history. Even if she wasn't lying, I accept that she might be mistaken.

"What do you need from us, Nigusi?"

"I need you to watch the Tanishi. Don't touch her and don't speak to her. Just ensure she remains in my chambers. I don't know what damage she's caused yet, but I intend to find out. I'll be back shortly."

And I am.

I don't bother investigating anything. I just walk the tunnels all the way down to the village. The Eastern tunnel system is forbidden for prisoners for this reason. They are not allowed entry into the village. Only the breeders will be and only once they're broken and absorbed into our tribe.

Shallow river enters from a branching tunnel, wetting my feet and lapping around my ankles.

Eventually, those droplets fling out over the world, forming a trickling waterfall.

A hundred feet below, the water forms a pool. It branches off to either side and the river continues forming a liquid barrier around my village. It's not a large village, but our numbers are robust — less than the Wickar, but stronger and less diseased than the Kawashari given that half of them are inbred.

From where I stand high above, I look over the stone homes carved into the walls of the immense cavern. A large opening above lets in light and sand. We covered it with an iron grate once, but the grate is worn now and needs replacing.

Sand showers the market in the center of the village, so the stalls there use leather awnings to keep the sand off of their wares. Sand piles up everywhere the awnings are not, spreading annoyingly to cover many of the roads winding through the market. Eventually, we'll have to carry some of it back up. A useless exercise…

Looking down at the men, women, and children of my village mingling so far below, I feel a sudden exhaustion settle into my bones.

Nigusi I may be, but I'm nearly as much a captive to the Pikosa as the captives that I keep are to me. I don't have many choices. There is only protecting the village. There is only bloodshed. Killing those that would destabilize our way of life. Killing foreign tribes that come for our water supply. Killing prisoners that would otherwise escape and bring Kawashari and Wickar tribes to my door. Killing, killing, killing. I've been doing it for so long, I don't even remember a time when I didn't have souls in my sword and the faces of ghosts painted on the insides of my eyelids.

Maybe I deserve something I want.

I wince as I lean against the rock opening and stare up at the skylight hundreds of feet above.

Maybe I should just kill her and remove this unknown from existence and go back to the ways things were before.

Perhaps for the first time in my life, I have choices with her, but I can't decide. I feel unsure, shaken, and like something even more dreadful is soon to come. But it doesn't stop the relief I feel when I finally make my way back to my chambers in the mines and find Brin standing outside of the door and Tenor standing diligently inside.

"Did she do anything?" I ask Tenor as she steps out of my room.

Tenor makes an unusual expression that makes my stomach clench. "Uh. She..." Tenor clears her throat, uncommonly clumsy. "Well, you told us not to interact. She started drinking spirit wine and then she started...I don't know what to call it." She glances at Brin for help, but he only shrugs.

Strangely, his expression is less steely than usual. In fact, both of my warrior helpers seem to be on the verge of something I haven't heard in a long time — true laughter. Not brought on by bloodsport but brought on because of something — what was that ancient word she used? *Transcendent.* Yes, transcendent.

I glance to the door, curious — nervous, too. From within, I can see low torchlight flickering against the dark rock walls. I can also hear a soft mumbling — words that, from here, I can't make out. But they don't sound Pikosa from now or any other history.

"You are dismissed. You did well. Thank you."
Thank you? What am I doing? I am Nigusi. I thank no one…

My helpers must find it equally strange because they share a look before bowing and scurrying away. I don't have the energy left to correct them. Instead, I edge towards the cracked doorway and peer in.

The Tanishi is *jumping* around my room. No, not jumping. The movements aren't frantic, but quick and then suddenly slow. Like syrup. Her hands are above her head and she's gyrating her hips in a way I've never seen anyone move.

It manages to be sexual even though it looks nothing like sex. Sex with a woman is a battle, a fight that ends in brutality and there's nothing brutal about this.

I cannot look away. I refuse to blink for fear of missing one single swish of her hips, twist of her fingers, kick of her broken feet. *She's wearing shoes. The shoes I made for her. She must have completed them. And now, that's all she's wearing.*

My mouth dries. She rolls her stomach and when she inhales I momentarily think of how much more arousing this would be if she were wearing light linens in shades of green. She'd look stunning in red, too.

My thoughts twist out of my grasp too quickly for me to strangle them and break their necks. I'm supposed to be breaking hers but now, she's looking over her shoulder with her eyes half-lidded, very much alive.

I advance on the female just as she dips her hips, changes the placement of her hands, and slowly rises with her ass pointed towards me. My feet slow even though I tell them not to. Whatever this is, I'm caught in its trance. This is not done. I don't even know what this is.

"What is this movement?" I bark.

She doesn't use the moment to her advantage. She could have because I'm genuinely curious as she spins, bringing herself closer to me. So close that I can feel the brush of her hair on my chest. I grab it before I can stop my own hand and, using her hair as a rope, I reel her in.

She doesn't stop moving.

And then she does something truly malignant.

She *laughs*. She laughs a true laugh and it kicks the dull organ in my chest, forcing it to stir.

"You don't have *danssing*?"

She says a word that I don't know, but I'm rendered entirely mute when she sinks her hips into my crotch, the warmth of her rear pressing through the barrier of my linen pants. They're thin. Too thin. I groan. A kilt would have been better. Battle trousers I wear on the surface even better than that.

My hands drop to her waist, fitting almost completely around it. She's so small. A true Tanishi. And she has the gall to call *me* Tanishi. *But maybe that's not what she meant. Maybe, she just means that we were once able to adore each other freely.*

I tell myself that I'd like the sensation of her ass against my cock more if she were thicker, but that doesn't erase the fundamental problem, because there's no question — I *do* like it.

"We don't have this," I whisper against her hair, pulling, pulling, pulling. I want her close. I want to enter her badly.

Meanwhile, her voice sounds entirely unaffected when she says, "You don't *danss*?"

"What is *danss*?" I growl, throat muscles working overtime to swallow when her back arches.

She rubs her ass up and down the column of my erection and I drop my face to her mineral-scented hair. I close my eyes, then am left empty-handed when she spins away from me and continues her hypnotic movements in the open center of my sleeping chamber.

"*Danssing* is better with music. I haven't heard music since I woke, but when I drank a bunch of your yummy drink, I started to hear it in my head. Hum hum hmmm…hmmm hum hummm…"

She makes these sounds and then starts to speak in a tongue I don't know in a language I can't follow. The cadence is up and down and flows in no speech pattern I've ever heard before. Is this the language of the Tanishi? I don't think so. I haven't heard anything like this.

Tender in ways that are alien to me, I have no words for it.

I want to move towards her but, at the thought, force myself to move back. I sit on the edge of the mattress and dig my fingertips into my kneecaps, hoping to regain control, hoping to find some kind of reason in what she's doing so that I can better understand the reaction I'm having to it.

But there is no understanding of any kind. There is only watching completely mesmerized as this drunk captive does her *danss* around me and speaks in these patterns that dig into my soul like the edges of a dull spoon. It hurts.

My insides all tighten in a way they never have. My cock is hard against my will, jutting up and leaking from its engorged head. She does her *danss* for me back and forth and the lulling lilt of her language gets louder and then softer. She pauses only briefly to twist her way over to the wall where she still has spirits in her wine skin — *my* wine skin — and brings it to her lips.

She misses her own mouth and spills some of the deep blue liquid down her chin and chest. It makes her laugh that true and torturous laugh. That laugh that makes the tightening in my stomach and the pressure of my cock even less bearable.

She starts to come towards me and I flinch, prepared to force her back. Women prisoners are known to try to use their sex to get them out of work or curry favors, but this is not allowed. There is nothing that will get you anywhere in this world without strength. Only the strong join the village. Only the strong survive.

She will have to die eventually and I will have to kill her, I repeat for the thousandth time, but it's rote and feels very much rehearsed.

It's also a lie.

She touches my shoulder and I hiss loudly between my teeth. My cock has never been harder. It juts between us like a damn stake in the soft earth, but she ignores it — for the most part.

For just one moment, she glances down at it and swallows and it wrecks me, tears me apart, slaughters me in ways Wyden never could, no matter how many spears he leveled at my heart. My throat dries and I have the audacity to hope that she reaches out and touches…

Ignoring my pleading cock, she takes hold of my right wrist with both hands and starts to pull. Curiosity. It's not a good thing. It's a very, very bad thing. But she's pulling me now and both my cock and I want to see where this goes.

I'm up on my feet, erection still poking out the front of my trousers while she pulls my arms back and forth. Her face is bright red and her pupils are so large as to subsume all color.

She laughs and it hurts me. "You're not even trying," she slurs and she's slurring badly.

My mouth twitches. Bad, bad, very bad. Worse, she *sees*. She laughs, "Did you *smile?*"

"*Smile?*" I repeat and my mouth twitches again and this time, I'm unable to catch it. I grin at her. Grin. Something I haven't done in months, years, at least…not like this. Not in true pleasure. "You mean *feel?*"

"Feel?" Her face scrunches. "Smile is for…"

I cut her off, refusing to hear more of her *history*. I can't afford to. Not tonight. "Smile is an old word. We don't have smiles anymore. Just feel."

She shakes her head. "Feel can be good or bad. Smile is only good."

My heart is a box of rocks that rattle, unsure. "Feel is good enough."

"Not for me," she answers quickly. "Feel is any sensation. I want to feel good, so I smile. You feel good, so you smile because of it."

I swallow hard and ask her a question I shouldn't — the last question that should matter right now. "Do you feel good?"

She laughs. She laughs so spontaneously and so loudly, the sound makes my stomach hurt. "Of course. I always feel good when I *danss*. You should try it."

I force a frown. "What should I be trying?"

"To *danss*! Obviously. Here. Hold my hips. Follow the movements."

She presses her belly to mine and my threadbare smile dissolves immediately. She's evidently unconcerned that she's entirely naked except for those shoes and my erection is poking into her abdomen — but I'm not. Just thin linen separates us. *It could be less.*

Her hands are light on my shoulders, fingers tangling in my hair. I freeze. I shudder.

"What was that?" She says on a laugh. Her breath smells like spirit wine, heady and delicious. I find myself leaning in towards it, towards her. I'm enjoying this far, far too much.

"Pull," I bark.

"You mean, your hair?" Her fingernails scrape across my scalp and she tugs my hair softly, *gently*, and in a way that sets all of my nerves aflame.

I release an animalistic groan as I snatch her around the waist, toss her onto the bed and climb onto it after her. I grab her wrists in one palm and slam them down above her head, unsure of how to proceed from here.

"What are you doing?" I grumble, low and so gravelly, it's a wonder she can understand me. But she does. She always has.

"*Danssing.*"

"*Danssing.*"

She smiles and it brings my focus to her mouth. I drag my thumb over the bottom lip, and then the upper with a frown. I wish I'd left her covered in shit.

"You said you were lost in the tunnels, but I know that isn't true. If you were truly lost you wouldn't have been found. You'd be dead. What was your plan? What are you planning?"

I expect a defense, a rebuttal, an elaborate explanation, but what I get instead is a single word. "Escape."

She laughs lightly and her body becomes boneless. Her reactions are all unrehearsed. She is not here with me right now. No — that's not it. I'm not here with *her*. What if…no…what if, in her mind, I'm someone else?

"Who is your mate?" I say, like a coward, when I should be asking her about her plans and her prowess with my language and the history she spewed and all of her lies and worse than her lies, her *danss* and the willing way she touched me.

My face and chest flood with heat when she doesn't answer immediately. Instead, she starts her melodic way of talking and I find my gaze roaming over her strangely colored flesh, lingering over her breasts. They are small and her nipples are dark and sinfully soft, but when I slide my thumb roughly over one, it does not peak.

"What man out there claims you?" I all but shout.

She just smiles that snakelike smile and I know that I need to remove myself from her presence, one that emanantes such….peace. *Yes. That's what this is…It's what I felt before when she shared my bed last night.*

My heart starts to pound to a pulse that doesn't match the one in my cock.

Peace.

I've never seen it before in a person. In nature, yes. In the subterranean caves much deeper than these. In the pools that shine completely clear with a hint of liquid green. That's the only peace I've ever seen before this, now, and somehow that natural beauty created by the awesome force of nature doesn't hold a candle to the thing she calls *danss* or the way she looks at me when she's smiling.

My hand goes to her neck, my lips follow. I lick a line up her throat, tasting the salt on her skin. Then I kiss the space over her pulse, just a little. Then I bite, just a little bit harder. She releases a fluttery laugh, but her eyes are closed. She is not here. *She's with him.*

I roll out of my own bed and ruffle my hair. I pace around the room. I will leave, but only after my erection has gone down and it hasn't yet. I need some space to clear my head and compose myself because it's clear that staying here, my thoughts will only become more dangerous. I pace away from her to the door, but then I pace back. *Don't touch her. Don't touch her. Don't...*

I reach down and wrap my hand back around her neck. I force myself to wrap the other one around, too. Kill her, I tell myself, just do it!

I squeeze and her eyes open. She sees me and exhales. *Peace.* It wraps around my bones, bleeds into my blood, murders all thoughts of committing murder — every one — and fills me with something even more deadly. It fills me with peace, too.

"It's alright," she whispers and I wonder if I've spoken my uncertainty aloud.

She meets my gaze and gives me a little nod. Her left hand clumsily whispers over my arm, knocking against my elbow, then my wrist before molding to my palm. She squeezes very gently, or perhaps as hard as she can.

"It's alright..."

I let go of her and show her my back and, as I do, I'm faced with a crushing, crippling awareness. *I won't kill her. No. I won't. Not just today, but maybe not ever.*

And…

I swallow hard.

And if anyone else tries, maybe I'll have to stop them. But at what price? My title, that's sure. But maybe more. *My life?*

Abandoning thoughts of leaving her on this night, I get into the bed and pull the blanket balled up at its foot over the both of us.

She turns her face to mine and sighs and I rub my thumb over her wine-stained lips. So burgundy. So red. I lean in and, cautious so as not to wake her, take her bottom lip between mine and taste it.

I'm doused in fire.

She sleeps like the dead.

7
Ero

I return, expecting her to have understood my meaning and how tenuous her life is in my grasp. Instead, I open the door to my chamber, reports from Tenor and Brin that she has surprisingly *not* tried to escape, nor has she done anything at all disruptive and find her standing at the foot of my bed like she's been... waiting for me.

More shocking than that is the fact that she's *clothed*. I ordered Tenor to bring her linens, but I didn't imagine that seeing her *in* clothes would stir me more than seeing her out of them. Because seeing her in clothes makes me want to see her out of them.

She's draped in a tapestry of blues and greens. Clearly bits and pieces from garments left unclaimed by those in the village, but on her, she makes the combined fabrics look like the gown of a Nigusi's queen.

My blood boils, but my body relaxes. My flesh drapes down my bones and I am immediately ready to sink into whatever it is that she's offering.

And then, on the inhale, I smell her skin and I feel lucid and alive and ready — for a trap. I snatch up her wrist.

"What are you doing?" I ask her, though what I should have said was, *what treachery is this?*

"I'm just..." She flounders. "I wait for my Nigusi."

"Nigusi... You haven't used this word before now. Who told you what it means?"

"I...y'ani..." She uses a strange word while she searches for an explanation to my question.

I'm compelled to ask her another before she can voice the response. "What is this yani, thing? You've said it many times."

She grins at me. She grins and it's full of feeling. So much feeling. So much good. "Oh, it's a word to fill spaces when I don't know what to say. It's an *Ahrabiq* word."

"What is *Ahrabiq*? Another Tanishi language?"

Her eyes get large at that and, whatever pretense she'd been protecting, is shed. She looks around, searching for something. She doesn't find it. Instead, she comes to me and takes me by the hand.

"Yes, it is a Tanishi language, but I...I don't know how to say it. I must show you."

She leads me by the hand to the tray of food, most of which is empty. I'm pleased by the sight of it. She uncorks the wine, releases my hand and repositions her fingers around my wrist.

She dips my longest two fingers into the wine and my fingers drip onto the stone, but she moves them to hover over the half-eaten tablet.

"*Ahrabiq* was the language I spoke first. But it isn't like *Inglesh*, another Tanishi language. *Ahrabiq*...you have to feel it."

She smiles up at me as she says the Pikosa word for *feel* and it makes me feel strange, like we're sharing something private.

She takes my wine-dipped finger and moves it across the tablet to form a peak, then brings it down and to the right before sweeping back in and up.

The long upward stroke links to another upward stroke, this one much shorter, before creating a fluid circle and then another shape that's somewhere between a triangle and a circle. She concludes by adding two dots above the triangle and two more dots below the shortest line.

حليمة

"Ha-lee-ma," she whispers. "That is how you illuminate my name, how it should be inscribed." She lowers my hand and I suffer from the loss of contact.

I stare down at the tray. The foods pushed aside. A bone that's been gnawed at. The wine stains the dry stone in loops and swirls that don't mean anything to me. Only that isn't true, is it?

Halima. In her language. The language she learned first, long before she learned Pikosa. She learned so many other languages between now and then. It makes me jealous of every single person she spoke those languages with.

"And this," she says, moving my hand again in a different pattern this time, "is Ero. This is your name in *Ahrabiq*."

ايرو

I drag my fingers over the letters and *feeling* hits me with sharp suddenness — a full frontal assault — and I find myself incapable of fighting back.

"You…" I watch the letters disappear, evaporating against the stone until it's blank and bare. My voice is thick with *feeling* that I can't seem to swallow as I say words I didn't think myself capable of. Gentle words. "You *miss* this language, don't you?"

She smiles weakly, but her gaze is pinned to the tablet between us. Her fingers on my wrist smooth down my palm and my eyelids flutter. I want to put my arm around her shoulder…and then I do.

She jolts, as if surprised by the contact, and when she looks up at me, there's a wetness to her gaze that makes me feel like I've somehow failed her.

"Don't do that," I whisper.

Her gaze flicks up to mine and she sniffs and shakes her head, like she's shaking off a weight far too heavy for her slim shoulders to bear.

"You're right. I don't miss it," she says, but it's a lie I can feel to my core.

"Don't do that," I growl. I snatch both my hands away from hers and use them to cup her face.

I stroke the sides of her cheeks, disconcerted that she feels so soft, but not disconcerted enough to stop touching her. I smooth one hand down her throat and touch the tender lines of her collar bone, then smooth that hand underneath the linen flaps covering her shoulder.

My other hand slides around her neck, fingers threading through her tangled curls. I angle her head back and before I can interpret my actions, catch them and stop them, my mouth is covering hers. I kiss her hard, crushing her lips, shocked by how they feel and how good this is.

Feel. That's what I told her.

Pleasure. That's what she's teaching me.

Her lips are parted and she's making no move to keep me out, so I pillage her mouth with my tongue, tasting everything. She tastes like minerals and salt, a sweetness that I like. I pull at her lips with my teeth, wanting more from her than what she's giving.

Her surprised gasp fans breath over my face and spreads warmth through me that competes with the fire slowly building in my gut in a most discomfiting way. Because that warmth feels more dangerous than the flame.

And then her response goes from hot to warm to deadly.

She touches me back, her grip tentative and unsure, but fueled with a passion that I hope to the universe isn't manufactured. Her fingertips touch my bare sides and I moan deeply, loosing my rhythm. My lips break from her lips and I kiss her face, planting open kisses across her chin.

My response must surprise her, because she flinches again and lets go of me. *Still afraid of retaliation. She doesn't know that I've already decided so many things about her. The first and most important being that she won't die by my hand. She may even be protected by my life.*

Frustrated, I release her hair and grab her right hand, slapping it over my ribs, just where she'd need to slide a spear if she wanted to reach my heart. I anchor it there and bend low enough to speak into her ear.

"I won't hurt you. Don't be afraid to touch me, if that is what you want."

"What changed?"

"Everything."

Impatient and needy, I nip and suckle my way across her jaw and pull her soft earlobe into my mouth. I marshal my excitement so that I don't bite it clean off. I want to inhale her. Consume her into me. But first, I want her to want me back.

Nervous myself, I drop my hand from hers. The micro-flinch in her fingers tells me she isn't sure of my words and that pisses me off.

Anger and sexual fucking frustration and a desire that has tripped over the border and fallen face-first into the realm of all that's painful tug me back, away from her before I do just what I told her I wouldn't. *I'm better than that.*

I shake my head, retracting myself from her terrified embrace. *What the fuck is going on with me?* I touch her throat, feed one hand up the back of her neck and the other up over her chin to her mouth. I keep my eyes closed as I bow my forehead to her lips, chasing a kiss I have no right to and that has no place here…not in this world, and never between us…

But she shocks the hell out of me when she responds without the heat of her earlier passion, but with something as sweet and as tender as a droplet of water, so perfectly formed.

She sweeps my hair back from my face with her soft fingers and pushes my tangled curls behind my ears. She pulls on the tips of my hair, sending ripples of cascading energy down my back all the way to my ass and upper thighs. She presses her lips more firmly against my forehead, their softness bending to my hardness, cutting through it without claws.

She strokes her hand across my scalp, nails catching and soothing and I moan like a beast. My desperation triples. I want her with a numbing intensity that makes it impossible for me to see past her or think of anything else.

Stumbling slightly, I back her up towards the bed. I feel, rather than see, as the backs of her knees hit the edge and buckle. She would have dropped onto it had I not caught her around the waist, lifted and tossed her further onto the mattress.

I climb after her, my gaze devouring her as I move. I bury my face in the pile of blue fabric that covers her chest, breathing hot and hard, seeking a tit, which I find and wet through the linen.

"Ero," she says and my mind stutters to a stop while my cock writhes beneath my trousers maniacally.

I glance up into her eyes and see her looking dazedly into mine and I have to wonder absently if there wasn't something potent in the wine or maybe a toxin released into the air making me feel like this. Completely drugged.

And it's because I'm completely drugged that I whisper back, "Halima."

Her pupils flare and her lips part and I lower my body onto hers and take her mouth once again. My body is moving over hers in small pulses, hips desperately seeking her heat through the barriers that separate us.

I want nothing more than to ram deep into her delirium-inducing form but, even though her lips move against mine with an urgency that suggests she's not totally unaffected by this, there's still a tension laced throughout her bones.

"Stop this," I snarl, grabbing her wrists in one of my hands and slamming them onto the mattress above her head.

She jolts a little and licks her lips, then shakes her head, not understanding.

I glare at her, but my body is shaking — *shaking* — with need. I don't have the words to describe what I need from her. I have only feels that I want her to feel with me.

I lunge for her right wrist and her pulse flutters beneath my tongue as I taste my way down her forearm to her elbow crease, to her chest to her ribs.

I slide my fingers into her garment, eventually finding the edge of her tunic. I edge it up to the top of her pants. Tight around her hips and small, pert ass, they're an effort to wiggle her out of.

Shock. It hits me first as I slide her pants down to her knees and look down at the slit at the juncture of her thighs where there was hair yesterday. And then comes interest and curiosity. Without the hair, I can see more of her and, while it irks me slightly and makes me think of a child, I know she is not.

My thumbs pull at the skin of her most sensitive region to expose the inner parts. Her legs tighten and clamp together around my shoulders. I hold down her left leg with my free hand and use my shoulder to brace her right knee open.

"You see how beautiful you are when you open for me?" I hiss. She whimpers and I become feverish. "You're wet for me Halima, soaking wet."

I open her for further study, parting her brown lips to reveal her hot, wet core. It's bright pink and glistens like gemstones. A shudder wracks my entire body and for a moment, my thoughts short. *I want to enter her here. And I will. But first...*

I lean in closer, biting the insides of her thighs hard enough that my teeth leave red marks. The scent of her is pure female and heightens my lust. My back muscles bunch in painful convulsions as my hips plunge into the mattress underneath me as a surrogate for her heat. A piss poor one.

But I don't want her when she's stiff as a board. I want her body to be as soft and submissive. I need her to relax. I'd do anything in this moment to have her fingernails score my back and her legs wrap around me and her thighs hug my hips tight as she fights to have me closer and inside of her, where I want — where *she* wants me — to be.

Fuck that she's a slave. Fuck that I'm her master. None of this matters. Not today.

I can relax her. I am not skilled in this, but I am a warlord, capable of conquering anything.

I lean in and lick a line right up her center but she jerks wildly and lets out a scream that is tinged in fear.

Looking up her body, I can see that her hands are fisted in swatches of fabric covering her chest and her eyes are wild and wide even though her cheeks and mouth are relaxed and pink.

"No damnation," she says to me with a small shake of her head. "No damnation."

I make the mistake of loosening my hold and she's quick to scramble away from me, tucking her legs beneath her body and cowering against the head of the bed against the stone wall. I frown.

"Damnation?"

She bites her bottom lip, chest heaving. *She wants me. I know she wants me.* Then she glances down to her scarred forearm and presses her finger against the wound.

"Damnation." She turns around, pulling her rags aside to reveal her shoulder. Fuck! It's swollen, healing poorly — possibly infected — likely because of her adventures down the shit tube.

Furious for so many fucking reasons, I surge across the bed, grab her around the waist and throw her over my shoulder. I walk into the cleaning room, while she remains quiet, likely waiting for her *damnation*.

"Punishment. That's what you were trying to say," I grumble, lowering her down onto a stool at the edge of the pool of water. I go to the metal drawer in the stone cabinet and wrench it open angrily. I pull out healing cream, scissors, a needle and thread. "I need to restitch your shoulder. It's infected, your wound."

She says nothing as I sit her on one stool and drag another up behind her. I straddle her hips with my thighs as I clip the threads in her shoulder, rinse out the wound, cleanse, heal and reapply the stitching.

"It's infected. Why didn't you tell me it was infected?" I snarl. "And why do you speak of punishment?"

She doesn't answer. I can see her tongue reach out to wet her lips, but she still doesn't speak. There's a redness in her face I don't know how to make sense of.

I prod her in the spine with two knuckles, my cock still hard, my whole body still thrumming with unspent energy. "Answer me, Tanishi."

She shivers in a way I don't like and her lips come together in a thin line. "I didn't think you would concern. And I speak of *punishment*," she sounds out in my own tongue, "because of this." She points to her forearm. She points to her back. "Because of the women you have tied to your chair in metal." She bows her head and her hair falls forward in two curtains, blocking her face on either side. "I don't want that."

"You think I would tie you to my throne if you chose not to fuck me?" My chest clenches. My stomach tenses. I wait.

She just shrugs, but only with one shoulder as I keep the other anchored in place. I snarl and say nothing. I'm thinking of what to say. What to tell her to get her on her back, relaxed beneath me. I want her fingers in my hair again. I don't want her screams, her flinches, her fear.

"I wouldn't…" I start.

She cuts me off. "Leanna and Kenya."

I wait. She doesn't say more. "What?"

"Leanna and Kenya. Those are the names of the Tanishi tied to your seat."

I growl. "They don't need names. They are Tanishi."

She makes a soft sound, shakes her head, her hair falls even further forward. "And you ask me why I feel terror. It is clear, like river water. Soon, you will need to kill me."

I pull her hair to the side, my lips finding the side of her neck. I whisper against her skin, "What if I don't?"

"You can't keep me in this room forever. Eventually, I will find the surface or the crocodiles in your river."

I laugh but there is no humor in it. "You will do what I tell you to and you will stay here for as long as I tell you to."

"And you ask me why I feel fear of damnation," she whispers again even more quietly. Even more bitterly. "Of punishment."

She turns around on her stone stool and slides her knees between mine. They press dangerously against my erection, which has yet to fade, and I drop the needle, let it dangle from her back, and slide my hands between her legs.

She clenches her thighs together and tightens her stomach and sits up straight. Still, her hands slide back to latch around my neck and comb through my hair along the way. She leans in and kisses me, her lips tender and sure in ways that her body is not.

I moan and pull on her waist, trying to drag her into me desperately, but as I get ravenous, she breaks the contact. "I have not done that before. At least, not that I can remember from before."

I suck in a breath and hold it. Fuck. I start to grin. I touch her chin and sweep my thumb over her mouth roughly. "No Tanishi has kissed you here?"

She yanks her head back, free of my grip so that she's touching me, but she doesn't let me touch her. I fucking hate that. "No man has kissed me there. Or anywhere."

I reach for her again and when she dodges my hand, I curl my fingers into claws and angrily grab hold of the flesh on her hips. I spread her legs apart and wrench her body onto mine so that we're almost pressed together at the groin. It isn't enough.

"I am your first, then."

She nods, her gaze drops to my mouth and she leans in, sweeping my lips tenderly with hers. Too tenderly.

I start to pull her closer, but she drops one hand from my neck to my crotch and awkwardly palms my erection, but I don't care how she touches it, just as long as she keeps touching it.

It's been too long since I've been with a woman. But I know that isn't it. There's something wicked and tempting about this one and knowing she hasn't been with another man fills me with something primal and heady and dark. It's a drug.

I reach for her core, wanting to feel her wetness, but she blocks the advance of my hand with her elbow and presses harder against my cock. At the same time, her other hand pulls softly on my hair. The pain and the pleasure roar up and drown out any other conscious sounds. Any other conscious thought.

"I will be your first in this, too…"

What I would have said, had she let me finish, is that I would not just claim her virginity for my own, I'd be the only male to claim her *ever*. But she instead, she interrupts.

"I don't want my first time to be you." She combs her fingers across my scalp, as if to soften the blow of her words, but it doesn't help. They hit like anvils to the shins. Like axes to the skull. "I don't want my first time to be fear of punishment. I want my first man to be good."

I wrench her away from me and place her back onto her stool, spin her back around so that she faces away from me and force her head down between her legs. I win a pained, startled yelp from her and the desire to harm the one who has caused me harm is making my hands both shake.

My soul shakes on its rickety fucking frame.

The marbles that are my heart shake in their cage.

"I am keeping you alive. I am keeping your people alive. You still think you're too good for me?" I laugh. "I am the armor that my people wear, but you want someone soft and gentle. Soft and gentle will not keep you breathing. Only I can. Don't forget this. *Never* forget this. And remember this the next time I ask you for what I want."

I apply the final stitch to her shoulder with hands that are steady despite the pain lancing the rest of my body. I clip the thread, tie it closed, smear more cream over her shoulder and lift up from my seat uncomfortably, erection still jutting angrily towards her. I turn and head for the exit. I don't know where I'll go only that I can't stay here.

Just as I reach the doorway, she calls after me. "I'll still remember that their names are Leanna and Kenya next time you ask me for what we both want. I will not forget them so easily."

8

Halima

My second escape attempt is through the chute — not the poop chute, but the one for old food and bones. I don't make it far, though — it's too narrow. But Frey did teach me that it leads somewhere important: directly into Ero's harem.

Now, I'm too big to get down the chute and they're all too big to come up, but there are a ton of whips in Ero's closet and, when I tie them all together, I wonder if it will be enough to send a message and since I don't have paper or anything to write on or with, I have to get creative.

The first message I send down is a slab of meat tied to the tip of the whip. When that comes back up meatless, but fixed with a tuft of what looks like cabbage, I send down my second gift — one of Ero's knives.

That comes back up empty, so I send another, and then a third. But after that, I worry he might notice they're missing — he has a few knives stored here, but not so many — so I send the whip back down empty. What comes up is…interesting.

What comes up is a skin of liquid. It smells like wine, but there's a chalky X drawn on the side of the skin that makes me reluctant to try it. I glance at the full wine skin on the tray Ero's female helper, Tenor, left me earlier. I bite my bottom lip.

I smudge away the X on the side of the skin and then quickly trade it for the skin beside the tray. I lower the clean skin down and, when nothing comes up, I get nervous. *Is this it? Is this how I kill him?*

I'm in the caves. I just promised Frey toothbrushes. She's speaking to me now, less nervous than she had been when I introduced her to Jia, Chayna and Haddock. I can see that she's pleased with the toothbrushes as she eyes the sticks she has now bunched in her hands.

"Bye Frey, thank you for your help," *I tell her clumsily, the only way I know how.*

She looks into my eyes and hesitates before she whispers, "Your leaders suffer. You should speak to them."

She shows me the way to the main cave and I'm surprised to find it empty, for once. I have no trouble approaching Leanna and Kenya. They look surprised to see me, relieved, too.

"We thought you were dead," *Kenya says.*

Leanna scoots closer to me on bloody knees. I wish I had something of my own to give her. Something that could help... but covered in poop, I'm not doing much better. "How are you alive? You defied Ero. You should be crocodile meat."

"That isn't important," *Leanna says, pulling at the metal collar around her neck.* "We don't have much time. Tell us how you're alive. Why didn't he kill you? Where were you last night and why are you covered in..." *She sniffs the air and then sniffs again.* "For fuck's sake, Halima, are you covered in shit?"

I grin. "Yes. I am. I escaped down the poop hole in his private quarters. That's where he's keeping me."

At that news, Kenya and Leanna exchange a look, one that speaks a dozen words. Maybe thousands. Volumes of history. "You should be dead," Kenya tells me.

"I'm not. But I have spoken to the Omoro and they want to work with us to escape. The Danien are already planning and I think I can persuade them to work with us as well."

Kenya grins broadly, eyes flashing with sparks that look like hope. At least, that's what I want to believe. "Leanna, looks like you were right to spare her."

"For more than one reason. It's great to work with the other prisoners, but our true advantage lies in her power over Ero."

"What?" I almost tumble backwards off the rock.

"You think she..."

Leanna cuts Kenya off, scoots forward some more, grabs my hand. "You have to seduce him. Seduce him and then kill him."

But after the way he showed me his *feeling* and offered me tenderness even when he was mad, I have a hard time believing that he's someone who deserves to die. Maybe most of him, not all of him though.

I have an even harder time believing I'm going to be able to kill him. Because what I told him was true — I don't want him to be my first. Not because I think he's a monster — I know he is — but what would that make me if he were my first and I killed him?

A monster, too. Just like him. No, perfect for him.

I glance again at the wine, getting increasingly nervous the longer the day labors on. There's nothing for me to do in his chamber except plot. And so I plot. I know I've exhausted my options for going *down,* so I spend a good half a day studying the bigger cracks in the ceiling through which light filters down.

Assessing them all, I decide that there's no way in any of Dante's Circles that I can make it up through the cracks. They're too high to reach, for one, and look treacherous, besides.

Maybe with tools, I might, but I don't have a lot of options. I've got the whips, which function as sort of a rope, but among the other tools I do have, none of them are a pick axe.

Which means my final and only option is...I swallow hard...going right out the front door. Past Ero. *Once I've killed him.*

I spend the rest of the day drenched in cold sweat and by the time night rolls around and Ero doesn't return, I'm relieved. I sleep a deep, dreamless sleep.

I have four long sleeps. Four interminable, stress and boredom-filled days in between but, on my fifth sleep, I wake up to a body at my back and lips on my cheek.

"Tanishi, wake up," comes the gruff voice. His heat folds over my body like a cocoon while his breath shoots down my ear canal making me think terrible, carnal things.

"Fuck," he curses, and the sound shocks me because the curse somehow, over the course of thousands of years, has hardly evolved at all. "You're wearing one of my tunics."

"I found it," I murmur, still trying to drag myself from such a pleasant warmth.

I try to jerk up, but the weight of his body presses me down into the mattress in a way I don't mind at all. I wonder what the mattress is stuffed with. It's comfortable and so is his weight on top of me.

I blink quickly and am surprised to find that the room is so light. I'm less surprised to find that he isn't smiling at all. His face is stone, rigid, almost…angry. Khara! Cold trickles through my bones as I dare to wonder if he drank the wine that I think might kill him.

Or worse — does he know what I've done?

Is this my time? After so much deliberation, Leanna and Kenya and the Omoro's plans have failed before they've even begun?

I try to sit up, but his fingers tighten around the back of my neck. He shifts more of his weight onto me so that our hips are lined and I stifle a moan.

But he still hears it.

"Halima," he growls against my mouth and I squeeze my knees together as a surge of heat hits the space between my thighs and then crawls down them.

I love the sound of my name in his accent. It's entirely new, and all his own.

I make another small, involuntary sound and his free hand finds my hair and fists it. He tips my head back and I whimper louder, in overlapping waves of fear and desire. I'm not sure which sensation is more powerful. Perhaps desire. I feel it slowly begin to beat fear away.

"Ero…"

He growls against my neck in the way he did before that set all of my nerve endings — and my restraint — on fire. The only reason I don't just spread my legs and let him do what it is he wants to do to me is because of the monster that it'll make me when he drinks the wine.

But those were my orders. Seduce him. Kill him.

"I like you in my tunic," he says against my lips.

"It's comfortable," I tell him, feeling a little uncomfortable with how dramatically this situation between us is progressing. He's touching me too freely. Like I'm already owned.

He huffs out a laugh. A *laugh*. "*Comfortable*," he says, repeating the word that I did. "This is an old word. You mean *unharmed*."

"There is a lot between unharmed and comfortable."

He shakes his head. "There is in pain or no pain. And then there is this." He fans his fingers over my left leg and pulls the fabric of my tunic up so he can palm my hip with his bare hand.

I suck in a breath...and let myself go. I circle his neck with my arms, comb my hands through his hair, kiss him back. He kisses me hard and his hips start to pump against mine. I'm overwhelmed by the sensation and what a fucking sensation. It feels so damn good.

"Ero," I mewl, my breath getting harder, my body heating up.

He tears his lips away from my mouth roughly and plants a kiss on the corner of my jaw and it's so soft as to nearly be described as tender. It nearly breaks me. I squeeze my knees even tighter together and then I throw them open and pump my hips up into him.

"Fuck, Halima." He shudders above me and curses again. "I did not come here for this. I came to bring you to the main mining cave. Put on your shoes and don't take off that tunic."

He pulls himself off of me and stands at the foot of the bed, watching me as I slowly amble off of it and obey the commands he gave me.

I try desperately not to stare at the wine as I do, wondering if he drank any of it and how much he drank if he did. He chuckles slightly and the sound makes bubbles surface in my chest and explode in my mouth like tiny fireworks.

"Don't worry. We can drink wine later when we return. I'd like to see more of your *danss*."

I shudder a little bit as I straighten up, my shoes safely laced up over my bandaged feet to my shins. My heart beats harder as I nod in agreement. "Maybe this time, you can join me?"

"Maybe," he says.

I smile, but a bit sadly. *He can't dance with me if he's* dead.

I cross my arms and look down at the floor, trying not to let my guilt play out over my expression. That wine has been sitting there for four days. Maybe whoever put whatever into it won't be good anymore — or maybe it will be even more potent.

"What is it? What's wrong?"

"Nothing," I lie.

"You're lying. Look at me."

I look up and try not to make a face, but I'm not sure how much it works. I get the sense that he knows I'm lying. How he knows is anyone's guess but his expression immediately cools — but it doesn't frost over, like I thought it might — and he narrows his gaze. Hawkish doesn't begin to describe him as he scours the place.

"Did anyone come into my chambers while I was gone?"

"No."

"Not even Tenor or Brin?"

I don't know how to answer. I don't want to get them into trouble. "They brought me food, on your orders, I think."

He looks at me over his shoulder. He's standing very close to the tray of food. Now, he glances down at it. He pushes aside the things I didn't eat and frowns. "You didn't eat much."

I wonder at his tone. He sounds unnerved by that fact. "You sound worried." The hilarious thought makes me smile and eases my guilt until his gaze sharpens and then the frost rolls in. Oh khara...khara khara khara khara...no.

He sounds worried...because he is.

He looks away from me quickly and the tension in the room couldn't be thicker than if it were the lust that ordinarily clouds the air like a poison between us. Poison? Stop thinking about poison!

"I y'ani...you...I shouldn't...I'm ready for the crocodiles now," I blurt suddenly.

He looks at me and his face wrinkles up. "Crocodiles? What about them?"

"I'm ready. Isn't that where we're going? To the croc pit? To throw me in?"

He growls as he charges at me and grabs my uninjured shoulder. Steering me towards the door, I stumble over my feet, grateful for the shoes I haven't needed to wear until now. They fit me surprisingly well now that the swelling in my toes has gone down and I blush all over at the memory of him making them for me with his own two hands.

"I'm not throwing you in the pit," he says as he leads me through the open door out into the cool hall. It's refreshing. Already, I can feel some of my earlier tension slough off. And then it all comes back in a rush when I hear the sound of voices coming from the main cavern. They are Pikosa voices, judging by the volume alone, and they don't sound happy.

I press my heels into the ground, trying to halt our progress. What little good that does. Ero comes up behind my back and grabs me by the neck. He gives me a slight squeeze before trailing his fingers down my arms to my wrists. He squeezes those, too. It's nice. It's reassuring. It's…*confusing*.

"Nobody will hurt you," he says to the darkness of the hall, which is illuminated only by mounted torchlights. "I have claimed you for my own."

"What does that mean?" I whisper, again thrown off by the strange change I sense in him.

"It means that you are under my protection. When we absorb the strong prisoners into our ranks, you will be among them and I will keep you with me in my home in the village."

Shock. He wants to *keep* me? I have the audacity to feel slightly flattered, and then guilt hits. This is *Ero* we're talking about. Not what I told him, not a male that's good.

"But what happens to the rest of the prisoners after the selection is made?"

"Nothing. They'll stay here and work until the end."

"Until the end," I whisper, reminded, ever reminded about Kur and it's bleak, unfathomable depths. I shake my head.

"You do not seem pleased by this." He's watching me over my shoulder, mouth turned down in a frown so severe it could cut glass, but in his eyes there's a rawness, a certain vulnerability that hurts me in the center of my heart.

"Did you think I would be?"

And then the vulnerability he showed cuts off like a severed limb beneath a sharpened sword point.

He spins me around so that my back hits the wall of the tunnel and slams both of his palms against the rock on either side of my face.

He dips his own head until we're nearly at eye level and I hate the closeness because it makes me lust for him. He grinds his teeth and looks at me madly, half-rabid, before all at once, he surges forward.

He takes a heaving breath and then another and even though I'm a little scared to touch him, I do it anyway and touch the top of his crown. I comb my fingers into the satin curls, so different from my own even though they're the same color. My hair is rougher somehow, less silken, but also lighter. His is heavy and reminds me of the rocks on the bottom of the river, weighted and smooth.

He exhales deeply as Pikosa voices get louder and then recede again. As he lifts up, he comes very close to me and presses his mouth to mine. I don't know if the kiss was meant to be brief or not because it doesn't end that way.

I can't help my body's reaction, starved for contact, needy and so desperate for this monster who, with or without wine, has already been poisoned by this world and his brutal life. I use my hands in his hair to keep his lips fused with mine and I try to suck out the venom. *It doesn't have to be this way.* I know that truth in my soul even if I am as naive to this world as he says.

He grips my waist with one hand while his other fists the front of my tunic — his tunic — before pulling back as abruptly as he descended. His breaths are labored, even more so than mine.

Slowly, after some time, he opens his eyes and looks at me before finally dropping his gaze to my scarred forearm. He rubs one thumb across it. His other hand, he moves to my shoulder which he pets very gently.

"Does it still pain you?"

For a second, I don't have any idea what he's talking about and I nod dumbly.

His back teeth bite together and a crinkle pops up between his eyebrows. He opens his mouth to say something that I can sense will change things between us…something profound…

"Come." The moment passes like a storm cloud.

He leads me forward by the hand out into the main chamber where Pikosa soldiers speak loudly and Danien slaves work to clean clothing in the river and Omoro slaves run back and forth carrying supplies from caves to other caves. The monotony of it kills me — it *will* kill me if I don't escape. Does he really not know that?

I glance at Ero nervously, but the raw Ero capable of gentle kisses, bawdy laughter and wolfish grins is gone and in his place is the cold, mechanical Ero capable of violence and only violence.

The cave quiets. All eyes turn to us and remain there as Ero suddenly scoops me up into his arms and crosses the river. He doesn't put me down either, but waits as the Pikosa warriors scramble to clear a path to his throne where he ascends the stones and promptly sits down on the warped heap of metal with me on his lap.

He slides one hand on the arm of his throne, the other over my bare thigh up underneath the hem of his tunic. It arouses me and embarrasses me in equal measure.

"Shh," he murmurs. "You're safe here."

I hate that I calm under his touch. I hate that I believe him.

Pikosa warriors look up at us and I can't tell which is worse — the surprise on their faces, or the anger. One male warrior looks particularly pissed. He's got a scar running down the right side of his face and has what looks like fresh bruises covering his jaw. His mouth is purple and his bottom lip is split down its full center.

I look at Ero's hand covering the arm of the throne. More specifically, his knuckles. They're bloody, decorated in healing scratches and yellowing bruises and I shiver, reminded that the man beneath me is a violent man. They're *all* violent men and women because this is a violent world, a savage place, one not meant for souls whose only weapons are words.

But the only way out, is through the wine... I bite my lip and shiver. Parts of Ero may not deserve to die, but maybe those parts are too small to protect. Maybe, they aren't worth it if it means freeing so many others who are made up of mostly good pieces.

I swallow hard, guilty and afraid. Ero's hand creeps up my thigh, rubbing at the seam where my leg meets my thigh. I grab onto his wrist. My embarrassment flares and I look into his eyes with a fire I have to draw from way down deep. From Hades itself.

"No," I hiss, voice low and filled with meaning. Meanwhile, my eyes burn hot even though my fingers are cold and clammy. "Ero, no. Not here. Not like this."

He meets my gaze evenly and there is no recognition there. He isn't even here. There's someone else wearing his skin.

"Nigusi," I whisper and something dark flashes in his gaze.

Frowning, he pulls his hand out from under my tunic and, when he shifts his legs, he makes it impossible for me to keep my seat. I find myself standing up on the stony ledge just in front of him before I know what's happening.

"Kneel," he says without looking at me.

I'm sweating again. Sweating all over. I don't know what to do. Part of me *hates* him for debasing me like this. The other part of me is too afraid to defy him.

As I stand there, unsure before him, it's too easy to understand how factions formed.

I just want to stay alive. I should just give in.

No. "Ero…"

He leans forward and braces his right elbow against his right knee. His other hand still grips the arm of his throne. "This is not a punishment."

His gaze drops to my arm and then to the ground to the right of his throne where an empty set of chains dangles flaccidly. "Halima, kneel."

My breath gathers until I think my lungs might burst. I kneel next to the chains, careful to stay away from them, and rub my sweaty palms off on my tunic.

The stone is cool beneath me, but it makes absolutely no difference. I'm *stressed*. He says this isn't a punishment, but all I can think about as I stare at the unlocked shackles is what he did with Leanna and Kenya. I glance towards the river. Are they croc meat now? Because I told him I didn't want to give him my virginity?

"Wyden, you seem worried about my Tanishi. It's so *kind* of you to concern yourself with her wellbeing. Maybe you should make yourself useful and get her a tray of meat, some wine, too."

Shock rattles me, just as it does the accused. "You're fucking joking," comes the male's reply. "I'm not getting anything for a Tanishi. I'm not a servant. I'm a Pikosa warrior. You insult us all by demanding this of me."

"You are a Pikosa warrior and your Nigusi gave you an order. Are you challenging me again? Twice in three days? That's a record no Pikosa warrior has ever matched."

He clicks his tongue disapprovingly against the backs of his teeth. "And yet you think yourself a warrior. You are nothing, Wyden. I'd feed you to the crocodiles if it didn't bring me so much pleasure to defeat you in combat again and again and again and again."

"You would put one weak, pathetic slave above the tribe?"

Gasps and outraged cries pull my attention up. The man with the scar — Wyden — has pulled his whip out of his belt and unfurled it. He's looking at me and I gasp, unprepared for the pain that's soon to come.

I see him raise his whip. I see three other warriors lunge to stop him — one of them being Ero's young female apprentice, Tenor — and another warrior try to hold two of them back. They're too slow.

Wyden lunges at me and the whip flies. I don't have time to scream. Pain. White hot. I'm revisited by the brutality of the memory, but...it's a phantom pain. His whip doesn't touch me.

Ero lunges into the path of the whip, moving impossibly fast. He's sitting down, relaxed in his seat one moment and in the next, he has the tail end of Wyden's whip wrapped around his forearm and then, equally as quick, he yanks the whip hard and it flies from Wyden's outstretched hand.

Ero jumps down onto the smooth stone arena and the other warriors clear a circle and then I watch Ero wrap the whip around his fist several more times before raising that whip-wrapped fist and beating Wyden to death with it.

I watch the first few punches land and then I close my eyes. *My soul is from elsewhere and I will end up there.* Sounds of pain. Of flesh smacking against flesh. I recognize that Ero is doing this for *me* and there's a distant recognition that this is not easy for him to do, either, but I cannot forget that there is always another way. Another option.

There is always good feeling. There is always dancing. *I was drunk, but I haven't forgotten what it was like to have him* try *for me.*

More laughter and shouting. The other soldiers are betting, but I don't think it's a hard guess to understand the outcome of this match. Ero was clearly provoking Wyden and the junior warrior fell right into Ero's trap. Because the male who has laid claim to me is a madman. *He's not Hades. Even Hades would be frightened of Ero.*

"Halima."

My whole body jerks at the sound of my name. I was dazed a moment ago, but when I look back down at the pit, I'm alert and then horrified when I realize that Ero's got his arms spread to the sides and is willingly taking punches from Wyden while his head is thrown back on his neck. He's laughing. He's laughing sick, dark laughter that I've never heard and that makes me want to run. But he isn't the one who called for me.

"Halima!" I glance over my shoulder. On the stones below, behind the throne, stands Frey.

My face squinches up. I shake my head. "What are you doing here?" I ask her in my best Omoro.

She nods and even though she keeps glancing over her shoulder every few seconds, she seems oddly calm. "Leanna and Kenya sent me...why haven't you given Ero the wine?"

"Leanna and Kenya are alive?"

"Yes. Ero took away their chains..." More words I don't quite grasp pass before I understand her meaning, "...the day after he took you away. We thought you were dead...until weapons exchanged with the harem...we thought you drank the wine we sent...that you died..."

I can't help but grin more genuinely then as the sounds of violence recede behind me. This is more important. "What?" She says.

"You said *we*."

She blinks, surprised understanding dawning in her bright eyes, and then she smiles with me. "Yes. *We* want to know when we should plan... When you will give him the wine..."

Tension and terror ripple through me. He is a madman and a monster, but is it not better to stand at the Devil's right hand than in his path? I'm a coward because I'm not a soldier. I'm the interpreter. I'm not cut out for mutiny. I'm not a harbinger of death. *But for them, I will have to be.*

"It must be tonight," she says. "Leanna says to say *ziss is ohrdor*." Order. An order from my commanding General.

I wring out my hands. "I don't know if I can seduce him."

She shakes her head, not understanding. "No time. Gerd and the Danien go tonight. We must...with them or not...closes..."

I understand what she means and my heart beats even harder. Anidi laye, I can't forget. It's not just about Ero and I. It's about us all.

"Okay," I say, nodding, terror blurring my vision even as resolve stiffens my spine. "Okay, I'll do it. I'll kill him tonight."

She smiles, her teeth flashing *mostly* white against her face and I think of Jia and the toothbrushes. Frey nods and tucks her grey hair behind her ear. "I will tell the others. Haddock, Gerd and I will come for you."

I nod, mute, voice hoarse.

"Anidi laye," she says finally, giving me an unsure look.

"Anidi laye," I answer, but for the first time, I don't feel it in my whole heart. I don't want to be like him. I don't want to become a monster.

"See you tonight."

"See you tonight."

9

Ero

I worry that Halima does not understand the significance of my display. That I both freed her Tanishi leaders from their chains and that I openly challenged my warriors to keep her is a step no Nigusi has taken before — not at this stage.

Of course, Nigusi have claimed captives in the past but it's been a rare occurrence and *never* has such a claiming taken place before those slaves have proven themselves in combat and gone through the process of initiation.

I don't intend for my Tanishi to go through such a process. I won't take any risks with her. I want her. Perhaps after I have her submission, I'll get bored and decide that she's for the crocs, but I won't count on that eventuality.

But when I brought her here to the main cave, she was blind to what I'd done for her. She'd been afraid, unable to meet my gaze. She hadn't even honored me enough to watch me fight. I didn't like that. I wanted to reprimand her for it, but I was distracted afterward by the look on her face.

As soon as I finish destroying Wyden, I order Lopina to take him away to the village healers and I return to my throne...only to find her standing beside it.

I jump up onto the rocks and advance on her. My blood is rushing in my ears and the battle has me feeling restless. My tunic drapes off of her right shoulder and the brown of her skin gleams gold beneath the brilliant daylight.

Fuck, she's beautiful. There. I said it. An oath I've denied for too long. I don't know when it occurred to me that she was stunningly beautiful, but somewhere along the way it did and now I'm confident she's the most stunning creature I've ever laid eyes on.

And she belongs to me.

Pride swells in my chest, along with a small dose of fear — fear that she doesn't understand the lengths I've gone through and will continue to go through to keep her — but suddenly, she takes a breath and offers me one of her smallest smiles. One of her *good* smiles.

"Nigusi," she says breathlessly. She shuffles to the side, angling her body towards my seat. I take it, grabbing her by the waist and dragging her against me. I inhale deeply against the curve of her neck. She smells so perfect.

The battle has my blood racing with want — and it isn't just a generic want — it's a need for *her. I broke the rules for her. I risked my throne for her. Now, I want my prize.*

But part of wanting my prize is having that prize want me. And now?

Now as I sit with my arms around her body, she doesn't fold on herself, but sits up straight and meets my gaze with trepidation. She's unsure about something, even as the little succubus presses her thin body against my chest, reaches both arms around me and gently threads her fingers through the hairs at the base of my neck.

Good feeling cascades down my body in waves, making my toes curl, making me forget about her uncertainty. Fuck it. I'm sure enough for us both.

My head drops back, hitting my metal throne. I feel nothing but her touch. Her weight in my lap. Her hip and the soft muscles of her ass pressing against the stiffness forming between my legs. My pelvis jerks and I pull her harder against me, my cock desperate for a relief I want to feel from her and only her — *now.*

"Soon," I hear myself growl without meaning to.

"What?" She pulls my hair again so softly, too softly. "I didn't understand."

"Harder," I rasp, fingers grabbing her so hard I worry I'll hurt her, but she doesn't complain. She pulls my hair harder, but not hard enough. "Harder," I tell her again.

"No," she whispers.

I open my eyes and she quickly looks away from my face. I pull her attention back to me with my hand on her neck. She struggles to meet my gaze and, when she licks her lips, I fight a losing battle not to taste them. *She's my prize. I have every right to her.* But instead of forcing my lips onto hers, I fidget and find restraint.

"No?" I snarl.

She shivers just a little and bites that lower lip again, looking far too young for this world — for me — and it doesn't matter at all.

"No pain." She pulls my hair with that same bone-breaking tenderness and, at the same time, leans in and kisses my left cheek and then my jaw.

I freeze, relishing and worshipping this far more than I should. It just…isn't often that I'm touched by her. By anyone. And never like this. Like she cares for me more than this world will ever allow for.

Distracted, I answer, "A little pain lets you know you're alive."

"No pain. Not this time."

I smile. She tugs on my hair a little harder. "Alright, Halima."

I open my eyes and see hers. They're large and brown and full of glittery surprise. Fuck, she's going to be a problem for me. She is already. I smooth my thumb over the mark on her arm and try to calm myself. It doesn't work.

I stroke the stitching on her shoulder, feeling the urge to see the signs that spell *El-li* — that brought us to this moment. "Can I look at it?"

"You…you're asking?"

"I'm asking if I can undress you, check your wounds, and then if you're healthy enough, kiss you."

I curl my fingers into her hair and then into the fabric at the small of her back. *Restraint, restraint, restraint…*

"Don't you want to do more with me than that?"

Fuck. I crush her body against my erection, grinding up against her through our clothing. My forehead is hot and my heart beats harder than it did when I fought Wyden. I lean in and press my mouth to her bare shoulder and drown in the taste of her skin.

"You don't want this from me," I say, trying to remember, wishing I could forget. "You want a good man," I seethe.

"I want you, Ero." Her voice trembles. I don't like it.

I jerk back, but she leans in and kisses me and I'm unraveled by the passion in her lips. She tastes me deeply before placing open mouth kisses across my blood-spattered cheekbone to reach my ear.

"I do want you, Ero," she says, and this time, she sounds nothing but sure. "I don't want to want you, but I do. I've wanted you ever since you *dansst* with me."

I bark out a laugh and reposition her on my lap, just for the friction of her hip against my erection. I'm hard as a goddamn stone, now.

"I fight and kill for you and you want me because of your *danss*?"

She pulls back and looks into my eyes and there is a shocking wetness there that makes me terrified.

"What is wrong?" I say, but she interrupts me in a way only she has the right to.

"You put your hands around my throat." She puts her hands around my throat. "You squeezed." She squeezes.

My entire chest pounds, furious and worried. "I did not kill you," I offer and it's a pathetic thing.

She smirks and looks up at my forehead, traces my hairline, and it's as if the cave system has entirely fallen away. We are alone in the universe — perhaps, alone in *her* universe — where the Tanishi way of gentleness is the only one that can survive.

She reaches between us and palms my hot, steely shaft and every muscle in my body flexes. My fucking ass lifts from the seat of my throne, bringing her with me. I look like a fucking fool. I feel like one. And it doesn't matter. She's ruined this for me, too.

"You say you did not kill me because of this." Her hand smooths my erection. "But it's not true. You did not kill me because of this." She touches my chest, placing her palm flat over my heart. Can she feel the way it stutters for her? Unsure in ways a Nigusi is not?

"Enough," I snarl. "If you want to fuck me, you will have to fuck all of me, not just the pieces you believe to be good. And Tanishi, I promise you, your search is in vain. Those pieces are not there."

I hold her still, hungrily, mind racing. I'm fucking pissed, but what's worse? The fact that I'm still trying to marshal my touch into something less aggressive, something that might distantly resemble something good because that's how I want her to feel. That's how I want *all* her feels with me. But I don't want her forgetting that I am Nigusi and I will slay every single soul under this mountain to ensure it because only by ensuring it can I keep her with me forever.

"What are you thinking?" I say when her smile falls and some of the light leaves her eyes.

Something flashes behind her gaze that I don't like. She licks her lips and starts to smile again but it isn't the smile I've seen of hers that I've come to hope for. It's a different smile, but one that's just as easy to read. It's fake, forced, trying to persuade me of something she herself doesn't believe.

"You're right…"

I smirk. "I am…"

"…but I still want to return with you to our room."

"Oh?"

I lean back in my seat and pull my hand from her hair. I comb a few stray curls behind her right ear and feel my way down the dark textures until I reach those feathery tips. They lay tangled against her chest. Against her breasts. I mold my hand to her left breast through my tunic and squeeze in a way I know she won't like.

Her fingers flutter over my wrist. She wants to stop me…but she doesn't and my suspicion explodes into full blown accusation. There's something wrong here. She wants something from me…but it isn't my body. The true question is, can I convince her otherwise?

"Yes. I'm eager. I'd like to go back to your room now."

"To my bed?"

She nods, looking so unsure. I'd laugh in her face if I wasn't so interested in playing along.

"You'd like to spread your legs for me now?"

She nods again. "Yes. I'd like to give you what I haven't given any other man."

"Hm. I see." I press my palm over her sex through the tunic, rubbing it crassly, making the false smile still plastered between her cheeks jerk wildly.

"Is it because I released Leanna and Kenya? You no longer fear being shackled to my throne, so you're ready to relax for me?" That was my plan. I didn't think it worked and, when the surprise registers on her face, I'm sure it didn't.

"Oh yes. Yes, that's it. For releasing Leanna and Kenya, I want to…" She says something then, using an old word for a concept that we no longer have.

"You mean to fuck."

She hesitates, then nods. "What is the difference?"

"There are no good feelings in fuck. Good feelings happen only in *Xiveri*."

"Xiveri?"

"It doesn't matter. It's not a concept for you or for us or for this. There is only fucking, which you want to do now because you are pleased that I fought Wyden and released your prisoners."

"Yes," she answers quickly, chewing hard on her bottom lip.

Funny, that she can speak so many tongues, but be unable to form hers into the words she'd need to convince me that she wasn't up to something. The only true thing is what she says next.

"And because you dansst with me and because I see those parts of you and I know they are real."

"Halima," I seethe, but I meant to call her Tanishi.

I pull her against me and rub myself against her body, making myself wild with need. Her eyelids flutter. Her fingers curl against my bare skin. I wonder if she even knows she's inched them lower and lower. Now her right hand is still caught in my hair, but her left hand is splayed over my bellybutton. *Just a little lower...*

"Can I kiss you?" She has the audacity to ask.

I have only one answer. "Yes."

She stretches up and I tell myself not to react to the pleasure of her mouth on mine — to try to see this investigation through to its end — but I'm standing up, carrying her out of the main cave before I realize I'm even moving.

With her legs wrapped around my waist, I can feel her hot center pressed against my abdomen. I rub her against my body, wanting to feel her everywhere. Wanting to mark myself with her scent.

Her breath is coming quicker and hotter — shorter, too — and I don't know if it's because of her lust or because of whatever it is she has planned, but I'm aroused by the sounds regardless. If she wants to play this game, then fuck it. I can play, too.

I push open the rolling stone blocking the entrance to my chambers with my foot, but I have to lower her and use both hands to slam it back into place. In the time it's taken me to release her from my grip, she's already moved to the foot of the bed. She's sitting on it when I turn around, wiping her hands off on her thighs. They must be damp. She looks nervous. It makes me just a little...sad.

"Are you going to relax for me now that you know I won't lock you up?"

Her chest rises and falls in waves. She licks her lips. "I'm going to try."

An honest response. That sadness morphs into something else. It tings inside of me like the tiniest of bells.

"Are you going to accept that you'll be fucking someone you hate? Someone with no good pieces? Someone who isn't and will never be a good man?"

She looks at me so softly, so tenderly, I'd have killed her if she were anyone else. "Only two of those are true."

Fuck me, but I know which two. "I don't care, Tanishi."

By the time I reach her, the fire in my groin has stoked into a roaring flame, but my concentration manages to cut through it unscathed. I palm her cheek, tilt her head back so that she's forced to look up into my eyes.

"No pain," I tell her.

She nods and her lips part as I sweep down to taste them. She opens for me and I don't miss how her legs spread just a little wider.

I don't grab for her sex, but spend the next moments worshipping her mouth. It isn't a hard thing to do. She tastes divine. We kiss for what might be an hour or just a few minutes.

I break our kiss with a throaty laugh that makes her smile.

"What?"

"You look drunk," I tell her.

A flash of that earlier lie passes across her face, but I don't understand it. And I'm too distracted to care when she glances down at the fastening of my kilt and starts to undo it.

Her fingers are trembling as she slips the belt free and pushes my kilt down until it's caught on my erection. I fist the shaft and pull it out, careful with it because it's as tender as it's ever been. She swallows again and reaches for it, hesitating in a way that I hate.

"Are you going to hurt me, Halima?" I ask. *It feels so good to say her name.*

"Are you severe? This looks like it could punish me. I could not punish it."

Smiling at her sometimes perfect sometimes broken speech, I grab her wrist and place her hand on my straining erection. The blood has rushed from all other parts of my body to this one mast, flushing the brown skin a dark and dangerous red.

"I will be gentle," I choke. "And in this — only this — good."

She scoffs. She has every right to because I'm not so sure of the declaration myself. She drops her hand from around my cock and I curse between my teeth, furious at the loss. Slipping my hand under her arms, I toss her back onto the bed and chase her onto the pillows.

I grab her beneath the knees and wrench her towards me, winning a small gasp from her. Her tunic rides up, exposing her lower lips and the soft skin above them. I reach for it, and pass my thumb gently over it. Her back arches and she makes an expression of pure shock.

"Khara," she says and it must be a curse in her *Ahrabiq* tongue because it bursts out of her with force.

Smile uncomfortably big, I begin smoothing my thumb over her soft nub in gentle circles. I can't remember the last time I had to concentrate so hard on my touch. It's important for me though, that she stays like this. I don't know what she's lying about, but I don't want this to scar her. I'm not a good man and I have no good parts, but I'm a selfish fuck and I want this to be good for me and to do that, it has to be good for her.

I'll use the opposite strategy I use on my warriors to win this war — instead of my fists, I'll use my tongue.

"No pain," I whisper, dropping my tone in a way that makes her look at me with wonder. She has not heard me like this before, I'm sure of it. Because, perhaps for the first time in my own memory, I want to be earnest.

"Do you understand me?" I trace the tips of my fingers up to the crease of her thigh, teasing it gently.

She shivers. "Yes…" Her voice comes out breathless and even though her hands are shaking against sheets, the muscles in her legs are making no move to close and keep me out. Not like the last time.

"Good little Tanishi…" I have her where I want her and I may only have seconds to act.

Moving fast, I lift her knees and hook them over my shoulders. I bury my mouth in her sopping wet center and drink in the heady scent that is her arousal. She screams and her whole body tenses, but only for that breath. Because on her next, a tremor rolls up her right leg and her head kicks back into the mattress and she reaches for me, unable to touch me but that doesn't stop her from trying. *Fuck, she's stunning like this.*

I settle in, prepared to lavish her pussy with the lies I'm so capable of — lies of a male that is gentle — for hours, working her over and over until she crumbles into pieces in my lap. But she forces a laugh from my lips when she comes apart. She only lasts seconds.

She shivers and shakes and her leg muscles spasm as she opens them as far as she can and then farther, arching her lower back and then grinding her hips up. From lies to this, I'm amazed she wants me closer. I'm amazed she wants me at all.

"Ero!" She screams, her eyes flying open and finding me.

She watches me through her orgasm and I damn near come all over the bed at the sight of her shock and her alarm and her gratitude. She looks so grateful for this, it's hard to imagine I was ever any other way with her. Or that she was ever any other way with me.

As soon as her tremors die and her legs stop twitching, she squirms away from me, laughing as she wriggles her way down the bed. She stares between her wet, messy pussy and my mouth and chin and I wait for her to scream in horror as she realizes what she's just done, or incriminate me in some other way. She doesn't.

And I don't see the lies in her eyes either when they crinkle and she says, "That felt good. Thank you, Ero."

"Just *good*?"

She hesitates, then shakes her head. "Transcendent."

I growl, a charge lighting me up like flint on rock. I surge forward, smothering her body to the mattress with mine. I yank at her clothes until they're off and her small breasts are bared to my gaze. But I don't lavish them as I should. Instead, I find myself more interested in her face.

Her expressions are fascinating. So unsure one moment and then ravenous the next. She throws her hands into my hair and wrenches me closer — and then she slams her palms against my shoulders and shoves me back. And then she grabs me by the neck and crushes her mouth to mine so hard our teeth clack.

A gust of laughter bursts out of me and for a second, I forget that she's lying to me about something or that I bloodied Wyden's face to get her to this point, that she was horrified when I meant to impress her, or that she's a Tanishi who isn't ready for what I'm offering.

No. In that second, she's just Halima.

And I'm just Ero, a male left wanting.

Her legs part around my hips and guide me closer. I reach between us and sweep the head of my erection through her wet heat. She gasps and her eyes flutter and so do mine when I grind my erection against her sensitive flesh.

She shivers and clings to me and it's a…a precious thing. I plant both elbows on either side of her body, fully eclipsing her. She's so much smaller than I am and I'm not a small male anywhere.

I kiss her lips tenderly and then kiss her cheek gently, and then her ear. "Halima."

"Ero…" Her voice is shaky.

"Are you sure you want this?"

"Yes." I search for lies in her gaze...but I do not find them. Or maybe, I'm too far gone to see.

I'm lined up with her core, pressing gently against her entrance, probing, trying to gauge how much pain I'm going to cost her at the expense of my pleasure and reveling in the knowing that I am her first male. *I will be her only male.* The thought troubles me. I shake my head and seek her mouth again, offering her a possessive kiss.

She tastes like herself. I don't know how to describe it. The taste is so distinct I know I'll never taste anything like it. She tastes like peace. Like *Ahrabiq*. Like a distant sun. Like a history lost to darkness and unearthed by her tongue.

"I want to melt in you," I tell her.

"What? I don't understand."

And then some kind of demon takes hold of my vocal cords and speaks without my permission, using my voice and my lips pressed against her salty cheek.

"Anidi laye," I whisper.

She shivers and her arms circle my shoulders, trying to reach but not managing. "Anidi laye." She pulls back just enough that I can see her face and look into her eyes as I melt into her, which is what I meant to confirm was alright.

Too late for that shit now.

Because she's so wet, the slightest movement sends me flying and none of my movements are slight. I thrust forward, spearing her heat with my girth. I hit several points of resistance when her walls squeeze tight around me, and I can tell that her body is attempting to push mine out.

"I'm stronger than you are. I will win this battle." Despite the sincerity of my words, my voice is still strained.

I slide one hand down her body and lift her ass off of the mattress, changing the angle and my ability to find the root of her core. Her sloppy arousal is mine. Her body is mine. Her tongue is mine, her lies, her smiles, her screams.

"Ero!"

My eyes flutter open. I glance towards her arm, but it's hidden from me. I have the sudden strong urge to see it, to revel it in, to capture her scars in my memory. But I can't move. I can't change the trajectory of my hips or my thoughts or my intent, which is only to sink into her as deep as her small body will allow.

I slide in even deeper, stretching her past the point of no return. "Halima," I growl.

She makes gasping, pained sounds and I stop, look at her face, wait for her to meet my gaze. "Relax with me. Please, Halima," I beg. I fucking beg.

"It hurts a little."

I growl, not wanting to break a promise. I sit back and grab her waist, my fingers meeting around her middle. She arches back, her body going boneless as I lave my tongue up and over her chest. I capture one pert brown nipple in my mouth as I pull down, sheathing my cock with her body. I'm almost there. Almost all the way in. Her hips are squirming, making it hard to focus, but I repress the fuck out of my own pleasure as I work to guarantee hers.

Because when this is over, I want this scarred into her memory: That the first male she was with was a bad male, but he did not treat her badly. I want her to remember that it was me that claimed her for my own. I want her to remember...fuck that. I never want her to *forget* that it was me.

I grab her roughly and give her one last jerk, yanking her down onto me fully. She whimpers, but I remember where I am and that she's hurting and I lick a line down her sternum before sucking her other nipple into my mouth. I bite hard enough to leave marks on her breast, hoping to distract her from one pain with another. Her hands drop to my shoulders and hold me with a certainty I don't deserve.

I move forward, covering her fully and keeping her hips up so that I can grind my pelvis against her soft bump and win another tremble from her. Her eyes fly open and meet mine. Like this, we stay connected as I start to move. Fear flashes plain in her gaze and I slow.

"Pain?" That's all I can wrap my head around now. That one word and using everything in my power to prevent it. I grind a little more gently and move a little more fluidly.

"Pain?" I say again, trying to keep my head on straight and not lose my fucking mind as I wage countless battles inside of my own body as I struggle to care for hers. She isn't ready. One day she'll be ready, but that day is not today. One day, I'll fucking savage her. But today, I'll let her savage me.

I am no male that I recognize as tears well in her eyes and her mouth quirks up and she uses her tongue to wet her bottom lip and hangs onto my shoulders for dear life as I pound into her as gently as I can.

"No pain, Ero," she says. *She says my name.* "Just inundation."

I smile. "Overwhelmed? Many feelings?"

She nods. "I'm overwhelmed."

"Then be overwhelmed."

She gasps and I almost lose rhythm right then and explode into her body. Instead, I hold her still, needing a moment to pull my shit together. I kiss her neck, burying my face in the cavern above her shoulder.

"As I am overwhelmed," I grunt against her flesh.

I continue to move, sliding in and out of her heat as the day fades into hours and hours become seconds and Halima sheds some of the fear she'd been wearing. Not all of it, but some.

Her hands still flinch towards my shoulders, but she touches me instead of holding back, spearing her fingernails into my back hard enough I hope they leave marks. She kisses me more freely, biting her way down my jugular.

I worry, but only fleetingly — after I remember that I'm the only murderer here and that she isn't here to kill me. Instead, I let her touch me where she likes, kiss me where she likes, bite me wherever she wants. No one else has ever had such a privilege. No one will ever have such a privilege.

I flip her onto her stomach and yank her hips up. She's shaky, but I'm also shaky. I don't know how long we've been at this. I reach around her body to stroke her clit and her inner walls pulse around my erection, squeezing the fuck out of me.

"Fuck, Halima." This is the third time tonight I've felt her core ripple around me, and I'm barely hanging on. "I can't...much longer...mine!"

I slap her ass when her torso falls forward. She's giving up. Her body's giving out. She's mewling nonsensical things to the sheets and to the rocky room around us in languages I can't identify or interpret, but I feel like a fucking thunderstorm every time I hear her whisper my name.

"Ero...this is transcendent..."

I drag her damp hair over her shoulder. She's sweating and I fucking worship it. I fucking worship all of this. "You're mine. And I'm going to fill you now," I growl, except I'm not. I can't. I can't risk a child. That's a weakness I'm not ready for.

Nigusi only have children when they step down, and almost none survive that long. And I refuse to let this little human with a thousand weaknesses walk this world with our child alone.

Bowed over her shoulder, I bite down and start to pull out, intending to come on her back, but she gasps as I slip free of her and her ass plunges clumsily backwards.

"No. Please. You can...inside. No baby," she babbles.

"What?"

"No baby. I haven't..." she says a word I don't know, then clarifies. "Blood. No blood. I haven't...bled yet. None of us have. You can't...get us pregnant."

Panic rises. The idea of pregnancy deters many of my warriors. The idea of disease deters the rest. But if she's a virgin without the ability to get pregnant, all of her Tanishi women are at risk.

Rage makes my blood hot as I think of one of my warriors with Halima. Her body is so pliant. Would she go to him willingly?

I snatch her hair in one fist and she whimpers. I struggle to release the hold as I plunge into her deeper. And then restraint flits from my palm like a leaf in the river's current.

I rut her, the only thing on my mind the thought of her with someone else. No, not the only thing. Because there are other thoughts there, too. Thoughts of her pregnant, thoughts of her with my kids...

The slapping sound of my hips against her ass is all I can hear. She tries to prop herself up on her arms and hold onto the sheets to keep herself still, but she's just here for the ride, bouncing in every direction, absorbing every thrust, sweat dripping off of her body and mixing with the sweat dripping off of my body.

I grab her neck again, desperate for her attention. She tries to look at me over her shoulder, but my fingers are working on her clit again and she's falling...and this time, she's taking me with her. Anidi laye. We fall together.

I fight against the pleasure threatening to warp my expression and keep my gaze trained on her eyes. I want to watch her, want to see everything as my balls hitch up against my body and I slide home, emptying into her with force.

I hope to fuck she wasn't lying to me, because there isn't a chance in my mind she wouldn't get pregnant from this. I've held on for fucking ever — at least that's what it feels like. The last woman I was with...fuck it. I can't even remember.

As far as my cock's concerned, there never was another.

As far as my cock's concerned, there never will be again.

"Mine," I groan, falling on top of her as my hips continue to slam against her thighs and my cock continues to pound unevenly into her body.

I touch her everywhere, hands roaming blindly, desperately. I squeeze everything I can, squeeze everything together, squeeze my eyes shut. I can't keep hold of anything, my sanity, my spirit's all that's left. And it's a weak thing. I didn't think it would look like this...like a husk compared to her greatness.

She's pure life.

As I bury myself in her body and try my fucking hardest not to crush her, a sudden creeping realization starts to move over me like a shadow shifting beneath the sun...she may be a Tanishi and she may be mine, but I may have to fight just as hard to keep her as I do to *earn* her. *I'm not ready.*

I feel so unprepared. I should get out of the bed and put some distance between us, because I feel cracked wide open as my balls give up every drop of cum that they have left. But I don't do that.

Instead, I squeeze her within an inch of her life, coiling myself around her. I grab her neck, either side of her face and I shove my tongue into her mouth and taste the salty tang of her lips. They're slack and her breaths are jerky and it doesn't matter at all. I can't stop fucking her with my tongue.

I grab her around the waist and hold her so that our stomachs are pressed together. My cock is still deep inside of her body, jerking, twitching, needing. Needing. It's a dangerous word, but it's all I can think about now.

I grip her jaw in a shaking hand and she licks her lips and, when I pull back, she does the fucking damnable. She chases me, peppering my face with soft presses of her mouth and kissing me so sweetly, too softly to survive.

Against my whip and my blade, she wields a sword made of flowers, and she'll vanquish me every time. I stand no fucking chance against her.

"Fuck," I curse.

"Mhmm," she moans.

"I'll swallow you whole."

"What?"

"Nothing." Everything. "How was it? Did you feel pleasure?" I'm speaking quickly because I'm desperate to know. I can't stop touching her and I touch her with an intensity and urgency I worry will leave bruises.

Meanwhile, she lazily strokes my back like she doesn't have any of the same pressure in her chest that I do. But she also strokes me like nothing else in the world matters besides me and us and this. She isn't retreating. She's here, too.

"Tell me, Halima." I push her hair out of her face and watch the stars clear from her eyes. "Please."

Her mouth works, her eyes gleam, she grins back at me but her expression is shaky, her lower lip is trembling. She doesn't speak. She can't. And I can't read her. Not right now. Because right now, I'm as shattered on the inside as she looks on the outside.

"And you say you aren't good..."

Fuck. She sounds so wounded, I can't make sense of her expression coupled with her words. "Fuck. Did I hurt you? Pain?"

I start to draw back, trying to pull myself out of her, but she moans and her hands firm around my shoulders and she yanks me down.

"No. No! Please don't." Her thighs squeeze my hips and she exhales deeply when I settle my weight more firmly onto her. My cock is screaming at me, sensitivity riding it to the point of pain, but I don't give a fuck about that right now.

I stay because she asked me to stay and because I can't remember anything ever feeling better than the weight of her body in my arms. I kiss her forehead, tasting her salty skin. And then because she tastes so fucking good, I kiss her again. I hold.

Time slows and stretches, bleeding out into the river and following the currents. The history that she spoke of and that's weighed on my sword arm my entire life bleeds out, too, exercised like demon from a body.

"I lied to you before," she whispers.

Ahh...here it comes. "About what?"

"I don't hate you Ero. You are not a good man, but you have good parts and I don't hate those parts."

I smirk and shake my head. "Your willingness to believe this would get you killed were I someone else." And were she not mine, as written by the laws of the universe and the masters of time.

I stroke my hand down her back, trying to mimic the gentle way she touches me. My fingertips scrape over stitching and she jerks.

"Your stitches. I didn't think. Come. I'll wash your wound."

"No. No, Ero," she sighs. "I'm okay. It was just... inundation."

Carefully leaning over to check her shoulder, I see that her stitching looks neither torn nor enflamed and has already started to scab.

"Good. You should feel overwhelmed."

"Inundation — is that the wrong word?"

She wrinkles her nose, dropping her head back on my arm. She looks up at me and I stare into her eyes and they're so fucking brown. My cock twitches in the home it's found and a surge of stress and panic cut into me. *She needs to stay here. To stay forever. As long as I tell her to. Safe and happy and alive.*

"It's the perfect word. I want to inundate you, so that you think of my cock in you all the time. I want you to crave it. To wait for me when I come back from slaughtering our enemies with your fingers in your body, spreading yourself so that you're ready to receive me. Will you be ready for me?"

She blinks slowly, lazily, looking so fucking sweet. I kiss her chin and against her throat I exhale, "You will be ready for me. Because you're mine."

I reach above me blindly and pull a fistful of pillows beneath us and around her, cocooning her so that she can't escape. I drag a blanket over her and she starts to laugh.

My erection has started to die down. I could take her again easily, but I don't think she's ready for more. The sheer force of my will is what keeps me from mounting her into the next sunrise — that, and a very real fear of my newfound desperation, the one driving me to mania and violence.

I look down at where our hips are joined and then back at her face and can't help but laugh at her expression. "What is it?"

"I can't…can't believe…we made a chaos. Is that all…from you?" She's looking down at where our stomachs meet and the clear and milky liquid that adheres us together.

I shake my head and rub my fingers through the slick stickiness, gathering some and bringing it to her lips. "No, Halima. This is yours. Mine is in here. Open."

She opens, her gaze never meeting mine. Her tongue swirls my longest finger before letting it pop free.

"Swallow," I order and she obeys me.

Then she mimics the motion, gathering some of her slick and my cum on her thumb and pressing it to my lower lip. "Open, Ero."

Ero. That's my name, but I don't think I've ever heard it spoken like this. "You dare order your Nigusi?" I ask her, but I'm teasing her...*teasing* her. Unfuckingbelievable.

I open my mouth and she grins rapturously when I suck the jizz from her finger onto my tongue. I don't swallow though, but lean in and kiss her, thrusting my tongue into her mouth.

She sucks.

My eyes roll and my hips jerk inside of her once more. "Fuck, Halima," I hiss, wrenching back. "If we don't stop soon, I'm going to fuck you again and I'm never going to stop." I press my palm to her lower belly, passing my thumb over her skin. "I'm going to come out now."

"Mm mmm." She shakes her head. "Ow."

I stop moving. "I'm not hard anymore. It isn't hurting you."

"You can't tell me that," she pouts and I can tell she's very fragile. She's joking, but there are tears in her eyes, too.

"Don't do that." I press my thumb to her bottom lip to stop the slight way it quivers. I'm powerless against it. Make this face with that lost, young, look in her eyes and I'd hand over my throne. *My life.* I swipe my thumb underneath her eyes.

"I'm not crying," she whispers. She touches my hip, nails catching in my side. She sniffles.

"Stop that," I bark, confused by the sudden change I see in her. "Why are you doing that?"

"I'm not doing anything."

"I know when you lie." I slide a thumb underneath her chin and tilt her face up. "Why are you like this?"

"Because it wasn't supposed to be good." She leans forward and kisses my pectoral. "I will expect the next man to be just as good and I don't think he will be."

Fury stabs through the preciousness of this moment. My grip turns hard. "What next man?"

"When I escape to the surface. Or when you kill me. In the next lifetime," she whispers. "I think I will not forget even then."

Fuck. Fuck fuck fuck. I roll onto her and kiss her deeply, tasting her fear and her pain as if they were mine. I hate everything she's saying. I hate her for saying them.

I snarl, "You're right. You won't forget me because you'll have me like this every single day for the rest of your life. There are no other men. There's nothing but my bed and if another man dares approach my bed, the last thing he'll see is the sword I impale him with."

But she just shakes her head. She touches my chest. She smiles. "You can be *shar-ming* when you want to be." She calls me a word I know, but that has an unfamiliar meaning.

"What is this word? Boyish? You're calling me a child?"

She laughs and it lights up my entire body, my entire room. "No. The word must be an old word. Sad, that it reflects a child now. What I mean is…" Her gaze settles on my chest where she brings just her fingertips together over my heart. "What lives in here. Those good pieces? They *move* me."

My heart beats harder, faster. I open my mouth to tell her that I'm equally moved — ravaged, destroyed by her little touches, little kisses, and the way she is when she opens, but her next words cut the tongue from between my teeth with one single stroke.

"But they cannot stay."

"What? Why do you say this?"

"Because I will either escape and be free of you, or you will have to kill me. Either way, I will be free of you," she whispers so sadly, stroking me all the while. "We will never be here again."

Furious, I rip my erection out of her ruthlessly and her body curls, like I punched her in the stomach. Hearing the sound that comes out of her makes me feel like shit. It doesn't help that the pain she shows is one I feel mirrored acutely. My cock is sensitive and exposed and pissed off at what I've just done.

I rub my face roughly, still awkwardly bowed, unable to stand tall. She's made me this way. I should punish her, but the only punishment I want to inflict is between her thighs and only if she feels pleasure from it and no pain. Never pain.

Never again.

"Fuck." My heart is a war drum and I struggle to breathe through the tune. It wants something from me. *Say it. Just do it. Tell her you're sorry. Make her stay.* "I..." I can't. I've never said the word before. "It will not be this way. It will be how I say it will be and if I want you forever, then you'll be here just like this, legs spread wide and waiting for me to pleasure you."

I don't wait for her answer — I don't need one — but quickly go to the washroom and grab a rag, a stone basin of water and healing cream. I return to the bed and set the items down on it, then grab the flagon of wine from the food tray. I uncork the wine stopper with my teeth and pass the wine skin down to her only to find something odd.

My Tanishi is staring at me completely frozen. I glance behind me, suddenly concerned that maybe my chambers were stormed while my back was turned and my focus was so wholly concentrated on her. But there's nothing. We're alone.

"What?" Her gaze passes to the wine. I extend it down to her. "For your nerves. To dull any lingering pain."

Her fingers in the blankets curl. Her voice catches. Then she shakes her head and her eyes round and understanding falls into place. *The lie. This is the true lie. The one that she decided upon back in the caves.*

This little Tanishi poisoned my wine.

She must have been holding onto this lie for some time then, because I haven't returned to my chambers in several days. *That means she must have decided on this lie before today...*

A small needle of something dark stabs my gut, but a needle isn't anywhere near enough to hurt me. *But it does hurt, though. Much more than any wound I've ever sustained.* Maybe what hurts more is knowing that the poison in the wine is something she thinks I deserve. I know it's something I deserve.

But I don't want her to think that.

I think of her words. *Either way, I will be free of you.* So, here it is. Was that a warning? Or a threat? Because this is the play.

I smile down at her and wonder what she sees. She tenses. She waits for me to pull out the knife. Instead I smirk, "If you don't want any, I'm not going to force you."

I bring the wine to my lips and make a great show of gulping down several thick swallows. I stopper the opening in the leather skin with my tongue, but let a few droplets escape and dribble down my chin for show.

Bringing the wine down, the expression on her face guts and cuts. Her eyes are filled with water and her lips are slightly parted. She's clutching a blanket to her chest like it's a shield. The needle in my heart retreats a hair at that look. She may want to kill me, but at least some part of her might regret it, too.

She's not a killer. I doubt she'd willingly ever kill anyone. If her life were in danger? I wonder, I hope. But I'm not even sure of that. So fucking fragile. And she wants to escape me? She wants freedom? I shake my head. She is so wrong. On the surface, alone in the mines, anywhere, she'll be killed. She needs me and I will make her see it. I *have* to make her see it.

"What?" She whispers, voice trembling and afraid. *She's afraid of me again. She thinks I suspect her. She thinks I'll kill her. She doesn't know what's changed, that everything has.*

"You know there is a third option from the ones you described?"

Mute, she shakes her head.

"You could kill me."

I take another fake swig from the wine skin and watch her jaw work. Still, she says nothing and pain digs its heels into my heart, trying to stop it from beating.

I flip the blanket and hiss at the sight of her legs, still slightly parted as if awaiting my return. I almost give in to the compulsion until I remember that she's just killed me. At least, she thinks she has.

"But there's even a fourth option," I whisper, hand finding her ankle and moving across the arch of her foot. "One where we live like this every day. Where neither of us has to die."

She makes a little choking sound and her gaze drops to the blanket. *No, my little Tanishi does not have a murderer's heart.*

"Fuck." I shake my head and grin, gaze dropping to her exposed inner thighs. "That's more than one rag will handle. We made a mess didn't we?" I look into her eyes. She nods just a little. "Anidi laye."

She doesn't repeat the word, perhaps for the first time. She just swallows and looks wracked with guilt. *No, not a killer, my Tanishi.* But she doesn't need to be when I'll kill for us both. But for now, I'll continue to play along. The ruse is not yet finished.

"Wait here." *Drinking* from the wine skin, I make my way out of the room, but as soon as I'm out of sight, I stopper the bottle and drop the leather skin into a pile of armor, way down deep where there isn't a chance she'll find it.

Then, I take a fresh wine skin from the cabinet in the entry room. I uncork it and drink from it freely before grabbing a large white linen cloth and returning to the bed where I carefully spread her legs apart and even more carefully clean her up.

"You're quiet," I say as I drag the damp rag over her slit and clear as much of my semen away as I can. It makes me restless, seeing how the white drips from her pink core to stain her brown skin. Like rain. Ha. Like anything but. This is *filthy*.

She nods and looks rather weepy again. To drive this home, I drain the rest of the wine skin and watch her expression twist. *No. Not out for blood, this one.* Perhaps the only one in the caves who isn't.

"Are you in pain, Halima?"

She sniffs and shakes her head. She pulls the wine out of my hand suddenly and tosses it off of the bed. She takes the rags and tosses them away, too, then grabs both my wrists and pulls me down against her. I wrap my arms around her and am immediately annoyed that the torches around my room are still lit, but I have no intention of doing anything about it.

No, I'll stay here until she kills me.

Not with her poisoned wine, of course, but with the beating of her heart and the tender way she pulls my hair and the soft way she squeezes my back as she holds me.

Several times she starts to say something, but she never does. In the end, I reluctantly start to think that I've waited long enough and I pretend to drift to sleep.

She waits a long time before doing anything. So long, I fleetingly wonder if I wasn't wrong. Maybe she *didn't* poison me and her weird expression stemmed from the rough way we fucked. I'd tried to be gentle, but maybe she is hurt. Maybe I wasn't gentle enough. When I was cleaning her up, I didn't see any blood...

She shifts, moving not at all quietly or carefully, but I suppose she thinks I'm dead or at least incapacitated, so it makes sense. She doesn't reach for my pulse or stop to check my breathing because she either is so confident in whatever she used to drug me or her killer instinct is so weak as to be entirely ineffective.

I wait for the telltale sign of her trying to roll back the door and sprint down the corridor before I get up to follow her, only to be shocked when she doesn't move towards the door at all. Instead, my ears perk to the sound of her rustling around...it sounds like she's handling leather.

Curiosity pries at my eyelids, but I can resist this temptation. I listen instead as she goes through my cupboards and finds linens. I can tell by the sound of fabric rustling as she dresses.

She whispers softly to herself as she moves, amassing items from around my room that I wish I could see, but I can't risk opening my eyes. Not yet. Not until I know exactly what her plan is so I know next time how to stop it before it occurs.

And then, to my horror, the door to my chamber is opened — but not from the inside, from the outside — and fucking captives walk right in.

They speak. There are three of them, plus Halima. I cannot identify any words in their language, but I can hear the stress in Halima's voice as she urges them to do something. And then footsteps get louder. I struggle to keep my breathing even and my pulse long and low. Playing dead is an art mastered by every Pikosa warrior. It helps when you're being tortured.

Fingers touch my throat and then my wrist and the hand is large enough for me to think it might be male. Is this him? The male she thinks of when she fucks me to the stars and back?

Words are rasped and every ounce of restraint in my body steels as I fight to remain grounded and see this through. Because a Tanishi man came to Halima's rescue. A Tanishi man has come to take from me something I have no intention of losing.

I focus hard on the sound of his voice, knowing that this is all I'll have later to identify him by and I wait moments after they leave before getting up, arming myself to the teeth, and heading after them down the tunnel. Every thought that takes me after her is of bloodlust. Every ounce of tenderness is vanquished.

Because the thought of her trying to kill me doesn't bother me half so much as the thought that she's trying to kill me so she can be with someone else. Unacceptable. And this knowledge comes with another promise, a vow that is as simple as it is sure. To eliminate my competition, I will kill every single Tanishi in my caves tonight, male or female.

Every single one but the one that is mine. I need no more convincing. Universe, save your signs.

10
Halima

The trio that comes to rescue me from Ero's chambers is a surprise. Haddock I expected, but with him are Chayana — the person least capable of sneaking around in the entire cave system — and Frey, who I didn't think would trust us Tanishi enough to join a group of them by herself.

Both women are staring at me as we stand in the stone corridor, waiting while Haddock struggles to roll the boulder back into place.

Chayana continues speaking the whole time, her English too quick and quiet for me to catch until she groans, "Fine!" Even though no one asked her anything to prompt her answer. She trudges over to Haddock and applies her strength to the door. Frey flinches, like she wants to join them, but seems stuck in place.

I shrivel under her inspection and clear my throat. "You came."

She nods, evidently understanding my Omoro even though my voice is hoarse and I'm unsteady. That unsteadiness makes it hard to understand what she asks me next. When I struggle with her for clarification, I realize what she means and wince.

"No. No, he didn't rape me," I say, using the same horrible word for it she had. She doesn't seem to understand me though, so I repeat myself once, twice, a third time. And then I add, "I give him my body. It helped him to drink the wine."

Why did he drink the wine? I'm furious with him for it. He sees everything. Why didn't he see this? Why did he let me become a monster, too? Why did he let me become just like him?

Understanding settles over her expression, concern too, but understanding is the more prominent emotion of the two. "I understand."

I sniffle, feeling so horrible I can't even categorize what hurts worst. My body? My spirit? My heart?

"Are you in pain?"

Pain. This is a word I know in every tongue. I shake my head before realizing that I actually *am* in a bit of pain. Not a lot but there's a pressure in my gut and my lower lips feel sensitive and raw even though they're hidden by a pair of Ero's linen pants that I've cinched at the waist and cut off at the ankles. *They're also still dripping with his cum...his and my own.*

"I'm...okay."

Her dark eyes roam over my body and I wonder if she believes me. I don't. Because it isn't just my gooey core that's bothering me, it's the way my whole chest feels like it's caved in, my heart wrenched out and cut open.

Please don't be dead, please don't be dead, please don't be dead.

I hope I didn't kill him, but...I also hope he never wakes up — not because I hate him or want him dead — but because I don't want to have to meet his gaze ever again knowing that I betrayed him. *The monster look suits me well.*

"Alright. Let's go." Haddock squeezes my shoulder and we're off, racing through the tunnels. Well, not racing so much as shuffling quietly, and that's all the chance I have to mourn the loss of Ero, all his little good parts.

Frey leads the way, maneuvering the cave system in ways I don't expect. As we move, I remain at her right hand, offering translations to the best of my ability as we sweep the Northeast tunnels first before moving directly North where the Omoro stay.

We pass through the chamber full of candles and she passes them out to us and we use them as we maneuver the dark. It's so dark where the Omoro are kept. So dark that I can't see the bodies we run into at all until Frey comes to periodic stops.

I don't know the plan, but I'm grateful. I don't want to be in charge. I'm not meant to be. I'm glad that I played my part and helped make this possible, but my mind is still reeling.

All I can do is concentrate on taking one step after the other and keeping my candle held high, keeping my heart from breaking. I betrayed him using what he wanted — a little tenderness. I'm just as bad as he is. *He was.* I hope we're long gone when he wakes up…but I hope he wakes.

Please wake up when I'm long gone.

I translate for the apprehensive Omoro that join our growing group. They stay as far from the Tanishi gathered behind Haddock and Chayana as they can. Chayana still hasn't shut up.

"We need to be quiet," Frey tells me as we enter a small, un-mined and fully pitch black tunnel and she lowers into a crouch. I can hear the thirty bodies behind me shuffling onto their bottoms, too.

I utter a quick order to Haddock who slaps his hand over Chayana's mouth, winning a small giggle from the Omoro kneeling closest to them — a man or maybe a boy, he looks far, far too young to be here fighting for his life like this. The woman kneeling next to him looks older.

She takes his wrist and shushes him. Catching me staring, she offers me a small, white smile. I smile back at her and wonder fleetingly about Jia's toothbrushes. These past days in Ero's care, I've been missing mine and using linens to rub at my teeth. It's just not the same.

I open my mouth to ask Frey what we're waiting for, but I don't suppose it actually matters, so I don't. But then time trickles by and Frey starts to fidget.

Haddock curses behind me. "Leanna should be here by now."

The tunnel we're in is tight. I have no idea where we are in the cave system, only that I haven't been in this tunnel before and I don't know where it leads. In the darkness, I can't even see how long it is, if it turns or branches off, or anything.

Frey glances over her shoulder at me and the girlish look she'd had when I first found her in the caves is gone. She looks like a warrior. Every bit Pikosa and then some.

"We are out of time. We need to go now. We only have a short...time before the Pikosa guards come back. Your leader and the Danien will have...go...to the surface without us."

I piece sentences together from the words I understand and relay their meaning to Haddock. Haddock bites his back teeth together. "Will we be able to find them again on the surface?"

I translate to the best that I can. Frey shakes her head. "If your people are with the Danien, then they will go to...Danien village...we cannot find...their locations are like ours — hidden."

I relay her words to Haddock and he shakes his head. He has dirt smudged all over his cheeks and hands and he looks truly menacing in the low candlelight. "Then we go back."

"If...caught, we are all dead. If your leader...caught *and* we escape, then she will...better chance...survive...if we're gone. Pikosa then have...less slaves. Those left will be more valuable."

Haddock listens to what I've translated and meets my gaze squarely. "What do you think?"

I don't hesitate. "That we need to get far away from here. If Ero does wake up, he'll turn me inside out and anyone that I'm with will go down with me. We can't risk it. We should listen to Frey. She knows the tunnels, the Pikosa and the surface better than we do. This is her world."

Haddock doesn't speak. Chayana grabs his elbow. "I'm with Halima and Frey."

"You'd abandon them?" Haddock snarls. "What about anidi laye?"

And that's how Ero ruins me a second time. Killing him makes me a monster just like him. Fear that I *didn't* kill him makes me a monster, just like him.

Either way, I'm just like him now.

"Khara," I say, shaking my head. "You're right, Haddock. We have to go back for them..."

Frey rips around and slaps her dust and wax covered palm over my mouth. "Tut!" She barks and we all fall quiet. Even my shattered heartbeat suspends itself in terror as we wait....

...and wait...

The tunnels are eerie things, echoes traveling from what feel like other worlds, other histories separated from this one by magical doors in the stone, if only we could find them.

Now, it sounds like I'm in a TV sitcom broadcast from the old world. There are muffled words and then a murky roar, like many people laughing. And then the voice gets louder.

Frey's eyes get so round, I can see white on all sides of her dark irises. She says something in her language that's either a curse or a plea.

She releases me and stands up and issues orders to her people and I don't have to know her language to know what she's telling them and I stand up after her, turn and repeat, "The Pikosa are coming! We've been discovered. Everybody run!"

Behind me, Frey screams and, when I turn, it's to see a huge shadow that could only belong to a Pikosa warrior emerge from around the edge of the corridor and pull her body into the dark.

I run blindly, tripping over people. A hand on my arm keeps me upright and I find myself pressed against Haddock's side. In his other hand, he holds Chayana by the wrist.

"Move, people!" He roars and feet are running — Omoro and Tanishi alike.

Some eyes look to me, as if I might be able to help them, but I'm not their leader. The leader we were all following was just taken and now there are more Pikosa filtering into the caves, either taking or slaughtering. It ends in screams, either way. People die. *And it's my fault.*

A knife flashes and Haddock pulls me out of the way, down a tunnel that branches right. Most of the Omoro go left, though neither turns out to be a good option. More Pikosa are there waiting for us. Everywhere. They have us surrounded.

"There!" Chayana gasps and I look to where she's pointing and see several Omoro disappear into a crevice in the cave wall. It's narrow.

"Haddock, you won't fit," I breathe when he shoves me toward it.

"Go!" He pushes my head down and I bash my forehead on the floor and the crown of my head on the upper edge of the opening when I drop to my belly and wriggle through, following the path three Omoro have taken.

I can hear Chayana whispering curses to Hindi gods behind me and am surprised. Most of us had religion wiped from our memories, yet she speaks to her gods now as if she knows them. Like they're family.

Wriggling through to the other side of the opening, I pull Chayana by the arms and help her and another Omoro through. When no one else follows, I try to ignore the sounds of screaming from behind us, muted now through the cave wall that separates us from the tunnel where the massacre occurred.

A massacre I caused the moment I betrayed him. I should have just stayed in his bed where things were tender and feelings were good. I could have changed him with small acts of kindness. I could have shown him that things could be different. I could have proven anidi laye to him. I could have shown him love.

The Omoro make a left and head down another tunnel. I follow them until we hit another large cave. There are Pikosa here, too. They manage to snatch two Omoro while the third Omoro grabs my wrist and pulls me right.

I drop into a pool of water and, against the gleam of my wildly flickering candlelight on the water's surface, I can see that the tunnel is half-submerged.

"Oh shit...I don't think I can do this, Halima," Chayana says as water reaches our chins. I keep my hand flat on the ceiling above me so I don't bash open my skull, but there isn't anywhere to go.

And then the Omoro in front of me looks back and says a single word that fills me with terror. "Under." And then under she disappears.

"Oh no. Fuck that! I'd rather fight one of those hunky meatheads." She starts to go back, her tattered grey garment clinging to her frame. Her long black hair sticks to her neck and arms and floats between us. The candles in her hand and mine are all the light we have left.

"We can't. We don't have that option...I...we need to follow!" Terror floods my lungs as I drop my candle under the water, letting it go out.

Chayana screams a blood curdling scream and starts to back away from me. I try to swim towards her and grab hold of her hand when, all at once, she disappears under the water completely and, when she shoots back up, she isn't alone.

A Pikosa warrior is standing just a few feet in front of me, Chayana securely wrapped in his muscular arms. He grins at me and it's a terrifying expression. His eyes are full of heat, the thrill of the chase infecting their carnivorousness. Heightening it.

I back away and, when he doesn't follow me or grab me, my heart almost explodes. Abandoning Chayana like a coward, I dive underneath the water and swim after the Omoro. I keep my hand on the rocky ledge above me as I swim and swim…and swim…

My lungs start to jerk. Oh no. This is where I die. There was a turn off somewhere…something! I must have missed it. I need to turn back. Better die gutted in Ero's arms than die here in the dark where someone will find me months from now, a bloated corpse.

My mouth opens, I take in water, my lungs jerk… and then my fingers stab up blindly, expecting stone and finding…nothing. I plant my feet on the rock floor below me and push.

Breaking the surface of the water fills me with fear and with a savage desire to live. I flail helplessly until my wrists bang on rock and I use what little arm strength I have to heave myself out of the water and onto the rocky shore.

I breathe. I choke. I lay dying. I stand living.

Wavering on my feet, I can't see anything and I mean *anything*. It's pure darkness — the inside of an eyelid doesn't compare — and there are no sounds except the water gently lapping behind me. The Omoro I'd been chasing must have gone on ahead, must have escaped already…*Please, don't let her be dead. Don't let her die.*

I stumble forward, going nowhere, and when I take another step, I hit a wall. I brace my shoulder against it and curl my hands up into fists. I squeeze my eyes shut tight and try to think about something else for a minute, something nice. I hate that my first thought is of Ero kissing me so, so softly.

"Be overwhelmed...as I am overwhelmed."

I stagger as a faraway sound pulls my attention left. It's distant, but it sounds manmade, not from an underwater canal. Maybe...metal on stone? I'm not sure, but I take a shaky, terrified step towards it and then another. A few steps later, my hands find another rock wall. I edge to the right and find an opening.

"Thank you," I whisper to no one but the cave around me as I turn into the next tunnel.

The corridor is a little brighter — at least, it is to the right. I can't tell what it's illuminated by, only that at the far end of the tunnel, I can see grey rock before the tunnel bends. That's also the direction the sound is coming from. It sounds...strangely familiar. A whistle, maybe? A common Tanishi song? One meant to rally us without being obvious?

I don't know, but when I hear splashing in the river behind me, I don't have the stomach to wait and see if the body emerging from the river is an enemy or a friendly. No, I damn near shit myself and take off at a full sprint, grateful for the shoes Ero made for me with his own monstrous hands.

I run and run and run, taking the next right turn and then the next before I emerge suddenly into a well lit cave. It explodes open in front of me in acts of violence as my thoughts — like my gaze — both stall.

Ero's alive...*and he's humming.*

That's *my* song. I was drunk off wine — wine from a skin just like the one in his hand now — and I'd sung it to him and we'd danced and he'd looked down at me with such…hopelessness. With such need. And I'd betrayed that and he has every right not to forgive me.

And seeing him? I have no right at all to feel such overwhelming relief.

Pikosa ring the room and, at its center, Ero sits on his throne. The main cave is somehow where I've ended up. *Ended up, or corralled?* Behind me, rocks scatter over larger rocks and when I turn, I see Tenor, of all creatures, standing right behind me.

I jump. She doesn't react at all, mouth remaining in a thin line like she's either deeply unhappy to see me or bored with her assignment. Her assignment? Water drips from the braid that hangs over her shoulder. Was she following me even then?

"Were you there the whole time?" I ask her.

She tilts her head, her face stoic, betraying nothing.

"Even in the dark?"

She just blinks, but I know her answer.

"Thank you." She makes a face, one of confusion. I smile awkwardly in response. "Just…you know, for not trying to scare me. I was pretty scared. And also, you know, for bringing me food and not being mean to me these past days. You could have been cruel, but you weren't."

She looks away, likely annoyed or disgusted by my small admission, but I don't really care. I step forward and, seeing me, Ero smiles. He lifts the wine in his hands to his lips and drinks deeply, and I recognize that he's made his decision. Today, he will punish me. Today, there will be pain. And it will hurt so very, very badly.

Inside out? Is that what I said to Haddock? Flayed, perhaps? Burned alive? Fed to the crocodiles? No, that would be too easy. What he's going to do to me is something I likely can't divine.

Ero turns his head just a little and he sees me and he smiles, like he's been sitting there all day waiting for me to arrive.

He turns his wine skin over and lets the wine splatter all over the stones at his feet. The red looks like blood. He's covered in blood already and if I had to guess, I'd assume most of it is Tanishi and my soft little heart hurts. He owes me nothing. Not my life and certainly not theirs. What we shared doesn't matter at all.

That's what I tell myself, but I don't know if I believe it. There were good pieces in him. But I gathered them all in my hands and shattered every one of them.

I sunk to his level when I should have brought him up to mine. *It didn't have to be like this.* We could have had good feelings, all of us, anidi laye.

Dropping the empty skin, he beckons me forward with the sultry wave of his hand. I take a step. Torchlight mounted high in the walls flickers across the faces of so many eyes as they turn to see me, making it clear that I wasn't the only one corralled.

Every member of every slave tribe is present here. I can tell because their numbers are overwhelming, even though I know some lives were lost in this attempt. One in which I failed. But Haddock *checked* his vitals. He assured me that he was out cold, but not dead. He'd promised. How could Ero have deceived him?

I frown, lower lip trembling as I feel the fool all over again. Ero would have no problem deceiving

Haddock. He doesn't have any problem deceiving anyone.

Or killing.

And if I don't do something, we're all going to die here tonight. Starting with Haddock.

I take another step and my gaze drops to the body sprawled across the rocks at Ero's feet. I sniffle, tears welling in my eyes at the sight of our doctor, possibly dead or at the very least beaten within an inch of his life. Though Kenya's back in her chains again, Leanna's been replaced in her chains by Haddock.

As I walk numbly forward, my feet squish in my shoes, the leather unhappy with how I've just wet them. When it dries, it's going to hurt, tightening around my calves like constrictor snakes. I should just wrap some of that leather around my throat and spare Ero the trouble and the time — and spare myself the pain.

"You really thought I'd let your lover walk into my private chambers and take you from me? Just like that?" Ero's voice rings out in the quiet, carrying far even though he hardly raises his voice.

He speaks to me as if we're alone. As if this is a private conversation, one I might be able to use reason to explain my way out of. But we're past that now. Yes, we're past that.

I think about contradicting his idea that Haddock and I are lovers, but the futility of it prevents me from wasting the words or sparing the effort.

I shake my head and clear my throat. My voice is thick with tears as I say, "I thought you'd be asleep."

A rush of whispers stirs and startles the Pikosa gathered around the perimeters of the room, blocking all of the exits. An older male warrior steps forward, kicking a Danien slave in the process.

I wince at the action, bleeding for the Danien who rights himself and looks at me. I hold my hand to my heart as if to convey my sorrow and my apology and my regret for the way this day could have gone, but didn't.

He just nods and I see no incrimination in his gaze, just a mirrored regret. At least this we feel together.

"You taught your Tanishi our language?" The warrior shouts.

"I taught her nothing. She learned it in the days since her capture. When I discovered this, I kept her sequestered so she wouldn't teach the others. Why else do you think I kept her in my chambers, Gerarr? It certainly wasn't for the pleasure of her company." He sneers the man's name like an insult.

"You *claimed* her. You claimed a Tanishi who broke the laws of this place. If your father could see you..."

"You assume that because you are his brother I will show you leniency. Remove yourself from here or die by my sword. We both know I have wanted to gut you like the fish that you are for a long time. That you are kin to me means nothing. Now bow to your Nigusi or I'll force you by cutting off your legs at the knees."

The older warrior — Ero's uncle — clenches and spits but eventually drops down among the slaves. I wince, gathering my breath as terrified heartbeats pulse through me, making my whole body feel like one exposed pulse.

My feet bring me to the edge of the river and I look down at its frothing, biting waves and wonder...maybe, I should jump in. That end would surely be faster than whatever Ero has in store, wouldn't it?

But no.

No, I can't do that.

The slaves are mostly all crowded beneath the throne, on the other side of the river from where I stand. My gaze scans their faces now. *Be brave, Halima. Be brave,* I hear a voice whisper from deep in the dark cavern of my forgotten memories. Erased...or repressed?

Be brave, he whispers...a man, a *father? Mine.* I can't be sure of this, but I can be sure that I can't and won't abandon the other tribes to their suffering. If we could not escape together, at least we'll die that way.

Ero hisses, "Halima."

"Halima." *I blink and see waves, but they don't belong to the river. They belong to the ocean. I look up and a man is smiling at me. He has my eyes and my stubborn chin, at least, that's what my mother tells me. I'm crying but he's chuckling lightly as he reaches forward and pulls the plastic bag out of my hand.*

I'd been devastated to see so much trash on the beach, but my father just grins gently and says, "It resists. That's how the ocean survives, despite all the harm we do to it. It resists, remaining unbroken. And though it is unbroken by us, it can break us so easily. There are too many droplets and, when they gather, they are capable of magnificent violence. Its calm now is just an illusion so be careful, habibty, with the ocean.

"Respect it, but know that if it can remain unbroken by us, then you should not be broken by this." He holds up the plastic bag and stuffs it into his pocket. "Now come. Let's catch up to your mother, aunt and uncle, and all your cousins. The family is waiting."

"Halima." I look up. Ero is frowning at me and the entire room falls away.

I waver as I come out of the dream and my slick leather sandal slips on a couple of the rocks. I fall back onto my butt, quickly pulling my toes out of the stream. When I look up, Ero is perched forward on the edge of his seat, veins in his forehead popping proudly. I can see his tension even from here. He opens his mouth, but doesn't say anything, so I use the opportunity.

"You shouldn't have done that to Haddock. It was my betrayal. I wanted you to sleep, not to die. I don't want anyone to die."

Leaning his elbows onto his knees, he sneers, "It is a bit late for that now, don't you think?"

"No. I don't."

His expression flames, becoming even more dangerous. He tugs hard on the chains that connect his throne to Haddock, sending Haddock's body rolling pitifully down the rocks.

Kenya roars, but a bandage has been wrapped around her face and mouth to muffle her voice. She fights against her chains, but she doesn't get anywhere. Ero looks at her when she lunges for him but her chain is too short to reach.

My breathing hitches and I feel inundated all over again, but in fear this time. Not at all like I was inundated earlier. Fear and guilt. They're going to die because I showed Ero kindness, then took it back.

"You should not be broken by this."

I blink down at the river, and then I look up at Ero. I hallucinate momentarily, unsure of what I'm seeing. Maybe it's the adrenaline or the exhaustion or maybe, it's what happened when I hit my head on the stones before. I'm beginning to feel the soft, featherweight touches of distant, distant memories. *Repressed, not erased.*

I hear the ocean on the rocks. I feel something warm and rough against my palm...Ero's hand. No, my father's, my mother's my aunt's... I don't know what this pressure in my chest and both of my temples is, but it doesn't feel like surrender. It feels like the ocean. It feels like this river.

"Halima!"

I look up and time slows. I don't bother looking at Ero. He doesn't concern me now. Instead, I calculate my options — not just to save my life but to save us all. I'm not the physicist or the mathematician, but I'm sure I can add all these pieces together and find a way out for us now.

Haddock was right back in the caves. We should have turned around right then — the moment that I forgot anidi laye — and gone to save Kenya and Leanna and all the rest. Because that was the moment that I forgot that a single droplet has no power, but the ocean cannot be destroyed.

I glance at the exits. Ero's too quick for me, too quick to read my face. "Grab her! Tenor, grab her now!"

The rushing of feet tells me that Tenor is almost on me. Even though it puts me closer to Ero, I scramble across one of the bridges to the main landing where all the slaves are gathered.

At least forty Omoro are on their knees on the ground directly in front of me, some beaten, others whipped, some dripping wet. I meet the gaze of one Omoro who I might recognize, but I'm not sure given the state of his face. He has one blackened eye and a busted lip, but he holds my gaze as best as he's able.

"Run," I whisper, scrambling for Omoro words. "Run! You are many bodies. We are many, many bodies together. They may catch some, but not all." I repeat the directive in French and Spanish and in every dialect of both languages that I can think of.

I wade into the center of the group, wide eyes and grey faces turned up towards me in pure fear. No one moves, so I scan the crowd as Tenor draws her blade.

"No!" I scream as she slashes an Omoro across the back who's blocking her path.

"Omoro, move! Listen to the Tanishi!"

I whirl around in time to see Frey wobble to her feet just paces away from me, but separated from me by dozens of kneeling bodies. She's limping on one leg, but there's a resolve in her expression as she turns to face me, her wet hair whipping around her shoulders.

I tell her, "Ero will kill any who helped me. Run!"

"She speaks the language of the other slave tribes and yet you forbid me from killing her!" The older male warrior roars. He rises from where he's kneeling among the slaves and advances on the throne with his blade drawn. "We should rise up and tear our Nigusi from his seat. He is bewitched by a Tanishi!"

I use his distraction to my advantage. "Frey! Order your people!"

"Omoro," she calls after me, accent high and sing song in a way mine was not. "The Tanishi translator says that Ero has ordered us all to die." It's not quite what I said, but I appreciate the collective gasp it brings from the crowd. "We will flood the North cave."

Tenor is nearly to me now and I fight to get away from her as Omoro start to panic. The Tanishi don't need my help moving and even though I haven't said anything to them in English, Leanna is somewhere in the crowd and is already ten steps ahead.

"Follow me! We head West towards the Sucere Chamber. Those of you who arrive there, gather the weapons from the armory and come back for the rest. We leave no one behind!"

"Danien!" I scream, wading towards the Danien still crowded, mostly still on their knees. "Run now! Ero wants all to die. The Omoro run to the North cave entrance. We Tanishi go West. You go South. Find Tanishi on the surface! We Tanishi have machines the Pikosa cannot fight against. Run! Run now!"

I shout, louder now, hoping against all hope that my words in any language have any kind of meaning, pushing my way through the Danien, fighting not to fall. More of them are standing now and their pale bodies are shifting like a cruel current. Every so often, I catch glimpses of bronze skin and a hint of dark grey steel, but I manage to evade it.

Soon, I find myself stumbling into Tanishi prisoners, most of whom are already running and following Leanna as she and the other Tanishi fighters — few that are left — violently clash with the Pikosa guards blocking the large cave leading West.

Soon, battles rage on all sides of me as I stumble into a Danien whose name and face I don't know. He's not moving anywhere, so I grab him by the shoulders anyway and shake him hard.

He stares at me with saucers for eyes as I tell him in my bad, pitchy Danien, "West exit! Go west. Follow Gerd!"

I keep shouting the orders at every Danien I come across and I'm still shouting them when I trip and fall. I catch myself on the heels of my palms and running feet scurry over my back, knocking the wind out of me.

In the deluge, I hear competing orders being shouted. In Pikosa, Ero orders the warriors to block all the exits. By the sounds of it, even those that are complying are being overpowered in some cases. Outnumbered. Overrun.

"The ocean cannot be dammed," I shout to myself, to no one. Omoro shout nearby in Omoro. Danien in Danien. Pikosa in Pikosa. Tanishi are the only group here shouting in multiple languages. I hear cries go up in English, Russian and Mandarin.

Struggling up onto my knees, I taste blood. I'm woozy. It's been…a long day. *Ero peppering small kisses over my chest. He suckles my breast. I am overwhelmed and I tell him that. "Then be overwhelmed," he says, "as I am overwhelmed."*

He may be a wholly terrible man, but it was not a wholly terrible day. No, it wasn't. And if I die today, I will not forget that moment or the Ero that existed just once that I almost…sort of…cared for.

I hold onto that sense of serenity as feet step onto the fingers of my burned arm and pain lights up my entire left side up to the shoulder. The Omoro on my hand is shoved away roughly and hands slide underneath my armpits and lift. I look up into a face I didn't expect to see.

"Gerd." I smile at her.

She shouts at me. "Ero is coming for you!"

"I know."

"You cannot come with us. You need to go alone."

I don't understand what she means when she says more about a life debt that she owes and I understand even less when she takes me to the river's edge and abruptly shoves me into the water.

I gasp and I swear I can hear Ero roar my name, but soon the water is rushing over my head and I'm drowning...but unlike the last time, I'm not drowning alone. Gerd is still with me, her hand on my wrist. She's swimming somehow and I don't know how to swim, but I do my best to kick my feet as I try to stay with her.

Gerd jerks me abruptly to the right, against the whims of the river's current. My arm feels like it's popping free from its socket when she whirls me into her body and her arm, which is *way* stronger than it looks, is wrapped around my torso and she's urging me to do something...something...

"Swim!" She screams.

I gasp and lurch and try to haul myself up using the stones she places beneath my hands. Eventually, I manage to drag my own dripping body out of the water and onto a stony bank. We both flop free onto cold stone and though I'm shaking and shivering and sure that I'm one wrong turn away from death's door, Gerd hasn't given up yet.

"Come, Tanishi."

"Halima," I correct as I jerk up onto jelly-filled knees.

She pauses just a moment and her blue eyes are piercing in the low light, a darkness that is only disrupted by flickering light filtering in from the cave behind her. Her skin is light and her hair is almost white, her eyes are blue. Just as different from me as the Omoro are different from her.

"There's no time." She grabs my wrist and turns down the tunnel, flying while I stumble.

My injuries feel the abrupt movements and my sensitive thighs tingle and smart. She turns left and then right and the tunnel opens up and the lights get brighter and the sounds of chaos, much louder. *We're back.* We're in the East tunnel and we're heading straight for a room I know all too well.

When we come to Ero's room, the door is still open and I have to laugh. "The last place anyone would expect?"

I must say something wrong, because she gives me a curious look and doesn't answer me. She surges into the room and looks up at the ceilings. "You have been here some time. He has to have access to the surface. The East caves all do. Which is the largest shaft...we go up?"

I nod, surprised by her genius considering that she's never been here before. I've been here a long time, but I'd never have thought to come back this way to get out now. I was ready to die back in the river, or even before that, trampled under escaping feet.

"Here." I grab her by the worn hide on her shoulder and pull her into Ero's bedroom. My feet stumble at the smell. It smells like sex. Like sex I was a part of, back when the world seemed a little less horrible and maybe even, a little good.

She looks up the shaft I point at and nods. "Good. Is there rope?"

"No, but I have this." I show her the whips I tied together and stashed at the bottom of Ero's armory. There, I also find something that surprises me. A wine skin. I reach for it, distracted when I don't have time to be. Is this the poisoned wine? Did he switch it out on me?

My lip twitches and painful heat makes my eyes water. He held me with all the desperation of a drowning man, and me the lifeline. When I let him drink from that wine skin, it was like, I let him fall.

I don't deny that he deserved to fall — he did — but I can't help but wonder if I'd stopped him, if things might have turned out a little different. Then I remember Haddock's broken body...

Maybe not.

"Good. You...help me up and then I will pull you up. Okay?"

I haven't agreed before I find myself up on the bed with Gerd standing on my shoulders. She has the whip around her neck and screams as her fingers fight for purchase in the bare stone. She doesn't have shoes on and the bottoms of her feet are black and so calloused they look impermeable. Little pebbles fall from a jutting ledge she manages to get her heel squarely planted on. When it falls into my eyes, dust blinds me for a moment.

The sounds from the East tunnel get louder and I look back over my shoulder, staring at the door as I wait for Ero to fly through it and tear out my throat. Instead, something hits me in the head from above. I look up and see the whip dangling in front of my face. I glance past it at Gerd.

"You think you can lift me up there?"

"You use funny words. But if you're worried, I can hold your weight. You are half my size. But you need to help. I cannot pull you all the way."

I fall three times before Gerd huffs, "Wrap the tail around your leg three times." I do. "Now step onto the tail with your other leg. On your calf. Yes, just like that. Now lift."

Khara! It works! With the whip wrapped around my calf, I can essentially use it as a ladder and inch my way up without having to rely solely on upper body strength. I'm giddy with this information and smiling until I realize that Gerd is grunting under the labor of carrying my whole weight, so I hustle a little bit faster until I reach the ledge her feet are on.

I climb all the way up until our hands are nearly touching, and then push my feet into the wall. Thank all the gods of all the universes that the inside of this light shaft is so uneven it creates small ledges. I'm able to drop onto one now. Gerd releases the whip with a pained groan, but she doesn't stay inert for long. Instead, she loops the whip around her neck and looks up. She starts to climb.

I follow the path she's making the best that I can, but it's hard work. A few times, I think I'll fall. Though we're lucky that the inside of this crevice is rocky as hell instead of slick and smooth, the rockiness presents problems in other ways when stones jut too far out to pass.

We have to squeeze our bodies around them — an easier task for me than it is for her — and several times I wince at the sound of her screams as she cuts herself open in order to get by them.

I only cut myself once when my stitches meet a rock and reopen. Blood drips down my back as my wound is made anew. I concentrate on the paths it makes as it swirls down my spine, instead of on the pain. I keep moving.

My inner thighs are shaking so badly I'm sure I'll fall...but when I hear a female voice directly below me, followed immediately by Ero's, *"Halima!"* I know that falling is no longer an option.

I wipe off my right palm and jerk up, catching hold of the next rocky protrusion while little pebbles scatter underneath the shoes Ero made for me with his own hands.

The rocks have bent together too unusually for me to be able to see him, or any part of his room, anymore, but I can still hear him as he seethes, "Halima, you don't know what you're doing. You'll die from exposure on the surface if the snakes don't get you first! Come down and I'll let you live."

No way. No freaking way. I don't answer, just keep climbing.

"Halima, come down and I'll let your people live."

Tempting, but I'm too close. I can feel the heat from above caressing the top of my head already, making my dark hair hot. The humidity of the previous cave system falls away. I can feel sand on the air, taste the grit between my teeth. We're almost there. And I'm both too curious and too terrified not to try for it.

"Halima! I swear to you that your people will live! I swear it on my sword arm. Just come down." I hesitate, but only for a breath.

He sounds so desperate, I want to obey him and comfort him on a deep instinctual level. I don't know why. I hate him. Maybe it's because he took my virginity. Maybe, it's because after everything, I don't hate him. Maybe I'm not capable of it.

Out beyond ideas of wrongdoing and rightdoing, there is a field. I'll meet you there.

Rumi said that. Rumi. Jalal al Rumi. My father's favorite poet.

So grateful to have that knowledge back that I say it out loud, "Jalal al Rumi says, out beyond ideas of wrong and right, there is a garden. I will find you in the garden, Ero." I simplify the language, at least I think I do.

Ero roars, sounding pained in a way that hurts. But once the pain is gone, all that's left is anger. His voice is the tips of a thousand knives wet with the blood of my kin and his when he says, *"You think you will escape me? I will find you and when I do, I will cut off your eyelids so you have no choice but to watch as I impale your people one by one and mount them on pikes so that they are constantly looking down at you, reminding you of what happens if you try to escape me again. You are mine, Halima! The signs have decreed it!"*

I want to climb faster, but I slip when I do. Calm. Calm, I remind myself, the ocean is calm before the storm. I take a deep breath and try to shut Ero out as his words ricochet up the tunnel in threats of increasing violence. This is not Ero. This is Azazel, Baal, Hades, Lucifer. And in the lore there was always a way out of Hell. Always a foothold back into the realms of all that is good.

I still remember in Ero something good.

Something gone.

I scramble up, looking for the handholds Gerd shows me, as Ero's voice cuts out. The abrupt silence frightens me even more. I'm sweating as I climb in silence. It's a painful thing. Everything is painful. My arms are singing and my muscles are aching and my bones are snapping apart and reorganizing themselves into new shapes until finally, *finally* Gerd disappears and all that's left is her hand reaching down.

I take it and she hauls me up and we land side-by-side on our backs on hard, packed sand. After however many days I've been reborn into this new life, I finally see the Earth that's abandoned us — no, the Earth that *we* left in ruination and then abandoned.

I blink back the wind that pulls large sheets of sand over me and stare towards the horizon. Pale, purple light glows on the edge of a flat, desolate world, marred by a few stony outcrops.

"It is always light here. Never dark. This was a good time to escape. Before sun comes up fully. Now come, Tanishi."

"Halima," I gasp, chest still heaving. I don't know how she's moving. She hardly is, wavering on her feet like that. Her eyes look bloodshot and her once pale complexion looks sickly in this light.

"I don't have much time." She lifts a hand, like she's going to defend against the horizon, and for a moment, she looks me directly in the eyes and I feel as if we once shared a lifetime. A lifeline. Maybe not. Maybe just a moment. "Halima."

"Thank you for saving me, Gerd," I tell her as soon as I'm upright beside her. It's hard to be upright. My legs are shaking so badly, my left knee buckles three times before I'm able to lock it.

"We are not safe yet. We must find your people or mine."

"Or the Omoro. They will shelter us if we find them."

She understands me. I can tell in her eyes but she doesn't acknowledge what I've said. "The west entrance. I think I can find it from here." She sets off and I follow her.

We run for a long time. Longer than I expected us to have to. We run so long, I start to see polka dots on the horizon where I'm sure there aren't any. But eventually, I start to wonder if Gerd sees them, too. She's wavering as she walks, no longer running, no longer even walking in a straight line.

"Gerd?"

"We need to make it to your people. There is underground safety there."

"Yes, there is. But Gerd, do you need to lie down? We've been going for a long time. Maybe we need to rest."

"I can't. The sun. It poisons my skin. The Danien suffer from sun sickness. That's why we live underground." She stumbles and I lunge, trying to catch her, but I'm just as delirious as she is and it's worse now that the sun has started to rise.

Underneath the suddenly bright light, the skin on my bones feels heavier. It isn't so hot though — not yet — but already the once black and then blue and then lavender light has shifted to white and it stings wherever I see it. I blink a lot as I try to grab her wrists and arms and haul her upright.

"You can't stop here." I lob her arm over my neck and lift. She weighs a ton. An unapologetic ton. I can't carry her. But I'm not going to stop trying. And so I don't.

The three-legged beast we are staggers towards an unknown goal that I start to think might not exist. "There…Gerd." My throat is starched. I see blurry shapes on the horizon. "Could that be them?"

"Yes. Yes, it could. But it could also be something else…"

"What?"

And then I hear it — a horrible shriek that, in no possible way could belong to a human. It's followed by the sound of voices and then a bang so loud it might be an explosion and then, finally, a human cry of pain.

I think about leaving Gerd there and going to investigate, but when I glance around, it's with the knowledge that there are absolutely zero landmarks out here and there's a chance that, if I leave her, I won't find her again. So I drag her along for this horrible ride until my mouth and skin and flesh completely dry out and are nothing more than sheets of hide draped over my skeleton.

I drag her until the sun hits the horizon and I understand why Gerd seemed so grateful for the night because it's *painful* in its intensity. I drag her until the blurry figures on the horizon crystalize. And then I stop dragging.

I can't believe what I'm seeing.

The beasts that dominate the sandy plane are unlike anything I've ever seen. Looking like the wild offspring between rhinoceros and horses, tough grey hides cover their long, horse-like limbs while a single huge horns spirals out of their foreheads. Like a unicorn. Like a weird, grey, leathery, armored unicorn…Huh.

And I'm so transfixed by the beasts themselves that I don't notice the men on top of them until Gerd screams, "Kawashari!"

Another explosion goes off and one of the three males — a Kawashari — flies off of the top of his beast. He moves in slow motion. Everything is suspended. The sand in the air, the sun on my shoulders, Gerd's heavy, labored breathing at my side. She's pulling now, trying to get away from me and I'm so confused, that I don't bother trying to understand why.

Leanna roars something I can't make out and my gaze drops to her. She's surrounded by the other two Kawashari males and their beasts while twenty, maybe thirty Tanishi crowd behind her.

I smile a watery smile and sniffle deeply. *I didn't think so many would make it.* We were billions once, now reduced to this. But this is more than nothing.

Little droplets forming whatever ocean they can, the Tanishi surge forward as one to attack the man on the right on top of his terrifying unicorn.

Among the Tanishi gathered are a few Danien and even one Omoro, made distinguishable by his dark skin and hair. The Danien and the Omoro fight with the Tanishi against the men on the beasts, thrusting all kinds of crazy makeshift weapons up at the animals. They have to move fast to avoid getting trampled and I hold my breath when one Tanishi rolls underneath the creature's hooves. He screams in pain, but two Danien manage to grab him by the arms and pull him out of harm's way before he gets even more hurt.

Anidi laye.

I sniff, feeling full in this moment, even though I'm terrified.

Another boom sounds so loud, I can feel the ground shake underneath my feet. It sends a Kawashari male soaring through the air, his body an impossible shadow against the bright white sky.

Like the first fallen Kawashari, when he hits the ground, he no longer moves. The beast he was on rears up and back and takes off, hooves pounding with surprising panic over the ground. I wouldn't have thought these demonic horses from hell would be afraid of anything — least of all a gathering of Tanishi — but maybe, it's Leanna's weapon?

Or maybe, it's something else.

Maybe, it's *that.*

My gut hollows and my mind spirals out of control. I hustle faster, drawing closer to the sound of cheering Danien and rebelling Tanishi, still fighting off the last of the Kawashari males. It's easier for them, because his beast is agitated, too, and I seem to be the *only* one who has any idea why.

It's on the horizon. It's unmistakable. It's terrifying.

"Halima!" Chayana cries out. She starts to run towards me, but I point past her.

"Khara! Alhaouny!" I shout, begging for help from the universe around us. "What the fuck is that, Gerd?"

She hangs off of my shoulder, head lolling as she tries to keep herself upright. She's doing worse than her Danien counterparts, who are all able to walk on their own. Two are staggering, but they don't look as bad as she does.

Her voice croaks, sounding half dead when she says, "Desert snake…"

"Snake! Snake?"

This is a word I've heard before in the caves in every language. But I pictured a small little garden snake with a cute little tongue and little beady eyes. Not…not *this!*

"A snake! Are you fucking kidding me Gerd? That's not a fucking snake! Chayana!" I shout in English now, urging her to turn to face the creature crawling towards us out of the light.

It's slippery-brown carapace reflects the sun as sand sloughs off of its shell and it emerges from beneath what I *thought* was a dune, not a cute little snake house. As it sheds the rest of the sand and rises up into the light, its stinger rises with it, curving on its enormous tail.

Three heads have three sets of eyes, but only one set of arms between them. Its spindly, spidery legs move as one and number in the hundreds.

"That's a massive, three-headed fucking scorpion!" I scream.

Gerd, though she doesn't speak English, just nods at me and repeats. "A snake. Yes. A snake. We should lie down…be dead while it eats the others. Maybe…not eat us."

"What?" I screech in Danien before staggering forward faster than my bones want me to. My insides are screaming as loud as my outsides as I get closer to the Tanishi. "Leanna!"

"They are dead. Leave them. Save yourself."

"Shut up, Gerd. Leanna!" I shriek until my lungs get so heavy they weigh me into the sand below. *"Leanna turn around!"*

But she's too slow. The Tanishi are still distracted by the Kawashari male and Chayana and the Omoro are the only ones who turn when I tell them to.

Chayana screams louder than I ever could. "Holy fucking shit! Leanna, look out!"

But the scorpion snake is spurred by the increased agitation and scuttles rapidly, moving so fast my breath gets caught in my throat. It's already on the group and, while others run, Leanna doesn't.

She turns to face it, firing the gun in her arms at its underbelly, but it doesn't so much as flinch against the onslaught. Instead, its stinger floats high and then strikes low. It flashes in the light, moving so quickly the whole attack takes only the beat of one heart, maybe two.

Leanna's caught mid-turn and I think the thing manages to snag one of her arms. Either way, it sends her spinning. The gun she was holding tumbles out of her hands. Another Tanishi — Donovan — runs to it and picks it up. He plants one knee on the ground and starts firing up at the creature in rapid bursts.

It releases a shriek and canters back against the onslaught of bullets, but the tail is a wicked thing. With one swipe, it sends Donovan flying, the gun tumbling again out of his grip. The rest of the group is sprinting away from it, running towards me and Gerd.

"Gerd…any ideas?"

"It is too late now for ideas. It has seen us. It will eat what it can, but it does not eat so quickly. Your best chance of survival is to leave me…try to make it to your boat where you keep machines…That machine your leader uses might wound the creature. I think I see…" Her voice fades. "…it is leaking…"

"I'm not leaving you!"

"Then you have already lost…" With one final huff, she puffs out a breath and sinks to her knees. I can't support her weight by myself and she ends up taking me down with her.

With hard sand grating at my shins through my pants, I look up at the approaching horde but my gaze snags on something else. A dark smear against bright yellow-white. *The gun.*

I point at it and shout, "We need to get the gun! Fire at the thing!"

I point around at anybody — at everybody — the little good it does me. They're all running toward me in panic and I'm the only one running towards it. And did I say running? I mean crawling because that's what my jellied limbs allow for, which isn't ideal since the scorpion is closing the distance between me and it.

As feet pound past me, the scorpion turns its attention to me and I duck, flattening myself to the ground to avoid the swipe of its tail. I might not have avoided it at all had a high-pitched whistle not captured its attention at the last second. At the sound, I look up to see the creature twisting away from me.

It's tail lifts up even higher and rattles a terrifying ballad. Plastered to the ground, I can taste the charred earth and feel its grit between my teeth.

My thoughts flicker back to the beach...to the one I called father. Strange how *this* memory comes back to me when I can remember so few others. It came to me when I needed it. Father, thank you. *Ebi, bahibak...*

Halima...

"Halima!" My chin jerks up, caught in the tide of memory and unsure whether this voice is real or imagined.

And then I see the figures in the distance. Murky and disfigured, they are a Fata Morgana in the making and I know that it's Ero and his warriors. Despite my betrayal, he's still coming for me.

No, he's coming for his slaves, for all of us. To punish us himself. Hmm. That thought doesn't make much sense. If he wanted me dead, wouldn't it have been a better, easier option just to let the scorpion have me?

But he doesn't.

"Where are my armed soldiers?" Leanna's voice cleaves into my thoughts. I look up, shocked to see her standing just a dozen paces away from me, between me and the scorpion.

She's holding a knife — one I recognize from Ero's quarters, one I gave her — and she's closing in on the scorpion from behind, all alone. A warrior I could never be. Right now, I am in complete awe of her. *No wonder she's our general. She's a leader easy to follow.* And I intend to. I won't let her stand alone.

Anidi laye.

I glance to my right and see the gun and I go for it. Scrambling over the sand, catching it under my nails, I haul the weapon off of the ground and lift it even though it weighs a goddamn ton. I start after Leanna and, when I reach her, hand the weapon over.

She hardly looks at me, keeping her gaze focused on the creature waving its tail back and forth. It strikes without warning, stabbing down and landing like an explosion that sends three Tanishi scattering. One of them is Chayana.

She screams and flies back, landing near one of the Kawashari bodies. Two bodies, but when I glance around, I see the final Kawashari is still standing, still here. Though their skin tones range in shades of brown from light like Haddock's when he's tanned all the way to Chayana's darker hue, just like the rest of us on the surface, they are distinguishable by their hair.

The manes flowing from the tops of their heads and forming the thick beards on their faces are all the same shade of red. It's the color I see when I'm lying on my back, blinking through my eyelids at the unforgiving sun. Blood red.

He's on the outskirts of the crowd, behind me, like he's trying to decide whether to attack or retreat. His gaze is pinned ferociously to Leanna, though, like there's nothing else here that concerns him at all. Not the advancing Pikosa army or the cute little garden *snake* that's going to kill us all.

"Halima," Leanna barks and I stagger up. I touch her shoulder. There's something wrong with her arm but before I can ask her if she's okay, she jerks away from me. "Tell them to fan out. They do us no good all bunched together like that. Alpha formation," she shouts to the other Tanishi.

I don't know how to relay her orders until the other Tanishi form a double-layered semi-circle around the creature, Leanna in the center position. The Tanishi that gather carry an unfortunate array of weapons between them, ranging from long and short steel swords and knives to stone spears to pieces of metal and stones.

Chayana, staggering into formation, has the gumption to approach the massive scaled creature holding a wooden slingshot. A slingshot! Fearless, she is. And my heart beats harder. I don't think I've ever been so proud.

"You ugly piece of shit!" Chayana shouts at the creature as she and the other armed Tanishi close in from behind while Ero and his warriors close in from the front in no formation or pattern I can make sense of.

In Danien, I shout first, "Spread out. Fill in the gaps between the Tanishi. Hold your weapons strong!" I repeat my intention in Omoro, grateful that enough gets through — or maybe they're just interpreting body language of the others, because they move when I tell them to move.

"Halima, ask them if they know this creature's weakness."

I do as I'm told, first in Danien and then in Omoro. It's the lone Omoro who says, "The breathing flaps. Stab inside."

"Where are they?"

"Lower left and right sides."

"Leanna, this creature has gills of some kind," I shout at her back while the sand swirls harder around us and the sun beats hotter onto my shoulders. "Underneath the belly on the left and right sides."

She nods once and I'm distracted by her right arm holding the gun. It's turning *blue*. "Leanna, your arm…"

"Soldiers, we go for the gills on the left and right sides of the creatures' underbelly on my command."

I tell the Danien and Omoro to wait for Leanna's signal. Meanwhile, in front of us, Ero engages the creature first. He launches a steel spear at the creature that sails true. It glints in the light, moving in a strike of color to spear one of the creature's three heads, right above the mouth.

The creature shrieks so loudly I have to cover both of my ears while the center head sinks down to touch the sands. Enraged, the tail flies and my heart lurches up into my mouth. *Ero…*

Leanna shouts, "Now! Left and right forward flanks attack!"

Leanna doesn't have to tell me to translate as I relay orders to the Omoro and Danien who then do as the Tanishi do and lunge for the creature's sides. Leanna meanwhile plants one knee in the ground and opens fire on the tip of the creature's tail. She must know what she's doing, because I'm shocked when her machine gun kicks over and over again, penetrating this red, swollen sac just below the stinger until it finally explodes.

A small cheer goes up — the Danien and Omoro cheer the loudest. One of the Danien turns to me and shouts, "It cannot poison us now! We must attack!"

"Only on Leanna's word. Leanna, should the second row attack yet?"

"No! Hold! Fall back! Left and right forward flanks, circle around the creature to join the Pikosa!"

The Tanishi fall in line, but the Omoro and Danien don't move when I tell them to get closer to the Pikosa.

"Halima, give them the order!"

"I did! They won't go closer to the Pikosa!"

"Fuck!" Leanna curses and struggles to stand. I rush to her and shove my shoulder under her armpit. She leans more weight on me than I can carry — and the scorpion is fast approaching when it turns around.

She tries to lift her gun — I try to help her — but we're too slow. The tail plunges towards us, the venom sac depleted, but the stinger still shiny and chrome.

I scream and something must throw the creature off of its course because when it should have stabbed, it only swipes for us.

Doosh! That's the sound I hear. A thud as the impact of the tail with our bodies rings in my thoughts and then a whoosh of the wind as we sail through it.

We land hard a few moments later and the ringing in my ears recedes just enough for me to be able to hear a male voice calling my name. Roaring it.

I blink my eyes open and the scorpion isn't done with us yet. Leanna is moaning, her limbs tangled with mine. Somehow, the machine gun is still caught in her limp and yes, very blue hand. Leanna isn't moving.

"Halima," she groans and I know what she's asking me.

I reach for the gun and prop it up some kind of way even though I have no idea what I'm doing. I find the trigger and pull and the gun kicks back so hard, the butt nails me in the center of the chest. My shot goes wide and I keel over.

I try to stay lucid and present even though my mind has had enough. My body isn't ready to let go, though. I sit up and try to cover Leanna with my own body while she tries to pull me back. The creature is almost on us now, close enough that I can see the twin pincers in two of its mouths working, while the third center head sinks around the handle of the spear, not yet dead but trying to dislodge it with its crab-like pincer hands.

A brave part of me wants to lunge for it and try to finish the job Ero started, but that is only a very small part of me. The other larger part of me wants to close my eyes and look away, unwilling to watch myself be killed, but I don't do that either.

Instead, I sit and stare horrified and mesmerized as the shiny tail lifts up, looking like plates of metal stacked on top of each other and spray painted the color of liquified earth. It's made more terrifying by its beauty. I take in a breath. The tail moves too fast for me to track. But...death falls short because a sword comes down, moving even faster than the tail, somehow managing to catch it and sever it at the final second.

So close to death, the depleted venom sack and sharp, serrated stinger, along with the entire tip of the tail, falls into my lap. Blue blood leaks all over my knees and the sand beneath. I wrench away from it and look up to see Ero with his back to me.

"Tell them now, Halima. While Ero has it distracted. Tell them to attack the gills. And here, give this to Ero. Tell him to keep the thing distracted."

Leanna's voice is weak and I don't dare look at her because worry will distract me from my task. I just let her push the gun that fell out of my grip further towards me. I nod, grab it by the heavy handle, and use it to help me stand.

I try to yell, but we've been separated from the crowd and they won't hear me, so I get up and scramble quickly around Ero's body. The scorpion screeches out its desire for revenge, or its anger or its pain and its bajillion tiny feet scutter as I move. The creature is tracking me! But when it lunges in my path, Ero lunges, too.

He brandishes his sword and keeps his body squarely planted in front of mine. My heart beats harder and my throat contracts, his actions begging consideration if only I had the seconds to spare.

The creature lunges for him with its pincers, but Ero deflects with his blade. I move up until I'm right at his back. "Ero, take this."

I nudge his arm with the gun and he glances quickly down at it.

"It's a weapon." I quickly check to see that his sword is in his right hand and say, "Hold here with this hand."

I reach forward and take his right hand and he shocks the bejeezus out of me when he lets me take his sword away from him. I fit his hand to the trigger and take his left hand and fit it around the grip.

"Use this hand to help aim." I pat his left shoulder and then pat his right when I tell him, "Keep the end in your shoulder. It will kick you." That's the closest I can come to kick back.

Ero doesn't wait for more instruction but braces his feet, one slightly in front of the other, as the scorpion dives for us again and I scream at the suddenness of its reaction. The gunfire plugs into the creature's open right mouth, but it isn't enough to kill it.

"Distract it! We will kill it!"

I start to run, but his hand is suddenly on the collar of my tunic, yanking me back. "Stay close."

"I can't. I need to give the orders from our Nigusi," I improvise, knowing there is no Pikosa term for general. There is only Nigusi, warrior, slave and enemy.

"I can't protect you when you're far," Ero says releasing me long enough to firm his grip around the weapon. He fires again.

"Yes, you do. Protect me while I deliver the orders. Distract it. And protect Leanna."

I don't know if he would have let me walk away willingly, but when the scorpion lunges again, he has to use both hands and brace his feet apart, one in front of the other, to keep himself stable as he fires at the thing again and again.

I run around, meeting the Pikosa warriors first who seem flustered — at a loss of what to do — and I bypass them entirely, heading straight for Donovan.

"Now! Head for the gills! Leanna's orders!"

"Leanna's orders! Split! Head for the gills!" He leads the charge towards the left flank, taking four Tanishi and the Omoro with him while a screaming Chayana is the first one to break right. Panicked that she's screaming like a banshee, but glad that she's at least managed to find herself a knife in this mess, I quickly follow her. Then I remember the Danien.

They look lost as they cluster together, looking wilted, their weapons looking so feeble. Only one of them has a spear and it's chipped at the tip and the other one has a sword half that's shattered and broken. I approach the man with the broken blade and offer him Ero's sword.

The moment I hand the sword over, a heavy hand whirls me around and I come face-to-face with a Pikosa warrior I recognize. She is always around Ero in the throne room, looking mean and angry but not defiant like the one called Wyden. Now, under the blazing sun, she looks meaner than ever.

"That is the Nigusi's sword! You can't give it to a slave!"

And then a second voice, also female rips between us. She grabs the woman by the arm. "Take your hands off of this slave, Ellar. She belongs to the Nigusi."

Rage surges up inside of me and makes it possible for me to shove the much, much stronger female off. "You stupid idiot!" I shout in Pikosa. "Who gives a *khara* about the sword or the slaves? There's a fucking scorpion on the loose!"

I don't know what I say. I'm sure it means nothing because every third word is a Pikosa substitute. But my vehemence must be enough to startle the warriors standing here claiming to be warriors but doing *nothing* because the mean one — Ellar — flinches when I lunge forward and grab her by the shoulders and shake her.

"Get to the left and right flanks. Stab the creature there! We need to kill it! Go! Those are your orders, warrior!"

The warrior blinks at me and her eyes round and the warriors behind her shift like they're uncomfortable or restless. And then the moment is over. The other woman — the woman who'd been there to defend me against the first — straightens and whirls around, "The Nigusi relayed orders through his female," she shouts to the other Pikosa gathered.

"We attack the left and right flanks with the other war...slaves." I heard it. We all heard it. There's a momentary lull that's broken only when the scorpion screeches behind me. *She was going to call them warriors.* "Are you with me?

A collective cry comes from the Pikosa contingent that surprises me considering that these people that call themselves warriors do nothing together. They don't even fight together.

The female turns, but Ellar grabs her by the upper arm. Their leather armored chests clash as they go nose to nose.

"What the fuck do you think you're doing, Lopina?"Ellar hisses.

Lopina surges out of her grip with violence and when Ellar starts to advance on her, she holds up her sword, looking very prepared to use it. "What we should have all done a long time ago. Now move, or do you want to be seen as the only warrior who didn't fight?"

"You are mad," Ellar hisses, but she turns regardless and joins the kind one as the other Pikosa filter around me like wind around trees until I'm left standing with Lopina alone.

She starts to sprint off to join the rest, but before she does, I whisper, "Thank you, Lopina."

Her gaze hits me and narrows. She doesn't seem convinced by my presence now that we're alone here, but after another momentary consideration, she tilts her head forward, almost as if in…respect? And then she's gone.

I turn and track her to the others as they swarm the scorpion. On its other side, far from me now and separated by what feels like legions of terror, Ero is on one knee, firing up at the creature…but he's also doing something strange. He's kneeling right in front of Leanna…almost like…he listened to me. Like the Nigusi of the Pikosa tribe is following my orders. Even as the scorpion closes in.

"Take it down!" I shout, panic clawing at me, but I don't approach. Weaponless, I'm useless. No, the only thing I can do is try to help the others that are wounded. And there are quite a few who are wounded, especially considering how susceptible the Danien are to sunshine. The Omoro is kneeling on the ground nearest to me, so I go to him first.

He's holding his side and, when he pulls his fingers back, I see a gash. I pull my tunic off over my head and quickly start shredding it into long strips. I tie a few of them around his waist and he thanks me while I scamper off with my rags to try to help someone else.

A Pikosa warrior is next on my list. She doesn't seem to have any wounds anywhere, but she's holding her head in her hands like it might fly away.

"Did you hit your head?" I ask.

She shoves me in the chest when I try to touch her shoulder.

"If you put your knees up and put your head between them it will help," I offer, but that's all that I offer because I'm distracted by the sound of a woman's shriek coming from the opposite direction as the scorpion.

"Gerd." I take off. "Gerd!" I shout, unable to see her.

"Halima!" She screams. She's apart from the fray, forty paces back the way she and I came. She must have been trying to escape, maybe even go after one of the Kawashari horses. I can see its tracks leading up to her, but the beast is nowhere to be found. No, all that's left of the beast is the man that was riding it. Straddling her chest, his hands around her neck, it looks like he's trying to either assault or kill Gerd now.

Not on my watch.

I have my destroyed tunic in my hand and I wave it over my head like I would a flail, had I happened to have one handy or know how to use it, and I release a battle cry in imitation of the Pikosa's.

The Kawashari looks up and his eyes register surprise seconds before I barrel into him. I use my momentum and my full bodyweight to throw him off of Gerd. Unfortunately, I don't know how to *stop* that momentum and it sends us both toppling head over heels over one another and leaves us tangled together. I have sand in my mouth and an enormous weight pressing down on me. I think he might be sitting on my chest.

"Ow..." I moan pitifully, totally incapable of movement.

The Kawashari recovers faster than I do and is on me in a second. He has a bushy red beard and brown eyes that sit uncomfortably close together on his face. I wait for him to do something and then when he doesn't, I try to wrestle my way free. He pins me down easily, knees trapping my legs together, hands holding me down by the neck.

Alright, freeing myself this way isn't going to get me anywhere. He's four times my size, at least as big as the Pikosa. So I stop. I lay still, still straining and fidgeting — I can't help my body's natural response — but I open my mouth and ask him, "What do you want?" In every language I can think of ending, finally, in English.

At the English word, he slaps his hand over my mouth and stares at me, shocked. He says something and I catch one single word — and that word is *langudar* — and I laugh behind my muffle, and then out loud when he releases me.

I nod. "Langudar English."

"Langudar Kawashari."

"Sure. Same same. Just a few thousand years' difference."

He shakes his head, eyes meeting mine and then staring intently at my mouth. He says something that I don't understand, but I know what he's asking based on the signs and I give him the answer he wants.

"Yes, I speak langudar Kawashari."

"Yesra?"

"Yesra," I repeat, tucking that word away in the vault and saving it for later because, in this world, there will always be a later, I'm sure of it.

I scream when he vaults off of me and grabs me by an arm and a leg. He throws my naked body over his shoulders in a fireman's hold while I scream bloody murder. "Stop it!"

I scratch his back with my free hand, but he doesn't seem to notice as he takes off at a bloody good sprint away from the devil that I know, who doesn't seem so bad right about now.

"Ero!" I shout — not Kenya, not Leanna, not Donovan, not Gerd, not Frey. I shout for Ero.

A beat passes when I think this unknown male might actually get away with taking me away before a huge impact hurtles into us from behind and sends me flying — or would have, had a meaty hand not closed around my arm and reeled me into the cavern of a warm chest.

I fly, but in the cage of arms I know well. I close my eyes, waiting for the fall, but all I feel is a jolt as his body hits the ground underneath mine. The cage of his arms firms around me as we roll together. They hold me tight and then unfurl as we slow.

He keeps rolling, never stopping, while I lay on my back trying to figure out what in Kur just happened. He's up, lunging onto his feet in one fluid motion. He has a dagger in his hand and pulls his arm back and I follow the direction he's pivoted towards and see the retreating back of the Kawashari.

But I've seen enough death for one lifetime. For every lifetime.

For the third or maybe fourth or fifth time today, I defy the Pikosa warlord.

Flat on my stomach, I grab Ero's left ankle and yank back as hard as I can. Ero's knee gives and he collapses down onto it. He snarls at me rabidly over his shoulder and I cower, throwing both arms over my head, but when he doesn't hit me like I thought he might, I look up and see him pull back his throwing arm again. I lurch up and grab onto the leather sling crisscrossing over his chest and back.

My muscles are soup but my dead weight is enough to disrupt his aim when the dagger in his hand releases. It plummets short by twenty feet of the retreating Kawashari and I quickly release Ero, prepared to face the unblemished purity of his rage as he rounds on me.

He roars in my face and I inhale in a jerk, spinning onto my back as I await retribution. He snarls and growls and seethes and makes so many violent gestures, reaching, reaching, reaching for me. But he doesn't touch me. Not once. Not in anger.

And then he squeezes his eyes shut tight and everything about him clenches together. He lifts his right hand and I sort of gasp, but mostly shriek, as he brings it down and punches the sand just above my left ear. He roars down at me the whole time and when he's finished, he swings his left leg over me, bends it, and drops his forearm onto it. His leather skirt swishes over my naked body and I can feel his thick trousers beneath it as they press against my belly. I wait...

And wait...

Wondering if this is it, knowing that it has to be.

But he just tightens more and more, squeezing together so hard that I'm sure any second now, he'll break apart and disintegrate into nothing. He lunges to his feet in a burst and grabs my hair so hard it sends pain shooting down my scalp to every other part of my body. Involuntary tears come to my eyes as I reach up, fingers slippery with sweat as they claw at his hand, trying to free myself. It's a wasted effort.

He shouts at me unintelligibly and shakes my whole body. My eyes rattle around in my skull, clanging around like loose marbles. And then suddenly, I'm up against him, our bodies flush, tied together by the thin threads of the sun.

"I should strangle you, Halima," he says against my cheek as he pulls my feet off of the sandy floor and fixes his grip more ferociously around me. "That Kawashari could alert his tribe to our location. They could come back. He could come back *for you*." He holds me to him so tightly I can barely breathe. My temple touches his jaw, and then his lips when he turns his face towards mine. "Not even the full strength of the Kawashari could keep you from me."

Sensations light all over my skin when his meaty hand closes around my left butt cheek and squeezes in a gesture I'm not sure whether to interpret as a good thing or a threat. I clench my buttocks and angle my hips closer to him, trying to escape. He growls again, but this sound isn't like the others, because he chokes halfway through it.

I keep my eyes closed, waiting for the fall. Waiting for what comes next. My hands grip his shoulders and I try to climb higher onto him to alleviate the tension in my hair. The easiest way to do that is to hook my leg around his hip. He drops his hand to my thigh and this new position brings my hot core right against his even greater heat.

"Ero..." I whisper.

"You let another male into my quarters," he rumbles directly into my ear, his breath shooting through my temples, his tongue reaching out to taste my earlobe. "You let him take you from me."

Wait...what? "I tried to poison you..." I offer stupidly, but he cuts me off.

"I don't give a fuck about that. I care that you went with that male. Is he your lover? Did you lie to me before? How many times has he had your body beneath his?"

"That's what you're mad about? You think Haddock and I had sex?"

"Had-dock," he chokes out the word in two parts, each one equally ferocious. His hand tightens around my leg, inching closer to the danger zone. "Tell me how many times, Halima. If you tell me, it will lessen his punishment and yours."

"No! No...Haddock and I have never, ever, *ever* slept together. We've never made love. I've only done that with you. I didn't even know he was coming to take me away. I thought Leanna or Kenya would come. And when I saw him there, I only asked him to come into your room to check your pulse. I wanted to make sure I hadn't killed you."

"Don't fucking lie to me, Halima," he roars. "I will rip out his eyes and feed them to you if you lie to me again."

"I'm not lying," I scream, panic making me desperate. Strange that in my desperation, I cling to him so fiercely. I speak against his neck, inadvertently tasting his skin with every word. Maybe not so inadvertently. He tastes like salt and heat and blood, a reminder that twice today, he's saved me and once today, I've killed him in return.

"I'm not lying. You know I'm not. I don't know how. If I did, you would have drunk the wine I poisoned."

A pause. A long one. At least, that's how it feels to me. It lasts an eternity. Thousands of years. We are not Tanishi and Pikosa anymore. For just a moment, we're both human.

His fingers twist out of my hair and his hard, heavy hand slides around the back of my head, fully cupping it. "Halima," he exhales. His breath trickles over my forehead as he rubs his lips over the crown of my hair. He bites my hair and pulls with his teeth, not hard, but hard enough to send feeling down to my toes.

"Ero." He clenches again when I say his name and secures my head against his shoulder. "You aren't mad that I betrayed you?"

"No." A bark of grim laughter bursts out of his mouth. It's dark and terrible and in contradiction to the tension in his chest, across his shoulders, down his abdomen...

It kind of makes me want to cry. It sounds so...sad and in that sadness is an Ero that I recognize.

"I didn't want to betray you. I didn't want any of this."

"What do you want?"

"I want us to be together. All of us. I want everyone to live."

"That's not the way this world works."

"It is," I say, fire encroaching on my tone, hardening it like clay in a kiln. I look up at him and meet his gaze immediately because he's already looking down at me.

My fist thumps lightly on his chest and I shake my head. "You see now what we can do together. We can be this way, always. No more betrayal. No more lies. Only truth."

The hard edge of his mouth twitches and I wonder what wrong word I've used, but I don't ask and he doesn't tell me. Instead, I lift my finger and rub at the edge of his lips, wishing...

"I don't know what to do with you and your soft heart," he snarls against my hairline. He hoists me up, slides his hand across my lower back and holds me like this, very gently. "You've brought chaos, Halima."

"I know."

"I will have to punish you."

Tighter, I wheeze, "I know. But Ero?"

"Yes, Halima," he chokes.

"I won't let you punish any of my people. You will regret it if you try."

"Is that a threat?" He breathes into my ear, making me shiver.

"Yes. I will make trouble for you."

He groans, like he couldn't imagine anything more pleasing than that. "I think you already have."

"I'll make *more* trouble. I promise. I'm not lying."

"I know."

"But first..." I swallow hard. "You have to save Leanna."

"I *have* to save your Tanishi leader? Is that what you just said to me?" He grabs my neck from behind. It isn't the first time. He pulls my head back just enough that he can see into me and I can see into him. I lick my lips and ignore the dizziness crawling up the back of my brain towards my eyes.

I nod. "Please, Ero. Please."

"You dare," he seethes, but he doesn't tighten his grip. Instead, he starts off towards the scorpion and the people crowded around it staring at each other as if they aren't sure whether or not a second and even more terrible battle is about to begin — this battle against each other, because it appears that the creature is now dead.

In the time it took for me to tackle the Kawashari man and for him to escape, it seems that the group managed to kill this cute little garden *snake* because it lies dead on the sand, taking up an unfathomable amount of space. It's massive. And terrifying. And even though he may be my death, I cling to Ero as we pass by it and I appreciate the way he squeezes me tighter to him.

"It can't hurt you," he whispers just before he sets me down.

I'm left blinking up at the unexpected kindness, mute, as he barks an order. In the next moment, he's tugging a tunic over my head that belongs to someone else — a Pikosa warrior, I think, because it's a nicer material than any seen on a Danien, Omoro or Tanishi. It drops to my thighs. Ero has my upper arm in a vice grip.

"Ellar, give me your sword," he barks to the female who shouted at me about giving away his sword before.

"You don't want your own sword back from the Danien?" She says, handing her own sword to Ero anyway.

"No. He laid the final blow to the snake." Snake! Are they all mental! "He has earned it."

His words are met with rasped whispers and stirs of chaos from the other Pikosa warriors. It makes me worried, anxious, afraid, and despite the stupidity of the situation, I still find myself pressing closer to Ero's back.

I press my hand just below his shoulder blade when he releases me and withdraws his whip.

"Hold the Tanishi warrior up. Bare her wounded arm."

Protests erupt — not just from the warriors now, but from all corners of this bunched group. What surprises me the most though, is that the group is somewhat...mixed. Like, whatever attack formations they had in the beginning when they went for the snake, they just kept.

Pikosa stand shoulder-to-shoulder with Danien who stand beside Tanishi. The one Omoro kneels on the ground, still nursing the wound in his stomach tied with my tunic. Khara. What I should have said to Ero earlier is that I'll accept the punishment, but he has to save *all* of them.

"But...but she is a Tanishi slave, Nigusi," a warrior starts, but Ero cuts him off.

"Grab her arms!"

Two Pikosa warriors lift Leanna up under her arms and hold her blue arm out to the side, but Donovan tries to attack Ero, somehow having reclaimed the gun. I gasp and shout at him to stop, but Ero advances towards Donovan and, in a flourish, disarms him and pushes him to the side.

"Do not *ever* point this weapon at my Tanishi again," he hisses.

Surprise makes me shake. I blink quickly, confused, and I look down at Donovan when he asks me to repeat what Ero said. "He um...he thought you were threatening me. He doesn't like it."

Anyone that can understand me grumbles and whispers. Donovan looks downright stunned at my mumbled confession. He glances between me and Ero over and over again. Ero grunts and shoots a foot forward threateningly.

"Oh. Don't, Ero," I chirp. I start towards Donovan to intercede in his death, but Ero uses the tip of the gun to hold me back.

"Don't move." When he looks over his shoulder, his gaze pins mine and is so heated, I can't maintain it. I look down. "Don't you do that, Halima. Come stand beside me. Tell your Tanishi to brace herself."

"What are you going to do?" I ask, stepping up to his other side, *away* from Donovan. My head is hotter than hell's fires. The sun is so bright. It's been too long. I'm sweating profusely. I can't keep up.

"You want her to live?"

I nod.

"Then we have to remove the arm up to the infection point. Everything below the elbow has to go before the venom spreads to the rest of her body. Warn her if you must. Otherwise, I'll start now."

My stomach goes straight to my throat. I step forward next to Ero and pitch my voice loud. "Leanna, can you hear me?"

Her head has fallen back. She stares at me through slitted eyes but still, she's a fighter, and nods. "Tell them to take the arm," she says, with no prompting. "I'm not ready to die."

Tears well in my eyes. I glance up to my left, up at Ero. He's watching my face and his expression goes from hard to harder when an errant tear escapes. I nod because I can't say anything more. At least...not to him.

Instead, I clear my throat and pitch my wobbly voice louder. Speaking to the Tanishi, I say, "Crowd around our general. She needs your strength. Ero's going to take her arm to save her life."

Leanna's name is whispered on repeat by so many different voices speaking in so many different accents — Tanishi, yes, but also Danien and Omoro.

They move closer to her, too, and I sniffle a little bit harder. The Pikosa make room for the others to gather around Leanna, but only on Ero's command. I step past Ero. He tries to stop me, but I hold his arm — the one blocking me — and look up into his face.

"Please," I say.

A battle plays out in his expression until finally, his jaw sets. He drops his arm, freeing me to go to Leanna. Two Pikosa warriors hold Leanna's forearm steady as they wait for Ero's next order.

"You're going to be okay, Leanna," I say. It's a lie, but I say it anyway.

Voices echo the same words I've said. Others are more realistic. It's Chayana who blurts, "It's going to fucking hurt. Here baby, bite this."

She thrusts a piece of leather between Leanna's teeth. I reach past a body in front of me — a woman I think is called Meera — and touch Leanna's neck and arm. It's so sweaty. We're all dripping and we all smell wretched, our rank odors cooking together under the sun.

The sound of the whip crackles and jerks Leanna's body in our collective grasp. I glance at her arm even though I tell myself not to and see that the tail end of Ero's whip coiled firmly — what looks like painfully — around Leanna's arm just above her elbow crease.

Behind me, Ero says, "Is she ready?"

"Are you ready, Leanna?" I say.

Leanna nods. We all squeeze around her. I mutter a prayer to the sun and the stars. Over my shoulder, I shout, "She's ready, Ero."

The words have barely left my lips before her body jolts. Her mouth opens. Her scream rises up and I can't help it, I scream with her. We all do. Her pain feels collective. Shared. As we all lose something significant to the sand. Anidi laye.

We scream.

We scream until her cries fetter out and her body drops into our waiting arms and, together, we carry her out of the light and back into the dark.

//
Ero

"What now?" Ellar stands in front of me, asking the question that all my warriors want answered as we rush the main cave where the other captured slaves have been contained.

With seventy-eight Pikosa warriors assembled alongside fifty-four Danien, another forty-two Omoro and one hundred and thirty-three Tanishi, every slave is accounted for except for six. Three Tanishi and three Omoro. One of the escaped is the Tanishi leader who was chained to my throne earlier and now, isn't.

My neck flares with heat and I glance down at Halima again, knowing that she will be to blame if the slaves are captured by the Wickar or the Kawashari and are able to direct our enemies back to my village. And then I inhale a breath.

When they come, we will be ready because I have an answer for my warriors, but they won't like it. I don't like it. I fucking *hate* it. But if the day's events taught me anything, it's that together, these captives are much, much more than they seem.

"Take the Tanishi to the village," I command. The violence of my warriors' response is immediate. Immediate...and expected.

"What?"

"What!"

"He wants to take the Tanishi..."

"...to the village."

"He said to take them to the village..."

"You dare!" Gerarr is sitting on my throne. Between him and Wyden, it's a miracle I still have it. But — I glance down at Halima — there's not a chance I'll give it up now. Not when we're on the cusp of something great. Something Halima tried to tell me before with all her words, but I ignored. She had every right to try to kill me, to try to run. I should have listened. What would I have lost had I not seen her Tanishi's success with my own eyes? No...what would *we* have lost?

Gerarr stands when I cross the river, Halima still in my grip, but I leave her behind me just long enough to pull the mechanical weapon around my body and point it at him. I press the button that releases the metal pellets. They sail into his body and he's dead where he stands.

Behind me, Halima gasps, feet slapping over the stones as she backs away, but I'm sick and fucking tired of her trying to run from me, so I wrench her forward until she collides with my back. I need a chain to anchor her to me because I'm not fucking losing her again.

"Do not feel sorry for him. He'd have killed you a thousand times," I rasp into her ear, but she's shaking her head, still fighting. My lips perform acrobatics in ways they shouldn't as I think that perhaps, she will always fight me and maybe that tenacity will be enough for her to live.

She jerks in my grip, almost freeing herself. Her eyes blaze as they meet mine. "What you did to Haddock? He…" She calls him a word I don't know, and I'm frustrated that our communication falls apart here.

"I don't understand."

Halima huffs, her face turning a bright and glorious red. "Wounds. Healing. He heals us, but now, he needs healing."

"He was never supposed to survive."

"He must!"

I laugh. I laugh hard and viciously and drag her closer to me. "You think I'm going to give the male who stole you from my chambers access to healers? You are mad."

I round on her, but she's also rounding on me. She rips her arm down so hard that the sweat on her skin makes it possible for her to free herself. Furious at the loss of contact, I shake with wrath and a sickening anger that festers and spits.

But Halima's anger looks near equal to mine as she shrieks, "It is not madness to want to save lives!"

She surges forward, outmaneuvering my grasp — not because she's faster, but because I'm slowed by the pain and hurt in her expression. She makes it to the stones and shakily, starts to climb.

She's the tiniest thing in here and she doesn't give up. And even though I want to kill her in this moment, I don't want to give up on her either.

"You do not need him. You will not die," I tell her and I can hear my warriors shift with unease at my declaration, but right now, I don't care about them. Any of them. There is only Halima and me and this.

Halima scoffs as she climbs up to the stone where the Tanishi called *Haddock* lies on his back, unmoving. "He has knowledge of the past. He can help all of the tribes here, not just Tanishi."

Her fingers flutter over his body as she tries to help him. She's defending him, as tiny as she is, but would she do the same for me? She did once when she asked this Tanishi healer to ensure I still lived after she poisoned me, if what she said is true. And it occurs to me that if this Haddock male dies, maybe, she never will again. Maybe, the bond will be broken between us.

My gaze flashes to the blood dripping down her back, staining the outside of her tunic, and there's a tightening across my chest that makes me despise her. "Halima, if you don't get away from him, then your punishment will be even more severe."

"Then why do you wait? You will kill me! Just do it. If there are no good feelings left, then just bring me pain!" Her voice climbs the decibels and comes out in a scream.

She watches me and I watch her for far, far too long. I can't admit to what I'm feeling, because I don't understand the feelings. More than good, they are overwhelming. Inundating.

Transcendent, perhaps.

I vault onto the rock between her and my throne and she cries out as she bows over the male's torso, protecting him with her little body. The wounds on her back have reopened. Do they still spell *El-li*? Does it even matter? The damage is already done.

"No."

She blinks, not understanding, but I don't need her understanding. I'm too angry for it anyway. Gerarr's limp body emits a groan and I glance up at my throne seat where he lies slouched, pellet holes studding his chest and abdomen.

I frown, checking his torso for marks. Three pellets hit his right side, but my shot must have gone wide of his heart. I think about ending his life, but one glance at Halima cowering underneath me like I'm some dreadful thing to be feared and *not* the male who had her soft, relaxed body beneath mine and the invitation to press my mouth to her dripping heat, and I don't.

"Lopina, Ellar, Goja, Quin, and Meret." I pull the male who is kin to me out of my seat and let him fall onto the stone below. I don't care if he survives this, but I won't ensure he doesn't. Not yet. Not in front of Halima.

"Take anyone with an injury directly to the healers. Tell them to look at the Tanishi leader first. Tell them to look at Gerarr last. I do not care if he lives."

Lopina, Quin and Goja move to action, but Ellar holds back. She crosses the river and dips her chin towards Gerarr. "Why should we help their people before our warriors?"

My poorly leashed rage presses against the underside of my skin, wanting out. I glance at Halima. She's sitting up, watching me now with lips slightly parted, but she cowers when I meet her gaze and I fucking hate it. I inhale deeply, fighting for calm, and look away.

I jump up on top of my throne and keep one foot planted in the seat, another on the arm and I pitch my voice loud enough for every one of my warriors to hear. "Fifteen Tanishi took down a fully grown desert snake."

Murmurs strike up among my warriors, though none are loud enough to issue open challenge. "It sounds unthinkable, but I invite any one of the Pikosa warriors there to deny this." I wait, but there is only silence.

Finally, Ellar clears her throat. "They weren't alone. They had help."

"They had help, but it did not come from us. While they fought side-by-side with Danien and Omoro, our warriors lingered behind, unsure, unwilling to fight beside slaves. Let me ask you, Ellar, what prompted you to join the fray?"

Her face glows as color floods her cheeks. She has the decency to hold my gaze, only flicking hers away long enough to glance at Halima.

"We fought on your orders relayed through your Tanishi."

I laugh, "I did not give that order. The order you followed today was given by a Nigusi, but it was not given by me."

A warrior shouts, "There is only one Nigusi!" Cries of assent rise up around him.

"There is one Nigusi and I will not allow any to challenge my throne, but what I saw today was something no Nigusi has ever seen before. The Tanishi tribe fought side-by-side with the Danien and the Omoro and they fought..." I struggle through the word that comes next, because it feels foreign and ugly, "*anidi laye.* They fought together.

"The orders given by the Tanishi leader brought the fighters into *formations*. The Danien knew the weaknesses of the snake. Acting quickly, they were able to work together to bring it down while we Pikosa warriors had only the simple task of distracting it.

"And the Tanishi had this." I lift the weapon in my grip high. "It is an instrument of magic. According to my Tanishi..." I stop. I think hard about what I'm about to do. Sweat breaks out over my face. I clench my teeth together. "According to *Halima*, the vessel we pulled these Tanishi from has more magic like this. According to her, there are even instruments that would enable us to build on the surface and even replant the earth."

I shake my head. It sounds farfetched, even to me. I did not believe Halima the first time she told me. I should have. I could have avoided all this. But maybe it wouldn't have mattered. Maybe my warriors, like me, needed to see to believe. Because seeing the formations they assumed when they fought has changed everything. With those formations and with their instruments of magic, these Tanishi were able to fight a sand snake. They fought *together* and together, they did not need us.

Does that mean that Halima does not need me? I rage against the idea. She needs me and if I have to change to prove it and bind her to me forever, so be it.

So be it.

I shout, "At minimum, even learning some of these formations would enable us to take on greater opponents. We could expand and take back some of the oases our ancestors lost."

"They will need to be broken if they are to be of any use to us," a male called Carven says.

I shake my head. "We will try another way. We will try to communicate."

"Halima, communicate between the tribes. Tell your Tanishi and the Danien and the Omoro what I have decreed today."

There's silence after my order. Too much of it.

I look down at Halima then, luxuriating and falling into the inferno of her eyes, which continue to blaze. "And if I do, you will spare them? Truly?"

I nod, wondering if I'll have to break that promise. Hoping, for her sake, that I don't. "Yes, I will spare them. They will all be one tribe." I try, but don't manage to say we. I'm not ready and am not sure I ever will be. Despite my words, this is not easy for me.

"Even Haddock?"

I clench my teeth, blood hot, head hotter. She went with him willingly, he cannot survive because I will not survive the insult. The jealousy. I glance at his body and see that his eyes are open. His breathing is shallow. He looks somehow more injured than the last time I left the caves and I wonder if one of my other warriors had at him in my absence. I frown, not liking that either.

"He can live for now, but if I ever discover that you have given any part of yourself to him — your body or your heart — I will destroy him and I will force you to watch."

She frowns, her lips curled in tight and her dark eyebrows pinching together. Her rubicund cheeks betray her rage as they tremble. Tears wet her lower eyelashes, but I do not let them affect me. I cannot. Jealousy is not something a Nigusi is known to contend with. That I let him live at all is a mercy. My first one.

Perhaps, my second, for all the times I should have killed Halima but, instead, found myself falling further and further towards her in a frighteningly warm, tender abyss.

She nods and gently sets Haddock's head down on the stone. She whispers something to him that makes me rabid and he nods, but she's in motion too quickly for me to decide whether or not to kill him now or wait until after he's healed.

She pushes herself up on her knee, but wavers dramatically where she stands. She lifts a hand to her head like she's woozy and for every display of pain that plays out over her body, my heart is crushed again and again.

"Ooph." She falls into me, but only because I take the step bridging the gap between us and catch her by the wrists. I pull her against me and turn her around in the cage of my arms. Her back to my front, her hands on my wrists, I exhale a little more easily, a little closer to calm.

"Tell them," I whisper in her ear, tipping my head towards the crowd.

She licks her lips and after a final hesitation, she pitches her wobbly voice loud and says in Pikosa, "I will communicate between the languages. I will make it possible so the other tribes can, too."

More enraged and surprised shouts come from my warriors from those who still cannot believe her ability. I can hardly believe it myself. But I don't care about them. Because as they shout at her angrily, she leans further into my chest. Her fingers curl around the leather bracer covering my left forearm. *Does she know that I will protect her?* Yes, even though she hates it and even though I love it and hate that I love it, she does know because I will.

How had it felt seeing the surface snake point its venom-laced stinger directly at her? How had it felt watching her naked body bounce across the Kawashari bastard's back? How had it felt watching the Danien throw her into the river? She should have *died*, but somehow, miraculously, Tenor found me and told me that she'd returned to my chambers. I had half my entire war party looking for her — just her — when they should have been concerned with catching the other slaves.

It'd been a close call, too, because I thought she'd gone into the croc pits, and I'd been close to going after her to a sure and bloody death.

"Halima," I say, but my voice comes out in a groan.

She shivers and, realizing our positions, starts to try to push away from me, but I don't let her go. Finally, she looks up at me, eyes full of stars, and licks her ashen lips to bring them shine. My cock stirs when it shouldn't and I'm angry all over again at how easily she affects me, making it hard for me to think. So disruptive, it's like *she* owns *me*.

"Can I communicate your words to the other tribes, Ero? They should know that you don't want to have them killed or they might try to run again."

My jaw sets, but I nod down at her and keep my hand wrapped around her waist, securely fitting my palm to her hip. Her eyelids flutter and when she sucks in a breath, I hold mine. Rage-filled tension fires between us.

Quickly turning forward, she speaks first in her own Tanishi tongue before switching to the others. One of her statements is met with laughter from the Danien and I frown, hating that I don't know what she's telling them.

"What did you say?" I snarl against her cheek.

She hesitates and I squeeze her hip harder, until she winces. "I told them that I speak much shit. I don't know the word in Danien for *mistakes* or *wrongs*."

My own mouth twitches in response. And then I remember that this is the same female who sought to betray me hours earlier. "You did not tell them something else? Something about rebelling?"

Her gaze steels and she twists to look up at me. "I told you already, Ero, I cannot lie. I fail at it."

"Good." I curl my hand into her hair, tilting her chin up so that I can speak against her mouth. "Good," I exhale, leaning in for a taste. She looks dazed and angry, but she doesn't pull back.

I taste one edge of her mouth softly before jerking up. "It is done." I look back up at the crowded mass of bodies, so many colors and shapes that I've never considered might have value.

"Malachi, Ovid and Chalor — head back to the surface to recover the snake. Take it to the village and let Berna take it apart. Tonight we feast.

"The rest of you, take the prisoners to the village. Let them fill the empty houses on the center island so they can't escape. Feed them from our reserves. Not slave portions, but true portions. Those ordered, tend to the injured. Do not let the Tanishi leader die," I rasp to the ones currently holding the female Halima calls *Leanna*.

More of her Tanishi people crowd around Leanna, looking agitated as I make them wait to carry her East. And then even though it kills me, I grind out, "Do not let the Tanishi healer die, either. Halima, communicate."

She does and a final moment of waiting follows her last pronouncement. I can't have that. Silence allows for reflection. Like Halima, I just need them to obey.

"Move!" My voice echoes throughout the cave, spurring everyone to action simultaneously.

Even Halima starts to pull away from me, but I just hold her against my chest, absorbing her heartbeat through the thin linen she wears until we are completely and entirely alone. The sounds of footsteps have receded and, in the silence, the cave seems enormous.

She moves and this time, I let her. Spinning around, she backs up until her heel reaches the smooth curve of the stone. She'll have to jump down onto the stones below to get down, but her legs are shaking and it's a far drop for her.

I take a step forward and she wobbles in the leather sandals I made her. I frown. The leather bands around her calves look tight. I also hate seeing her in the tunic she's wearing. It belongs to Brin. He'd been sleeping when I'd woken the warriors and he hadn't had time to change. Smelling his scent on her skin makes me lethal.

"So this is where we do punishment? Where you give me pain?" She says and I can tell she's trying so very hard to be brave. Lightning shoots up and down my fingertips.

"Do I look like I want to punish you?"

"Yes."

"You got that fucking right." I close the gap between us, grab her by the hair and around the waist and I crush her to my chest. My mouth finds hers and is utterly unforgiving in its attack.

I kiss her like a madman, devoid of reason, reduced to want. I slide my tongue into her mouth when her lips part in shock and I lavish her tongue. My lips press against hers so hard, I can feel the pressure of her teeth. I don't expect her to respond. I expect her fury. But she lunges for me, her arms circling my neck. She grabs a fistful of my hair and yanks so hard I see stars and am forced into retreat. And then she lays a siege all of her own against which I have few defenses left.

She leans in and bites my neck so hard, for a second, I allow myself to wonder if she's trying to break skin and drown me in my own blood, but she's too good for that. Instead, she laves her tongue over my beating pulse and kisses her way down to my collar bone, to my chest.

I groan and drop her and when her feet find the floor, she keeps kissing her way down. She reaches between the flaps of my armor and grabs my cock through my thick hide pants. I don't have time for this and shed them.

I pull my dagger out of its sheathe and cut her tunic right down the middle and shove her linen pants down her hips. I throw all of our clothing off of the stones, kicking everything aside, and grab for her a second time. She jumps up onto me and I capture her against my body, her wet, hot pussy smearing across my abdomen. I reach for it roughly and shove two fingers inside her and she tosses her head back and screams my name.

I growl and kiss my way across her jaw, working from ear to ear as I work my fingers inside of her. She starts to tremble too quickly, her body primed and ready for mine because it knows we didn't finish what we started earlier. We didn't. I intended to rut her for hours, into oblivion, while she intended only to distract and then kill me.

"Ero, I'm coming," she gasps and it's her undoing. I wrench my hand out of her hot, tight slit and she bucks with desperation.

I hold her hips away from my body, making sure that she doesn't fucking come. I'm still kissing her jaw while she fights to fuck me, scoring my arms with her broken nails and biting my jaw and my collar bones in a way she knows I like already...or maybe that I only like because it's her. I think I'd like anything she did to me, I realize with frustration.

Releasing my anger in a short growl, I carry her to my throne and set her down on top of the pocked, blood-spattered metal. Then I drop onto my knees and hook hers over each of my shoulders.

She can't catch her breath as I cover her entire core with my mouth, rubbing my chin through her folds, creating friction for her that she responds to with squeals of pain and squeals of delight.

"Ero, I'm..." She gasps.

I wrench back. "Lick yourself off of my face," I order.

Her eyes are glazed and her lips are fighting to form words. Her hands are balled up against the arms of my throne and the insides of her thighs are trembling violently. She looks like she's about to cry.

Good.

"Wh...what's happening?" She says, voice breaking.

"Your Nigusi gave you an order. Are you going to follow it?" I challenge.

She frowns, her nose scrunching up. She winces away from me, cowering against the back of my throne seat, and I let her. My cock is aching and my balls are threatening me with mutiny right now, but there's one thing I'm sure of — that she'll break before I do, because I'm fucking furious.

Her hands flutter uselessly towards her sloppy, dripping cunt. Her hair is a disaster, all fallen to one side and gathered in a sand-filled nest. She has cuts and scrapes all over her body. She's much too thin. There's blood on her arm and I know some of it's her own. There are scars on her body, scars that I made and even though I hate the sight of her in pain, I can't come to regret them.

They brought her here and me before her and even though this is very much a battle between us, I won't lose. I can't afford to lose her.

"You're a...a beast," she says, though I'm sure if she had the words, she'd have called me much worse.

"I can't have you trying to run from me again or disappearing into the caves or trying to explore the surface alone. You say you come from another time where Tanishi ruled. Tanishi are no longer strong enough here. There are sand snakes and crocodiles and Wickar and Kawashari tribes. There are poisons in the minerals, traps in the sand, waters that are unsafe to cross. So I may be a beast, but I'm your fucking beast and you need a beast to survive this world. I can only protect you if you obey me. Are you going to obey me, Halima?"

Her face twists in defiance and she leans back against the stones and reaches her hand between her legs. She closes her eyes and I'm so fucking turned on by the sight of her touching herself, I'm almost distracted from my goal.

Blinking back into awareness, I grab the offending hand and wrench it away from her body. I grab her other wrist, too and stretch her arms to either side, anchoring them to the arms of my throne. When she whimpers and tries to clamp her thighs together, I slide one knee between each of her feet and force her legs apart.

Holding her spread eagle, I look down her body and my eyes nearly roll back into my skull at the sight of clear, viscous liquid spilling from her brown, petal-like lips onto my throne. Water wells into her eyes and she makes a sound of fury as she tries to break away from my hold. She knows she can't. Just like she knows this is the only offer she'll get from me.

I lick my lips and offer her a gift far beyond any I've ever given anybody and ever will. "If you obey me, Halima, and keep yourself safe, I promise you that none of your precious tribesmen and women will die needlessly by my hand or on my command. I promise you, that I will listen to you when you speak and when you offer me council and I will believe you. I will attempt to trust you. But if you ever run from me, and if you ever break this trust again, things will be difficult. I do not forgive easily because I have never forgiven anyone. But I will forgive you for almost killing yourself by going onto the surface alone."

She's listening to me now, hearing me, at least half-focused. Her watery eyes are pinned to mine and I try to ignore the pounding of my heart as I'm lost in them. She jerks again in my hold but knows her defeat. She sniffs. "What about trying to kill you?"

"I told you already, I don't care about that."

A single tear plummets from her left eye, damn near sending me into cardiac arrest. "Say the words," she says thickly.

"I don't understand."

"Forgive me for giving you the wine with poison." She bites her bottom lip and gnaws on the inside of her cheek. "Please, Ero." She releases a shuddering exhale and my entire heart, body and soul breaks.

Panic and something else, far darker and more demanding seize me, and I can't stand the look on her face. I release the hold I've got on her wrists and slide my arms further up her body. I dig my fingertips into her lower back and wrench her closer to me. I breathe into her inner thigh and bite lightly at the delicate skin there. She smells like sand and smoke and the fiery surface above our heads.

"Halima, your heart is too soft for this world." I kiss the place where I've bitten and say darkly, "I forgive you for trying to poison me, but only if you forgive me for this…" I smear blood from her shoulder on my fingertips and bring them to her scarred forearm. "…and this."

She looks down at me and she shakes her head. I harden, but then she says, "I forgive you for the pain, Ero, but not for killing that sick Omoro and not for hurting Haddock and not for making captives fight each other and not for what you did to the women you kept in your harem."

I move rapidly, lifting up and surging forward and crushing my mouth to her cheek, fighting, but losing this battle that's so important for me to win. "I did not touch those women, Halima. They were kept aside because they were beautiful and I did not want my warriors going after them. Pikosa do not rape.

"And for the other things, you will forgive me. This is how we live. You will need to accept violence as a part of your life and though I will not kill for the sake of killing, I will not hesitate if it means keeping you safe. I don't care who the person is or their tribe, but if they get in between us or interfere with the way I protect you, they will have to die."

She jerks more forcefully now and this time, I let her push my shoulders and put space between us. "That isn't good enough."

"It isn't good at all," I sneer. "But you were right before. I am not a good male and I will not compromise on this."

"Then I will not forgive you."

"You will in time."

"I won't."

"You will have to, because I'm not giving you up. That mark there on your arm? The one I branded you with? That was the first sign. In ancient Pikosa script, it spells a word — *anidi laye* — and the mark on your back is the sign that solidified it — *el-li*. It means mine. You are mine, Halima, as decided by the universe, and I protect what's mine.

"For now, I don't need your forgiveness. I need your agreement that you will help me keep you safe by not running away and obeying my commands and I will give you all that I promised. Respect for you, for your people, for the Danien and the Omoro. We will rebuild, Halima, as you once said, and we will do it together. But I cannot lead and protect everyone without you. I need you."

She waits for a long, long time, but I let her, easy as I wait for I know already that there is only one answer she could give me now. Eventually, she nods a jerky nod. "Fine, but I'm not going to like it."

"You will like it." I smile and her eyes widen in alarm, causing me to laugh. I prowl towards her and she spreads her legs, eager still, despite the bargains brokered on these stones that have never seen a Nigusi negotiate, on top of a throne that has never before held a captive.

Bracing one hand on the metal arm of my throne, I slip my free hand through the wetness coating the insides of her legs before reaching their juncture. There, where her slick is hottest, I penetrate her with three fingers, stretching her to the point of discomfort.

"Ah…" She moans. "Yes…" She sighs. "There…"

I pull out of her and smile down into her furious eyes. "Why are you torturing me?" She whimpers.

"Because it's all I know how to do." I lick my pointer finger clean, before offering her the other two. Hesitating just a moment before leaning in, she licks my middle finger clean of her juices, sucking it deep into her mouth so that I can nearly touch the back of her throat. As I do, I can't help but imagine what it would be like to swap my finger out for my cock. I growl, yank my fingers out of her mouth and lick away her spit, just for the sheer fuckery of it.

"I could ask you the same question. What's your excuse?"

She pouts, looking fucking adorable. "I'm not doing anything."

"Don't you see all that you've done. You've changed everything. Everything I've done now I've done for you. My tribe may be ruined…"

"It won't be. You know this is the right decision." I do, but it doesn't change the tension and fear I feel. "And even though the things you've changed are good, it doesn't change you. You're still a monster and I hate you. You were right. There are no good pieces," she asserts, but she's lying. For once, I do not call her on it.

"No, I'm a Pikosa warlord, a protector. And I will protect you even if I have not been able to protect myself against you. So hate me all you like Halima, it does not matter to me. All that matters is that you live."

I turn around and leave her there on my seat, jumping to the landing below. "Come. We have work to do. But first, I need to dress your wounds and feed you."

She makes a strangled sound and I know what it means, what she wants, because I want the same thing.

I wait and watch her face contort. She wrings out her hands and staggers awkwardly to the edge of the largest stone. Every instinct in my body is firing, wanting to go to the edge of that stone and help her down from there. She's too small, she can't get down on her own without difficulty. And her feet...they're tracking blood. Fuck.

I want to go to her with everything in me, but I don't. I hold.

She shuffles forward, looking every bit the wounded animal and me, the eager predator. I close my eyes on an extended blink and lick my lips, swallow. "I... can we...finish?"

I snort and shake my head. "You're being punished, remember?"

She gasps in this over the top way that might have made me smile, but at the last moment, I show restraint. "But...but, you're punished, too." She points at my cock, still fully erect, still bobbing when I walk, and I nod.

"I've been slow to learn, but I will not disobey the signs anymore."

"What do you mean?"

"From now on, we do things together. Anidi laye, Halima. Now, come."

"Ugh. Wait, Ero. My legs...pain...I can't..."

I inhale deeply, fighting that urge to run to her. I say softly, "What do you need, Halima?"

Her head whips as she looks at me. "You...are asking me?"

"Yes." My chest rumbles.

She shakes her head, looking confused. "I need your help getting down because my legs..." She doesn't even finish her sentence before I'm on her. Her ankles are at my shoulder height and I grab onto them and lift. She yelps and doubles over, grabbing onto my shoulders to keep from falling.

I pull her off of the stones and then drop her ankles and catch her around her ass. I kiss her between her upper ribs, right below her breasts, and then quickly toss her into a cradle hold and carry her down the Eastern tunnel to the village.

12
Halima

The village shocks the khara out of me.

"This is the village where your people will stay from now on," he says while I fight the urge to sink into the calm, welcoming warmth of his body as he carries me to the end of the Eastern tunnel to a massive platform that juts out into completely empty space. It's utterly terrifying, but what lies below? Absolutely transcendent.

"What do you think of it, Halima?"

I don't think. I don't have any thoughts other than jemila jemila jemila...beautiful beautiful beautiful...

The cave around us, if you can even call it that, is so huge it must be at least as large as every other cave in the upper system combined times ten. Massive, it spreads far and wide, so far, that the horizon feels distant from here. Cracks in the world above let in light and it shines bright now, covering the village below in tender sunshine. It's surreal.

The village itself is entirely made of stone houses carved directly into the walls all around the edges of this massive place. I notice though, that there is no city center. There is no place where villagers would...

converge, at least none that I can see, though there would be space enough for it.

The river empties into the cavern from a cave somewhere directly below us. I can hear the spattering of the water as it thunders down into a lake below us that's large enough for boats to fish in. Two are still on the water now.

The lake winds through the massive cavern in a sort of lazy river and anywhere the river isn't, is either stone or moss-covered stone. There are people dotted across them, working at various tasks now. I wonder if they ever just lounge out.

One mossy oasis, in particular, looks inviting. I wonder if Ero might let me go there sometime and swim — so long as there aren't any crocodiles.

"Tell me, Halima. I won't ask any more if you respond better to commands."

I nudge him in the ribs with my elbow and I hate that he fights off a grin when I do. He looks like someone I don't hate when he smiles and I'm reminded that maybe, just maybe, there are still good pieces in there... maybe more than just a few.

"It's incredible. I see why you fight so hard to protect it."

"Now that we are so many more, it will be more difficult."

"I'll help you," I say and he looks reluctant to answer.

He swallows and searches my face with his gaze. "Yes, we will work together." He leans in and licks the seam of my lips but when I moan and try to chase the kiss, he stands up straight, pulling out of my reach.

"Is the punishment over, Ero?" I ask, squeezing my thighs together.

"No, it isn't."

Fifteen days go by and the punishment doesn't end. Inside of his mossy stone home, we even share the same bed every single night and every night he tortures me like the monster that he is, touching, petting, groping… but never giving me the release my body so badly craves. And worse, I'm never alone so I can't exactly help myself.

If I'm not with him, I'm on the center island where all the slaves are housed. There are only about eighty small huts on the island. They're all made huge sheets of moss draped over stone and steel structures. They offer protection but, unlike the dry stone caves, these are quite damp. They aren't great, but they're a five-star hotel compared to the cramped, wet, dark caves that Ero had us in earlier when we were prisoners.

We still are prisoners — there's no doubting that. The island all the *former* captives are now housed on is in the very center of the lake, only reachable to one of the main walls by first passing several other islands, all of which are inhabited by Pikosa.

Otherwise, you could snake between them if you had a boat, which we don't, and it's far, far too far to swim — not that any here but a few Tanishi and the Danien claim to know how to swim.

So when another seven days go by and my punishment only ramps up and the captive tribes start to get antsy, I decide finally that I should do something to deserve my punishment. I know Ero will be pissed, too, because it has to do with wine…not poisoning it, but stealing it.

I raid his stash and bring over two dozen skins with me to the island. Tenor doesn't approve, but she doesn't stop me. Ero's only orders to her were to keep me alive and in the caves but beyond that, my only tasks have been teaching the tribes to speak English.

Yes, English.

I'd been sure Ero would want the tribes to speak Pikosa, but instead, he's asked me to teach them — *all* of them — Tanishi and since English is our only unifying language, English it is. I didn't understand why until Leanna explained it to me.

She'd laughed and said that she was actually starting to respect the bastard. That it made the most sense for him to keep Pikosa as a private language and for him to learn our language so that we'd no longer be able to keep secrets from him.

I didn't like her answer. Why I'd been expecting something more altruistic is beyond me, but I had been.

So I steal the wine, the petulant thing that I am, and I take it to the island with Tenor's disproval, and I pass around all *thirty* sacks that I brought and soon, we've managed to clear out a space in the center of a ring of huts and use blankets that look like they're made of woven moss nets to sit on.

We pool our food and drink and set it out on a long stretch of stone. It's a full days' rations — plus stuff folks have squirreled away for later. The Danien and Omoro donate less than we Tanishi do, but they still donate to the cause and that's okay.

The sky darkens above through the grate-covered opening in the massive cave system and oil burns in pits around the outskirts of our little party, the largest in the center.

We eat and drink and then eventually, a Tanishi woman called Sorena shows us the thing she created in her spare time. An instrument, it stands almost as tall as she is and looks like a bow, but strung with patchwork pieces of hide instead of strings. It looks crazy, but it plays beautifully and I'm surprised and elated by how many different people manage to cobble together different slipshod weapons and make *music* together.

The Danien and the Omoro are confused as hell, mostly watching from the outskirts of the dance floor, and Tenor looks horrified by all of it. Never more so than when we do actually start dancing.

I start dancing first.

Chayana joins me soon after. Jia and several of the others are missing — still assisting the Pikosa healers with the wounded. Haddock was returned to us just yesterday, cuts all mended, looking okay. He seems...off though. As more get up and start to dance and the dancefloor becomes nearly overcrowded, I find him in the shadows.

"Mind if I sit?" I tap the edge of the moss blanket under him with my toe.

He struggles to meet my gaze and shrugs. Weird. "I get it if you're worried about Ero, but he did promise me that he wouldn't hurt you again."

"You actually believe him?" He scoffs and brings the wine skin in his hands to his lips.

His knees are propped up and his elbows are draped across them. He looks closed off, not at all open and I wonder what's changed other than, you know, being beaten to an inch of his life. Maybe...because of Ero...he's upset with me?

I shrug and sit anyway, reaching across his arms for the wine skin in his hands. Taking it, I drink from it, sure that I'll hate myself tomorrow for it but not caring right now. Right now, I'm dancing and singing and surrounded by a tentative, wobbly joy. I'm happy. All my feelings right now are good.

"I think I do."

"You can't trust him." The word tears out of Haddock's throat with violence, so violent that I spill my wine all over the front of my tunic. Ero, he…he tailored it himself from one of his own shirts to fit me. He makes all of my clothes.

"You can't trust anyone, Halima. Not even me."

I frown. "What's that supposed to mean?"

"I mean the guy you're shacking up with is using you just like the Sucere Project used you and for what? In exchange for your life? Is it worth it, knowing what you've done to save yourself?"

Haddock's gaze is glazed and his hands are fists. His hair grew out in his time with the healers and now falls to his shoulders. His beard is also thick and untrimmed and I know that whatever he's seeing now in those bright orange flames is something other than fire.

My pulse picks up and cold sweat breaks out across the back of my neck. I'm actually *scared* as I reach forward to gently touch Haddock's upper arm. "Haddock?"

He jolts and I spill more wine. He snatches the skin away from me and upends it into his mouth and, when he's finished, he throws the skin so hard into the nearest hut, a patch of its mossy exterior falls off in a chunk.

"Haddock!" I jump and lean away from him. He seethes anger.

"You know what? Maybe you should trust Ero. He's never claimed to be anything but a murdering lunatic. Meanwhile, look at us. Look at what we've done and all for the sake of *humanity*," he spits and as he speaks, he rounds on me, body hovering over mine so large that he casts a shadow from which I cannot escape. "What humanity? I'd rather abandon it than live with monsters — that's the last thing Kenya said to me before she escaped."

I blink shocked, confused. "What? She escaped and she didn't free you?"

"Free me? Hah! She knows who I am. Why do you think she did this to me?" He gestures to his face where there aren't any more scabs or scrapes, but there are scars. "Though I only got my memories back because of her. I was so surprised." He shakes his head. "So surprised when she started beating me. And after? It makes perfect sense. She should have gone farther. I should be dead."

My gut churns. "She...she did that to you?"

"Yes." He rubs his face roughly, stretching out his already stretched collar. He looks unhinged.

"What are you saying, Haddock? You're freaking the crap out of me..."

He grabs me by the front of the shirt and shakes me so hard my teeth clack together and I choke on my spit. I release a high-pitched squeal, but my cry for help is drowned out by Haddock's low snarl, *"Don't trust me. Don't trust any of the Tanishi. And above all else, don't trust Leanna."*

"Haddock!" I shout.

And then comes the crackle. It's a sound I know well by now, though I haven't heard it in some time. It fills me with fear at the thought of the destruction it causes, but also a sick pleasure at the thought of the man behind it.

Haddock's hand rips away from my clothes and my whole body jolts in the process but when I land back on my butt, rolling onto my right hip — away from him — and I open my eyes, I see why.

Ero's whip is wrapped around Haddock's wrist, stretching it across his body. Meanwhile, Haddock doesn't even seem to register what's happened because his body is still turned toward mine and his eyes are blazing. His face is bright red and so consumed by stress and rage and the darkest sides of all good emotions.

Spittle flies from his lips as he seethes, "Don't trust Leanna. Don't trust me. Use your monster to protect you from us. At least he'll be good for this one thing."

My mouth is hanging open and I'm confused and shaken. I look up and push my hair over my shoulder, combing it behind my left ear. I fidget, starting to stand, but I've had wine and struggle to get off my bottom and when I look up and see Ero, getting up becomes impossible.

The fires are still burning, but the party is dead. The music is gone. Everyone is holding their breath. All I can hear are Ero's heavy feet hitting stone. Thwack, thwack, thwack.

"Ero, please," I say breathlessly, already panicked. Why did Haddock have to do this here? Why did Ero have to see? "He wasn't hurting me. He's just…in pain." I'm scrambling and Ero's crossing the center of the square and almost on us now.

He comes to a stop four feet from us. I'm up on my knees, holding up my right hand and holding my left back towards Haddock, as if to separate them. As if I could somehow be the blocker Haddock would need.

Muscles ripple across Ero's chest and down both of his arms. His stomach is so taut and his jaw is clenched so tight, he looks like a statue.

"Ero," I say.

His gaze jumps from Haddock to me, sweeping... assessing. His focus hangs on some part of my shirt and when I look down, I see that the top button is mangled, dangling by a thread like a fish on a line, and some of the fabric is ripped around it.

I open my mouth to try to explain it away, but Ero speaks first. "Halima," he says. He takes what seems to be a bracing breath. "Tell me why *Haddock* had his hands on your tunic in anger."

I'm so shocked, my mouth works without speaking. "He...y'ani...he..." I gulp. "He's angry with the Tanishi leader who beat him. I thought it was you, but he says it was her who did most of the damage. Kenya."

I glance at the bodies at his back, watching this scene play out to its end. And it has to have a good one. I only like stories with good endings. *My father didn't. He loved tragedies.*

"Why didn't you tell me?"

His eyebrows draw together. "Is Haddock a threat to our tribe, Halima? To you?" *Our. He said our.*

The moss crinkles under my knees, smelling so rich and fragrant. Smelling like Ero and all of his violence, but right now, he's restraining it for me.

"I..." I refuse to lie. I glance at Haddock, lowering my arms. He's back to kneeling, but he doesn't look afraid of Ero or any impending punishment. Instead, he's staring at the distant fires again, looking so sad, so lost.

"I don't think he is, but he's very angry with Kenya." With all of us, or at least some of us, it would seem. Something about trust and memory… "It might be smart to have someone keep an eye on him, but I promise you that he won't hurt anyone."

"You can't promise that." He flicks his wrist, releasing Haddock's wrist. He reels the whip back in and stows it on his belt and I exhale, relieved.

"Halima?"

I turn and see Leanna slightly behind me. She's standing there next to Donovan and two other Tanishi men who fought the sand snake with us. "You can tell Ero that I give him my word that I'll keep Haddock away from you if he spares him this once."

Haddock chuckles darkly. "I'd thought you'd want me out of the picture, Leanna. Or is it guilt? Guilt is a powerful driver."

"What did he say?" Ero says.

"He said something I don't understand. He is angry with Kenya, but with Leanna, too. Leanna promises that she'll watch him though and make sure he doesn't do anything strange."

"Here, let us take him." Leanna steps forward, but Haddock shoots up onto his feet. He sways and swerves dramatically to avoid the Tanishi group as he staggers away.

"Stay close to that barbarian of yours Halima. I think I'm right. He's the only honest piece of shit here." He swipes a wine skin from Donovan's grip as he passes him and brings it to his lips. He disappears around a hut and Leanna goes after him.

Ero jerks and his hand twitches to his sword, but he doesn't take it. Instead, he shifts his weight between his feet and inhales deeply, then exhales just as deep.

"Tell me how he insults me."

"He didn't insult you. He actually told me that I should stay close to you."

His eyes narrow. He doesn't believe me.

I stand up and face him fully. "He thinks that the Tanishi leaders are liars and that I shouldn't trust them. He thinks you're the only honest being here."

He rolls his tongue against the roof of his mouth as he weighs my truth in his gaze. And then he shifts suddenly. He looks over his shoulder at the people gathered, all of whom are still watching us. He lingers over the sight of the instrument we've taken lovingly to calling *harp,* even though it's more like a drum, before turning back to face me.

"You're okay?"

"I'm okay," I exhale and relief, like warm syrup, slides through my bones.

"No pain."

"No pain." My mouth quirks. "I feel good. We're having a *party,*" I say, improvising with a word I think hopefully means *congregating.*

"I saw you dancing with other Tanishi. You weren't dancing with them like you danced with me back in the upper caves."

"No," I say, surprised he was watching me for so long and even more surprised that he saw me dancing and his first thought was to join me, not to stop me. The warmth thickens in my blood. "I didn't dance with them like I danced with you."

"Mmm." The rumbling that comes from his chest *does* something to me. And that feeling only intensifies when he says, "I would like to dance with you again like we once did. Now. With the *party*." He licks his lips. More feet shifting. A warm burst of air touches my cheeks from the flames dancing not too far off. "Will you dance with me, Halima?"

The smile creeps over my face slowly, but there's no fighting it or him. He is warlord for a reason. "Yes, I will."

He steps up to me, his heat crashing over me, hotter than the surface up above. He slides both of his huge hands back through my hair, tilts my head back and speaks against my jaw.

"I have only danced with you, Halima. I don't know how. You will have to show me."

A shiver runs up my body from my heels to the top of my head. My mouth is dry. My voice is thick. All I can do is nod. "We need *music*."

"What is this?"

"Music," I tell him in English, pointing over to where Sorena stands with her harp on display.

"Moo-zick," he repeats, accent clunky and thick.

I smile again. "Yes."

He follows the line of my finger to Sorena and jerks his chin at her. "We need moozick," he says in English, shockingly given that, of all my students, Ero seemed to be one of my bigger projects.

Sorena's mouth falls open and I can't help but laugh. "The party isn't over yet!" I shout in Tanishi, then Omoro, then Danien, then in Pikosa say, "You all should dance with us. The Tanishi will show you how."

Leading by example, I take Ero's wrist and pull him toward the central fire pit. The space has cleared out around us and I'm a little embarrassed that everyone is staring — including the ten or so Pikosa warriors that must have joined Ero on the boat over here — but I pretend I'm not, turn around so that my back is to Ero's front and begin to sway my hips side to side in half-time to the beat of Sorena's harpdrum.

Though he's slow to learn English, he's a quick study in this. His hips follow the motions of mine and his arms circle my arms. He takes my hands and brings them up to his shoulders and I circle them back around his neck. I play with his hair. My hips sink deeper. He bites the side of my neck.

A few other brave souls eventually trickle in around us — obviously, Chayana is first. Even bolder than that, she grabs a Pikosa warrior by the hand and drags him with her into the circle and proceeds to start dancing around him in a traditional Indian dance whose steps are so quick, he can't possibly hope to catch her. But he doesn't leave either, though. Instead, he watches Chayana, occasionally bobbing his head and the gruff male warrior manages to look *amused*.

Leanna appears and pulls two Omoro into the circle with her, both young women who look mortified. Donovan starts dancing with a Danien called Illyara and Frey starts dancing with Marlene.

Eventually, the dance floor fills back up and more wine is passed around, so much, that I'm not sure where it even came from. "Would you like more wine? I see you counting the skins," Ero says in my ear.

I shake my head. "No, I only stole thirty. There's at least fifty skins here on my count."

"I brought more."

"You did? Why?" I look up at him.

He slides his hands down to my waist and lifts, pulling my feet nearly off of the floor in order to grind his hips into my ass. "For your good feelings."

"But I stole wine. Won't you have to punish me?"

"No, Halima. Your punishment is over."

I burn all over and tilt my chin up so my head is resting on his chest. He kisses my jaw and cheek, but when he moves for my lips, I yank on his hair, keeping a splinter's distance between his lips and mine, "But what about yours?"

"My what?"

"Your punishment."

"You dare." He narrows his eyes in a frightening display, but I refuse to allow the fear to enter my blood. *He won't hurt me.* If he didn't hurt Haddock. He might not hurt anyone.

"Yes." I turn in his arms and reach down his abdomen, tracing the line of every scar. I drop my hand abruptly and grab his erection through his hide pants. They're thick, so I don't get a good feel, but it doesn't seem to matter to Ero. He still moans like a wild animal, like I'm touching him for the very first time.

He grabs my hair, scrapes his fingers along my jaw, wraps both hands around my neck and squeezes. "You are playing a dangerous game with me, Halima." He squeezes just a little harder, just enough for me to panic, before releasing everything. He drops his forehead onto mine. "But I will play."

And then I say something I didn't even expect myself to say. "Good. Then take me back to the pools in our home." I don't know why I said it. It just slipped out.

His nostrils flare. His lips part. "Our home," he mouths, without saying the words aloud. His eyes flash to my shoulder, though I'm sure it's too dark for him to see the scars. I know that's what he's looking at. "Not mine," he says, he chokes, "but ours."

"Yes. Ours, habibi."

He jerks and suddenly I'm being crushed against his chest. There's nowhere left for me to move. Just mineral-scented skin at my front, hot as an iron, and his warm breath on the top of my head, ruffling my tangled curls. "I'm ready for my punishment now."

13
Ero

My chest is heaving and the muscles in my lower back are all knots. My arms are spread out to either side, hands clutching the lip of the pool as if the bottom of the pool has opened up and the strength of my fingertips is the only thing keeping me from plummeting to my death.

I can't take it. My hand unclenches from around its perch and aims for Halima like a pellet from a machine, but she blocks my hand with her forearm and stops what she's doing, which causes me even greater pain.

"No touching. This is your punishment."

I firm my grip on the lip of the pool with a roar and throw my head back. The caves here go deep into the mountain and my voice echoes and for a moment, I force myself to focus just on the sounds and block out all other sensation before I descend further into the sounds Halima is making.

The splashing.

Her moans.

Her high, breathy gasps.

She's riding my cock for the third time and, even though I've come each time she has, she doesn't let me touch her. And I know now, if I ever doubted it for a moment, that she's the only female I've ever wanted and will ever need. Made for me, as if by some greater, universal power. Because she's depriving me of something I did not know I ever wanted. *Not touching.*

It's *painful* but only because it feels so fucking good and I'm fucking petrified that, at any moment, she's going to stop and there won't be anything I can do to prevent her. She's stripped all of my control and worse, the little fucking savage, she's forced me to relinquish it willingly.

Her hips swirl in patterns that make no fucking sense. She has her fingers twisted together behind my neck and she bounces on my cock, using me for her pleasure. My restraint breaks and I grab her hips and slam her down onto my lap. Her inner walls contract around my length and the moan that flutters out of her sets me alight.

"That's it, Halima. That's it." She shudders in my arms, but she stops herself. She fucking stops herself.

Blinking rapidly, she pulls off of my cock, ruining both of us just long enough to return my hands to the smooth, wet edges of the stone pool. I let her. I don't understand what she's doing, but I let her do it anyway.

"This is for me," she whispers. "Not for you."

And as she continues to rub herself on my body, holding onto my neck, pressing her lips to my chest, grinding her hot clit against my pubic bone as my cock thrusts in and out of her at whatever speed she chooses to set, I finally understand *anidi laye* in all of its meanings. This is pleasure yes, but it's incomplete.

We aren't together.

I want all of her, but she's keeping pieces of herself from me.

"Stop this, Halima," I snarl.

"No." Her eyes roll back as her pace picks up. She has her feet on the bench on either side of my hips and is moving slower than I would like her to, but she doesn't stop me from thrusting up.

She orgasms on my cock, her inner walls trembling and I grab onto the slippery lip of the pool with so much force that pain shoots up both of my wrists. I'm arching up, leg muscles stiff, back muscles blazing. My ass is flexing forward, hips pistoning up into her hips as my cum explodes into her just as I do all things, violently. She wrings me dry and when she finishes, I'm exhausted, depleted, *needy*. Left so fucking wanting.

"Halima," I moan, pulling forward against my invisible restraints.

She's draped over my chest, damp forehead pressed against my shoulder. Her hair sticks to my chest in dark ropes. She needs to cut it. I'd cut it for her, if she let me. I want her to cut mine. I want to be close.

I thrust my hips up just one more time as the last tremors of her body begin to fade and she hiccups and smiles lazily up at me. She sits there for a while and I can't decide what's better — fucking her or having her near me like this. I like this nearness a lot.

I love this nearness.

It ripples through me like the lapping waters of this pool. I nuzzle my lips across her hairline, but she pulls up and off of me, slowly climbing down and, even though she smiles at me lazily over her shoulder as she turns away, she leaves me where I am.

My breaths aren't coming any easier as I watch her turn her back to me and wash herself with soap. Her cheeks are flushed, her eyes are glassy. She looks at me without shame or embarrassment, but also without releasing me from this prison.

"How long?" I say. My chest is heaving. My nails score the stone. I want to rail and rage against her, but I also...don't.

"What do you mean?" She climbs out of the bath and pulls a large swatch of linen from a stack against the wall. I watch her dry herself and I hate everything in that moment.

"How long is your punishment going to last?"

She shrugs. "I don't know."

"How will I know the rules?"

"There aren't any."

"I need to know, Halima. If you do not set terms, I will ravage you whether you want me to or not. I'm not used to being denied. Tell me now — how long will I have to wait?"

She dries her hair, squeezing, squeezing, squeezing... Even that slight motion arouses me and I growl. I should go to her, tear the cloth from her body and fuck her against the wall for her defiance. But I don't do that. Because I want her to want me *more*.

It shouldn't be possible, but my throat dries at the same time that my mouth waters. I glance down. The distance between us is so little now but...too great for me to cross. Like the river rocks that form bridges over the river. I need her to push those rocks into place. Instead, she looks down at my chest as she continues to dry herself.

"How did you get so many scars?"

Her gaze lingers over the largest, most visible of my scars. It starts at my lower left rib and goes almost all the way to my groin and I'm reminded of the warrior who gave me this particular scar. I think taking my cock had been that particular warrior's intent. It was Ellar's mother. She had been a fierce warrior in her prime, but she was beyond that when she challenged me for my throne seat. I'd taken her head, but the pain of the marks she'd given me hung with me long after I'd taken my title.

"How do you think?" I hiss.

"How many slaves have you killed?"

"Why does that matter?"

She doesn't answer and I can't decide if she's mad or if it's her intent to kill me. She's baiting me and I have never been baited before. I uncurl my fingers from around the stone edge of the bath. Water cascades down my body when I push myself up out of the pool and stand on its edge. I don't go to her, but I tower over her even from here. She watches me without moving. She's waiting for me to strike, expecting me to react with violence.

But that violence doesn't come to my fingertips as it once did. Because now, my fingertips know danssing, they understand gentleness, they are familiar with closeness and wanting and they understand the impact of punishment. Since hers has ended, she is so much more confident — *confident in me*. I want to be confident in her equally.

I want to trust her with this. With my body. With my dick. With my heart.

I try to marshal my pitch and speak evenly. I don't. But I try. "Sixteen. I've killed sixteen slaves. Nine that I killed were either injured or sick, two were trying to hurt other slaves, three attempted a rebellion and one..." My voice isn't easy, but I still tell her, "One was a man. Healthy, able-bodied. The Nigusi before me ordered me to kill him in order to initiate into the tribe. He was the first person I killed."

"You remember?" Her eyebrows pull together and she uses that damn linen to cover herself up. "You remember them all?"

"Yes. Now take the fucking towel off."

She ignores my command, the little beastly thing that she is. "And how many others have you killed?"

I huff angrily, "I don't know. At least that many Pikosa warriors to fight for and keep my position. At least twice that many from other warring tribes who invaded or crossed our land with the intention to take."

"But you remember the Danien and the Omoro that you've killed? Why?"

I don't understand her questions or why they matter, so my voice is rough when I blurt, "Because they aren't warriors. Warriors know that to cross another warrior is to accept the possibility of death. The weaker tribes are just that — weak. They aren't warriors. Killing them felt worthless."

No. Killing them made *me* feel as if I were worth much less. Like weighted stones I've carried every day, I've allowed them to make me heavier and heavier. And worse, is knowing that they'll be there forever, lodged in place for eternity. Not even Halima can do that, and she's light as breath.

"You deserve punishment, Ero. For everything you've done, you deserve my hate, too." I both freeze and immolate from within in the time it takes for her to say, "But, I don't seem to be capable of hating you."

"You've said the words often enough I thought that you believed them." I rise out of the water, letting it sluice from my skin across the stone floor. I look down at her and grip the edge of her towel and she resists, but not enough. I take it away from her and dry myself perfunctorily while my gaze gobbles up the sight of so much bare flesh. Her stomach is flat, her nipples are dark and so is the thickening hair growing again between her legs. I ache to touch her fire, but for now, she lets me only bask in her glow and oh how she glows.

"I wish I did, but I'm glad I don't."

I reach for her chest, wanting nothing more than to rub the backs of my fingers down her sternum, just a taste...but she stops the progress of my hand in hers and my hand forms a fist instead. "How long?"

"Sixteen days plus the fifteen days' worth of punishment you gave me makes thirty-one."

"And then?" I gruff, not liking the math or how she arrived at such a number.

"And then we see."

"I want guarantees, Halima. I want to be able to touch you freely. I want to call you mine forever. I want there to be no misunderstandings between us. You will help me keep the tribes safe and you will also give me this." I touch her chest, thumping her twice in the space above her heart.

"You have already had my body many times today, Ero." She laughs and I'm dazzled by it, grateful for the cave's echo which lets me hear it far after it's stopped.

"Not that. This." I thump twice more.

Her smile becomes wistful then. She steps a little closer and smoothes her hand over my own heart and for a moment, we just stand there together. "I think your heart and my heart are very old friends." She sniffles and flexes her hand repeatedly as she breaks the bond between us. "Come. Let's go to bed where you will be *respectful*."

"*Respectful?*" I repeat.

She nods. "No touching when I don't want. No pushing me. You have thirty-one more days."

I growl, knowing that I can be this thing, but also that I don't want to be. "Fine. Though you tested my patience during your punishment. You cannot expect me not to test yours."

"Ero…" She says, confusing me. Her voice is in reprimand, but she's also smiling at me.

"Confusing, fickle thing."

"What? I didn't understand the words."

"They were insults. Now go. Let me show you just how *respectful* I can be."

I follow her at a distance all the way to the bed and, when she lies down, I lie down beside her. The bed is large enough that we don't need to touch when we lie flat on our backs, but I pretend the space is less than it is so that at least our shoulders brush.

"Is this respectful?" I tsk.

She makes a soft sound. Her breath fans my bare arm. I glance at her and see that she's rolled onto her side facing me and I inhale deeply, freezing, wanting to memorize this moment.

"Yes."

"Respectful," I exhale in her Tanishi tongue, trying to balance the word on my tongue so that the syllables fall perfectly on either side of this invisible scale. "You have so many words in your language that we do not in Pikosa."

Her eyes closed, she answers sleepily. "Then *ya'ni* maybe you should try harder to learn Tanishi."

I growl, "Don't test me, Halima, or when this is through, you may deserve further punishment."

"You know, I may consider reducing the time of your punishment, if you let the captive tribes off of their island to help with construction on the surface," she says to me.

I hate how easily I want to agree. The idea of having captives off of the island where they can go anywhere and escape and bring rival tribes to our doorstep frighten and alarm me. But...I want to touch Halima again.

Reluctantly, I whisper, "What did you have in mind?"

Twenty-four days later…

14
Halima

"Pull!" Leanna's voice makes my bones harden and my adrenaline surge. "Pull!" I pull.

I know my contribution doesn't do half as much as the Omoro man standing in front of me, and even less than the Pikosa boy on my other side, but I also know that I have to try, because if Leanna can be here — voice hoarse, face turning a blotchy red underneath what's already very clearly another layer of red burn, missing her right arm and in pain because of it — then so can I.

"Pull, goddammit! We're almost there."

We. That was my idea. I told every Tanishi to use the word *we* as much as possible to reinforce the idea that there is no them or us anymore. There's just us together trying to build something never before seen in this new world. And never before seen in the old one, either.

Finally, after much cajoling and many promises — and after sucking his dick deep down my throat half a dozen times — Ero finally agreed to let some of the captives move off of the center island and into some of the stone houses on the perimeter of the village, against the outer walls. Now, some Tanishi and Omoro and

Danien even live side-by-side with Pikosa warriors who sued to hurt them.

No one has tried to escape so far. I'm worried they will, but I made them promises too, and so far, with Ero's help, I've been able to deliver.

We have new tasks, new purpose, now. From the Sucere Chamber, we were able to harvest enough building materials to build a city — not a huge one, but a small one — and possibly even enough for a couple more outposts.

Our urban planner, Malachi, as well as Chayana, Marlene and two engineers, got together with Omoro, Danien and Pikosa builders and experts on the terrain to come up with the design. Ero made the final adjustments.

I was surprised that he thought to ask Ellar and Leanna what they thought of some of his changes — like adding additional reinforcement to the bottom of the outer walls to prevent sand *snakes* from burrowing beneath the steel walls and adding steel beams to reinforce the overhead dome, rather than letting them be entirely made out of biological materials — apparently, the Kawashari use burning pitch as a weapon and have the tools needed to lob it over the height of our walls. The steel beams will help keep the bulk of it from totally decimating the area the botanists and horticulturalists have reserved for planting.

We've got fertilizers that are meant to make the soil workable and seeds for fruits, vegetables and legumes that are supposed to be robust and capable of withstanding the harsh climate.

Marlene has even insisted on planting cactuses — both as a natural barrier to keep creatures out of the fields, and because cacti evidently can be used as everything from anti-inflammatories to combs.

But!

Before we can do any of that, we need to finish putting up the barrier.

Ero was panicked that we would take too long to get the barrier sections up, would be spotted by a scout from a rival tribe, and that they'd lead an angry horde back to us. That, in a moment, everything would be lost.

Correction. Ero appeared calm, but I could sense his panic. He tends to look at me a lot when he's worried. I don't know if he realizes he's even doing it. It's impossible for me to ignore.

"Pull!"

My heels dig into the ground. Sweat drips down my back. The sun glints off of the steel surface of the wall as bright as a torch in the dark. It blinds me and I remember that disguising the steel is the next step. My hands slip on the rope and blood smears from my palm onto its rough surface. I don't let go — at least, I wouldn't have, had the Pikosa boy behind me not grabbed me by the shoulder and pushed me.

I hit the dirt hard and sand puffs up around my butt. I cough and look up, squinting against the sunlight and very, very eager to get the bio-netting stretched across the roof of our city to block some of the harshest rays out.

The Pikosa warrior-in-training stares down at me with a sneer. "Tanishi are weak. You are useless here." He kicks me in the thigh — not hard, but enough to let me know just how he feels about my being here in case his words left any doubt.

The Omoro in front of me steps toward the Pikosa and holds up one hand. "No pain Halima," he says in severely broken English.

The Pikosa boy flushes and squares his shoulders. Though he likely can't understand the Omoro, his intent is clear and I don't want to start a fight. Already, there have been too many scuffles to count. Ero has dealt with perpetrators severely in ways I haven't approved of, but his methods have been — dare I say, effective? Because the fights have been getting less.

"No fighting," I say, trying to stand again, but the Pikosa boy shoves me down.

Another Pikosa woman rushes over from another line and grabs the boy by the back of the neck. She throws him forcefully away from me and whirls around on me. She thrusts her finger in my nose. "Do not tell Ero about this."

I wasn't planning on it, but I don't want her to think she can threaten me or any other Tanishi or Omoro freely so, even from my position so far below her, I set my own shoulders and narrow my eyes.

"If you promise me that you will control your boy, then I won't."

"Boy?" For any Pikosa warrior, even one in training, it's a great insult. "I birthed no boys, only warriors."

She's terrifying, this warrior woman, but I swallow my nerves and grunt out, "Warriors follow orders and your Nigusi ordered you not to fight the Tanishi. So, if he is not capable of following orders, then your son is a boy. Not a warrior."

The woman gapes at me and, as I try not to gag on the smell of her clearly unbrushed teeth, I also let the

Omoro help me to my feet. Standing, I cross my arms over my chest and try to mirror the way Ero stares people down. I think it'd be more effective if I were a million feet tall, too.

This staring contest lasts for some time. Long enough for Leanna to shout at me from above and ask me if I'm okay. I don't reply though. I don't break this Pikosa warrior's gaze. I hold and I'm honestly a little surprised when she grunts and steps away first. She moves back and we're both startled out of our skins when she turns and we see Ero feet behind her with his arms folded across his chest. The Pikosa boy is on his knees beside him looking petrified.

"Is everything alright here?" Ero says in Pikosa.

He's talking to me, but my gaze is on the woman. She swallows hard and is speaking to me when she answers, "Yes. We had a misunderstanding."

"Yes," I agree slowly, trying to communicate just what will happen to her if her progeny decides to attack any other Tanishi through my gaze alone. I don't know if it's working or if I'm just squinting at her like a lunatic. "A *misunderstanding*. But we have an understanding now."

"Good. Rita, you may go and take your *boy* with you."

Rita staggers at the use of the word, but ambles off regardless. I want to exhale relief, but suddenly Ero's surrounding me. "That was the sexiest thing I've ever seen."

I grin against my better judgement. "Getting pushed onto the ground was sexy?"

And then his brows furrow. "Verik touched you?"

"Oh um, no." I apparently misjudged how much of our interaction he saw. "I misspoke."

"Halima…" He snarls and lifts up, but I grab him by the leather belt across his waist and draw his attention back to me. I touch his cheek and smile up at him, loving the way his pupils dilate.

"Why am I sexy, Ero? I want to know."

"Because you savaged a Pikosa warrior with nothing more than your tongue."

"Only because I have your sword arm at my back." I tug on his belt for added meaning.

"And you always will," he snarls, eyes blazing suddenly. His arms both simultaneously jerk, "Let me touch you, Halima."

"It hasn't been thirty-one days."

"I don't fucking care." I catch his wrists when he reaches for me and I get the sense I'm about to lose this fight when a voice calls out to us.

"Uhh lovebirds?" Ero's defiant fist escapes my hold. He snags a lock of my hair, but I've already turned toward the sound of Chayana's loud voice crashing through the bubble Ero and I have built out of nothing but ourselves. "We could use some help here." She waves at me from her position at the front of the line on the rope I'm also holding. Sweat is pouring down her face, like it's pouring down mine.

"On it!" I brush Ero's hand aside and grab the rope the Omoro male hands out to me.

"Needing help," he says in English, "with the… what is this?"

He gives the rope a shake and I open my mouth, but Ero's deep voice booms above me, "Rope. This is rope." And then I'm flying.

Hands close over mine and pull and I know it isn't possible that he lifts the huge fifty foot high steel wall all by himself, but that's what it feels like.

He steps in and takes my position, maneuvering his body swiftly and in a way that makes it hard for me to understand what happened. One second I was there pulling on the ropes at Leanna's command, the next I'm being boxed out, pressed away from the rope and a giant four times my size is pulling in my place.

"Pull! We're almost there! We're so close. It's the last piece and then the wall is...it's up!" I lift my hand to shield my eyes from the sun only to realize — I don't have to when a harsh shadow falls over me now that the wall has risen. "Goddamn good work, soldiers! The wall is up! Engineers, bat it down! Chayana, you, too!"

"Oh shit. That's me!" Chayana rushes away from the rope. She trips...over nothing...and she'd have gone sprawling if I hadn't gasped.

The sound pulls Ero around in time to catch Chayana's arm as she sails forward. He rights her and she gives him a pout and then a laugh and then waves like a goon and half-skips, half-stumbles off.

"That girl is a clutz," I mumble.

"What is clous?" Ero says in English.

It's still a shock to hear it. His voice is so rich and his accent is something totally foreign. Alien, even. I look up into his eyes and my skin sizzles and it has nothing to do with the sun. *Maybe, just maybe, thirty-one days is too long...*

"What's wrong with you?"

I bark out a laugh and shake my head, turning to face him as the Omoro waves goodbye and heads to his next assignment. The other helpers scatter around us, giving us a wide berth as they walk.

"Nothing's wrong with me, habibi," I say in Pikosa with some Arabic added in. It's been happening more and more often lately as distant memories of my parents fade in and out along with tastes of pistachio and sesame. I'm not the only one, either. Those of us with the most head injuries seem to be remembering more. Some have even recovered *all* of their memories. *Like Haddock...*

"Clutz is someone like Chayana. Who falls all the time."

He snorts. "I'm glad you're not this. Otherwise, I'd have to build the entire city out of pillows."

I slap his stomach and he grins. Thirty-one days is way, way too long. I'm about to tell him so when he says, "Are you happy with your city as it stands now, Halima?"

"It's transcendent, Ero. Bigger and better than I thought it would be."

I look around as the people holding onto the ropes disperse. The huge walls fit into grooves we dug into the sand in the days leading up to this one, but several strong Pikosa warriors have to hold the wall steady from both the inside *and* the outside while six Omoro hold the huge tubs of concrete and three Tanishi use these sort of strange metal spoons to carefully lay the concrete in.

"Don't you think so? I mean look at it!" I clap and turn, well aware that I'm in the way. "Do you think we can celebrate here tonight, habibi? Have another party? After the last one, there were so many good feelings between the tribes.

"I know we're low on wine, but did you hear from Jia that she and Marlene were able to make wine from the pink flowers that grow in the south cave system? But I still feel like there's so much tension between the groups. Maybe celebrating and relaxing would be…"

My voice trails off as I register the look on Ero's face. His eyebrows are drawn together, his arms are crossed, his lips slightly parted. He looks…not worried…but interested. Maybe *too* interested.

"What did I say?" I start to laugh as I realize I've been speaking English this entire time. "Am I going too fast?" I say in Pikosa.

He shakes his head, then nods, then takes a step closer. He touches my arm, just to bring me closer, or maybe not. A clearing has formed around us. Maybe he's touching me just to break the rules.

"Ero, it hasn't been…"

"What is *huh-bee-bee?*"

Khara. *Habibi. I called him habibi.* I've called him *habibi* many, many times. I immediately try to swallow my tongue back down my throat. No. Why did I call him that? The word just slipped out. "I mean…"

"No. What does it mean? It not English. It *is* not English."

"No, it's…it's not important. I didn't mean to say it." I'm not sure if that's true, but he's still being punished, isn't he? He's still a violent warlord, isn't he? Ending his punishment and letting him touch me when we fuck seems like one thing, but confessing to *loving* him seems like a step far too far. Do I though? Do I love him? Can you love someone and hate them at the same time?

"It is Arabic," he says.

Shock. "How...how do you know?"

He stares at me with his same critical, hard expression, only this time there's a wicked gleam in his beautiful eyes. "What is *hub-bee-bee?*" His pronunciation might have made me flounder in any other moment. But not this one. Right now I want him quiet.

I cross my arms over my chest and insist, "Nothing."

"Is it bad?"

"No," I blurt, cringing at the truth.

"Then what is it?"

"I'm not telling you." I chew on my bottom lip *hard* and beg him with my eyes.

Suddenly, he clicks his tongue against the backs of his teeth and he straightens. He's reading my face again, trying to suss out what he can't understand in my language and what I won't tell him in his and he seems to have come to a decision.

"Arabic. Who Tanishi talks Arabic?"

I know what he's asking me instantly and the answer is *yes, there are other Tanishi who speak Arabic.* An Israeli born in London and a Palestinian born in Israel both do, but I shake my head. "No."

"Don't lie," he repeats, fingers twitching toward his belt.

Momentary guilt flares and I shake my head. "Sorry. I didn't mean to."

He's still...sensitive about my betrayal. It's the only sensitive thing about him. That, and his need for me to end the punishment. But it's the only thing I've got left to keep distance between us and if I admit to this now, it'll be over. All of it. Every ounce of control I've managed to gather will be stripped away. *Because I called him habibi because I meant it. Because in Arabic, habibi means beloved.*

He bows his head forward, as if to accept my apology. He repeats, "Who Tanishi Arabic?"

"Ero…"

"Halima…habibi…"

"No, Ero. I said no. Now, stop it." He bites his front teeth together, looking pissed, but I'm not feeling too cheery myself. "I asked you for a little bit of space, and you keep pushing it. You keep touching me in the night…"

"You touch me, too, *habibi*," he says, purely out to torture me now.

Frustrated at my lack of control I push his chest. "You can find out yourself. Maybe try actually talking to a *Tanishi* for once or learning something about us," I say, knowing it's unfair as I do.

He narrows his gaze and his hand at his side curls into a fist. "Talk to *you*. I learn you."

Oh fuck him. My heart swells, my body aches. Because the truth of it is that I want to be touched by him, too. I lick my lips. He looks instantly at my mouth. "Halima, it's been more than twenty days," he says in Pikosa. And then in English, "I miss you."

I freeze, heart clenching up, arousal pooling low. "I'm afraid."

"What afraid? Say in Pikosa."

I sigh and stare down at our feet. He made a new pair of shoes for me. These fit better. I watched him cut the leather down and stitch it himself, just like he stitched together the shirt that Haddock tore.

"I'm afraid of giving this to you." I massage the space over my heart where I can still feel his thick fingers thump.

Ero stalks towards me, sucking in a breath, prepared for a battle I know I've already lost. I just don't want him to know it.

"Halima, have I hurt anyone?" he says, switching tongues to speak in his native one.

"No, but that isn't what I'm..."

He doesn't let me finish, but says, "There is no but. I told you I wouldn't hurt anyone else, not unless absolutely necessary, and I haven't. Beyond that, I cannot unwind time. I am not a new man. I am still the one who gave you these scars."

I reach for my forearm and rub my thumb across the lines that spell a word not seen in this Pikosa tribe for generations. *Anidi laye.* My thoughts flick back to that very first moment when his gaze met mine and I knelt on the stone floor looking up at him and thinking he was... not a monster, but something worse — something undeserving of affection — because even monsters can be loved.

He must read something in my expression because he hardens, closing himself off. His vulnerability evaporates like a droplet of water on a hot stone. "I hurt you. I wish I hadn't. I wish I could take the blade to my own skin to show you the depth of that. But I cannot take away the marks or the memories."

He reaches forward and touches my cheek, so very, very softly. "If it is too much for you to overcome, then tell me, Halima. Because what I feel here is nothing I have ever felt." He massages the space over his heart and, once again, we're caught in mirrored gestures and both are gestures of love.

"I don't know this feeling. Maybe it is something you Tanishi feel all of the time, but I am weak in this. I am weak in many things when it comes to you. I cannot be patient. I told you once, I won't lose this, but I realize now that I don't want to fight forever for it, either.

"I need to know if you will open for me or if I should stop bothering you. Because I can't be close to you anymore and not touch you. For thirty-one days, maybe, but not for one day more."

He glances over my shoulder and retreats. "Tell me your answer tonight at the *party*. You can tell your people and the others that we will celebrate tonight as we never have before — under the stars."

He retreats from me while my lips continue to flounder. I can't believe it, but in my quest for self-preservation, I might just break a monster's heart.

"You okay?"

I look over my shoulder and see Jia standing just a few feet behind me, her face all scrunched. I wonder how long she's been there, what she heard, what she thinks I should do about it.

"I…" I shake my head and then when she takes a step closer to me, her fresh Pikosa linens billowing softly in the wind. Her skin is so much tanner than it was when we started. She looks healthy again. "I'm not sure."

"You want to talk about it?"

"Not sure what I would say."

"Do you like him?"

"No. But I think I love him." I breathe and I smile at her a little wistfully. It feels good to breathe. It feels good to say it. "I'd tell him myself if I weren't such a coward."

She looks appropriately shocked and stutters out about half a dozen sentences before she settles on, "You...I..."

I laugh. "Wow. Seeing you speechless was almost worth admitting it out loud. Don't tell anyone though, okay? I...I know how the other Tanishi judge me for this."

"Hey..." She steps up close to me and does something no one has done to me in a very long time. She hugs me. Her hair smells like the pink flowers she makes wine out of. I breathe in all the good and glorious feelings.

"No one that minds matters, and no one that matters will mind."

I belt out a wet laugh and shake my head as I peel away from her. "That's cute."

"I thought so when I remembered it."

"You...got your memories back?"

She tilts her head and something changes in her expression. Her eyes crinkle at the corners, but the smile has left her eyes. "Yeah. I did."

"All of them?"

"All. I remember everything. I wish I didn't."

"Haddock said the same thing. What is it, Jia?"

I touch her shoulder but she just exhales in a rush and rubs her bangs roughly. "I just remembered that desperation has driven people to do all kinds of terrible things." She shows me her arm, where she also wears a brand. Hers is much smaller than mine, but it's still there, a visible memory of the man that Ero was and still is.

She takes my wrist and tilts her scarred arm to the light so that it shines beside hers. I wonder what, in ancient Pikosa, it might read. If anything.

"But I know that those people aren't terrible themselves." She smiles a little more fully then and smoothes her hand over my arm. "Haneul-i muneojyeodo sos-anal gumeong-i issda. I remember that, too."

It takes me a moment — my Korean is lagging and badly out of practice and I worry that, one day, it will fade — but when I find the words, I smile thoughtfully at her. "Even when the sky falls, there is still a hole?"

"A hole to crawl out of, a way to escape, yeah. It's a Korean proverb and one I've been thinking about a lot. I mean, the parallelisms are too unmistakable."

"You mean literally crawling up out of the ground like worms? Something I really hope we don't ever do again."

"Chayana, Halima! Come here," Leanna shouts from the top of the supported wall just beside the one that was just erected. "I want to show these Danien how the lodestone machine works in the mines. Can you help me explain?"

"Just a minute!" I shout.

Jia rolls her eyes at me and offers me the heavy coiled rope on her shoulder. I sag under the weight of the rope and Jia laughs. They're thick ropes meant to help us scale the inner wall so we can reach the platforms at the top.

"Alright, you better go. I should go, too. I'm supposed to be helping a group of Omoro till a section of shade-covered soil." She shakes her head and lifts her hand to shield her eyes. "And no, I did not mean crawling out of the ground like worms."

She laughs. "I meant the Sucere Chamber. The world ended before. The sky fell, in a literal sense, after the climate apocalypse led to wars that unmade our civilizations. But we had the Sucere Chamber, those creepy pods, and we climbed out. It's even crazier to me that after all that, we haven't really changed."

"What do you mean?"

"I mean we were once savages and we stayed that way. But…" She takes my burned arm again and grips it fiercely and just as fiercely holds my gaze. "There are holes through which we can escape. Holes shaped like love and if you love your savage, then step up to the edge of that hole and jump. Don't look back for anything."

I don't know why, but her words make me want to cry.

"Halima!" Leanna shouts again.

I nod quickly and blink just as quickly. Thickly, I say, "I better go."

"Go. I have an escort, anyway." She blinks and turns and I'm shocked out of my senses by the male walking up to us with narrowed eyes and hostility rolling off of him.

"Wyden," I say, keeping my voice pitched strong, refusing to be intimidated, but Jia just smiles and Wyden's furiously bunched brow spreads and his eyes flare and his jaw works and he swallows again and again. He looks like he's sweating. Is he sweating at the sight of her smile?

"Hello, Wyden," Jia says in English.

He focuses on her face and swallows hard. "Jia." He knows her name. Holy shit. They know each other! They like each other! I gape, heart beating hard and fast, belly full of riotous butterflies all eager for an escape I no longer long for.

"Are you feeling better?" She gestures to his ribs.

Ero broke several of them and Wyden's been slow to heal. The shock of this interaction is enough for my rope to slide off of my shoulders.

Wyden lunges forward to catch it, but falls short. The motion, however, brings him right up against Jia's side. It also makes me jump. I'm still scared of Wyden.

"Wyden, you shouldn't lift that," she mutters in English, trying to take the rope from him as he lifts it from the ground with a pained grunt. He sidesteps her and tries to pass it to me.

"You are insufferable," she huffs.

They fight hilariously, locked in an awkward square dance that neither of them seems to want to participate in. But what shocks me most is that even though Wyden is scowling, Jia's still smiling.

"Wyden, no! You're not well."

"Well. Not sick," he says in heavily accented English and I'm shocked all over again. He's the *last* Pikosa I expected to want to learn English.

Winning the war, Jia straightens up with the rope on her shoulder. She gestures between Wyden and I and makes what has to be the world's most tense introduction before handing the rope back to me. I jump underneath his inspection.

"Ero say party." He glances swiftly to Jia and swallows. "You, me go? Date?"

Jia beams. She even goes so far as to laugh. "Who taught you about dating?"

Wyden even grins. He tries not to, but there's no mistaking the upturned right edge of his mouth. This... this isn't Wyden. This isn't the same man who tried to dethrone Ero and who hates me.

I can't help it. I laugh. "When did this happen?"

She looks at me and smiles and this smile is a real smile and it makes me wonder — could Wyden be Jia's hole in the sky? Has she already fallen through?

"After we tried to escape, I went with the team to help the healers. Wyden was still there, healing, and since Ero deemed him last priority, he got stuck with me and a couple of Danien and a young Pikosa healer-in-training. We managed to patch him up alright though, and I helped him through some of his anger. I'd say we're even friends."

She smiles at him and he must know that last word because he perks up and his cheeks darken. "Friends. Wyden, Jia friends. You and me, dating?"

It's Jia's turn to blush. "Yes, Wyden. Dating."

He beams and my jaw drops.

"Halima!" Leanna shouts.

"Oh khara...um..."

"We'll see you later at the party, Halima." *We. She said we.*

"See you, then. Um...of course!" I blurt, struggling to grab my rope. Completely tangling myself in it, actually.

I trip over a loose end, stumble and fall and Wyden — *Wyden* — catches my arm. He rights me quickly and takes a few steps back, keeping his hands up like he'll catch me if I fall again but not wanting to do more than that.

His gaze drops to mine and I just stand there looking up at him, waiting for…something…but he just takes another step back. "I…" He shakes his head and switches into Pikosa to say, "I know that I haven't viewed your tribe as anything beyond a slave tribe, but your magic, your knowledge, your seeds… You believe they will grow, that we don't need to fear the sun, that we can live even more openly than the other surface tribes. You believe the seeds will grow.

"I didn't see how it could be important, but I'm beginning to see now the importance of this belief." His gaze flashes to Jia and he quickly looks back down at his feet. He holds onto his side, which is still covered in thick bandages.

I can't believe it. I feel like I'm in a dream. My voice cracks when I whisper a word in English. "Hope. In our English language, we call it hope."

"Hope," he repeats.

"Halima! Come now!" Leanna again.

"Here," Jia says, "I'll help Halima get these ropes over to the wall then you'll help me till the soil with the Omoro."

He scrunches up his face and I translate what she said. He nods, his forehead relaxing as he blinks large, hooded eyes at her. "Yes. Because I and you dating."

She laughs and I feel memories pull themselves out through my ears, so easily discarded. Her laughter unwinds time. It almost feels like we're starting over.

Again.

She helps me carry her rope to the base of the wall, Wyden acting as her shadow. They leave and Donovan and two Omoro called Na and Toosh, fix one end of the rope to a pulley and drag it up the smooth, metallic edge of one wall for me.

"Alright, up you go, soldier," Donovan says when the folks at the top have it securely mounted. I look at his face, his easy smile, his stupid smug expression as he glances between me and the rope and back again. "What are you waiting for?"

I balk, "Are you for real? You think this little rope scares me? Watch how it's done."

The Omoro start to chuckle. Na approaches me and puts her foot on the rope at its base to hold it down. "Let's see," she says first in Omoro before repeating, "We see," in English. *Incredible.*

I start up the rope, thinking about how much easier this is than it was trying to go up the whip with Frey when we were running away from Ero, sure that he would kill us and that we'd never, ever get to this point.

I'm about halfway up when a voice calls my name from above. "Halima, how's it hangin?"

I tilt my head back, back, back until I see Leanna's face and red hair glowing vibrantly above me. I smile when she waves with her short arm. *Incredible, her resilience.*

"Never better," I shout back.

"Hurry up. We need you up here. Chayana's already up here and we're not making any progress getting through to these Omoro."

Her face moves in and out of shadow, her hair swinging wildly as she peers at me over the raised edge of the wall. There's something about the angle. The way the sun is shining down on me, blinding me, looking like a fat disc in the sky, that makes me think of Jia and what she just told me.

Even when the sky falls down, there are still holes to crawl out of. The sun looks like one of those holes now and Leanna's face looks like it's a part of it, or blocking it. Haddock's face appears beside hers and I blink and Haddock disappears...it's not Haddock at all, but another soldier.

I shake my head, confused by the strange sense of déjà vu that hits my belly, making me think of the memories Jia just pulled out from beneath my feet and before that, all the memories that climbing through that hole and out of those tanks cost us.

But some of them are coming back. Kenya was the first. Haddock the second and now Jia, the third. *Kenya, where are you now? Are you still seeing the same sun?* I hope for her sake, that she's found food and, more importantly, water. I wish I could light a beacon and call her back home.

Home.

"All language is a longing for home," I whisper out loud. My father told me that.

"Halima! Yalla, yalla! Get your ass up here, soldier," Leanna yells again and I'm distracted by the Arabic words coming out of her mouth. Strange, to hear them here from her.

I lift another hand over the other, the rope swinging wildly beneath me. I look back over my shoulder as noises rage back in and movement below grabs my attention. Ero is on the surface, shouting at warriors on the ground, shouting for Leanna.

"Orushar spotted! Defense formation three," he shouts in English, as if he's been practicing even in the minutes we've been separated, before he switches to Pikosa. "Orushar are on the horizon! They come with sand cats! Halima, to me! Where is Halima?"

"Halima," Leanna shouts down at me. "Yalla, Halima. We need you!"

"Halima, I need you!"

Memories blitz me.

"Halima, they need you."

"No!"

Hands reaching, reaching, reaching. I blink up and see my mother's hand, reaching down for me, only the hand doesn't belong to my mother, it belongs to Leanna. "Halima?"

"Halima, don't be afraid."

"No!" I stretch my arm up and reach, reach, reach...

Reach.

"Halima!"

"Halima!" Two voices, one male and one female, call my name as I fall. I fall because I've completely let go of the rope as I try to reach for the owners of the voices, speaking to me in Arabic, pronouncing my name as it's supposed to be pronounced. Deep hah-long E-short ta'marbouta.

"Halima, it's alright. They need you," they tell me and they speak in a language I know better than anything — no, a language that knows me better than anything. I speak the language that colors my soul in completely. Everything else is just a crude synthetic copy.

"No, I don't want to go, I want to stay with you," I tell them.

"You can't stay with us." My father blinks at me, his eyes crinkling at the corners. They're brown, those eyes, like mine.

My mother kneels beside him clutching a string of beads…prayer beads. She kneels on a dark green carpet because she's praying, she's Muslim, and she worships Allah. But my father, he doesn't worship. He's an atheist. He knows about the Sucere Chamber. He was the one who submitted my name knowing that the price he'd pay would be this.

What is the price?

Wind whistles past my ears. It seems to last forever as I blink up at the sun and the long fingers reaching, reaching…

My father takes my shoulder in one hand. He gathers my mother to his side with his other. "You are our daughter. We will not lose you to this world, but send you forward to rebuild the next."

"I want to stay here with you. I want to stay in this world. With you." I'm crying. I can feel tears tracking down my cheeks.

"This world is gone. There is nothing left. This is why we agreed to this."

I take my mother's hand in one of mine, my father's hand in the other and I hold them fiercely, willing what's about to happen, not to happen. I glance up, seeing my parents are no use and shout at the other people crowding the space in our apartment in Cairo.

"Please!"

Leanna's gaze meets mine from beneath the hood of a low camo helmet. She's in uniform, just like the other half dozen people crowding my parent's apartment — everyone except Haddock.

He hangs back up until Leanna lifts her hand, and then he strides forward purposefully, moving to my father's side.

I scream, "No! Stay away!" I lurch up onto my feet and call Haddock every foul name I can think of in every language

I know, but Leanna catches me around the waist and throws me back hard. I land against a small end table.

My father surges up onto his feet while my mother flutters. "Be calm, habibty, you will not be broken by this."

"But you will!" I scream.

I scream and I scream and I reach for her as hands hold me back and Leanna gives the order to Haddock to inject my parents.

My father nods calmly as Haddock takes his needle to the back of my father's neck, but it's my mother who, wavering there on her knees, says, "Remember, habibty, there are a thousand ways to kneel. There are also a thousand ways to go home again. Wahashteeny, habibty." I miss you. "Behibek." I love you.

I'm reaching, reaching, reaching...and I catch her hand, but only briefly.

Her clammy palm slips free of my sweaty one and she falls to the side, landing on top of my father's body. He dies with peace on his face. He dies with me screaming as Haddock stares down at them numbly and Leanna orders their bodies disposed of and I'm carried out of the apartment building by two soldiers wearing bulky black suits. They take me outside into a huge armored truck.

Explosions light up the sky and bullets ricochet off of the outside of our transporter, but it doesn't matter to me that the sky is falling and that my parents have shown me the hole that I would crawl out of four thousand years later and that would bring me into the Pikosa universe.

That would bring me to Ero. The man I hate and love most.

My eyes flare open and I see the sky.

I imagine for a moment that the sky is a two dimensional sheet. I've climbed up through a hole in its flat surface and fallen through that hole onto another plane. But, looking back up, the hole has disappeared above me.

A weight slams against my back. No. I slam against something. Darkness consumes my mind and consumes my thoughts.

"Halima!"

"No!"

"Nogora..."

"Havawe!"

"Khara!" Ha. I taught him that one.

The curse belongs to a voice that's shouting wretchedly, the sound getting louder and louder and penetrating the darkness in ways the light no longer does.

"Halima!" I blink. See his face. He reaches down. I reach up.

I palm his cheek with my hand, lean up and kiss him tenderly...no, I don't. I imagine doing all of these things, but I can't move as air enters my lungs with all the subtlety of a lightning strike.

I arch and heave. "Aughhahww." The sound that comes out of me is inhuman.

Ero holds me down, an expression breaking out over his face that I can't even begin to categorize. Gone is the stoic male who told me he didn't want to change, that he didn't want to wait.

Present is the vulnerable male who fists the blankets or keeps his hands planted firmly on the chair or the rim of the pool or whatever object is beneath him as he lets me use him for my purposes.

Savage, that's how I treat him. That's how he lets me treat him because he wants something else. He doesn't know it yet, but he wants to keep me and not as a captive. He wants to be my family.

"Haddock!" Ero roars. "Brin, fetch me the Tanishi healer."

Pain shifts through the back of my head through my neck down my sides. I can't move, but I know I'm fine. Tears swim, blurring my vision. I close my eyes, but I still smile.

A moment later, hands are pushing up on my eyelids, trying to see into me to assess what I already know to be true. This time, I see a face, paler than Ero's with dark hair splintered through with red strokes.

"Halima, can you hear me?" Haddock says. His cheeks are gaunt. His bloodshot eyes are parked in dark docks. He looks like a ghost and I understand why. I understand what changed when he got back his memories.

"I saw," I whisper. I meet his gaze. I watch it change.

Haddock jerks slightly, but Ero sees. He kneels on my other side and snaps his hand across my body to grab Haddock's shoulder. "What is it? Is she alright?" He shouts in Pikosa.

Haddock's whitewashed face betrays nothing, but he's saved the grace of having to answer when an Omoro voice calls Ero's name. "Ero!"

"Kawashari?" He shouts back, turning his head to the side, but keeping his eyes on me while I take my next wheezing breath.

"Ellar speak Wickar!" The Omoro male shouts back in badly broken English.

"Khara," he spits and it brings a smile to my mouth.

While my slow, thundering heart begins to regulate its tempo and feeling returns to the heels of my feet first, and then the backs of my palms, I recover enough to be able to say, "Ero."

His whole body is honed on me. Looming as large as he does, Haddock looks like a doll beside him and nothing seems so important now. Not Wickar scouts. Not the fear that kept me from telling him a truth Jia doesn't seem half so terrified to tell a man half as good as Ero.

"Halima. Speak to me, Tanishi."

"I love you."

Somehow, my pronouncement makes his expression even more grim. He pounds his fist into the sand near my shoulder and I jolt as feeling drifts up from my feet to my calves, from my arms to my torso. "You aren't dying. *You will not die!*"

"I'm fine," I say, chuckling as I dare to move.

Haddock is the one who tells me to stop. "Let me check you over first…"

Ero pushes him off of his feet and Haddock tips to the side. Ero pounds one fist onto either side of my head and looks at me upside down. He looks different from this angle, kind of funny, and all mine.

"You will not leave me."

"No, I won't." I shift again and breathe a little easier. "And I mean it, Ero. I love you. The punishment can end."

"Halima, are you…" Ero grabs his heart and rubs the space over his sternum ferociously. "Please," he whispers, but I know he's not talking to me. He's talking to the gods who no longer exist.

"Ero!" A new voice calls for him from much closer. This one, clearly Ellar's. "Ero, Wickar scouts are on the horizon and fast approaching!"

His back teeth grind together. He looks down at me. "I'm staying with..."

"No, no, no. Don't be silly. Ero, go," I tell him. I move my arms and legs and tilt my head to the left and to the right, just to show him that I'm still alive, still breathing.

His eyes widen at that. He slides his hand tentatively behind my neck. He doesn't pull up, doesn't squeeze, just holds it there. "You are good?" He says in English. "Truly?"

I laugh. "Habibi means beloved," I tell him in English and, when his face scrunches up, I sigh in Pikosa, "You can touch me whenever you want. However you like. I'm yours, Ero. I mean it. I love you. I hate you, but I love you even more."

He blinks. He just blinks. He blinks and blinks and his hand twitches and so does a muscle in his cheek. "Do not...do not lie to me."

"I'm not." I grab his hand and bring it to my neck where I know he likes to hold me and where I know I like to be touched by him.

He doesn't hesitate. He crushes his lips to mine and as his heat brands my mouth and a delirious surge of *life* zaps me, I remember how to use my arms. I lift my hands first as I inhale his breath and I slide my fingers through his hair. He shudders above me, like a storm cloud, like he does every time.

My back arches up and my muscles shake. Dizziness swims in the front of my thoughts as I push up from the ground and try to wrap myself around him.

"Easy, Halima. You might be concussed. Ero," he says, switching to Pikosa. "Halima pain."

The single word is enough to send Ero throttling back. He pushes himself so far off of me that it feels like he's ripped the skin on the front half of my body clean off. He grabs onto his chest and abdomen as he edges back on his knees.

Slowly, wildly, he grins at me. "We call this Xiveri in Pikosa, this thing you call *love* in Tanishi."

"Xiveri," I say, trying the word out on my tongue. "Well, it's true."

His brow wrinkles. "Because you fell?"

"Because of what I saw when I fell, yes." My gaze switches to Haddock then and Ero's expression hardens.

"Tell me."

"Later," I offer. Ellar's appeared in my peripheries alongside Lopina, but I don't need memories of ghosts keeping Ero here when he could be helping keep my parents' memory alive by helping keep me alive. To die now after all they've sacrificed would be to disgrace them. "Go, Ero. Protect our tribe. Protect me."

He drags his gaze, what looks like painfully, to Haddock and says, "She will live?"

Haddock nods, distracted.

Ero narrows his gaze and even though I know he knows something is wrong, he still surges forward and plants a demanding kiss on my lips.

Ripping back, he speaks to Haddock in his thick accent, "Save Halima."

"With my life," Haddock offers and I repeat it in Pikosa.

Ero puffs out a breath and turns fully to face Ellar and, without looking back at me, joins the trio and takes off at a run so quick it surprises me. The moment he disappears into a tunnel leading into the ground, Haddock whirls around.

I smile sadly, about to offer him words of forgiveness that he probably doesn't deserve, but before I can say anything, Haddock grabs me by the shoulders.

"Haddock!" I can hear Leanna shout above me as Haddock claps a hand over my mouth.

The sands around us are a chaos with people running every direction, but I catch the gaze of two Pikosa — one of which is the woman with the son who pushed me. I wave at her wildly as Haddock claps his hand over my mouth, wraps a heavy arm around my waist, and starts to carry me away, but the Pikosa woman just smiles impishly and looks away.

Progress, not perfection, is where we are.

"Haddock, stop!" Leanna shouts.

But Haddock ignores the orders of his general. He drags me to a narrow, rarely used entrance to the mines and though I wasn't panicking before, I start to panic now. Ero told me not to use this entrance, and I don't know why, but I trust him.

I writhe against Haddock's grip, but he's all healed now and even though he looks thin and waif-like, he's wraithlike in his determination.

"Haddock! Put Halima down *now!* Haddock, what are you doing?"

But Haddock doesn't bother to give Leanna an answer. He slides down into the darkness, scree falling with us as we hit the rocky ground below. Powdery sand chokes my lungs as I struggle to breathe past his metallic-tasting fingers.

"We're almost there," he says into my ear, releasing his grip on my face. I lurch back towards the entrance of the tunnel, but Haddock has his hands on the back of my tunic and drags me with him further into the dark.

I wriggle and writhe but his fingers pinch into my sides with enough force to leave bruises. *I'm not the soldier. I'm the interpreter. I'm going to have to reason with him.* "Haddock, Ero told me not to use this tunnel. We shouldn't be in here." He jumps down onto a rocky ledge and the tunnel bisecting this one widens. He heads right. "Haddock!"

He's jogging, breath heavy, when the tunnel splits. A narrow passage, bright with light from several cracks in the rock above us, leads up while a much dimmer passage leads down.

"Haddock, if you kill me, Ero will torture you..." I slam my heels into the ground, refusing to allow him to take me to the crocs. "After what you did to my family, you can't kill me! You owe me at least that much!"

"You think I'm trying to kill you?"

"What else would I think?"

I twist to look back at him as he loosens his hold on my shirt, but before he can reply, he pitches forward into the darker tunnel, tumbling head over foot with me in his grip. I take the brunt of it when we fall and my already tender skull clacks against rocks. I catch myself on my hands and *I can hear the sound of explosions blazing in the distance and behind me, a woman screaming, "Halima!"*

"Halima!" I roll onto my back and for a moment, I'm back at the beach. I can hear splashing and swishing waters, even though I can't see them. Yellow and purple lights clear from my gaze as I push myself up into a seat.

Leanna is standing in the cave tunnel, her arms raised toward Haddock, who kneels between us. She makes a move with her hand and glances briefly at me and in that small motion I know she wants me to try to get to her. I don't need to be told twice, but when I try to get around Haddock, I miscalculate his reach because he lunges out, grabs my ankle, and I go down on top of him.

Stunned as I am, I don't roll out of the way in time to avoid getting grabbed. Confused as I am, I fight when I shouldn't because the moment I jerk, I feel a prick of pain just below my right jaw and hot liquid rolls down to wet the collar of my shirt the moment after that.

"Haddock."

Leanna is standing in front of us, her palm facing up. The space where she ordinarily would have a rifle slung around her neck is empty and, when her short right arm jerks towards it, she bites her teeth together as if only now recognizing that it won't help her because it isn't there. Neither the gun, nor the arm she'd need to lift it.

"Haddock, easy."

"I can't. She knows. She got them back."

Leanna's eyes flash to me. They're brown and look dazzling when a burst of light strikes the side of her face as she steps forward. Freckles cover almost every inch of her skin, making her look like she's almost the same brown color I am, but spots of pale white peek through, especially on her arms and chest. She tucks her hair behind her ear and the gesture makes her look younger than she has a right to.

"Is it true? You got your memories back?"

I should lie here, I know I should. No. *No.* "Yes."

"Fuck." A muscle under her right eye ticks.

Haddock laughs wildly. "Fuck? That's all you have to say to her after you and I killed her family? You're *fucked*. What even are you? Do you even have a heart? Do you even care?"

"Haddock, the families agreed to the terms of the Sucere Project. And you know as well as I do that the orders came directly from our superior officers — from the Architect of the Sucere Chamber himself. No one could have any knowledge of the Chamber and families were too big a risk.

"We couldn't have them reconsidering their agreement and trying to recover their loved ones. And we couldn't allow anyone to reveal anything about who was selected. Once information got out, it would incite others to try to find the Chamber in the delusion that they could board and somehow live — or worse, come for the families in misguided revenge. You know how desperate and lethal people got at the end..."

"Bullshit!" He points his knife at Leanna while I sit in his lap in cold sweat, wondering if this is it — my moment to run, but too scared to grasp it. "You *swore* to me that my memory wouldn't come back. That I wouldn't remember what you *ordered* me to do to Halima's family, to Kenya's family, to my own fucking family!" Oh khara.

"Haddock," I whisper while Leanna continues to speak. He's got spit on his lips and tears in his eyes. He doesn't look away from Leanna, but I watch the way he winces when he hears me. "Who did you kill?"

"My wife," he heaves. "She was a scientist but her application was rejected. They already had a geneticist," he barks out a cold, hacking laugh. "They needed a medic and she wanted me to join the project for us both. I was the one who stabbed that needle into the side of her neck. I watched the light leave her eyes. I watched her die. And we thought the Pikosa were fucking monsters," he says, lifting my scarred arm. "I killed my wife on your orders because you lied to me, Leanna!"

Leanna stands perfectly still and speaks without any hint of remorse. It chills me. "What's past is passed, medic. Our tactics worked. The Sucere Chamber was undisturbed, and the families of those selected suffered a much easier end than any others did. It was a mercy, Haddock. Now, leave the dead where they're buried and move."

"You fucking bitch…"

"That's an order, soldier!" She roars.

"You made me kill those people!" Haddock cries. His hand is shaking and the knife in it is oscillating wildly between Leanna and me. He's going to kill me without even trying. I need to do something.

Very quietly, I say, "Haddock, I forgive you for the part you played in my parents death. I know what desperate people do to survive and I know that my parents were also desperate. They loved me too much. If your wife was anything like them, she'd understand… she'd be proud of you…she'd forgive you…"

"No…no…" He moans, wounded.

"I forgive you."

"You should kill me," he says against my ear, "or at least want to."

His mouth drops down to my shoulder and I can feel his wet lips press against me. "I'm so sorry, Halima. I don't deserve to live."

"It's…" I scramble. "We've all done things. Terrible things…"

"What have you done? You united the tribes. You gave your heart and body to a bad man to save us. You were willing to die for us. For your parents. I can still hear your screams." Water drips onto my shoulder and for a moment I worry that it's blood until I hear Haddock inhale a shuddering breath. A sob wracks his chest.

Leanna is fidgeting, tense as she takes an almost imperceptible step forward and then another. "Haddock, I can't let you kill her. If you do, Ero's wrath will come down on the tribes. Everything we've worked for will be undone."

"You think I want to kill *her*?" He laughs and that laugh sounds like barbed wire-wrapped misery. "The only two people that are going to die in this tunnel are you and me. Why do you think I brought you here? Do you not know where this leads?"

He starts to laugh wildly then and I shiver. "No," I whisper. "Where does it go?"

"To the croc pit. The Danien told me."

Understanding permeates the tunnel in one terrible breath as Haddock pushes me off of him violently and, without warning, cocks his elbow back and flings his blade directly at Leanna's stomach.

I don't have time to scream as Leanna twists, letting the blade catch her in the meaty part of her right thigh. She collapses onto her knee, her good arm going down to brace her fall.

"Leanna!" I scream.

"The Danien also told me something else — that the crocs will only come this close to the surface through *this* tunnel, and only if they smell fresh blood."

I charge forward and try to go to Leanna as she rips the blade out of her leg and points it at him, but he lurches up onto his knees, catches my stomach and drags me past Leanna towards the tunnel that will take me to the surface. But he doesn't come with me.

Instead he shoves me hard enough that I stagger back and fall against one craggy wall. "Go, Halima. Leave us. We'll give the crocodiles a feast they deserve." He spreads both of his arms.

I hear the distinct sound of scraping in the tunnel behind him. It sounds like stone against stone, but if what he says is true… I shudder.

"Haddock, don't do this. Come with me!"

"Halima!" My name shouted in a Pikosa-accented voice has me whirling around. Tenor is running toward me with her sword outstretched, Lopina charging down the tunnel behind her.

"Halima, Ero needs you," Lopina says, panting. Her eyes are on me and mine are on her and we're staring at one another when Tenor comes to a halting stop. Lopina slams into her back with an audible, "Oof."

I don't understand the sudden expressions of horror that have crossed their faces and turn to look over my shoulder at whatever they're staring at…

And then I see a *crocodile.*

I scream bloody murder when I mean to shout orders. Lopina handles that. "Leanna! Healer! Back!" She withdraws her own blade with a hiss. "Halima, get behind me. Tell them to get behind Tenor and then run!"

Run. I hear her say as much, but I can't seem to move my feet because what's lumbering up towards us out of the darkness is no crocodile I've ever seen.

15
Ero

"What happened?" I shout as I lead the small team of mostly Pikosa and Tanishi warriors back through the tunnels.

Beside me, Warren looks confused. He shakes his head. "Ellar said she saw them on the horizon. I wasn't at the lookout then, but you know Ellar wouldn't lie about this."

No, she wouldn't.

"Ellar!" I shout. The female in question pushes through the group and makes her way to my side, looking furious.

"I don't know what happened. I saw them and heard the roar of their horses myself. They must have been scouting from farther than it looked from up on top of the walls. The female Tanishi may have a better idea of the Tanishi device that allows us to see far. Perhaps, I do not know its perspective. We should ask her."

I nod. "Everyone back to the surface. I want the reinforced secondary wall up by nightfall. We'll push the *party* back until we're finished."

I repeat the ideas the best I can in the Tanishi tongue for the benefit of the Tanishi and the Omoro and a weary groan comes up from somewhere in the crowd and is echoed by the other voices closest to me — Pikosa, Omoro and Tanishi alike.

My mouth twitches, but I don't give in to the impulse to grin. There is still danger on the horizon. Halima is still at risk.

"Lopina," I shout, not bothering to look back and see where she is. "I want you to run ahead and check on Halima."

"Don't you already have Brin and Tenor assigned to protecting her?" Ellar asks, her braid whipping over her shoulder as she turns to face me.

"And?"

"And that's a lot of resources already spent guarding your female."

"Is that a challenge?" Irritation ticks the space over my chest — a space already ticking with the urge to pull ahead and push everything else behind me and simply run to her and touch her as I've been so long denied.

She said she loved me. She claims me for her Xiveri.

I want to speak to her, to know what changed in the matter of moments. I want to know why she let go of the rope, because I was watching her and it didn't look like she slipped.

My first instinct was to think that she was trying to harm herself on purpose and it gutted me. But then she smiled and moved, shifting to let me know she wasn't hurt badly. And she told me she wanted to be mine, as I'd been hers this whole time. I was just too fucking dense to see it.

I drew the sign on *her* body in a language that, between the two of us, only I could read. The symbol read *mine*. I'm sure of it now, if there was ever any doubt, that the sign was meant for me.

"Lopina!" I shout again, but a shoulder bumps into mine from the back.

Lopina's loose black hair falls halfway down her back and swishes against me as she shakes her head vigorously and says, "*Men*. You think your females are all delicate flowers. Your mate is tougher than she looks."

My mate. My chest puffs out and I brim with pride. "I know that."

"The fall was nothing that could have killed or hurt her. She even fell flat so that her bottom got the worst of it."

I glare at her sideways. "And?"

"And she won't die."

"If she does, I'll kill every single one of you."

Lopina blinks at me once so slowly it looks rehearsed. Then when I don't react, she blinks again. "You're serious?"

"Do I ever lie?"

She and Tenor share a look. "Then perhaps I should run ahead and check on our sweet, delicate Halima, and perhaps Tenor, you should also join me. You know her best." She laughs and even the rigid Tenor breaks just a little.

"Thank you," I tell them both in Tanishi.

Lopina makes a face, somewhere between an exasperated glare and a smile, but she still rushes forward at a sprint. I want to turn to Ellar and ask her to accompany Lopina and my fledgling warrior, but a Tanishi female has taken the place Lopina just vacated on my right.

"Hi?" She says to me in Tanishi and I force myself to smile. It doesn't come naturally and her eyes go wide. She stutters for a moment before continuing, "Hi, I just uh...wanted to..."

She says more words — *many* — more words, but what I come away from the conversation with is that this female is called Chayana. Chayana invented the journey stone machine. She wants to invent something else. What it is, I have not a clue.

She calls herself one of these *ist* terms that all the Tanishi seem to use to describe themselves as. I know my female has an important role among them as the *leengoo-ist*. Another ist. I don't understand why they all need to identify themselves by such titles, but I can feel Halima's pride when she does, so I don't question it.

"You are Chayana. Chayana *gee-awl-oh-jist?*"

"Yes!" She practically shrieks. "Geologist. That's me. What I am. You are Nigusi." She beams and I give her an odd look. "Nigusi, Chayana...friends?"

Friends. I've heard this word many times, though the concept still doesn't quite make sense to me. In either case, I know that my female views this one as a friend, so she is one I will have to apply the term to as well. I will have to try. *And there is nothing I would not try for her.*

"Yes," I huff, "Chayana, Nigusi. We are friends."

On my other side, the male beside Ellar — Carven — balks.

The female called Chayana is clearly rattled, but she's trying for me just as I will try for her. Her version of *trying* however, seems to include speaking rapidly and without interruption even though I can barely understand half of what she's saying.

We've just reached a fork in the tunnels — one fork leads up to the new surface encampment while the other fork branches down to another corridor that leads to the main cave in our mines — when I interrupt her next thought.

"Habibi?"

She makes a face. "Uhh...Halima?"

I smile. "Yes. You speak *Ahrabiq*?"

"No. A little words."

We've slowed substantially, the other warriors pulling ahead while Chayana and I fight to understand one another. I'm grinning ear-to-ear by the time we do and she explains this concept of habibi to me. *Another word that sounds like Xiveri and feels like love.*

I'm ready to find Halima now when again, my plans are disrupted — or perhaps, accelerated, but for all of the wrong reasons. Because Brin approaches from the main cave now. "Nigusi," he shouts at me. "Your female. Something's happened. Come quick!"

Fear replaces my calm and I bolt. I can feel bodies at my back as I follow the path Brin's taken to the main cave, several warriors — and the strange Tanishi female who speaks too much — in tow.

Ellar orders her back in Pikosa and the Tanishi — *Chayana* — doesn't seem to understand her in the slightest. She just offers her a wave and jogs faster and then prattles off a laundry list of things that I can only make out three words of. They are: come, help and Halima.

"Stupid Tanishi," Ellar hisses under her breath, winning a stern look from me which she does not see as she surges ahead.

I race forward, pulling ahead of the group while Chayana and her shorter Tanishi legs fall behind. But that doesn't matter. How can it, when there's a body wrapped in blankets at the foot of my throne?

My body and soul turn to ice.

Goja is kneeling over the shapeless form shaking his head as I charge across the river to get to them. To get to her. Four other Pikosa surround him. Not among my closest ranks, three are young and one is Gerarr.

"What have you done!" I roar, dropping down beside the motionless form. I rip the fabric concealing her back carefully.

But as the fabric pulls to reveal more fabric and as my thundering heart slows and relief washes over me, I start to laugh. My deep laughter echoes back to me in the vast, empty cave, much louder than Chayana's, "What… fuck?"

She panting as she catches up to us, and hasn't figured it out yet.

"Very clever, Ellar. Very clever. Did Gerarr put you up to this or was the idea all your own?" I say, turning to her as I fist the blankets and toss them aside, empty. They're empty. *Thank the sun.*

She stares me down and I divine her answer before she gives it and smile. "Ah. You hate me. For how long?"

Her face is impassive as she says, "You killed both warriors who made me who I am."

"You are a better liar than I gave you credit for. You laid in wait for years."

"Decades," she corrects.

I soften, feeling a sudden self-hatred that I'm reminded of because I felt it once before — when Halima asked me how many slaves I'd murdered. I close my eyes longer than the standard blink and tip my head forward.

"You *loved* them."

"This is a Tanishi word, overused and meaningless. They sired me, that's all, and I respected them in a way I once did you, before you were weakened by the Tanishi."

I continue nodding and sigh, "I take it that there are no scouts on the horizon, then?"

"Of course not. You've forgotten how to read faces, you've been so concentrated on only the one. If you'd have remembered who you are, you'd have seen the truth."

I turn on one knee to face her, aware that I'm now fully surrounded by enemies and unlikely to make it out of this alive. *But I will. I must.* I already told Halima that I will not allow her to walk this world alone. It does not matter whether or not she carries my child.

I look up into Ellar's face, smooth and the same color brown as mine. Her hair is braided back tight against her scalp and she carries only Pikosa weapons, despite the fact that she was offered Tanishi instruments.

I should have recognized that, at least, as a sign. But I didn't. I was more focused on Halima's lips as she translated the instructions on how to use the machines. And I don't regret it. I should, but I just don't have it in me.

"Yes, I suppose you're right."

Chayana chooses that moment to catch up to what's happening. "Oh shit!" Panting still from the run down here, she's breathless when she turns and tries to run, but she doesn't make it far when Brin surges to meet her, grabs her by the hair and whips her onto the floor. She lands hard on her side about six paces away and rolls over with a groan.

She blinks and meets my gaze and I give her a stern warning not to move. I wonder if she reads it because she's too busy muttering other curses in a language that seems to be neither Tanishi nor any other I've heard.

I could try to barter for the little Tanishi's life, but I don't. That would be a waste of time and right now I need more of it. I turn my glance to the other traitors.

"So, this is the mutiny." No one answers. I don't expect them to as I look into the faces of some Pikosa I've beaten, others whose lives I've saved. I glance at my uncle, at the fresh scars on his side and smirk. "My father would approve."

"Yes, I believe he would. After all, it was your blade that took his life."

"You forget, Gerarr, that you once tried to do the same. The only difference is the mercy he showed you after you challenged him and failed. Now, you have mistaken the affection I show my Tanishi for a similar mercy. I have none — I never did — and when this ends, you will be reminded of it."

Gerarr's mouth sets and the older warrior draws his sword with a familiar ring. "On your feet. Form a circle. I want to kill him myself. That is the price I will pay to help you kill the others."

"No," Ellar barks as the others move to action.

He may be her senior, but she's still a stronger warrior than he is now that he's injured — perhaps even without his injuries — and she's smarter.

"You old fool, you'll never win against him. None of us will. It's why he's Nigusi, or have you forgotten? No, we'll execute him now and then kill the Tanishi, every last one. We'll return to the old ways with the benefit of their machines and without the burden of having to share what little resources we have with the others."

I nod, considering. "It's a good plan. Why are you waiting?"

Ellar tips her chin towards the Northwestern cave entrance and keeps the tip of her sword pointed down at me. She knows me better than few other warriors, perhaps only Wyden. I'm surprised he isn't here now…

"Wyden." Ah. And here he is. "He's fetching your Tanishi."

I make no outward show of emotion, but my insides have hardened. *Gerarr and Ellar will die painfully when this is over and Wyden? If he's touched or harmed her in any way…he will die painfully when this is over, over the course of many lifetimes.*

"I'm surprised he didn't want to be here to lay the final blow."

"This is the final blow." Ellar looks at me and there is absolutely no light in her eyes. There is nothing. And I realize that yes, perhaps our hardness has spared us the cruel pain of death by the hands of tribes even more vicious, but what we have lost in the process is the ability to *live*. To party. To love.

Because without the foolish, gullible light that spills from Halima's eyes every fucking time she blinks, what's the point? Survival means nothing without whimsy.

I frown and Ellar seems to like that because she offers me a grim smile. "He wants to kill Halima in front of you. He says he understands you better now and that doing so will hurt you more."

Though her eyes remain dead, her grin gets more fiendish. I am unable to mask my response when Gerarr laughs. My jaw sets. I want to throw myself at the both of them. I want to dig my fingers into Gerarr's wounds and rip off Ellar's scalp by the hair. My right hand twitches and she sees the motion. I shame myself for not being able to get my reactions in check.

She smirks. "You are *weak*. Unfit to be Nigusi any longer. Our reserves are getting thin. The medicines are going to slaves who aren't and never should be Pikosa. The benefit to bringing them in is finished. They have served their purpose, and so have you."

I nod just once and keep my lips sealed. I say nothing, knowing that further communication will only serve to anger me. She does not see. Unless she has felt it herself, unless she has experienced pure magic, pure Xiveri, she could not know how worth fighting for it truly is. And she won't ever, because I will have her head in my hands, dismembered from her body, before the day is done.

The low sound of footsteps jerks the attention of the traitors in the room left. Wyden appears in the mouth of the tunnel, but I cannot afford to be distracted by the female in his grip.

Instead, I look right, directly at Chayana and hiss, catching her attention. She's watching me with terror and anger and neither terror nor anger will help her escape when she's not looking for exits. If she had been, she'd have realized that she'd just been given one. The warriors have shifted their attention to Wyden, which means her only obstacle to escape is Brin.

Brin, my protégé. I should have expected this from him. Was I not once in his same position? I smile, feeling pride and shame. I taught him well. I taught him wrong.

What would it have been like if we'd worked together from the start? Perhaps none of us would have survived. Perhaps, all of us would have.

"Foot," I tell Chayana in Tanishi.

She gives me an odd look, but follows my gaze when I track it to Brin's left ankle. He wears a knife there. Her eyes widen so dramatically, I have to roll mine. I grit my teeth and hold one hand low, cutting it through the air sharply. *Not yet,* I communicate with my gaze. She opens her mouth as if to answer out loud and I close my eyes entirely, waiting for her to give us both up. At the last second, a different voice cuts in.

"You've got her?" Ellar says and I freeze, careful now with my reactions, careful now with the sight of my only weakness so near to me. How I respond means everything. It means Halima's life.

A grunt is Wyden's only response and a hatred unlike anything I've *ever* experienced ricochets through my ribcage like a metal pellet. *He will die before the night is through in supreme and awesome violence.*

"She wasn't hard to find."

A small "umph" is followed by Wyden's hiss. I look over and see Halima with a canvas sack over her head being pushed towards us and my gaze bleeds red. *They will die. All of them. Every last one of them.* A Nigusi killing Pikosa in defense of a slave tribe? Ludicrous.

Necessary.

And they die tonight. She must be frightened. I don't want to see her scared.

She's got on light blue linen covered in brown sand and red dust and her hands are tied behind her back so I cannot see them. I want to see her eyes, I want to tell her that everything will be alright.

"Weak," Gerarr hisses above me and I grit my teeth and focus on anywhere but her chest, where her fragile heart beats.

And then my glance catches on her feet. She's wearing the same sandals most of us do...but those aren't the shoes I made for her. The leather is too light. And stranger still, the skin beneath the leather is lighter than it should be, too. *What is happening?*

I glance up at the sack on her head, wishing I could see her face. Instead, I notice her hair. It's dark and peeking out from beneath the canvas covering her head and yes, it's black, but it's not the same rough texture of Halima's. This female's hair is pointy-straight and smooth like still water, shorter as well. *This is not Halima. But...this is Wyden.*

I understand nothing.

Everything in my being wants to shout out the accusation that this is absolutely not my fucking Halima, but I stay still and I wait as Wyden's eyes look anywhere but at me.

What is he up to? What has he done with my Halima?

"Halima!" Chayana shouts, and I'm grateful for it. I don't want any of the others to see what I see. I doubt they would. These Pikosa see only physical strength and ignore the power that lies beneath.

Brin kicks Chayana in the ribs and she yelps, crumpling into a ball around his leg. I jerk, not liking seeing her kicked for reasons that surpass my understanding. She isn't Halima. But I still don't like it.

"Fuck..." Chayana shouts up at him, earning her another kick. "You..."

I don't even know what she says and I know Brin doesn't, but it's whispered harshly enough to know it's an insult. He kicks her again. And again, and that's when I understand a small piece of the madness that's happening here.

Chayana is going for the blade on his ankle...but she doesn't have it yet.

Brin stops kicking Chayana as Wyden approaches and I scramble for words, "You never did learn as quickly as Tenor. I'm not surprised to see you here like this, kicking a Tanishi who hardly looks to have felt it."

Brin pivots to face me. He never was a boy of many words — I liked that about him — but he's always been far too easy to read.

"Your lack of loyalty is about as impressive as the damage you did to that Tanishi," I insist again.

"Loyalty?" Brin tilts his head to the left and his long braid slides over his shoulder. I'd like to grab it and swing the boy around my head by it. "You never taught me about *loyalty*, only strength. And now you are weak, all because of this worthless female."

"Is that why you kick this Tanishi like a worthless female?"

He jerks, like he'll kick me, but he's too smart — and too much of a coward — to try. He knows if I got a hold of his leg, I'd break it along with every other bone in his body, so he turns his attention again to Chayana.

Her eyes widen, but she bites her bottom lip in concentration. She prepares herself in a way that is so painfully obvious, I want to bark at her to be more fucking subtle. She's lucky her opponent is a blind fool and that the others are focused on the female in Wyden's grip — a female who is many things, Halima not being one of them.

Brin kicks her and my skin feels uncommonly thin as my muscles struggle for control. I don't react, though I want to. Because even though Brin is much larger than the Tanishi, and it looks like he causes her great pain judging by her muted grunt, her louder squeal, and her high-pitched squawk, Chayana still does what she needs to have done.

When Brin pulls back, she stays curled on the ground around her stomach — around her knife — and moans *soooo* unbearably theatrically. I'm lucky Brin's opinion of Tanishis is so low that he pays no attention to it.

Instead, he turns his attention up when Wyden speaks. "You had this coming, Ero," Wyden says to me.

"I know," I answer, twisting to meeting his gaze.

I search for something in his expression, something to read...but he has suddenly acquired an ability he didn't have before I beat him brutally. I can't read anything about him.

If anything, what I see in his expression doesn't make sense at all. He looks *afraid* beneath all that apathy.

But what is he afraid of? He's never been afraid of me before. Hated me, sure? But feared me? No.

He holds the female against his chest in a way that would make me rabid if it were Halima, but doesn't because it isn't. He holds this female in a strange way... like he's not intending to kill her at all. He holds her like she's *his*.

It hits me like a fist and when I speak next, I feel every bit as theatrical as Chayana. "If you harm Halima, I'll kill you." A weak threat. I can do better than that.

Wyden pulls a blade from the sheath on his belt and brings it to his female's throat. She whimpers — the only decent performer among us, whoever she is — and murmurs words that sound a lot like, "Ero...help..."

Wyden tenses behind her, his arm holding firm. The knife cuts into the cloth at her throat.

"Are you done, Wyden? Kill the female," Ellar hisses. "I want this over."

"Hold. I didn't bring her here for this to be quick. I want her death to be slow," Wyden snarls. "Hold him down! I don't want him to disrupt this. Use your whips."

I surge up and am yanked back by the free end of a whip around my throat. It could only be Ellar and the act and the fact that Wyden ordered it makes me question his motives. I relax, knowing I won't be able to free myself like this, not after Ellar gives the order for the others to hold my arms and legs.

By the time they're finished, my arms are spread to the sides. I'm on my knees, stuck in this position. I'm going to need something I've never needed before in my entire life...

Help.

I'm going to need a Tanishi captive and my mortal enemy to save my life.

The thought makes my lips twitch, but I don't dare smile. Instead, I snarl up at Wyden, "Don't you fucking hurt her, Wyden! What do you expect to come from this? That Ellar will let you take my throne? That Gerarr will? You know he's wanted the Nigusi title since his brother stole it out from beneath him."

"I don't want your throne," he seethes, eyes narrowing. "I just want you to suffer like you've made me suffer ever since we were kids."

Ever since we were kids. I lick my lips, memories gripping me with suddenness. I remember playing in the river with Wyden. I remember learning to swim beside him. My first trip to the surface that I can remember, he was there and I had looked to him to be strong because I knew that if he was strong, I could be stronger. He was my constant motivation. More than a fellow warrior. A friend. He'd been my friend. And I'd tried to kill him. How many times now? I'm not sure. But I'm sure that I don't deserve his help. Why he gives it, just proves he's a better man than I am. Maybe even a good one.

"I'm *sorry*, Wyden." I say the word in Tanishi because in my own tongue, it does not exist.

His face falls. The sound of the whip jolts me out of the confusion of his gaze. There's a prickling across my back but I am too familiar with pain to be distracted by it. I simply blink long and slow and watch the female in his grip as she wriggles, like she's trying to get free — *or trying to free something Wyden is holding*.

"Do not take this out on the Tanishi." My Tanishi. Fuck. If anyone were paying attention, they'd know...

But they don't. Wyden continues, speaking quickly over me. "Collateral damage. This has nothing to do with her and everything to do with you."

"You can have my seat, Wyden! Take it!"

Ellar sneers, "You are pathetic. To give up your Nigusi seat for a slave...disgusting. Wyden, do it *now*! I'm tired of waiting."

Wyden doesn't hesitate another moment. He rips the canvas off of the female's head revealing a face I recognize — but a face that is not Halima's. This female is pale, her face flushed with adrenaline as she drops to one knee and lifts her hands up in front of her, not bound, but carrying a machine. She closes her eyes as she pulls the trigger, aiming for something over my right shoulder.

The response is immediate.

A grunt is followed by a dull thud and the whip on my left ankle releases. Meanwhile, another whip slashes down, aiming for the Tanishi. The aim is true. The whip splashes color, bright and horrible across the front of her chest, cutting her from shoulder to abdomen.

Wyden makes a brutal sound, but his weakness doesn't stop him from reacting in time to prevent her from being hit again. He raises the knife in his hand and throws it.

I turn to see Gerarr drop to his knees with Wyden's blade protruding from his right shoulder. He pulls it free and throws it back, but Wyden is throwing himself forward over the Tanishi, blanketing her as he takes her down to the cold stones below.

"Chayana!" I roar.

"Wahheeeeeeeee!" Comes the screech louder than any *seeran* could ever be. When the whip hit me, I felt nothing. But this makes me grit my teeth. *Fucking Chayana...*

I hear movement behind me but I can't turn, the whip around my throat holding me steady. I surge against my restraints and the whip on my right arm releases while the one around my throat tightens.

"Don't you dare!" Ellar roars as she pulls, her whip burning into me like a blade, but I'm stronger than she is.

I tighten the muscles in my neck to steel and roar as I lift up onto my feet. I wrap the whip around my left arm twice more and pull Carven toward me. He's smart enough to let go of the whip and stupid enough to give it up to *me*. I toss the hilt up and catch it in my hand as the tail end releases. I don't hesitate but whip it out and catch Carven around the throat. I bring him down to his knees. My next strike goes to Ellar behind me.

I turn at Brin's howl of pain and see Chayana chasing him toward the river while he runs with a knife sticking out of his left ass cheek. I almost laugh. Instead, Ellar roars and I turn and charge for her, but I'm intercepted by Carven. He's got his hands on the whip around my left ankle and when he wrenches up, I go down.

A kick to my cheek rattles me because Carven isn't holding back. He kicks me again, this time in the throat where Ellar's whip still burns me. Clever man. There is no honor in battle. There is only survival. His foot comes again and I roll out of its path. Landing on my back, I grab his ankle, blocking his incoming attack. Catching it, I twist wildly.

Spit sprays from his lips along with his scream when I break his ankle and push him off of me. He falls back, giving me just enough time to roll out of the path of Ellar's blade as she brings it down.

I jolt up onto my feet and Wyden calls my name. I turn and catch the sword he throws me, utterly incapable of understanding what between us has changed.

"Jia!" Chayana screams.

I turn to see Brin edging Chayana towards the river. He's recovered his weapon from his ass and even though he's only a fledgling warrior, he is still a trained fighter

— trained by me. Chayana will be no match for him and definitely no match for the crocodiles.

I surge towards her, but Ellar blocks my path. The injured Gerrar and Carven move to flank her. *Here they are, despising the Tanishi and still using their formations.* I shake my head and utter an expression Halima taught me in the Tanishi language.

"Bring it on." I swing my sword around and lunge for the kill, but before our battle can escalate any further, a voice pierces everything and it's a voice I know in my bones.

"Halima," I whisper, but she just says a word I've never heard before, but that sounds like *"Drahhh-gonnne!"*

The war around me comes to an abrupt and unsettling standstill and we look up as one and panic together. *Anidi laye.*

My mouth twitches and I feel a wondrous heat bloom throughout my entire body. And on the heels of that heat comes panic.

Halima appears like a dream, ringed in the darkness of the cave behind her. She's dragging Leanna on her right arm while Tenor helps support Leanna on her other side. The female is injured *again* and limping. Behind them, Lopina shoves the male who I fight every day not to kill and he falls hard, landing on hands and knees.

"Ellar, don't you fucking lift that sword!" Lopina roars, barreling forward and breaking the momentary truce that had fallen between us.

Ellar charges me as if afraid of these somewhat *decrepit* looking reinforcements and I can't help but laugh. Pleasure, or at least, *amusement* hits me at this inopportune moment and my desire to laugh only increases when Lopina trips and falls halfway into the river. She curses as she hauls her dripping wet body out again, crosses the bridge, and arrives at my side and in time to engage Gerarr while my sword clashes with Ellar's angrily.

I bat Ellar's weapon aside just as the Tanishi weapon in Jia's grip releases a small explosion. A body splashes into the river and I hear Chayana's voice call Halima's. Relief pours through me as I dodge Ellar's next attack, letting her drive me closer to the throne, closer to Wyden dueling with Carven at my back.

Ellar knows she won't win. I can read it in the lines of her face. And because she knows she won't win, she has already lost. I spin around her and bring my sword down through the back of her leg, spearing it clean through. I release the hilt of my blade and whip around her, grabbing her arm before she has time to fall. Then, I take the loose chains hanging off of my throne and shackle her before she even hits the floor.

And then I run. Turning my back on everyone else, I sprint across the bridge until I reach Halima and Leanna in her grip.

"Hi." She smiles, one side of her mouth quirking up.

"Halima," I breathe, bending down to kiss her, but she jerks back.

I frown. "What's wrong?"

"So, we came to rescue you."

I blink, surprised, not even having considered her presence. "You did?"

"Yes. But y'ani, we had a bit of trouble. You see, Haddock tried to kill Leanna because Leanna killed all of our families."

My entire body clenches as I look for the first time at the female gritting her teeth as she dangles off of my female's arm. "Yours?"

"Yes, but that's not important. I mean, it is, but not right now. Because we went down the wrong tunnel and now we've got company."

"Company?" I touch her face because I can't fucking help it. I want to touch her everywhere because I'm allowed.

She nods. "Yes." And her word is bisected by the sound of a familiar, yet terrible screech. The blood drains out of my body.

"You brought a *crocodile* into the main cave?"

Her eyes flare with a momentary anger that is entirely inappropriate and undeserved when *she* is the one who brought the beast into the cave system. "That thing is *not* a crocodile!"

"Halima! You brought it here?"

She gives me a shrug with just one shoulder while lines crease over her forehead that I've never seen before. "To save you?"

I balk, "I was coming to save you."

"I'm faster."

"Never."

Another screech rips through the world, making every single hair on my body stand on end. "And now?"

She makes a face. "Um, now, I'm definitely going to save you."

I bend down and rip a kiss from her lips before glancing quickly at Leanna. My shoulders sag for the briefest moment as I consider *why* Leanna is still here despite the accusations leveled against her.

"I take it you want to save this one, too."

She hesitates, but only for a breath before answering, "Yes, she gets saved too. Haddock, also. Everyone. Anidi laye."

I don't wait. I pull Leanna out of her grip and grab the male who does not appear wounded but who acts as if he is by the back of the neck. I carry her Tanishi back towards the throne as I survey the carnage that's left.

Gerarr and the other warrior are dead and Brin is missing — dead now for certain if he fell into the river. Ellar is tied to the throne and Carven sits defeated, holding onto his shattered leg. I start to run past them, intending to hide my Halima in the Eastern tunnel, but Halima's stopped halfway.

"We need to free Ellar."

Rage licks up my spine. "Ellar is the one who formed this mutiny…"

"And Leanna is the one who ordered Haddock to kill my parents and Haddock is the one who tried to kill Leanna out of remorse and you're the one who tried to kill me a dozen times. Now come on! We don't have time for this!"

And we don't, because the sound of the crocodile is louder than it was before. *It's advancing on us quickly now.* I close my eyes, wanting to throttle her as I sever Ellar's chains and mutter tersely, "Anidi laye." And then louder, "Lopina! Get the traitors into the Eastern tunnel then meet me back here."

Jia says something and I turn to see her standing next to Chayana with Wyden at her side.

I meet his gaze for longer than a moment, assessing him and the threat he poses. "I hate you, but I am no risk to you or your female. You now carry a shield I cannot cut through." He just glances down to Jia and I nod, a brief understanding penetrating the fact that I hate him, too. But I am bonded to him by the same adhesive that bonds him to me. Acceptance, transferred by the love we have of these strange Tanishi.

"Help Lopina, then return here. Gather any weapons the traitors carry and bring them. We'll need everything we can get our hands on."

He grabs his female and the others by the backs of their necks and the group moves, taking Leanna and Haddock with them. Glancing toward the Southern tunnel, I see the first glimmer of a snout stretching forward, sniffing wildly and snapping. The beast has caught the scent of blood and it won't stop until it reaches it.

"What's the plan, Nigusi?" Halima asks me in Pikosa.

"We won't try to fight it. You will go into the Eastern tunnel where you'll be safe. Lopina, Tenor and Wyden will guard the entrance and keep you safe. I will drag Gerarr's body to the river, which will take it to the crocodile den and, with any luck at all, the crocodile — "

"*Drahgone,*" Halima interrupts.

The crocodile screeches and steps into the cave just as she finishes speaking. We both look up and Halima's face falls. She glances toward the mouth of the Eastern tunnel and shakes her head. "You can't entice it with one body when there's so much blood leading that way. I'll help. I can carry…"

"No," I seethe, directing my fury at her in the effort of compelling her back towards the Eastern tunnel. Shockingly, it works.

She blinks at me once, twice, a third time. Her jaw sets in a grimace and when raw vulnerability crosses her expression, I almost agree to let her do whatever it was that she wanted.

"Don't...die."

I slip my finger under her chin and lift. I kiss her roughly. "And leave you? Never. Now go."

She fumbles around the bodies just as the crocodile emerges fully into the chamber. It stands up on its hind legs and whips its long neck back and forth. Its jowls open and it screeches out a high-pitched wail that makes my bones hurt.

Dropping back onto all fours, its massive, serrated claws scrape against the stone below. Its pendulum head swings back and forth as it searches by scent and sound since it can't see. I'm irritated to find that Halima is right — there are too many of them in the Eastern tunnel — and as the crocodile makes its way across the river onto the smooth stone by my throne, it pivots towards my warriors defending the Tanishi.

I shout indistinctly at the thing and start to move more agitatedly, causing its massive head to turn towards me. It takes a few slow steps, but I know not to underestimate the creature. Crocodiles are fast when they want to be.

The scales on its back glimmer and the gills on its sides lift. Water sprays out of them as it opens its mouth and roars again, the sound penetrating enough to make a Nigusi lose his mind — it's happened before — but I grit my teeth and brace through it.

I have Gerarr by the hair on his head and I pull him faster as the crocodile focuses its full attention on me now. I catch Wyden's gaze from the Eastern tunnel as I pull, watch him struggle to remain rooted.

"Don't move!" I shout at him. "Don't distract it! Protect the Tanishi." Protect the Tanishi? Did those words really just leave my mouth? To Wyden, of all the world's foulest creatures? My lips jerk in a near grin and then...I can't help it. I laugh. I laugh while a crocodile the size of sixteen Pikosa warriors rolled all together barrels down on me.

I glance over my shoulder at the short rocky bridge leading to the other side of the river. I take it, holding Gerarr's corpse as the shield between me and the beast. It comes to the other side of the river, directly across from me and snarls as it starts to approach over the bridge.

I wait, wait, wait...watch, watch, watch...its got its front legs on the bank of the river nearest me now and its back legs dragging over the bridge. *Now.*

I toss Gerarr's body directly in front of its nose, kicking him in when I don't fling far enough, and then I freeze entirely, waiting...waiting for the crocodile to turn and give chase. But right in that moment, a voice behind me says, "Leanna? Halima? Ero? Shit..." And then more Tanishi words, followed by, "...fucking *drahgon!*"

The crocodile roars and surges toward the Tanishi male walking casually into the tunnel through the Western entrance with two Omoro and a Pikosa warrior with him. The Tanishi male's face is dark brown and I believe I've heard Halima call him Donovan.

"Don't move," I shout in Tanishi and then in Pikosa, fearing that if they run and the crocodile chases them through the tunnels, it'll end in bloodshed for more than just us and them but perhaps for every single being in the tunnels — anidi laye, but in the worst possible way.

I draw my sword, intending to do what we Pikosa have been schooled *never* to do — fight it. But as the sound of my sword being removed from its sheath pulls the crocodile's big ugly head around to face me, my worst nightmare is realized.

"Hey! You ugly lizard!" Halima shouts. She says more in her own tongue and keeps shouting until the crocodile finally turns back around to face her. She stands directly across the river from me, so close but impossible for me to reach.

As it turns back around to face her, it brings its massive tail only a few paces in front of me. I will have to attack it *now*, but as I lunge forward to do just that, Halima lifts her hand and shouts, this time to me in Pikosa, "I have a plan, Ero. Trust me."

Trust her? And before I can shout at her that she's a fucking idiot and the next time I get the chance I'm going to strangle the life out of her, she does the unthinkable.

The only person I've ever loved releases a loud, whooping shout and jumps into the river.

And *then* the crocodile chases her.

16
Halima

On a list of stupid things I've done in my life, jumping into the river sits at the very top. The plan sounded easy in my head — simple, even.

All I have to do is just catch the same brambly vines that Gerd did when she hauled me out of the river and took me to Ero's room and let the dragon pass right by me and go back to its nice dragony home in the pools below.

Easy. Right?

I find the vines — no, I find *some* vines. The problem? There are vines growing *alllll* along the river walls. The first vines rip off under my hand.

I scream and then I hear the sound of the dragon. A lot of hissing and thrashing water. So I pull on the vines and I pull and I pull without finding the opening until I feel it...something hard and smooth brushes the back of my calves.

I freeze. I freeze as my entire life flashes before my eyes.

My mother and my father. Our little apartment in Dokki that was more bomb shelter than home by the end. The courses I took at Cairo University before it closed. The underground classes that persisted after the Water Wars began.

The people that I met from all over the Middle East and Africa — even some expats and tourists that got trapped in Cairo when things got too dangerous to leave and all flights were grounded except those operated by various militaries as different governments tried to claim what little potable water was left.

I translated for them.

I translated across military lines when the other translators were killed in air strikes. I translated the negotiated peace treaty between the Palestinian and Israeli governments. It lasted three days before chemical attacks were lobbed by and to both sides. They were the first governments to collapse entirely and when they did, they did together.

I feel the cool brush of a steely claw against my leg and I freeze, just as I was frozen in that tank after my parents put my name into consideration for a secret military project called Sucere.

I'm all that survived from Egypt.

I should feel lucky. Many countries were left unrepresented in the Sucere Chamber and now, all that they had and ever were is gone. Even the languages I don't know. And there are so many I don't know...

I blink my eyes open to darkness, remembering what it had been like to wake to such violence. Born from blue water, it took hard work and pain and tenderness, above all else, to survive. Forgiveness. Because we are all God's terrible things. God. Though I was my father's daughter, I remember the way my mother prayed to him five times a day every day and, right now, I can't help but bite my bottom lip between my teeth and think of him. *Please*, I beg to the water around me. *Please don't let this be the end.*

I hold as something cool and rock-tough brushes against my outer calf, knee, and thigh...And then whoosh.

It's gone.

The dragon travels right past me, carried by the river's grace. I hold steady for another half dozen moments as I double and then triple check that I'm still alive and that this isn't some strange new depth of Kur or darker Naraka or circle of Hell or any other afterlife.

When I realize my arms are shaking badly and a silent pang is radiating throughout my entire body, I let out a very audible cry of relief...but that relief fades to panic far, far too quickly.

I can't find Gerd's tunnel and the vine I've got my arm wrapped around is tearing free of the cave wall. I reach forward, but the river's current is strong and I've been holding on for at least sixty minutes — or sixty seconds, long enough for me to think that maybe, just maybe, this plan, though successful, might be my worst yet.

The vine rips free and I spiral out into the middle of the river with nothing nearby to grab onto...

A hot, hard body slices through the water and snags me around the waist. We careen down the river, but only a short distance before we jerk to a stop. I've still got hold of the vine and it must be caught on something.

"Ero?" I croak as water rushes over my head and chokes me. Ero, because it could be no one else, hoists me higher against him and is *swimming* with me in his arms *against* the current towards an unknown destination.

"Let go of the vine and grab onto me," he rasps, sounding like he's in pain.

I don't hesitate to do what he says. I reach for him, but slip too far back. Ero catches my elbow and brings my hands to his waist. He catches hold of the wall, digging his fingers into the shallow grooves. Then he starts to pull.

"Don't let go. No matter what, don't let go." Slowly, we make our way forward and Ero's grunting in pain and I can see the grim outline of his expression every third stroke when my head breaks above the surface of the water.

"Wait...wait! Ero, you're going too far. Here." Because he doesn't see the mass of vines I half tore apart. "It's just ahead of those...those vines," I sputter.

He listens to me without question and I can feel the angry muscles in his body react wildly as he pulls us forward. Ever forward, pulling and swimming one measured stroke at a time until finally...the current of the river cuts like a stoppered valve. We exit and enter the small cove and I flail wildly, trying to swim.

He grunts as he drags me up against him, treading water for us both. "You cannot swim?"

"No."

"Fuck. You should have told me. I...would have taught you."

"You still can...just up there, to the right." I point deeper into the cave and Ero swims with me in his arms away from the light, up until the point that the cove cuts abruptly to the left and a small ledge appears nestled into the flat face of the rock.

"Augh!" He roars as he grabs me by the back of the neck, likely hard enough to bruise me but I don't give a hoot about that at this point. He lifts me up where I can't reach and pushes me all the way onto the ledge before hauling himself up after me.

"How the fuck did you know this was here?" He says, chest heaving.

"This is how…we escaped the first time," I gasp. "You saw me before…falling into the river…with Gerd."

His hand snaps out and latches onto the back of my head, no warning provided in this darkness. I gasp as his lips come against my lips and he speaks against them. "Don't ever take this path again."

I just smile with half my mouth. "I saved your life because the Danien, Gerd, showed me the path. She has taken it before."

"Wild woman." He balks, hauling me up against his heat and charging down the tunnels toward the light. "And you did not save me. I saved you. You were dangling in the middle of the river when I caught up to you."

"But before that I drew the dragon away from you. So take that! I definitely saved you first."

I can't see his expression, but I feel his chest rumble beneath my palm as we surge into the tunnels by his room. "It leads *here?* Fuck," he curses, and then he laughs. "If you'd known about this tunnel sooner, I have no doubt you'd have killed me in my sleep."

"Good thing I didn't."

"Great thing."

He kicks open the stone doorway to his room and doesn't even bother to close it. He catapults us across his sleeping chamber and flattens me to the bed.

"Where it all started," I whisper as my back hits the mattress and his torso crushes mine to the sheets.

His mouth slants across mine heatedly as he touches me everywhere, pulling the wet linens off of my body like tissue paper.

"Where you deceived me," he growls.

"Only a little." I comb my fingers back into his hair, gently scraping my nails across his scalp in that way I know he likes and that makes him shiver every single time. He doesn't disappoint.

"Fuck, Halima, don't stop." His flat palms latch onto my waist and wrench me beneath him until we're at eye level. His eyes are so different than they were the first time we were here...not just *pieces* of goodness, they're entirely full of light.

"I won't."

"Don't deny me again, *ever*."

"I won't do that, either. I love you, Ero."

His eyebrows relax, the tension in his tone going unbearably soft, so soft it quivers...and then breaks. "I love you too, Halima. More than my throne. More than my life."

I exhale. He inhales and exhales. I have no idea how we both got naked, only that we are. We're skin to skin, knee to knee, my legs tangled between his legs. He edges forward into the trimmed curls guarding my softest place, where I'm most vulnerable, the glowing ember of his erection meeting my sopping core.

"I'm so glad I found you in this life, Ero."

He grins with one side of his mouth, leans down and brushes his lips over mine so tenderly it makes the thing in my chest swell up into my mouth and burst. My head tilts back as he slides forward, forward, forward, stretching me fully. My legs spread as wide as they can and I hook my right knee over his hip to keep him here, hold him close.

"Augh," he groans, his eyelids fluttering as mine are fluttering — in the fight to stay open. "You are wrong in this," he says as he presses into me and starts to drive in and out of my body. "You did not find me. I found you."

He picks up his pace, his body moving roughly as he catapults me to the brink of an orgasm. My head rolls and my heart bursts and as my soul splinters apart, he bites my earlobe and against my temple he says the last words I ever expected of him, "Ana behibek, habibty."

My body breaks out in sweat and I yelp as the magnitude of what he's said and this moment and this day and so many lifetimes lived and forgotten and lived again crash down on me. He learned my language from someone in the minutes he was away from me.

"Hhh...how?" I gasp.

"Chayana speaks much," he answers in broken English right before his body goes still. He roars. "Ana behibek, Halima."

He clamps around me, holding me as if he wants to pull me inside of him. I'm not sure I would mind. I've missed this closeness. I've missed it so much. I cry out and he releases a low moan as the heat pours out of him in a rush, filling me up, up, up.

I kiss his face mercilessly, trembling as waves of residual release make me insane, make me want, make me happy. I'm so happy.

I grip the sides of his face and between kisses practically yell, "Ana behibak keman, habibi." *I love you, too.* "Enta elshamps, enta el'amr." *You are the sun and the moon.* I shout as I layer sloppy kiss over sloppy kiss and am met by his huff of laughter that lets me know everything will be hard from now on, but it will be okay, too. "Enta elbi, enta hayati." You are my heart, my life.

I lean back and kiss just the tip of his nose as he relaxes his weight deeper and deeper onto me, neither moving forward nor back. Not moving, Just being.

His gaze searches my eyes, first the left and then the right. He strokes the sides of my body lazily then, as if moments before we weren't just fighting a dragon for our lives.

And then he smirks and says in his typical Pikosa brogue, a low voice that's gravelly and rich, "I think I might need you to translate that, habibty."

Sixty-two days later...

17

Ero

The walls are high and imposing, guarding rich abundance. The green area has been thriving with the help of the machines and herbs brought by the Tanishi's mysterious chamber, as well as new methods of pumping water up into the soil that the Danien used back in their home caves — caves they no longer claim to have any desire to return to. As a result, we have produced crops that I have never tasted, heard of or seen. Some taste incredible. Others...taste like dirt.

I stand at the top of the high walls now, looking out at the wasteland beyond our oasis. Wyden stands beside me, but we don't speak. We share neither camaraderie nor affection for one another, but what we do share is far more important. The love of Tanishi women. Wyden has been inseparable from the little female called Jia. He waits on her hand and foot in a way that would repel me if I weren't also guilty of it.

He's already turning, a warm brush of hot wind pulling through his waist-length hair, even before I hear the sound of her voice. He's so attuned to it, it makes me smile and I keep smiling, until I register her words. "Ero! Tenor...Halima...pain!" My Tanishi is improving worse than any of the Pikosa's and I hate it, but I understand enough for this.

There are stairs winding down between the inner and outer walls with doors that lead to the inner city. We keep the doors barred in the case of an invasion and in case any enemies ever make it to the top, we can lock them in between the walls and kill them quickly while they're trapped — of all the new constructs the Tanishi have proposed, this one was my idea.

I don't have time for the stairs now as I issue a quick order to Wyden to hold his position, grab one of the ropes that hangs over the side and rapidly repel down to the sandy floor below.

"Show me," I tell the small female. She points across the space to the shaded garden.

"Halima…helping…plants…"

She doesn't need to say more. I'm running, ignoring those that would attempt to speak to me in this moment of agony. Not being able to reach her — knowing she's hurt — is unbearable.

But my ruin only lasts until I pass beneath the canopy overhead, which provides shade and a surprising cool as the plants here release their gentle aroma. I follow the path between the wall and the tilled, brown soil through which stalks of *corn* have begun to grow. I follow the path a few moments until I hear her voice shouting louder than the rest.

"I'm not hurt," she says in Pikosa. "There's nothing wrong with me…" She sees me around Tenor's body and groans. "You told Ero?"

Tenor and two Danien are standing with her — one of them is a female called Gerd who helped her escape me before and to whom I'm forever grateful for having shown Halima the way out of the river.

Gerd is shouting down at Halima in Danien and Halima is rolling her eyes, shaking her fist, releasing theatrical groans from her position beneath everyone sitting flat on her butt on the sandy floor. Halima shouts back in Danien and I'm entirely lost in the conversation and irritated because of it.

"Tell me what's wrong," I order.

The three beings clustered around Halima turn to face me. The Danien shuffle back just a few inches and it irks me that they're still afraid, so I try to relax my fists and coax a softer expression onto my face as I step up beside Tenor.

"What's wrong?"

"Nothing's wrong!" Halima shouts.

Tenor just shakes her head and glares ferociously around at everything. "I came upon them like this. The Danien say that Halima is wounded, but your female denies this."

"I didn't say I wasn't bleeding…" Halima chokes.

Her gaze flicks to me and a rush of color runs up to touch her cheeks. I would have smiled if I weren't so worried. That color makes me think that perhaps she's remembering how I woke her up this morning. With my tongue wedged deep in her body, her thighs clenching around my ears, liquid moans pouring out of her lips. In a land with so little water, her scent is my favorite thing to drown in.

I crouch down onto my haunches in front of her, irritated that she jerks her leg back when I reach for her ankle. The blush in her cheek rises even higher when I level her with a glare.

"I have earned the right to touch you wherever I like, whenever I like."

I reach for her ankle again and she makes this breathy little sound that immediately makes me wish these others around us would disappear. My breathing gets harder, but then I remember she's supposed to be injured.

Taking her ankle in my hand and squeezing it gently, I shake off lascivious thoughts and say, "What's wrong?"

She chews on her bottom lip and watches me and I watch that lip with something bordering on madness.

"Halima," I bark when I realize she's distracting me.

She jumps and then says something in Tanishi I don't understand. When I ask for clarification she manages to look deeply embarrassed. Slowly, she unfurls, takes my hand and lets me help her up onto her feet.

"I got my blood," she says, turning around so I can see.

There's a red spot on the back of her tunic, having soaked through both that and her pants, and I can see traces of it around her feet.

"I got my blood a *lot*."

I grin at her and she starts, like she's surprised by my reaction. I don't know why she would be. I lean down and claim her mouth with mine. "Leave us," I bark to the others as I pull Halima against me.

She lifts up onto her toes and presses up against me in a way that makes me feel like my desperation is not so pathetic when it's met by a rivaled desperation.

"She got her blood," I rasp between her teeth. I slide one hand around her waist and pull her body flush with mine, not waiting as I tug my hide pants down and free my cock without even bothering to drop my battle kilt around it.

Tenor curses behind me, and I hear feet padding away as I back my female up against the steel wall. It's warm to the touch, but not hot as I brace her against it, yank down her pants, and drive inside.

She's panting hard now, gasping, her thighs squeezing mine even as she breaks the kiss just long enough to shout, "We — we'll get blood everywhere!"

"It's only blood." I crush her mouth with mine and slide home, even deeper. She's slicker than normal and that's saying something and I die a thousand times when her inner walls contract around me even harder than usual.

"Khara! Ero, it feels…it feels…"

"Like something new."

"Yes," she gasps, sweat already forming along her neck. I lick a line, clearing a path through the salt, up to her ear.

I bite her jaw, her chin, taste her mouth and watch as she goes boneless in my arms while my cock plunges in, seeking a bottom to this well of pleasure that it won't find. The pleasure is limitless and her body is well adjusted to my size.

"And the next time…" I pound into her hard. Harder than hard. With enough pressure to make my arms shake and my eyes roll. "When you no longer have your blood…I will fill you with my seed…and we'll make a child."

"You...you want a child?" Her face scrunches up and I laugh at her tortured expression when I slow. "Ero..."

"Open your eyes." It takes her a few seconds to blink and another few seconds after that to focus on me.

I grin. "I want you. If a child comes from your body, then I'll want it, too."

She fidgets on my cock, little mewls begging me to continue as my erection stuffs her full without advancing or retreating. It fills me with the most torturous, delicious sensation, knowing that I rattle her like this. "I'm not ready for a child, I don't think."

"You will need to be ready, because I have no intention of going a single day without fucking you for the rest of my life." I slam home between her thighs and she cries out, loud and high.

"Ero! Oh...khara! I'm coming..." She breaks apart and I don't stand a chance — I never do. I come right on the heels of her orgasm, her body rippling around mine and milking my erection dry. It's a miracle there's anything left.

Four times in one day is not enough.

It will never be enough.

"Are you the first Tanishi female to reclaim her blood cycle?" I ask her as I help her wobbly legs back into her bloody trousers. I don't want her to have to wear them, but I also refuse to let any other male see any part of her that belongs to me.

She shakes her head. "No. A few others have. Sharon actually thinks she might already be pregnant. She's been having sex with an Omoro man basically since we got here. She didn't tell anyone...Ero?"

I've stopped walking. My eyes are huge. All that talk of children felt a little outlandish — babies aren't that easy to come by — and to hear that a Tanishi female may *already* be with child from an Omoro makes me feel…well, honestly I don't know how to feel. I clear my throat as I stare down at her, gaze moving from one eye to the other. I find an expectation there that I will not ever shatter and carefully release my next breath.

"She will need extra meal portions, then."

Halima's face, drawn with consternation, floods with a light so blinding I can't help but blink it back. She's suddenly throwing her arms around my chest and nuzzling into my breast, kissing me right where my bloated heart now sits free and constantly ready to burst. It hurts like hell, too big for the cage initially made to hold it, but it's worth every torturous beat.

She exhales against my chest and for a moment, among the corn and some shorter, flowering crops that I've heard called *zoo-keen-ee,* she says, "Yes, Ero. I think she will need more meals."

I hear her say, *thank you,* without saying anything at all. It's in the lines of her body and makes me feel like a rat bastard for the male I was before and also, like a king deserving of a queen's adoration.

"Any pregnant females will be cared for, regardless of their tribe, habibty. You do not need to worry."

She looks up at me, resting her chin on my chest and grins. "I'm not worried."

I take Halima down into the caves to clean up before returning to the surface where the pounding of feet put me immediately on high alert.

"There you are! Come quickly," Lopina says.

Since the Pikosa traitors were exiled, Lopina has been taking on more of Ellar's tasks. Haddock left as well, a fact that I know troubles my female. When I approached him on her behalf to persuade him not to leave, he told me that some crimes weighed too heavily and we'd shared a surprising understanding. I hadn't attempted to convince him twice. All I'd done for him was prepare him a pack that should last him three weeks. After that, survival will be his choice.

Leanna has been helpful counsel to me, but as more and more of the Tanishi regain some or parts of their memories from their world before, there has been strain. She stays down in the village now and, while she provides advice and assists in running drills with my warriors, she no longer gives orders.

"There's an approaching caravan."

Caravan? "Wickar?"

Lopina shakes her head. "It's not yet confirmed…"

Wyden appears just behind her, his female never far. "It is confirmed now," he nods, looking furious. Looking murderous.

"Tenor! Take Halima and Jia down to the mines. Seal the entrance," I order.

"No way!" Halima shouts, heading straight for the staircase that will lead her to the upper platform.

By the time I catch up to her, she's already mounted her defenses and I've let mine down too easily. She rounds on me and stabs her finger into the center of my chest.

"You need me. If the Wickar are coming, maybe once they see our fortress, they'll want to reason with us."

"Reason is not something the Wickar are known for, Halima," I growl.

She plants her hands on her hips. Wind whips hair around her face and I don't restrain the urge to touch it. I tug it over her shoulder only to watch it whipped back out of place.

"Still," she says, batting my hands away, "There are alternatives to fighting."

I hesitate, debating for far too long.

"They're almost on us, Ero. We need to do something," Lopina says. "Should we take out the war machines?" The term we've given to the Tanishi's sun-powered machines that have wheels and rickety frames but enable us to race across the sand at a speed even faster than the Kawashari horses.

Halima huffs, frustrated, "Ero, for once. Just do it my way. I'm always right anyway." She rolls her eyes.

I bark out a laugh and grab her hand. I tow her up the stairs and onto the platform, telling Lopina to wait. Of course, Wyden had no better luck than I did with his female because they arrive beside us on the platform a moment later.

The female who never stops talking, Chayana, is with them, Tenor, Quin, Warren and Goja in tow. The latter four are well armed — Tenor and Quin with Tanishi weapons, Warren and Goja with bows that are taller than Halima. They sink down into position in the archer slits carved into the outer wall. I drag Halima down to one beside me as I survey the caravan coming toward us.

It is a sight to behold.

"Khara!" Halima curses.

On her other side, the talkative female blurts, "Holy fucking moly!" It's a curse I've heard before from her. "Is that a *maam-moth*?"

Jia says something I don't understand and Halima nods. "What is this animal?" She asks me.

"An elephant."

She bursts out laughing. "That's *not* an elephant."

"It is."

"Maybe an elephant the size of a small mountain! That thing must be ten tons!"

She isn't wrong. The tusked creatures that form the Wickar caravans are almost as tall as our walls, putting the large platforms that ride on their backs nearly at our level. There are six of these large beasts and, crawling across the sand between them are many of the smaller horses that Halima keeps telling me look nothing like horses.

The horses drag carts filled with people and goods. A few warriors walk beside the carts, taking turns to help navigate them. There are hundreds of people here.

It is a frightening thing to see. We built our walls high, never thinking that a Wickar horde would attempt to attack with the entire force of their caravans, but wanting our walls high enough just to be sure. Their height will be tested far earlier than I ever expected and the panic in my chest turns my heart to slush.

"You've seen your fill. I want you back down in the caves *now*, Halima."

"No! Wait..." Her face squints, her hollow, light brown cheeks rounding with her effort. "Jia, Chayana... white..." I don't understand.

The females go quiet. Wyden and I share a look over the tops of their heads. "We should prepare the war machines, Nigusi," he says, surprising me.

I'm about to answer him in the affirmative when Jia emits a shout. Halima jumps up right after and I damn near lose my mind.

"Halima!" I grab her tunic and yank her back down beside me. "What are you thinking? You could be…"

"It's a *white* cloth!" She shouts, as if that's got meaning to me. "It's a Tanishi symbol of peace. They have a Tanishi with them!"

"You can't know that for certain," I say, pulling her back down again.

"Chayana!" She shouts and Chayana is up on her feet, pulling off her damn tunic so that she's standing with her breasts exposed, dark nipples flat and large and distracting. She starts to wave it over her head like a madwoman.

"What is she doing?" Wyden hisses.

"It's a Tanishi method of communication. It tells them we mean them no harm," Halima explains, but it's a lie. We do mean them harm. We mean everyone harm who would dare attack our tribe.

I share a look with Wyden and I go to issue the order to release the war machines when Halima pulls my arm, turns me, grabs my face on either side and presses her lips to mine.

I'm momentarily unseated, so there's no choice but to hear her as she whispers… "Trust me, habibi."

I lick my lips and open my eyes and sink into hers. Indecision swirls through me, but I already know what my answer will be before I give it. I grunt. She smiles. She holds my hand and stares deeply into my gaze for as long as she can, distracting me until the very final moment.

"They're here, Nigusi. Within shouting distance."

I nod at Wyden, breaking free of Halima's trance. I push Halima's body behind mine and I do something I'd never have done in my own past life, the life before Halima — I stand and face the Wickar without a weapon, and without any intention of killing anything. For now.

Hmph.

I narrow my gaze against the bright world. Sand swirls lazily through the air, as if debating lackadaisically whether or not it wants to incite violence. The huge beast closest to us trumpets through its long nose, as if announcing its arrival, while the platform on its back sways delicately with each lumbering step it takes.

Padding separates the tough hide of the beast from the bamboo planks that make up the landing. A white tarp tents over the entire thing. Ten individuals stand on the platform, the one at the front I know instinctively to be the Wickar king.

He's watching me, one king easily recognizing the other, and he does the unthinkable. Without dropping his gaze, he tilts his head forward in a sign of respect. I repeat the gesture even though it pains me to do so and just as I do, Halima, the insolent queen, steps out from the shadow of my protection.

"Kenya! Hey, Kenya! Kenya..." She waves her arms over her head wildly and Jia, seeing her giddy tribeswoman, jumps up onto her own feet.

Soon, all of the Tanishi women are squealing like chickens while a familiar dark-skinned, bright-eyed female throws herself to the edge of the Wickar king's platform and offers returning waves.

Shock tunnels through me. The Wickar king and I exchange a look and I fight to keep hold of my own stony expression. The slightly older male has skin a shade lighter than mine and hair that's several rough shades of gold. Shaved on the sides, it's braided roughly down the center and falls in thick knots to the center of his shoulder blades. In single combat, I wonder how we'd match up. He's slightly shorter than I am, but bulkier in the chest and arms.

Yes, I think I'd do fine.

I wonder if he can read me as I can read him because he cocks an eyebrow. I know he's thinking the same thing I am.

"What...why...with the Wickar tribe?" Halima says in Tanishi. "Are you in pain? Hurt...injured?"

Kenya nods animatedly. She seems to be healthy, in good spirits. I ask Halima to translate her words and she says, "She says he was kind with her from the beginning. Interested in ways the Pikosa weren't with us initially."

Her words make me cringe. As I do, the Wickar king makes a face. He barks something across the sands at me, but I don't understand his language. Smoother than the Pikosa brogue and the Tanishi tongue, it hits my ears and means nothing.

Meanwhile, Halima beside me, gasps. She answers the male and I watch his expression change from one of scorn and confusion to one of pure shock. Beside him, the female Kenya says a few words, but they don't sound half so smooth as Halima's. She hits him in the shoulder as he turns his open-eyed expression to her and she grins and punches him again in the arm.

"Halima," I murmur. "Tell me."

"He speaks Spanish." She laughs. "Well, it isn't Spanish, anymore, but he seems to understand the words I'm using. Kenya speaks a few words of Spanish, which explains how she was able to communicate with him to now."

"Is she his female?"

When Halima repeats my question, Kenya laughs. She repeats it again for the Wickar king and even he smiles, slow and syrupy. I don't like the way he looks at Halima and step closer to her, slide my hand behind her neck beneath the curtain of her still-damp hair.

The man's gaze flashes to me and then settles not on me or on Halima but skips down until he finds Chayana whose chest is still bare. His gaze scours her frame in a way that makes her react immediately.

She grabs her tunic and shoves it back over her head and shouts at him in her own tongue, "...eyes... up...me!" She points at her face and the Wickar male answers slow and deep.

Halima's jaw drops when he finishes and I squeeze her neck, coaxing the next words out of her. She's holding back laughter as she says, "He says that Kenya doesn't like males and that his interests lie elsewhere." She does laugh then.

The Wickar king says more and Halima nods, then smiles very softly up at me. "He says that Kenya managed to convince him that the Pikosa had uncovered a gem — technologies and a woman who could explain them in their own tongue how to use them. He didn't believe her at first. He didn't believe her for a while, but eventually he said he'd take a chance so he sent out scouts that confirmed her reports. They saw the wall we were building and he decided that he'd take her up on her proposal."

"What was the proposal?"

Halima wrinkles her nose. "He wanted to raid and help Kenya free us from your evil clutches."

I tense, about to challenge the Wickar king right there for threatening to take Halima away from me, but then she says, "He says that when they saw Tanishi on the walls, they changed their plans. Now, he's more interested in a trade than a raid."

"A trade?" I say and, as Wyden and Goja and Lopina gawk, Halima translates his words to the other Tanishi.

"A trade!" Chayana shouts. "Sounds good." She speaks so easily, as if she does not know that the tribes of this world have never traded before or ever worked together on anything except mutual destruction.

"Yes, a trade," Halima says to me.

She reaches down and squeezes my palm while Chayana loudly shouts about trading and certain types of stones I know by name — likely to improve her magnet machine, but perhaps to further one of her many other inventions.

The Wickar king says something else and, beside me, Halima barks out a laugh. She glances sideways at Chayana and then says loud enough for all of us to hear, first in Tanishi and then in Pikosa. "He says that he's willing to trade a lot to take the loud one off of our hands."

I laugh. I laugh full and from the belly, so hard it starts to hurt. What the hell is this new world order where tribes can laugh between each other in moments brokered by beings from another time so distant, it's as if it's another world? And trading with the Wickar?

They are a nomadic tribe, but have permanent settlements that guard even more oases than we Pikosa have access to. We'd be foolish to deny them as we stand a lot more to gain than they do. *Or perhaps* — my gaze slides to the three Tanishi females lined up beside me — *not.*

Chayana removes one of her shoes and chucks it at the Wickar king, missing him by a mile. While she continues to shout variants on the word *No*, I meet the Wickar king's gaze and say gently, "Perhaps something can be arranged."

Halima elbows me in the gut and I smooth my hand over her shoulder as I bring her against my chest. I can feel her heartbeat through her body and nod. "Tell him that I will not trade any females, but that I will allow him and a small party through the gates to barter with representatives from each of our tribes out from under the sun."

"You want to barter together?" She smiles.

I massage my fingers over her scarred shoulder with one hand while my other grips her scarred arm. "Yes, habibty. Anidi laye."

"Ane behibak," she whispers.

I kiss her cheeks and then her mouth, struggling to control the desire building and budding in my tongue. I pull back and give Halima a chance to interpret. As soon as she's finished, she glances over at Chayana and says in both tongues, "Chayana. He says if you want your rocks, you're going to have to be primary negotiator on this one."

"Tell...big, ugly...no!" Chayana screams, limping on one foot since she discarded her shoe and is walking on a steel and stone roof that's hot to the touch.

Halima just grins and shoots a wink up at me before she speaks to the king. He grins and starts to back his caravan away, preparing to dismount.

"What you telling him?" I ask her in Tanishi.

In Tanishi, she replies, "I told him that Chayana would be happy to negotiate with him."

Chayana, overhearing us, squawks, *"What?"*

We descend the high walls and make it to the sands together with laughter on our tongues as this new world, filled with terrors and tribes and creatures born of violence, is reshaped like a sandcastle once blown away in the wind. Small sections have been rebuilt in shapes that resemble something like kindness, like courage, and like love.

And I plan to protect it with every violence I was raised with and that, with Halima at my side, I otherwise, no longer need.

I hope you enjoyed Ero and Halima's story! Reviews, even the one-liners, are very much appreciated on Amazon or Goodreads.

To get access to future books filled with hot, possessive alphas and the resilient, warrior women they worship _first_, not to mention freebies, exclusive previews and more, sign up to my mailing list at www.booksbyelizabeth.com/contact.

Until the next time,
Wahashteeny ¤°´´`°¤,,‚ø*

Elizabeth

A note from the author

Ahlan wa sahlan (welcome!) and shokran (thanks!) to everyone who made it this far into the crazy world that is Halima and Ero's universe — and perhaps other Xiveri Mates', in the future! I just wanted to take a quick second to say that I am not Arab, nor am I delusional enough to claim that I speak Arabic fluently.

I studied Arabic in college and lived a year in Dokki — right in the heart of Cairo. I lived there partially during the Egyptian Revolution, at which point I was evacuated with my university group to Amman, Jordan, where I lived an additional three months.

I had every intention of spending the rest of my life in the Middle East, but life got in the way, as did some more conflict when I moved to Lebanon after university to work for the UNRWA. I ended up staying in Beirut only three months before I moved to Switzerland and I haven't been back to the Middle East since.

And yet, Cairo remains the place that has touched me the most, the hardest, the most brutally. I am actually tearing up writing this now because of how deeply and profoundly I loved — and still love — that city.

And maybe it's only because of how beautiful and magical and mystical I find Cairo, but I believe Arabic to be the most beautiful language on this planet. Small examples to illustrate this include:

Fil mishmish, which is an Egyptian expression that means *in your dreams*, but actually translates to *inside of the apricot.*

Ana bemoot fiik, which means *I die inside of you*, and is a hardcore, deeply sentimental way of telling someone that you love them.

Your Egyptian lover will rarely ever tell you you're beautiful. No, no no no. Instead, he'll tell you that you are like the moon or that you're like honey, that you're full of color or that you're like jasmine.

If someone tells you that you shine — enti mulowenna — you'll tell them that you only shine because of their light.

It's a poetic language, rich with imagery that I hope I do justice in sharing here through Halima's lens. Of course, I'm bound to have gotten a lot wrong. Pronunciations and cultures are tricky to write about when they don't belong to you. So, to those out there to whom they do belong, I apologize and I hope that you can be sated with the knowledge that I don't aim to co-opt or disrespect by writing Halima as a culture outside of my own, but that I wrote her out of a fiery jealousy that I cannot claim Cairo and, more importantly, that I wrote her out of love. Because ana bemoot fii Qahira.

And as a random side note — my nickname that my friends call me, even now, is Ellie and in Arabic, Ellie means *mine*.

And as a second even more random fun fact — in Amharic, Ellie means *turtle*.

Continue the journey and be…

Taken to Evernor
An Alien Gladiator Romance
Xiveri Mates Book 8 (Nalia and Herannathon)

Nalia's goal is to escape the gladiator games because she hasn't been included as a fighter, oh no, she's the prize for the alien who wins. And there's one four-armed psychopath who's coming for her.

Available for Preorder on Amazon
Release date: April 19, 2022

———

Taken to Sky
A Cyborg Bounty Hunter Romance
Xiveri Mates Book 9 (Ashmara and Jerrock)

Most creatures in these cosmos know Jerrock as Sky's most sadistic and effective bounty hunter. To Ashmara, he's her ever present threat. To be free of him, she might just need to free him and become a bounty hunter herself.

Available for Preorder on Amazon
Release date: May 25, 2022

Or visit another post-apocalyptic world in...

Population

Like a good scavenger, Abel's got no problem looting the alien corpse. But he doesn't stay, erm, dead. He comes after her. And if he catches her, she'll be his.

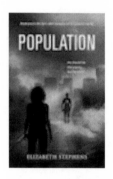

Population: A Post-Apocalyptic SciFi Romance
Population Book 1 (Abel and Kane)

Available in paperback anywhere online books are sold or on Amazon in ebook

Abel

— *Excerpt* —

I can hear a subtle scurrying, like rats, in the darkened doorways of the vacant buildings lining the street. Hollow shells that only serve as a painful reminder of the bustling life that existed just over a decade ago. Scavengers, but they don't show their faces. They remain in the shadows because they fear me. *I* would fear me. There aren't many scavengers that could take on one of the Others and live, let alone kill it, making me the most dangerous thing on the road at the moment.

I walk like that's true and pull off my outer coat. It's saturated with fiery crimson that smells so strongly of rotting eggs and piss that I start to feel light-headed. I pretend not to notice the bitter chill sweeping in through the holes in my men's tee shirt and jeans as I shoulder my pack and step into the center of the T-intersection, where all this senseless carnage began.

I stare in the direction that the cyclops went, but the grey is too thick to see more than two streets over. The grey presses in on me, heightening this new sensation of loneliness. It's invasive, more threatening than a blade. Humans weren't made to travel solo. I never wanted to travel solo. I kind of always thought, if I made it this far — to be the last one left of my pack — that I'd just…give up.

But I can't.

I made a promise.

I take a step to meet the grey and as my mind starts constructing the rudimentary outline of a very poor plan, I hear a cough.

Confused, I withdraw the sword from my pack and look around, frowning when I see nothing. Maybe my half-hearing? Maybe my imagination? Maybe my fear and adrenaline and shock? It could be all of those things, but I'm not in the business of being sucker-punched in the back, so I take a slow turn and then a tentative step towards the SUV — what's left of it — in the blood-basted intersection, where the sulfur smell and the metallicy blood lies thickest.

I freeze when I hear it again. A few seconds later, there's a short grunt followed by a cough that's too close to have been emitted by one of the scavengers lurking in the bombed-out storefronts. In fact, it's so close that I dare to believe for just an instant, something utterly unbelievable...

Caution tells me to press forward, but curiosity has me moving closer to the bus, the SUV and the Other lying between them. Well, what used to be an SUV, what used to be a bus, and what used to be an Other. None of them are recognizable, the loner least of all.

His face is mangled — nose bashed into his skull, lips sliced and bloodied, cheekbones shifting out of place beneath closed lids — and what was once black? hair stands up away from his face in matted chunks. His body didn't fare any better.

There isn't a single piece of him that isn't covered in that pungent, sickly red. His chest is concave, pockets of blood oozing out from beneath the patches of his tee shirt like little geysers, making it impossible for me to tell if he's still glowing.

His arms twist out from his sides like gnarling tree limbs while his shattered legs lay flaccidly atop grey ash that had at one point been cinderblocks. Now, they're just dust. I know that he can't be alive, but precaution keeps my sword angled down towards his neck, because despite the fact that there's not a chance in this galaxy or the next that he'll somehow muster the strength to attack me, my heart still hammers anxiously in my chest.

I see something glittering amidst the pools of sulfurous blood. Near his mouth, a shard of steel stretches up to meet his parted lips. I want to take it before the riff raff come and dismember what's left of him so I kick his foot once, just to be sure.

When nothing happens, I squat down and flick through the blood and teeth and chunks of whatever else he's thrown up. Finally my fingers close in around a slippery silver object. A hard object.

I wipe it off on my blood spattered jeans and tilt it towards the limited light shining down from the grey above me. It's a key. One of the big, old fashioned ones. A skeleton key. I scratch my head, understanding only that the key must be something important for him to have swallowed it. I think back to what the giant had shouted at him, and it's clear he'd been looking for something. Was this it?

I see no reason to leave the key behind even though I've got no clue what it's for, so I put away my sword, tuck the key into the side pocket of my pack and stand.

I take a step back towards the grey, but the instant my left foot touches down onto pavement, a vice clamps around it and I stagger.

Spinning, I rip the sword from my pack so fiercely I nearly shred it in two. I point the tip of the blade down, but the dead guy that has a hold of me doesn't react. Through the blood and the abrasions, I see that his lips are curled up in an expression that I recognize, but that makes my adrenaline rush in worry and confusion.

This dead guy is…he's smiling at me.

He says something that I can't make out, coughs, coughs some more, then coughs again. "That doesn't belong to you," he eventually croaks.

My jaw falls slack and for a moment the tumult of thoughts that so viciously assault my mind are silenced. "What?" I manage to stammer, sounding like an idiot.

I yank my foot back but his broad, flat hand is unyielding. He grits his teeth and I can tell that it causes him great pain to hold onto me, but he holds me nonetheless. How is he alive? And more importantly, how is this dead guy stronger than me?

"You have." He pauses, coughs, then says, "You have what is mine, human." He spits this last word out disdainfully and the little sympathy that I once had for him when he was just a lonely loner with a glowing chest against a cyclops and his band of goons, evaporates.

I tip my blade down to the inside of his arm and press just hard enough for blood to well in the crook of his elbow. He releases a feral roar, but I can feel the pressure of his fingertips around my ankle relax ever so slightly. He scratches me as I pull away from him and I feel that he has drawn blood. And then I'm *sure* of it when he reaches his fingers up to his mouth and tastes them.

I shudder. "It's not yours anymore, demon." I try and mimic his tone, but fall short. Instead, I'm vaguely aware that some of the scavengers have crept from their hiding places. I look up and see a soot-colored face disappear behind the safety of an overturned car. I shudder again as I think about what's in store for him.

Meanwhile, he doesn't seem so concerned. Instead he just blinks up at me with one good eye, given that the other is swollen shut. His lips are tensed together into a thin bloody line, but he holds my gaze intrepidly.

Part of me almost wants to give the key over to him. But I don't. If this key is important, then perhaps I can use it to leverage Ashlyn's release. Plus, it's not like he really needs it. I know that he must know that we both know that he won't last the night. He coughs again, as if to prove my point, and blood spills down his chin in reckless abandon.

A sound catches my attention and when I look up this time, I see the faces of two men watching me from a second story window missing the pane in the apartment building across the street. They don't move away from the window until I glare, which makes me think that perhaps, having seen me, they're willing to chance death in order to get to him. I cringe.

I wonder if he'll still be alive when they start eating him.

Rule number eight sits heavy in my chest. Never help strangers.

But even though he *is* a stranger, *and* an Other, *and* scum, *and* probably deserves to die, I keep thinking about the way he fought that giant and those other bastards. I keep thinking about the way he looked at me when he collapsed onto his knees off of the bus, and then again when he held my gaze when he was being tortured. Something tells me that if he could have moved, he might have made a good ally in the fight to save Becks and rescue Ashlyn.

Or maybe I'm just tired of hearing things screaming.

But whatever the case, I've seen enough death for the night, and even if he dies — which he will — I'm not going to let the cannibals have at him. I'm not going to let his screams haunt me through the night.

I lift my blade over my head and bring it down so that everyone on the street can hear the ringing of metal against pavement. "Fuck you scavengers!" No one is close enough yet to see that I've missed his head by inches.

"He's mine you sacks of shit," I shout, and when I bend down close enough to feel the pressure of his gaze on my face and see his widening eyes — *they're green, his eyes* —

I grab a fistful of rubble, drenched in his blood, and lift it over my head.

I toss my hair back and disgustingly, let a few droplets of his blood shower my chin and chest. I want them to think that I'm drinking him, even though I'd never let an ounce of that toxic, fetid blood touch my lips. The smell of it alone is deterrent enough.

I make a great show of stowing my blade and dragging his limp body across the ground to the nearest building. He's heavier than lead and I handle him gracelessly because it's the only way I can move him at all as I kick open the flimsy wooden door and wade into the shadows.

Even though it's dark inside, I can see well enough to know that the place has been looted too many times to count. There's nothing left that a person could have carried out, and there's no smell but dust. Something old. Stale, but clean. Stolen, but forgotten.

This clearly used to be some kind of cafe or coffee shop — I can tell by the busted chalkboards against the back wall, the faux-wooden counter in the middle of the small space and the refrigerator by the front door where I'm standing.

After getting the dead guy past it, I heave my weight into the side of the fridge and let it slam down with glorious thunder. On its side, it successfully blocks the bottom half of the door, which is badly rotted. I just hope it'll be enough of a deterrent. He just needs a little more time to lose a little more blood and die in peace. Then the vultures can have at him.

Luckily the windows are all boarded up and seem more or less secure, so I don't bother with those and instead, drag what's left of the dead creature around the far side of the counter. I drop his arms and his head hits the fallen cash register with a sharp clang and a dull thud.

He releases a groan that startles me so much I jump. Our eyes meet and I don't like the look he gives me, that baiting condescension and impish curiosity, so I don't give myself time to think about the rules I've just broken or why I've broken them.

Instead, I scramble over the counter to the street-facing wall and wriggle through a high window, keeping my pack close.

Once my feet hit the pavement, I take off down the road at a sprint and I don't stop running until I can no longer feel the creeping chill of the night air numbing me. I run until I burn, inside and out.

Continue reading in ebook on Amazon
and in paperback anywhere online books are sold

All Books by Elizabeth

Xiveri Mates: SciFi Alien and Shifter Romance
Taken to Voraxia, Book 1 (Miari and Raku)
Taken to Nobu, Book 2 (Kiki and Va'Raku)
Taken to Sasor, Book 3 (Mian and Neheyuu) *standalone
Taken to Heimo, Book 4 (Svera and Krisxox)
Taken to Kor, Book 5 (Deena and Rhork)
Taken to Lemora, Book 6 (Essmira and Raingar)
Taken by the Pikosa Warlord, Book 7 (Halima and Ero)
*standalone
Taken to Evernor, Book 8 (Nalia and Herannathon)
Taken to Sky, Book 9 (Ashmara and Jerrock)
Taken to Revatu, A Xiveri Mates Novella (Jewel and
Gorak)

Population: Post-Apocalyptic SciFi Romance
Population, Book 1 (Abel and Kane)
Saltlands, Book 2 (Abel and Kane)
Generation One, Book 3 (Diego and Pia)
Brianna, Book 4 (Lahve and Candy)
more to come!

Brothers: Interracial Dark Mafia Romantic Suspense
The Hunting Town, Book 1 (Knox and Mer, Dixon and Sara)
The Hunted Rise, Book 2 (Aiden and Alina, Gavriil and Ify)
The Hunt, Book 3 (Anatoly and Candy, Charlie and Molly)

Made in the USA
Middletown, DE
31 December 2021

57375038R00227